HIDDEN  W9-BKI-052

"A fascinating and finely written exploration of the human and the alien."
Adrian Tchaikovsky, Arthur C Clarke Award-winning author of Children of Time

"Intriguing world building and complex cultures are a Jaine Fenn specialty, and *Hidden Sun* takes these elements to the next level. Fenn fans will enjoy this one!"
Patrice Sarath, author of The Sisters Mederos

"Fenn is at her best when describing the lives of strong women up against it, and excels at fast action thrillers."
The Guardian

"A vivid and unusual world, populated by an interesting array of characters"
The Times

"Jaine Fenn opens a window on a fascinating and vivid science fictional world."
Strange Horizons

"Both plotting and characterisation are handled deftly, while Fenn's world-building of exotic locales is equally impressive. You should read Jaine Fenn – she's bloody ace."
SFX Magazine

"Thought provoking science fiction with a memorable cast of characters."
The Eloquent Page

"This really is science fiction at its best."
Falcata Times

By the same suthor

JAINE FENN

HIDDEN SUN

SHADOWLANDS BOOK I

ANGRY
ROBOT

ANGRY ROBOT
An imprint of Watkins Media Ltd

20 Fletcher Gate,
Nottingham,
NG1 2FZ
UK

angryrobotbooks.com
twitter.com/angryrobotbooks
Shadow people

An Angry Robot paperback original 2018

Cover by Andreas Rocha
Set in Meridien and False Widow by Argh! Nottingham

Distributed in the United States by Penguin Random House, Inc., New York.

ISBN 978 0 85766 801 1
Ebook ISBN 978 0 85766 802 8

Printed in the United States of America

9 8 7 6 5 4 3 2 1

For Dr Iain Nicholson, for explaining
to a naive young arts student
how the universe actually works.

CHAPTER 1

Rhia looked up, and listened. Distant chanting drifted in through the study window but the house itself was silent. Probably just one of the cats, knocking something over downstairs.

She pulled the lamp closer and bent over her workbench again. The second lens was a tight fit but she mustn't force it. A smear on the inner surface of the glass now would be damned hard to clean off later. Her motions slow and careful, she eased the lens into the cradle of leather straps.

The lens dropped into place, and there it was: her sightglass, complete. The tube of dowelling and waxed paper was only the length of her forearm, but it was the culmination of many years' work.

Time to test her invention. Smiling to herself, she straightened and looked over at the wooden ladder leading up to the observation platform. One advantage of the drought: the sky would be clear. Both Moons were up, so she could start with them. She unclipped the sightglass from the vice.

A sound outside: heavy footsteps thundering up the wooden stairs. Her head snapped round. Surely the servants were not back yet–

"This way!"

Not the servants. And coming closer. She grabbed the sightglass and ducked down behind her workbench.

The study door flew open.

Peering through the workbench's legs, Rhia saw a heavy build and stained streetclothes; from here only the lower half of the man's face was visible. A stranger. A stranger in her house. "In here," he called over his shoulder. The light from his horn-fronted lantern showed a crooked nose, no doubt broken in a fight.

Rhia's breathing deafened her. Surely he must hear that. She must stay calm. Stay calm, and hide until help comes. But no help would come. Everyone was at the rain-vigil.

A second man entered. He was shorter, so Rhia had a full view of him from her hiding place. His long face reminded her of a horse – no, with those close-together eyes more like a donkey. Both men had large packs on their backs. *Thieves!* Lower-city thieves, taking advantage of noble houses left empty by the extended restday devotions.

The two men looked around, getting their bearings. Broken-Nose swept papers off a shelf near the door – Rhia winced as the stack of celestial tables cascaded to the floor – and put his lantern down.

Why come this far up the hill, why risk robbing a house so close to the palace? Rhia had a ridiculous vision of shadowy hordes of ne'er-do-wells creeping through the upper city, targeting every townhouse.

"You sure no one's here?" said the donkey-faced man. He gestured towards the workbench. Rhia's heart jumped. "They've left a lamp lit."

Broken-Nose shrugged. "For the vigil?" He scratched his chin. "Or maybe she just does that. Meant to be pretty kooky, this Countess Harlyn."

This was no random criminality. They knew whose house they had invaded. This was about Etyan, and the girl. About what her foolish brother had done. Might have done.

This, after three months of uncertainty, was retribution.

No. Stay calm. Stay hidden. Remember to breathe. *Quietly.*

"Let's see what we've got, then," said Broken-Nose.

He ambled over to her sandclock on its little table, staring at it like he'd never seen one before. Which he probably hadn't. Seeing him in profile Rhia realized the pack on his back already had something in it, a small but heavy item. Stolen from downstairs, no doubt.

Donkey-Face wandered over to her desk and began picking up papers. Rhia hoped his hands were cleaner than they looked.

Broken-Nose called to his companion. "Any luck?"

"Nah." Donkey-Face stabbed the papers with a bony finger. "We need to start looking in drawers and cupboards."

So, they were here for something specific. Maybe this wasn't about Etyan after all. The thought raised her spirits, and anger challenged the fear.

Broken-Nose was surveying the cabinets and shelves around the walls. "There're books and shit like that all over the place."

"It won't be *books.*"

What won't be? What are you after, damn you?!

Donkey-Face turned and joined his companion in a silent appraisal of the packed study. Then he paused. "Aha," he said.

Rhia followed his gaze. *No! No no no no no. Not that.*

Donkey-Face strode over to the heavy ironwood chest beside the door.

Even as Rhia straightened, her mind was screaming at her to *Stay calm! Stay hidden!* Striding out, lamp in one hand, sightglass in the other, she remembered the moment she had turned on the worst of the childhood bullies. He'd been amazed and run off. Same thing now. Show them you mean business.

"Get. Out. Of. My. House."

Each word was loaded with righteous fury. Donkey-Face

turned. He did look amazed, Rhia was pleased to note. The fact that she wore men's clothing and didn't have her mask on probably helped.

"Now!" she added, in case he hadn't got the message.

Movement off to one side. Oh yes: there were *two* of them.

But she had the fury now. When the man lunged at her from the left she lashed out without looking, without thought.

The blow connected; she'd hit him with the object held in that hand. *The sightglass!* Doweling snapped, leather flapped. The lens flew free.

Broken-Nose staggered back with an oath. The crash as he hit the table hurt her ears. Sandclock, table and intruder went down. Broken-Nose's cry of surprise became one of pain.

Rhia didn't see him fall. She was concentrating on holding Donkey-Face's gaze, trying to drive him off by force of will. She had started this. She had to finish it.

Donkey-Face's left eye was watery, a little red. Even from here she could smell him: fresh ale and stale sweat. He broke her gaze, his attention flicking to the lamp in her hand. She'd grabbed it half thinking to use it as a weapon, but doubted it would be much use against such types.

Rhia glanced down. Yes, the man had a knife on his belt. Yes, his hand was creeping towards it. She must be mad. These men were criminals. But she couldn't back down. Speaking with slow care she said, "If you lay so much as a finger on me, my cousin the duke will hunt you down and have you skinned alive."

Donkey-Face said nothing, but his hand paused. His gaze twitched between her hand and her face. To her left, Broken-Nose groaned and began to move. "I mean it," added Rhia when the silence stretched. Donkey-Face's odour gave way to a new and more pleasant smell, a sharp-sweet scent she knew but couldn't place.

Donkey-Face looked across at his companion and shook his head, *No*.

That's *No* as in *Don't attack her*, Rhia decided. But logic said they would. Why not, two armed men against one woman? Sometimes she hated logic.

Out the corner of her eye, Rhia saw Broken-Nose climbing to his feet. Blood dripped from his torn cheek.

She went back to staring down Donkey-Face. *Run away, damn you!* She wasn't sure how much longer her nerve, or her legs, would hold out.

Then she realized what the smell was.

Risking breaking Donkey-Face's gaze, she looked over at Broken-Nose. His filthy breeches had new stains on them. His backpack hung flaccid, and dripped into the redolent puddle he now stood in.

Rhia dropped the tangle of doweling, leather and waxed paper in her left hand, trying not to wince as the remains of her sightglass hit the floor. Her gaze flicked between the two intruders.

They met her eyes. No one spoke.

Still staring at the two men, she transferred the lamp from her right hand to her left, the side next to Broken-Nose. Then she smiled. At least she hoped the expression she pulled her face into would pass for a smile.

The three of them stood there, frozen. Rhia's guts had gone watery and her knees wanted to knock together. She ordered her body to tense up, to not move, not show weakness. Except for breathing. She had to keep doing that.

Finally, Donkey-Face nodded at his companion. Rhia tensed. Donkey-Face said, "Not worth the risk."

"But–"

"No." Donkey-Face cut him off. "Not worth it." He gestured at Rhia's left hand.

Broken-Nose grunted as realization dawned. He was soaked in lamp-oil and the crazy noblewoman held a naked flame. The man paled under the blood and grime.

He looked to his friend, then lurched into motion and limped over to him.

"Go now," said Rhia. The command came out as a whisper. She tried to find the anger, hoping the pair believed her sanity had cracked. Because if she did throw the lamp at Broken-Nose, none of them would get out of here unscathed. "Go!"

Donkey-Face turned, pulling at Broken-Nose's arm.

"Go on!" she cried, louder now. "Get out!"

Broken-Nose turned and staggered after his companion.

Rhia stood, unmoving, lamp still raised. Two sets of footsteps sounded on the stairs: one swift and light, the other heavier, slower. Both going away.

When silence returned she placed the lamp on the workbench. Her stomach was trying to claw its way up her throat. She swallowed hard once, twice, until the urge to vomit passed.

Then she walked across her study, leaned out the window and shouted for the militia at the top of her voice.

CHAPTER 2

"This time, my girl, you've gone too far!"

Dej stared past the crèche-mother's left shoulder. You got a good view of the citrus groves from Mam Gerisa's office.

If previous "little chats" were anything to go by, this would be the point when the crèche-mother gave a big, dramatic sigh, making it clear how *disappointed* she was, how much she *cared*. But she didn't. She leaned forward and put her hands on her desk. "Did you even realize the knife was a parting-gift?"

I had my suspicions... which you've now confirmed. Dej's bottom lip twitched. She bit it.

Mam Gerisa threw her hands up. "I despair, I really do. I've come to accept that items go missing around you, but this is different. To take a parting-gift... Such unacceptable behaviour is worth two full days of contemplation."

Dej's gaze swerved to the crèche-mother's face. *Two days in the hole? Unfair!* But she'd never owned up before, and she wouldn't crack now. That bastard had deserved it.

Mam Gerisa continued, "Your time in the contemplation room will start immediately after breakfast tomorrow. For now, get back to your chores."

I've still won this, thought Dej when she got up to leave. But as she reached the door the crèche-mother called after her, "You do know that nothing you do will change your friend's fate, don't you?"

• • •

She was on irrigation duty for the late afternoon shift; these days, she seemed to spend half her time in the fields hauling water. It was hard work, so Min was excused. Dej caught up with her in the supper queue that evening.

Min linked an arm with her and said, "So, was it the old she-goat?" Dej had been summoned from siesta by a house-servant and a trip to the crèche-mother's office was the obvious reason.

"Oh yes." Dej examined her nails, such as they were. "Apparently someone stole Pel's parting-gift."

"Really?" Min managed to sound shocked.

The girl and boy standing in line in front of them turned and gawked at Dej.

Dej met their gaze. "What?" The pair were middle-years; Dej didn't know their names.

The girl turned back rather than cheek an elder, but the boy shook his head and scowled before turning away. Dej had an idea why.

"We'll talk later," murmured Min in her ear.

After dinner everyone went outside as usual, to gossip, stroll or play games. Min and Dej took up their new favourite spot, a bench against the wall of the herb garden that caught the evening light; until recently it had been claimed by Jen and her cronies.

Min lowered herself to the bench. "The she-goat didn't put you in the hole, then?" Min didn't have to ask whether Dej had confessed to stealing Pel's knife; they knew each other better than that.

"She's planning to. Two days, starting tomorrow morning."

"Two days?" Min shook her head. "It's not worth it, Dej. *He's* not worth it."

"You didn't hear what he said about you!"

"You did tell me." Min was amused.

Dej didn't see the joke. Bad enough that Pel wouldn't admit to having got Min in this state; Dej'd already planned to get back at the bastard before she overheard him talking to his mates outside the kitchen while she was on scullion duty. The little shit had sniggered and snorted as he compared her friend to a ripe fruit, and then to a rutting pig. She was glad she'd taken his most prized possession. "I don't know how you can be so calm."

Min put a hand on her swollen belly. "Must be her influence."

"You're sure it'll be a girl?"

"I'm sure."

Min had always been the self-assured one, but this new Min was like some preSeparation saint. Even the dorm bully left Min, and by extension Dej, alone now. Perhaps they'd both be this serene once they had their animuses. "Have you heard anything more?" Dej blurted. "About what'll happen to you, afterwards?"

"After she's born, you mean?"

Dej nodded.

"I don't even know where they're sending me yet."

"But you could come back when you've had the baby?" Min was half a year older than Dej, so they might go to their bondings separately, but they'd meet up again afterwards, in the skyland, once they'd become their true selves. Dej was sure of that.

"I don't know. I just don't know." Min turned to her. "You need to think about yourself, Dej."

"I am. You know me: selfish to the core."

"Yeah, so selfish you'll risk time in the hole for me. I love that you'd do something like that." Min never referred directly to Dej's misdemeanours. "But you made your point. Don't suffer for it." Min took her hand.

Dej relaxed everywhere except the hand Min held; that

she squeezed. It wasn't a sex thing, whatever some of their bitchier dorm-mates said about the two of them. More like the shadowkin idea of sisters. She hated thinking about life without Min. "You're right. I suppose."

"Often. But not always. I've got terrible taste in boys." Pel hadn't been Min's first. She'd grown up as pretty as Dej was plain, and knew how to deal with the attention that drew. She called going with boys her own "little bit of naughtiness", referring to Dej's light fingers and the trouble – and fun – that led to. Except stealing just got a cane across the knuckles, or time in the hole. It didn't ruin your life.

"Can we not talk about that?"

"All right. How about a song?"

Dej straightened, and glanced around to check no one was in earshot. Then, pitching her voice low, she began to sing the one song she knew from beyond the crèche's gates, a tale about a fickle lover that she'd once overheard the yam-trader singing.

Min joined in whenever the repeated set of four lines with the simplest tune came around. Her voice was nothing like as clear and sweet as Dej's but that wasn't the point. They were singing together. Dej had only heard part of the yam-trader's song, and had made up more words since, some of them less than complimentary about their tutors and crèche-mates. She'd added a verse just for Pel last month. It still made them both giggle.

Singing felt as good as stealing. Not for the first time Dej wondered why it was as strictly forbidden, when it caused no harm.

She moved on to other songs she'd composed herself, most without words, or with simple words based on her life here at the crèche. Min sang along with the parts she knew.

When the Sun dipped below the garden wall Min said, "Best get back inside."

Dej stood, and offered an arm to help her friend pull herself up. "I'll see you at the dorm," she said. "Got something I need to do first."

CHAPTER 3

"How terrifying!" The Lady Alharet Heptar Trevane, grand duchess of Shen, leaned closer, covering Rhia's hand with her be-ringed one. "Though knowing you, you weren't even scared."

"Oh, I was scared," said Rhia. "But I was angry too."

"Of course…" the duchess sat back and flicked her fan at the plate on the lacquered table between them. "You must keep your strength up, my dear."

Rhia took a second butter-and-candied-peel biscuit; her favourite – as Alharet well knew. Not that she could eat much in this damn corset.

"Do you have any idea what the ruffians were after?" asked the duchess.

Rhia kept her tone light. "I'm not sure. Some of my papers, perhaps."

"I see how that would anger you."

Unlike many at court, who tittered at Rhia behind fans and spread fingers, the duchess accepted her eccentric interests. Rhia wondered, not for the first time, if Alharet knew about the natural enquirers. "So much in my study is irreplaceable."

"And your sandclock was broken." Thanks to the last traces of the duchess's Zekti accent, her questions sometimes sounded like statements.

"Yes, it was. But I can get a new one." Unlike the contents

of the ironwood chest. The bottom quarter contained Father's notes, valuable mainly for sentimental reasons, but the chest also held correspondence from her fellow enquirers; centuries of accumulated wisdom from dozens of shadowlands. And, unless she missed her guess, the intruders had planned to set fire to her study once they had filled their backpacks with the enquirers' papers, in order to hide the theft.

"Do you know how they got in?"

"The new housemaid admitted she hadn't checked the back of the house before she left. We found the back door unlocked." *Though if she failed to lock the door, why admit it?* One more mystery among many.

"And they were surprised to find you in, you say."

"Yes. Obviously whoever hired them failed to mention my godless ways." Rhia might still have attended the vigil were it not for the newly arrived lenses, brought by a red-cheeked glassblowers' apprentice that afternoon. At least the lenses had survived the break-in, even if the sightglass itself was ruined.

"There has been no trouble since."

"No, I'm glad to say." Though Rhia had not argued when Markave, her steward, had insisted on accompanying her up the hill to the palace.

"Bunny says it's a sign of the times." Despite knowing Alharet for most of her adult life, Rhia still started when the duchess used Francin's nickname. For all the stresses on their marriage, perhaps the duke and duchess did love each other. Alharet looked pensive, then added, "Perhaps we should approach this from another angle. Perhaps we should ask ourselves who might do such a thing."

"Do you have any thoughts?" Alharet would be the one to know.

"I did wonder about old Earl Lariend."

"Him? But why? Oh, you mean his recent bluster about uppity women?"

"He really believes it. If you were married–"

"Then no doubt my husband would put a stop to my work."

"Would that be so terrible? There comes a time when we must put aside selfish interests."

Sometimes Rhia wondered if Alharet really understood her. Despite the duchess's sympathy for Rhia's work, her friend was eager to see her married off. But she would be thirty next year, so if she was to take a husband it must be soon. "Maybe. If there's no other way."

Alharet nodded. "Even if, as we all hope and pray, your brother returns to us safe and well, you should still consider Viscount Callorn's offer."

"His House's offer, you mean."

"Forget the source, Rhia. Consider the future."

"I am."

The duchess's golden finch began to sing from its fretwork cage beside the window, heralding the evening. The two women listened for a while, the duchess deploying her fan as delicately as she would at court, while Rhia used hers more practically, seeing off the last of another hot, airless day.

The scarred skin around her left eye itched under her lacquered quarter-mask. The mask, painted by her late uncle, showed a realistic woman's hand, and to the casual glance it looked as though someone was reaching round Rhia's head. It was her favourite formal mask; she liked the way it made the smooth-faced courtiers look twice. She eased the point of her fan under the mask, scratching the itch as subtly as she could.

The finch fell silent, and ruffled its feathers. Alharet said, "I am sure you have considered this, but could the break-in at your townhouse be related to your brother, wherever he now is?"

Rhia fought the flush rising to her face. Alharet was her friend: she should confide in her, tell her about that awful morning three months ago. But to voice her fear was to give it substance. *Pale hair in bloodied water…* "I doubt it." Her voice was clipped. "Unless you have news?"

"I wish I had."

Rhia looked for some escape from the equally difficult subjects of the Viscount's proposal and Etyan's disappearance. She settled on the kind of gossip Alharet lived for. "Did I hear right, that Lady Emerlain is leaving?"

Alharet smiled. "She has already gone. Back to her family estate. Ill health, you know."

"Not…?"

"Oh no. Not another of Bunny's by-blows, thank the First. She just…" Alharet waved dismissively "… fell out of favour."

"Wasn't there a rumour she had also fallen into bed with the new music master?"

Alharet raised her fan to cover her mouth in mock shock. "More than once, they do say."

"What was his name again?"

"I forget. He's gone now too." She lowered her fan. "Still, he was awfully pretty."

Of course Alharet knew the young man's name. Rhia suspected she had hired him herself, probably for his looks, possibly encouraging him to deploy his charms with the duke's latest mistress.

Alharet smiled. "Now. Let us call for fresh tisane and have the servants light the lamps." She put down her fan, then paused.

Rhia heard it too: a low rumble from outside. Alharet stood, Rhia rising a moment later.

Both women went over to the window.

The duchess's apartments were on the third floor of the palace, to one side of the gatehouse. The skyland was visible as a bright line running along the horizon, fading now as the Sun set. Her window overlooked the wide and elegant curve of the duke's parade. Rhia had a clear view of the jostling mass of humanity boiling up from the lower city.

The people moved like a living creature, an amalgam of faces and bodies. Over mutters and jeers a sonorous male voice rang out, "The First is angry. The duke must pay."

The marchers responded: "Someone must pay."

Riots sometimes occurred in the lower city, over taxes or the price of bread or other matters which, Rhia was sure, must be of vital import to those living without her privileges. But the trouble never reached this far upslope.

The crowd took up the cry: "The duke must pay."

"It appears our citizens believe my husband capable of ending the drought with a wave of his hand," said Alharet from behind her.

Rhia turned to see her friend's wry smile. Alharet added, "You may wish to step back from the window."

"Ah, yes, of course." Rhia moved to one side, but could not look away. She peered out from behind the folded shutter.

The marchers were now close enough to start hurling more tangible items than shouts. A few stones were flung towards the palace, though all fell short.

A low grinding sounded from below. It took Rhia a moment to identify the cause: the great ironwood doors of the palace's main entrance were only closed for rare ceremonial occasions.

Presumably in response to the closing doors, the marchers' chants became angry shouts. A few sped up, breaking free of the pack.

Rhia flinched as a hurled missile smashed on the wall just below the window. Beside her, the finch twittered in alarm.

From her shoulder, Alharet said, "There was talk of a rabble-rousing priest." Her soft voice was a contrast to the growing hubbub outside. "It appears he has indeed roused the rabble."

The first rioters reached the gate, shouting at the top of

their lungs. Mostly it was formless noise, though some still cried, "The First is angry!" and "The duke must pay!"

As the bulk of the crowd flowed uphill in the wake of their braver comrades, Rhia glimpsed movement in the circular avenue that surrounded the palace. Men on horseback, carrying no lights.

The leading rioters saw the advancing dark mass; some turned, uncertain; some shook sticks or other impromptu weapons, shouting and jeering.

The mounted men kicked their beasts into motion.

The horses charged the crowd. In the fitful torchlight Rhia recognized the green uniforms of the city militia. Behind the mounted officers jogged ranks of footsoldiers.

Another sound, directly below: a second cavalry charge, coming from the far side of the parade. The marchers were caught between two sets of horsemen.

Shouts became screams. In front of the barred gates, batons swung. Men went down. She realized, seeing a flash of crushed diamond, that some of the officers carried swords. Just below the window, a boy fell beneath a horse's hooves with a shriek.

Rhia looked away from the unfolding carnage, back down the hill. The riot had stalled. People were turning, looking around, running away.

But there was nowhere to go. A line of militiamen, barely visible behind their shields, headed up the hill in a solid unbroken wall. The rioters were trapped.

A few individuals broke free, slipping into the shadows between houses, but most of the crowd milled in panic. Some raised their weapons in defiance. More raised their hands in surrender. The line of soldiers advanced into them, shields held firm; from the second rank spears poked forward, jabbing and harrying. It was all screams now, screams and cries for mercy.

"They're mowing them down, Alharet! The militia are killing them."

The duchess reached past her and closed the shutter.

CHAPTER 4

When Mam Gerisa called her out from breakfast, Dej was indignant.

Pel's knife was a lovely thing: no longer than a flint paring-knife, but made of bone, the tiny, worn blade shaped like a leaf, the handle's spiral carvings still visible through generations of handling. She'd have liked to keep it. But Min was right, as usual.

Last night, she'd retrieved the knife from the leather pouch on a high rafter in the west granary. This particular stash also contained a pair of baked clay dice and a goose-feather pen with a real bronze nib. Dej had an idea the dice belonged to the boy who'd glared at her in the dinner queue. She didn't always worry about who owned the stuff she took; the thing itself mattered less than the act, that pure and perfect moment when something that hadn't been yours, became yours. With little chance to use them, and limited places to stash them, most objects found their way back to their original owners eventually, though to return the dice now would be an admission of guilt, and she didn't do those.

But she had sneaked over to the boys' bathhouse and left Pel's knife in the middle of the floor. Surely, someone must have found it by now?

Not that she could say anything. She followed the crèche-mother out of the refectory with her head bowed, lips buttoned. Some of her crèche-mates giggled or muttered as she passed. Let them.

The contemplation room wasn't a room at all, but a cupboard, too small to stand up in, just about big enough to sit down in with your legs out.

Once she'd been locked in, Dej lowered herself to the floor in the hot, reeking darkness, careful of the jug of water by the door. Previous experience suggested holding off drinking that for as long as possible. Once it was gone it was gone, and once the jug was full again – there being nowhere else to relieve yourself – you had to pee on the floor, and any mess you made you'd be clearing up before you left.

At least she'd miss morning classes. Twice. Ethics and geography today. Ethics annoyed her. How could the shadowkin tutors know how real, adult skykin thought? Geography she liked. Getting a feel for what was beyond the crèche fired her imagination and, unlike most lessons, it would be useful after her bonding.

The worst thing about the hole wasn't the dark or the cramp or the smell or even the lack of food and drink. It was the boredom. She called up a mental map of the world; her own personal geography lesson.

The crèche was about half a day's walk from the edge of Shen. Shen, like every other shadowland, was a great circle of perpetual shade, four days' walk across. (She'd once asked the geography tutor how far "four days' walk" was, given different people walked at different speeds; he'd been surprised at her interest, but unable to give a clear answer.)

It would take between six and eight days to walk to any of the six nearby shadowlands: although every shadowland was the same distance from its six neighbours, some you had to cross mountains to reach. (Again she'd asked, is that a skykin's walk rather than a shadowkin? Because a shadowkin wouldn't live long enough to walk even half a day in the skyland, would they? At this point the tutor had put her on report.)

In her head, she named those nearest shadowlands – Marn, Oras, Dolm, Erys, Xuin and Zekt – then the shadowkin nations nearest each of them, all the way along the five-deep strip of shadowlands running through the skyland like a necklace of dark beads.

But her real home was the skyland itself, even if she had yet to see it. She named the features she would find when she did – deserts, mountains, rivers, plateaus, swamps, lakes, plains – listing their salient points and visualizing what they might look like.

It was getting hot, making it hard to concentrate. She took a sip of water.

She didn't want to think about the future and it went without saying she wouldn't be reflecting on her "unacceptable behaviour". That left thinking about the past.

She and Min had become friends thanks to the contemplation room. That thought made her smile whenever she was stuck in here.

It was one of her earliest memories. She'd been three or four, playing in the vegetable garden with the other youngers. They had no formal chores at that age, though they were encouraged to dig and rootle around using miniature trowels and spades, watched over by a house-servant. Dej had put her trowel down when she heard the hedge-thrush's song. The bird sat on top of the wall, head up, music pouring from its throat. What a wonderful sound! After a while Dej tried joining in, and found to her delight that she could.

A shadow had fallen across her where she sat on the ground. The house-servant shook her head and said, "You can stop that right now, young lady!"

Dej didn't. She sang louder, scaring the bird away. Now she'd discovered this wondrous thing, she'd never stop!

The servant had dragged her indoors, where she had sung at Mam Gerisa. The crèchemother said there appeared to be only one way to "stop this foolish noise", and had shut her in the contemplation room. Dej had heard older children whisper about this awful punishment, but going from light and song to silent darkness all at once was like dying. When she came out half a day later, tearful and shaking, the first dorm-mate she encountered was Min. She'd put Min in the same category as Jen, who was already bossing around the other girls in the youngers' dorm, but Min gave her a hug and told her not to cry. Then she asked, "Why did they put you in there?"

Dej had shrugged. "Don't know."

"But you must have done something bad."

Dej considered shrugging again. But this girl was interested in her, and the thing she'd done wasn't bad, it was amazing, as well as being something the adults didn't like, which made it even better. "I did this," said Dej and then, keeping her voice low to avoid anyone else hearing, she trilled out the hedge-thrush's song, note for note.

Min had clapped her hands and hugged Dej again. After that, she began to sit with her at meals, and join in the games Dej had previously played alone.

A year later they started lessons, some of which focused on their skykin heritage. When the tutor talked about parting-gifts he'd looked at Dej, and she'd wondered if he knew she never had one. She wanted to ask... but couldn't. Min could: she put a hand up and said, "Does everyone have a parting-gift?"

"About one in a hundred babies arrive at the crèche without one."

"Why?"

Dej would never have dared talk back to a tutor like that back then.

"We don't know. You should not let it concern you."

After class Dej asked Min if she'd been one of those children too. Min said she was. Dej's relief had stopped her breath, then released it like a dam breaking. With fewer than two hundred children in the crèche, this made the two of them unique, special.

From then on, it was Min and Dej against the world.

The door opened, filling the contemplation room with light and dragging Dej back into the present. A house-servant stood in the glare.

The servant let her out, and told her to get some food at the refectory, then assume her afternoon duties. "Did Mam Gerisa change her mind, then?" asked Dej.

"Just get to your chores, please."

Most likely the she-goat had found the knife this morning but decided to give Dej half a day in the hole anyway. Or maybe someone had found it and hidden it for a while. She'd probably never know.

She hated not knowing. Too much stuff happened without a good reason here, too many things didn't make sense. The shadowkin staff went on about acting in the skykin children's best interests, then made up arbitrary rules and expected everyone to follow them. Like banning music. Dej had asked the numeracy tutor about that when she was ten. In the class he'd mentioned "musical intervals" when he talked about patterns in numbers, then caught himself. Dej had stayed behind and asked why music – a term she'd only heard a handful of times – was forbidden to skykin children. He'd just said, "The crèche teaches you what you'll need for life in the skyland once you are bonded, no more and no less. And you won't need music."

"But I will need numbers? When? How?"

"If you want to be happy here, you should start accepting that we know what's best for you."

And that was what she hated, in a nutshell.

The real problem with the contemplation room wasn't that it was boring, it was that it worked. It got you thinking. Thinking never made anything better.

She didn't see Min all day, not even at supper. In the evening she went to the herb garden, but found the bench by the wall empty. She sat anyway, trying not to panic. If Mam Gerisa had sent Min away already, and put Dej in the hole just to stop her saying goodbye, then the shegoat was going to see some *really* unacceptable behaviour.

When Dej saw a familiar figure waddle towards her she jumped up. "I was worried."

Min huffed out a breath and sat down. "No need. I'm still here. Had a bit of a rough day though. My girl's making her presence felt."

"Can you actually feel her, inside you?"

"Reckon I can. The nurse says I'm far enough along now." Though Dej had known about Min's situation for months she'd only admitted it to anyone else when her thickening waistline became impossible to hide. "Heard you'd got out the hole early. Also heard that one of the youngers found Pel's knife this morning."

"Some might call that coincidence."

"I suppose some might."

They shared a smirk. Then Min said, "Mam Gerisa spoke to me today."

"About what?" As though she didn't know.

"She says I'll be leaving next week, probably on threeday."

So soon! "Where are you going?"

"She won't say. Maybe to the city," she twirled a strand of chestnut hair which had escaped from her loose plait, "perhaps I'll catch the eye of the duke." She released the errant hair. "More likely I'll end up on one of the farms we trade with."

"But she won't say which one? Probably scared I'll follow you."

"Don't even think that!"

"Why not?"

"Whoever's taking me in might not want you too." She grinned. "Which would be their loss, of course."

"Then we could run away together."

"I can't run anywhere in this state. And where would we go?"

"Wherever we want. It's not like anyone would know we're skykin." Unbonded, they could pass for shadowkin.

"But they wouldn't take us in. Not with the drought and all."

"Maybe not." Though they still got the odd shower due to being near the umbral, the farmers had less to trade and portion sizes in the refectory were getting smaller.

"The she-goat says wherever I end up, I'll have to work to pay my way."

"But you're in no state to do heavy work."

"I think she means afterwards."

"Oh." Dej didn't like thinking about "afterwards". "So who should I try, then? Cif was staring down my tunic again when I was weeding earlier." According to the boys, Dej's breasts were her best feature. Which just showed how stupid boys were. She'd fooled around a bit with a couple of them, and not been impressed.

"That talk about you getting knocked up too was a joke, remember?"

"I suppose." It didn't feel funny now.

"Is that a blackbird?"

It was, in the distance. Dej gave in. "I know that song," she said, forcing a smile into her voice.

Min put a hand on her shoulder. "Care to sing it for me?"

"My pleasure."

She knew all those possibilities – to follow Min, to run away with her, to get pregnant herself – weren't practical, but the easy way Min had dismissed them made her feel hollow inside.

Chapter 5

"C-C-Countess?"

Rhia turned. The pair of guards Alharet had pressed upon her in the wake of the riot paused. She had avoided this not-so-chance encounter on the way to her weekly tête-à-tête with the duchess by taking a circuitous route through the palace corridors, but was unsurprised to find herself accosted now. No doubt he had been waiting for her. "Good evening, Lord Callorn."

Viscount Callorn gestured to indicate the city beyond the palace walls. "A t-terrible business tonight."

"Quite so." Although now the militia had withdrawn and the rioters fled, the palace was back to its normal state of restrained bustle.

"And I h-heard there was some trouble at House Harlyn a couple of days ago."

Of course he had. "Just a couple of ruffians, taking advantage of the rain-vigil."

"I was glad to hear you were not h-hurt."

His concern sounded genuine. Perhaps it was. She did not dislike Mercal Callorn. He was always polite, and never flinched from the sight of her masked face. In turn, she made the effort to ignore his bulbous features and faltering speech – unlike those at court who mocked his disadvantages. She felt some empathy with him. Which was, of course, what his House were bargaining on. "I'm fine. Thank you for your concern."

"A-are you coming to the b-banquet?"

"Banquet. Oh yes, the farewell banquet for our visitors from Oras."

"Tomorrow n-night, yes. Did you not g-get my invitation?"

"Ah. Yes, I did." The formal invite had arrived three days ago but she had allowed the break-in to drive it from her mind. "I'm afraid that on this occasion, I must decline." She injected some feminine weakness into her expression, considered reaching for her fan, then decided that would be excessive. The man was no fool. "These last few days have been somewhat trying."

Viscount Callorn acknowledged this with a nod of his oversized head. "Of c-course. I understand. Next t-time, perhaps?"

Again, his disappointment sounded genuine. And probably was, given the chance she represented. "Perhaps."

"Then I shall not detain you f-further. The blessings of the First on you, Countess."

"And farewell to you too, Viscount."

If she looked beyond his unattractive exterior, then Mercal Callorn was pleasant enough. And his physical disadvantages gave him a humility rare at court. He was rather pious, but not critical of her own weak faith. There were worse men to spend time with.

That was, however, no basis for a lifelong commitment.

Although the streets outside were quiet, scraps of torn clothing, discarded impromptu weapons and disturbing stains on the cobbles bore testament to recent events.

The townhouse had not escaped unscathed: one of the small glass-paned windows flanking the front door had been broken by a fleeing rioter. Fortunately, the servants had locked themselves inside. She was glad now of her instruction, after the break-in, to shutter the unglazed windows of the empty ground-floor rooms. Rhia was concerned when one of the cats could not be found, but the daft feline slunk in as she was taking her evening meal alone in the dining room.

After her meal, she went up to the observation platform above her study. She tried not to dwell on how much more fruitful her observations might be with a sightglass. Markave had ordered more doweling. She would rebuild the device.

Up here, at night, the air was as cool as it got. The night sky enveloped her, a comforting cloak sprinkled with diamonds, the familiar constellations like old friends: the Twins; the Huntsman; the Stepping Horse; the Corn-Stoop; the Merchant's Scales; the Dancers.

In some ways earth and sky mirrored each other. At night, the stars were islands of light in the dark sky. During daylight, in the world below, the shadowlands were islands of shade in the bright and hostile skyland.

She had brought materials to sketch the Moons but found herself unable to concentrate. Perhaps she should get out of the house, maybe even attend the Orasian banquet. The visit from the neighbouring shadowland had been instigated by Alharet, part of her campaign to marry off her oldest daughter to a prince of Oras. Lady Yorisa would not come of age for six years, but Alharet planned ahead; her own marriage had been the result of diplomacy, and she intended to continue the tradition. And the duchess played the courtiers and nobles with such skill. It could be an entertaining evening.

But to attend the banquet after having given her apologies to the viscount would insult House Callorn. She had stalled them for a month, ever since receiving the marriage proposal. This invitation was the second Mercal Callorn had sent. She was lucky enough to have a prior engagement the first time but today's excuse was just that: an excuse.

House Callorn was one of the poorest Houses – but also one of the largest, with many titled scions and numerous dependants. House Harlyn was rich, but small. With her brother absent, she was her House's only representative on the Council of Nobles. The problem would not go away.

She had been planning to broach the subject of marriage with Etyan, having given up waiting for him to mention it – surely she had not been so immature at seventeen?

But then he disappeared.

Once he returned, took a wife and produced children, the future would be assured. But she had to acknowledge that he might not come back, even though the thought tightened in her chest like a grasping hand. Without a male relative, even if she managed to hold on to her position, once she died House Harlyn would be dissolved. The House's assets would be divided between the three powers: Church and State and Nobles. Francin would take his third, as Shen's ruler; the other Houses would squabble over their share; but the Church had first call on any potential "items of religious significance". They would find the natural enquirers' papers. And some of what they read would scandalize them.

Money, property, even honour were fleeting. Knowledge was eternal. Those papers were her true legacy, held in trust for future generations. That they might be burned as heretical was unthinkable.

Her pen dropped from her hand. Rhia sighed, folded her notebook and stood. She climbed down the ladder, pulling the trapdoor closed after her.

When she lay down to rest, her internal vision was filled with disturbing images. Not those that had haunted her for the last two nights, those of Donkey-Face's grin and Broken-Nose's idiotic features, nor the ever-present memory of pale hair and bright blood in dirty water. Tonight she endured images of screaming men falling under hooves and staves.

Acknowledging that sleep would not come, she got up and read. The threat to the enquirers' papers had prompted her to dig deep into the ironwood chest, to reacquaint herself with its riches. She continued her study of Engineer of Dolm's speculation on the properties and uses of friction in malleable materials. More Father's area than hers; he had been a tinkerer, while she lived up to the title she had inherited from him: Observer of Shen. Yet some of Engineer of Dolm's writings gave her an idea.

"Can you explain what the binding on the tube will achieve, m'lady?"

Rhia suppressed a sigh at the master woodcarver's question. She had endured interminable, fawning formalities before he would even look at her diagram, and whilst her drafting skills were not up to Father's, surely the principle was simple enough.

When she did not answer at once the woodcarver's gaze slid past her. Markave had accompanied her down to the middle city and now sat to one side. No doubt the guildmaster would prefer to talk to him.

Rhia resisted the urge to snap her fingers, and contented herself with clearing her throat to get the man's attention. "If the two tubes are positioned one inside the other without the leather binding they will not be able to move, or else will move too freely."

"And the device requires that they do move, but in a controlled fashion?"

"Yes. Movement is required to change the focus, you see?"

Rhia doubted he did, but she only needed him to obey, not understand.

"Perhaps if I could see the lenses, m'lady?"

While Rhia fanned herself against heat and frustration, Markave stepped forward and produced a package, then unwrapped it on the guildmaster's desk.

The woodcarver leaned across and examined the lenses – without touching them, Rhia was pleased to note – then said, "I am not sure we can oblige your brother's wishes."

As though Etyan would wish for such a thing! Still, if this fusty old greybeard felt the need to believe so in order to take the commission, so be it. "As I have said, this is the requirement of House Harlyn."

"We realize this is a complex project," said Markave smoothly, "especially given the current difficulties in the supply of raw materials."

Rhia felt her mouth twitch before cutting the smile dead. *Well done, Markave.* The door was open for the men to haggle without loss of face.

"Yes, indeed," said the guildmaster, looking up from the lenses, "these are hard times. I hate to bring up the matter of payment, but such bespoke work would require the highest quality wood and the best craftsmen..." Rhia sat back and let them bargain.

Markave knew how much the sightglass meant to her but, eyes ever on the household finances, managed to beat the guildmaster down to somewhere between excessive and exorbitant.

As they left she murmured, "Thank you," without looking his way. If Markave heard, he gave no sign. She would not expect otherwise.

Outside, the day was as hot as ever. Yesterday's unrest had passed through the middle city without leaving a mark, and the airless afternoon streets were emptying for siesta.

Markave had suggested hiring a carriage but the most direct route to the woodcarvers' was via streets too steep and narrow for wheeled vehicles, and sedan chairs would be unbearable in this heat. So they walked.

As they ascended the hill the thoroughfares widened and

the houses became larger, drawing back from the cobbles.
The stench of baked brick and warm sewerage abated but did
not disappear. The city was like a great organism, thought
Rhia, with different parts carrying out discrete functions, the
interactions between them governed by rules. She had read
a treatise on that once, who had written it? Meddler of Zekt,
possibly. It was his style.

A letter waited for her at home, a simple note with the royal
seal. The content was typical Francin: direct yet ambiguous.

*Dear cousin, if your schedule permits, please visit tomorrow, at
the thirteenth hour. I have news - F.*

She had been dreading a summons from the duke for over
two months. This looked like an invitation, but with Francin,
you never knew.

CHAPTER 6

The body was not as fresh as his source had claimed. They never were.

Sadakh still paid what was asked, or rather had the servants pay it. The first time the agents who procured bodies for him had rowed their covered boat to this nondescript house they had tried to make conversation. They knew better now. Hand over the goods; take the money; leave. Sadakh, listening from a darkened room along the corridor, heard sounds of movement, followed by a closing door.

His people, a husband and wife of unquestionable loyalty and near-complete silence, carried the box into the back room between them, communicating with soft grunts. Sadakh waited while they placed the box on the scrubbed wooden table and prised the lid off.

The body had been packed with herbs, but the smell still made his eyes water. Ignoring the brief rise of nausea, he approached the table and examined his purchase.

It appeared one of the claims was true. Unlike the other three bodies he had operated on over the last four years – one of which had died of a deep belly-wound that had gone septic and two of which had telltale damage to the head, making them useless to him – this skykin was more or less intact. She had broken her neck, probably in a fall, an injury even an animus could not heal.

She's quite young, observed his ghost.

It was hard to tell skykin age but Sadakh agreed. The dead woman had the air of youth.

He nodded at the manservant, whose name was Ritek. "Lift her, please," he said, and stepped back. The last, infected body had been so decomposed that they had had to break the box down around it. This one had been dead long enough that her eyes were gone, and the scales on her chest and arms were beginning to lift. But she had been healthy before death overcame her, if a little thin. No poison in her blood to taint the extraction. As long as she had not been one of the clanless; though they were willing to sell him their own, he hoped he had made it clear by now that only a fully bonded skykin would serve his purposes.

This could be the one.

As she often did, the ghost voiced his hopes. At other times, of course, she gave form to his fears.

The smell of putrefaction lessened as the servants washed the body in salted water. He spent a while praying, asking for a steady hand and clear mind, though the act of murmuring to the First was more meditation than supplication.

When the servants were done they stepped back. He nodded thanks and a dismissal. They turned and left. Both had been criminals in their youth: Ritek a speaker of sedition against the caliarch and Ereket a liar who conned foolish men. Both had avoided slavery by accepting the removal of their tongues. Both had later sought redemption. They had become lovers, and been married, shortly after their initiation. He had made this property available to them for a nominal rent eight years ago and provided the initial funds for their laundry business, with an eye to his long-term plans.

Most of the time these two were exactly what they appeared: redeemed criminals who had become devout lay members of the Order of the First Light. That they could not speak and wrote only well enough to conduct their business made them perfect for Sadakh's higher purpose. Between faith and limited communication, his secret was safe with them.

Alone again, he went over to the body. The servants had covered the lower half of the dead woman in a sheet. Nothing was of interest to him below the neck.

He stood over the body for a few moments, mind empty, even his ghost silent. Then he picked up his obsidian-tipped scalpel.

Thanks to his unique knowledge of skykin anatomy, the initial procedure was a success. Afterwards he stripped off his stained work-tunic and washed in the scented water left by the servants. He dressed in the clothes he had removed when he first entered their house.

According to the waterclock in the hall it was the twenty-sixth hour; the operation had taken longer than he realized and it would be dawn soon. Ereket emerged from the kitchen with a bowl of warm chocatl, a luxury that would have cost her half a week's takings. He thanked her and savoured the drink, sitting cross-legged on her finest mat while he considered the night's work. Ritek and Ereket would keep the treasure he had extracted safe in the conditions he specified, behind the locked door of the room they never entered. Safe... but not easily accessible. Sadakh silently cursed the need for secrecy. Few of his followers would understand the importance of the work he did here.

Their opinions are not relevant.

Sometimes his ghost merely stated the obvious. Sometimes he wondered, if he stopped listening to her, whether she would go away and leave his head as quiet as everyone else's apparently was.

Ritek was waiting outside the parlour when he finished

his drink. The servant took the bowl, and then – having first bowed and averted his eyes to ask silent permission – re-dressed his master's hair and beard. The man used more perfume in the oil than his usual bodyservant, but Sadakh made no comment.

He would not need to instruct the pair how to proceed now; the substances they used in their work would be helpful in breaking down the unwanted remains, and they had dubious contacts of their own. The empty body would be safely disposed of.

A punt awaited him at the slipway near the launderers' house. Night mist curled in around its blunt stern where one of his bodyguards sat, a man who had, in addition to his faith, an unfortunate past thanks to his criminal family. Sadakh had ensured his history would remain just that – history. He trusted the man with his life.

The guard poled the punt silently between the islets of the city, the lake water black as ink beneath it.

Sadakh entered the priory through a postern gate. Once he was safely inside he nodded to the guard, and the punt moved off.

Less than an hour before the first office of the day. No time to rest, but enough for a proper bath before he had to lead his flock in their morning worship.

As he entered the men's baths he passed the foreign boy, coming out. For a moment the youth, forgetting himself, met Sadakh's eyes. There was a flash of understanding – or rather, Sadakh realized as the boy's lips curled into a smile, of misunderstanding. The young man was typical for his age and background, and judged the world by his own, incomplete knowledge. He assumed the eparch's tired and heavily perfumed state indicated a wholly different night's activity. Once, it might have angered Sadakh to be judged like this but now he took the encounter for what it was: another sign. He sensed his ghost's humour and, he thought, approval.

Youth was foolish but also pure. Ignorance that looked like arrogance stemmed from self-belief, and from a hunger for all life had to offer. By the time he lowered himself into the pool cut into the room's floor, Sadakh had reached a decision. If all went well at the laundry house, then one day soon, this young man might receive a blessing he had never dreamed of.

CHAPTER 7

The audience chamber could hold a dozen potentates in comfort. Today it was empty. Rhia entered, dismissed the footman and took a seat next to the most sumptuous chair.

Grand Duke Francin of Shen entered, preceded by his two favourite dogs and a whiff of cloves from his pomander. He was unattended for once. Rhia was not sure what to make of that. She stood, and he greeted her with a kiss on each cheek before waving a hand. "Take your rest, cousin. No doubt you are working too hard, as ever."

She had not seen him since the reception for the Orasian delegation three weeks ago; today he wore unadorned doublet and hose in scarlet and emerald. His rich brown hair – dyed, these days – issued in coiffed curls from under a floppy cap of moss-green velvet.

He sat next to her, not on the throne-like seat but in the ordinary low chair on the other side. He scooped up one of the tiny dogs and deposited it in his lap; the other chased its tail at his feet. At least it wasn't yapping.

The duke looked at Rhia, his dark, limpid gaze as vacuous as his pet's. "You are all right, aren't you?"

Presumably he was referring to the break-in. "I'm fine, Francin. Thank you."

"Good. Good. We've found another cache, you know."

Rhia blinked, confused. "A cache?"

"Yes, of artefacts. Right on the edge of the umbral forest."

"And they're pre-Separation?" Curiosity overcame apprehension.

"I believe so. A sinkhole opened up in a fallow field – damned drought does have some positive side-effects – and revealed one of those underground rooms."

"What was in it?"

"Couldn't tell you in detail. Safe to say it's stuff we have no idea about but which has the cardinals frothing. I do know there was another book thingy."

"A glass book?" That had been a privilege, to handle an object made by the Children of the First.

"One of those, yes."

The artefact Francin once showed her had looked like a very slender book made of a greyish material somewhere between stone and glass. It was surprisingly light in the hand. Aside from a small indentation on one side it had been featureless. Going on its size and shape Rhia had mused that it might be some sort of analogue to a book, albeit without obvious pages. Given the object was thousands of years old and made by people whose wisdom and knowledge far outstripped anything still known, this was a guess, but the theory had stuck, in Francin's mind at least.

That was five years ago, a snatched opportunity between discovery and the artefact going to the Church for "safe disposal". These days, thanks to her recent research into optics, she might give such an object a proper examination.

"So, might we get access to some of the items? To the glass book, perhaps?"

"Alas no. That naughty clerical error we took advantage of was a one-off. And the Church are not too happy with me right now." Presumably because he had arrested one of their own for inciting the recent riot.

Rhia hid her disappointment. But to be told she was not

to have access to an ancient artefact was nothing new. She waited for Francin to offer more. When he didn't she said, "You mentioned having news, in your note."

"Indeed I did."

"So, has something come to light?" Rhia kept her question vague.

"Hmm. Yes. You could say that."

"Francin, stop it!"

Francin stroked the head of the dog on his lap. The other one had tired of chasing itself and sat on its haunches, looking at its master with mindless adoration. "Stop what, cousin?"

Rhia did not reply. Instead she drew a long, steadying breath. She had insisted on knowing everything the militia investigators had uncovered about Etyan's sudden and unexpected departure. Not that it amounted to much. Francin had never mentioned a link between her brother and the unfortunate incident in the lower city, but that did not mean he hadn't found one. "Please, can we bypass the verbal fencing? Just tell me what you've found out."

"Etyan is in Zekt."

"What?"

"Hah. You ask me to talk straight and then act stupefied! Really. I expect better from a mind like yours."

"Francin!" But her reply was distracted, as the news sank in. "Zekt? My brother's in Zekt?"

"It was always likely."

"A possibility, yes." Zekt was one of three shadowlands with a caravan departure around the time Etyan disappeared. "But now you're sure it's Zekt?"

"I have new information from a reliable source."

"A source you can share?"

Francin waggled a finger at her, making the dogs flinch. "I don't ask for details of your researches and investigations, do I?"

"Point taken." She suspected she would be happier not knowing. She picked her next words with care. "I don't suppose your source has any idea why he went to Zekt?"

"No. It appears only Etyan himself knows that."

"What will you do now?"

"Well, we can't have our nobles gallivanting off, especially not to Zekt. I'll send people to fetch him home."

To face justice? Rhia was glad they were next to each other, not eye to eye. "Who will you send?"

"My best. After all, Etyan is my cousin. Well, second cousin once removed or whatever the correct–"

"I'll go too." *Where did that come from?*

"What?"

"I will go and bring my brother home." Out across the skyland, to another shadowland. What a thought!

"That's out of the question."

"No, no it isn't. It makes perfect sense." And it did, for more reasons than she dared say. She searched for a safe argument. "We didn't part on the best of terms. The only way to show Etyan how much I want him back is to go myself. Sending a stranger might make him run again." *As would guilt.*

Francin turned to look sidelong at her. The dog on his lap gave a muffled half growl of protest. "Rhia, I let you have your way in many things. Not this time. Etyan is the only close family you have and of course you miss him. You want to do all you can to ensure his safe return. But it would be unthinkable for someone in your position to undertake such a journey. I will not have it." Francin picked up the dog and stood. "And that is an end to it."

Rhia knew further argument was pointless.

Rhia's only thought when she offered to fetch Etyan was of the journey itself, of the wonders she might see out in the skyland. But by the time she left the royal presence, her mind had come up with more reasons to go.

Ever since that dark morning when she followed her brother down the hill her world had been off balance. She had stumbled on a grim puzzle with no solution. Or rather, to mirror Francin's words, only Etyan knew the solution.

She would also be escaping the attentions of Mercal Callorn, a prospect which brought guilty relief. And once Etyan returned and proved her fears groundless, House Callorn's proposal would become irrelevant.

The only reason to stay was to guard her papers, and between the servants' extra care and the metal padlock she had asked Markave to buy for the ironwood chest, the enquirers' wisdom was as safe as she could make it.

It niggled that she had no idea who was behind the break-in. Given her papers had been the target, it must be someone who knew she was in the natural enquirers' network.

Could it be the other enquirer in her shadowland? Although face-to-face contact between enquirers was not encouraged, Father had taken her to meet Theorist of Shen once. The other enquirer had been perplexed, having assumed her brother would inherit her father's role. She'd had no direct contact with the man since Father's death. But why would another enquirer want her papers? Even if he had lost his, the enquirers' code allowed him to simply ask for access to hers.

Francin probably knew she was a natural enquirer. Despite his air of vacuous dissolution, little happened in Shen he was unaware of. But again, if he wanted her papers, he had only to ask.

Did Francin know of a link between Etyan's disappearance and that poor girl's death? *Was* there a link? Though her little brother was feckless and wild, he was a gentle soul. But he was too easily led by sweet words, too prone to buy the friendship of fickle companions. She should have done a better job of protecting him – from himself as much as anything. She should never have let things go this far.

But they had. And the only way to uncover the truth was to speak to Etyan before the duke's men did.

To do that, she must go to Zekt.

"Rhia?"

Rhia started and focused on her surroundings. She hadn't seen Alharet coming along the corridor. "Oh, Alharet. He's found him."

"Who...? Wait, you mean Etyan. Francin's found Etyan." Surprise lit up Alharet's placid face.

Rhia nodded.

"Praise the First! My dear, that is marvellous." Alharet looked at her more closely. "What is wrong? Is he... hurt?"

"No. He's in Zekt!"

Alharet's surprise turned to shock. "Zekt!"

Rhia cursed her self-absorption. Alharet rarely mentioned her old homeland; Rhia had the impression she was glad to have left it. "Yes. He's – Francin, that is – is sending someone to fetch him back."

"Francin's sending someone to Zekt."

"Yes. And I should go with them, Alharet. Etyan and I rowed terribly."

"Yes, but you must not consider going yourself! Last curse it, I'm on my way to an appointment, otherwise I would insist you come and tell me everything."

"Oh yes, how was the banquet last night?"

"Never mind the banquet. It was fine. You say the duke is sending an expedition to Zekt!"

"Yes, and I can't... I can't just sit by any more."

Alharet took both Rhia's hands in hers. "My dear, that is precisely what you must do. Anything else is unthinkable." She released her cool hold. "Now, I have to go. Come and see me soon."

Rhia nodded. As Alharet swept off down the corridor it occurred to Rhia that this was the first time in recent memory the duke and his wife had agreed on something.

CHAPTER 8

Four days before Min was due to leave, a pair of skykin arrived at the crèche.

Looking out the dorm window after siesta, Dej saw a solid-sided wagon approaching from the west through the barley fields. Today's first set of chores was turning hay. While everyone milled around by the back door, she "accidentally" stepped on the rake she'd just been issued, breaking its ironwood tines. She told the servant in charge of her work group she would go and fetch a new one. Somewhat to her surprise, he fell for it.

After selecting a new rake, she loitered in the tool store. When the courtyard gates opened she pulled the door shut to peer out through the crack. She'd be getting a caning, if not hole time, for dawdling like this, but she didn't care. Skykin visited no more than half a dozen times a year and the crèche staff kept them away from their charges. Wait until she told Min she'd been this close.

The wagon slowed and the rhinobeast pulling it tossed its head. Diamond studs in its hardened head-frill caught the light and Dej smelled the beast's musty, yeasty scent. The skykin driving the wagon clicked his tongue, and the rhinobeast settled. The driver got down to help his passenger: just the one this time, and no babes in arms. The skykin woman was further gone than Min, her naked belly round as an egg.

Mam Gerisa hurried into view. "Welcome, welcome. We wondered if we might see you soon," she addressed the skykin wagon driver, then turned to the female skykin, "and to have a new life come to us is always a blessing."

You didn't think that about Min, you bitch.

The woman said, "The birth may be hard. Have you a room ready?"

"Always. The midwife will meet us there." Mam Gerisa turned to the other skykin. "We will find refreshments and a place for you to wait. Will you take any this time?"

"Yes. Three." Dej hoped Pel would be one of them. He was a year older than her, and overdue his bonding.

Mam Gerisa nodded, then turned to help the pregnant skykin. Her companion climbed back onto the wagon. He murmured to the rhinobeast, which lurched forward, heading for the animal compound at the back of the crèche buildings.

As the skykin woman passed the storeroom she looked up. Dej, head full of dorm gossip about unearthly senses, ducked back, before snorting at herself for being afraid. These were skykin – her people.

Dej waited for a summons to the she-goat, but none came. Looked like she'd got away with being late for her shift. Perhaps Mam Gerisa had more important matters on her mind.

At dinner the skykin who'd driven the wagon ate at top table, sending an excited buzz round the refectory. The way Mam Gerisa had greeted him implied he was a regular visitor. Dej wondered how the old goat knew, given all skykin looked the same to her, wiry and hairless and covered in scales. That would change when she was bonded, of course.

There was no sign of the woman.

At the end of the meal Mam Gerisa stood up. Everyone fell silent.

"This is a joyous day," she said. "You have a new crèche-mate, a little boy, praise the First." Another brief buzz, though most people were more interested in the visiting skykin than in a new baby. She continued, "Our visitors will return to the skyland once the mother has taken her rest. And when they leave," she concluded, "they will take three of you with them to become adults."

The olders looked at each other, some smiling, some nervous.

"Those three are Pel, Mev and Dej."

Everyone at their table looked at Dej. Dej waited for Mam Gerisa to correct her mistake, but the crèche-mother was sitting down.

Min hugged her. Dej tried to hug her back, but between the baby in Min's belly, and the hollowness in hers, it felt like they were barely touching.

Restday was another stupid inconsistency.

The scriptures tutor said Dej and her crèche-mates had to study the ancient texts because they went way back to the Separation, when the Children of the First fell from grace and split into skykin and shadowkin. Maybe so, but ever since the Separation the skykin didn't worship the First in the same way shadowkin did. While the crèche staff packed into the chapel every restday to recite holy words – some in a sing-song way which always caught Dej's ear – then hear the travelling priest's sermon and mutter prayers to the pretty-but-too-large-to-steal box allegedly containing a finger-bone of Saint Yu, their charges just got a day off to sleep or play games or do whatever else they wanted, within reason. But if the skykin didn't keep restday as holy, why should it be different to any other day for their children?

Not that Dej objected to a day off from classes and chores. And this restday Dej was happy to give thanks to the First, because it might be the last day she had with her friend, and she wanted to relish every moment of it.

She walked the gardens and fields with Min, saying goodbye to favourite places: a lime tree with a low branch they used to swing on, the olive grove where they'd once built a den, the ridge on the edge of the crèche's lands with the best view across to the clouded silver of the skyland. They took it slowly, resting whenever Min needed to, telling each other anecdotes they both knew, revisiting memories and secrets they'd shared. And singing. Alone in the fields they could sing loud and long and no one could stop them.

Whenever they saw crèche-mates or, after chapel, crèche staff, people smiled but didn't approach. They didn't even get pulled up for going up to the ridge, which was out of bounds now it was too dry to grow anything on. People were being so nice.

Somehow it got to suppertime without either of them mentioning what was to come. At supper Dej got an extra portion. Everyone on the table was her friend, not just Min. Even Jen wished her the best though, typically, the dorm's own little duchess added, "Well, the best you can manage, anyway," as she walked off.

After supper, Dej was called away to the baths. By the time she got back to the dorm, Min was asleep.

CHAPTER 9

The priest who had incited the riot was executed by hanging and disembowelment. Rhia's two junior staff, the manservant Brynan and the new maid, Nerilyn, asked leave to attend. The execution was held outside the city both as a mark of how low the priest had fallen and to accommodate the crowds.

This was the duke's justice being seen to be done. Just as it would be seen to be done to Etyan, if he was guilty. When the sound of the crowd drifted up the hill, Rhia closed the shutters and lit a lamp.

The servants returned as darkness fell. Their voices carried up the stairwell, before being hushed by Markave. Shortly afterwards her steward entered her study with the newly arrived lock for her ironwood chest. As he turned to leave she asked how the execution had gone.

"As well as these things ever go, Brynan tells me."

"But there was no... unrest?"

"Quite the contrary. Before the execution the duke's representative announced that taxes on foodstuffs entering the city will be cut by a third."

"A popular move, I imagine."

"Indeed so, m'lady. And as a result, everyone will expect prices to fall. If the merchants don't cut their prices, then the people will have a new target for their anger."

"So they will." Typical Francin, to divert people's attention like that.

"Will that be all, m'lady?"

"Yes. No, wait." She had been so wrapped up in the news about Etyan she had failed to share it. Now she explained that young Lord Harlyn had been located and the duke was sending people to Zekt to bring him home. She did not mention her response to Francin's offer.

"This is wonderful news, m'lady," said Markave, "and I am sure the duke will keep you informed."

"With those details he feels I should know, yes. However, servants may discover things their masters and mistresses remain oblivious of."

"I am not sure what you are asking."

"Just that if you, or anyone you regularly converse with, finds out anything regarding the expedition to Zekt, you should tell me."

"What manner of thing, if I may ask?"

"Who is going, how they will travel, and when they will depart." If the expedition did not leave in the next five or six days, it would have to wait another two weeks. Whilst Shen ran multiple caravans to the other five adjacent shadowlands, the route to Zekt had just the one, shuttling back and forth, a week each way over the mountains.

"May I speak freely?"

"Always." There had been a time when he came close to being more than a servant, shortly after the rain-fever took Father. Just a hand over hers, unexpected eye contact, a soft word. That she had let it develop into adolescent infatuation was her problem, not his. After all, he was over ten years her senior, and had his own grief to deal with after losing his wife to the same disease. Nothing had come of it. He had remarried, and her feelings towards him had mellowed.

"We – your household – look forward to the safe return of young Lord Harlyn. But we would be distressed should your eagerness to ensure this lead you to do anything rash."

He knew her well. "Such as?" she asked with false lightness.

He bowed his head, the thinning patch on the top catching the lamplight. "I could not say, m'lady."

Or rather *would* not. "Your concern is…" she searched for the right words and settled on "… a credit to you. Yet I would still like to know anything you discover."

"I shall report all I hear."

Markave's unease with her plan gave her a moment of doubt. But only a moment.

The following morning another note from the duke arrived. Her hands trembled as she unfolded it, in case she was being summoned to the palace to hear the charges her brother would face. But the note merely stated that Francin would be despatching the expedition to Zekt "early next week" and that it was "travelling unofficially".

As must she. She *could* book herself onto the caravan and travel to Zekt openly. It would be scandalous, but not illegal or impractical, for an unaccompanied noblewoman to leave her shadowland. She had considered such travel before, had in fact promised herself she would see the world once Etyan was safely married. But she suspected Francin would stop her, just as he had stopped her late uncle.

Rhia rang for Fenera. The steward's wife arrived in the parlour with flour on her hands. When Rhia apologized for taking her from her duties she bobbed and said it was nothing.

"I would like to ask a favour of you," said Rhia.

"Of course, m'lady."

"I wish to borrow some of your clothes."

"I'm sorry, m'lady?"

"Just a few items, a loan I will reimburse you for. I'm after some practical women's clothing, just for a while."

Fenera started, then focused. "As m'lady wishes." The housekeeper blinked then added, "M'lady is somewhat smaller than I."

"Yes, but Nerilyn is a beanpole, so she'd be no good." Rhia tried to make her comment lighthearted, an attempt at womanly camaraderie. Fenera just stared. Rhia cleared her throat. "If you could put together a few pieces by tomorrow, please."

"Yes, m'lady."

The woodcarvers had quoted her "about a week" to construct the sightglass. With the Harbinger still some years off, she had seen little urgency. But now she was going into the skyland, and she wanted her sightglass for that journey.

She re-read papers on Zekt, on caravan etiquette and on the nature, geography and creatures of the skyland itself. Although the skykin shared a common origin with the shadowkin there was comparatively little written about them, at least not in her papers. Had she more time she might have requested further writings from the enquirers' network.

She packed, unpacked and repacked several times. She kept her baggage in her bedchamber to avoid having to discuss it with the servants, though from the looks she saw exchanged, they knew her plan.

Despite the preparations, she found herself noticing how quiet the house was. When Etyan first disappeared, the silence was disconcerting. Yet even as worry over her brother kept her awake at night, she had guiltily enjoyed the peace his absence brought. Etyan had filled the house with noise and fuss, never walking up the stairs when he could run, leaving every room he entered in a mess, pulling the servants from their duties to practise the latest courtly dance or play some fashionable new game. Laughing, even as he denied a minor misdemeanour or concocted a ridiculous excuse for skipping his lessons. Infuriating. Impossible. Full of life. But since coming of age last year, he had also started bringing home noble scions of other Houses, eager to impress them now he had assumed his role as head of House Harlyn, and Rhia did not miss that at all.

In these last months she had become accustomed to the house's air of quiet reserve, but as she climbed the central staircase she felt suddenly alone. First Ma, then Father. Then Etyan. But he wasn't lost yet. She would bring him home, and learn to embrace the chaos that came with him.

Markave brought news back from the restday service. According to a contact at the palace the expedition would consist of a couple of militiamen posing as traders. That she would be keeping company with the same men who had laid into the rioters with such efficient brutality was alarming, although if there were dangers on the road, the militia would be the ones to deal with them. More chillingly, if Etyan tried to run, they would be able to deal with *him*.

Markave said his contact would pass on the exact timing of the expedition once it was known.

The next morning, she awoke from another dream mish-mash of recent events: the body in the pool was Alharet's, until Rhia reached out, as she had not dared to in real life, and turned it; then Donkey-Face grinned up at her, starting her awake. Voices drifted up the stairwell. Markave and Fenera; arguing, though she could not make out actual words, only the aggravated tone. The steward shushed his wife and silence returned. She wondered if the disagreement had been about her before reminding herself that other people had lives too.

• • •

Twoday came around, and with it her regular visit to Alharet. The matter of the Zekti expedition was sure to come up and Rhia did not want to lie to her friend. Alharet had been so adamant she should not go. She quashed the thought that being unable to take the duchess into her confidence had cut off a valuable source of information about her destination. Instead she sent a note pleading indisposition.

She received the reply later that day.

Dearest Rhia,

I am sorry you were unable to visit today, as I do enjoy our weekly chats. I hope you will be fully recovered and in a position to see me next week.

In the meantime, I have a gift for you, which I was going to present when you came to the palace. It is a new sandclock, of a similar design to the one you lost. I hope you will find a place for it in your study.

Yours,

A

The sandclock was magnificent, a superior specimen to the broken one. The gift made her uneasy: here she was, running after someone who had run from her, whilst deceiving her best friend!

A second note arrived as night fell. She wondered if it brought news of the duke's party, who must surely leave soon to catch the caravan. But it was from the woodcarvers. The sightglass was complete.

"M'lady, m'lady, wake up!"

Rhia forced her eyes open. A familiar figure was bending over her, holding a lantern. "What is it, Nerilyn?"

"The men going to Zekt, they're leaving now!"

Rhia struggled to free herself from the tangled sheets. "Has

Brynan gone to the woodcarvers' yet?"

"No, m'lady, it's still dark. Shall I–"

"Yes! Tell him to meet me on the north road. Wait, where's Markave?"

"Downstairs, m'lady. He brought news of the departure."

"Right. Good." No, not good, it meant the expedition had a head start on them. "Go, girl! Send Brynan on his way!"

Nerilyn slipped out, leaving the lantern. Rhia staggered to her feet then lurched over to her dresser, sweeping off last night's dress in favour of the plain kirtle loaned by Fenera. If she laced it tight and cinched the belt it barely dragged on the floor. Men's clothing would be more practical, but Father's old breeches and shirts would attract even more attention than noble attire.

By the time she was dressed Nerilyn was back, asking if she was decent. Markave entered after her.

"Is this your pack, m'lady?" he asked, gesturing to the bundle by the door.

"Yes. Carry it, please."

Rhia looked around, knowing she had missed something – aside from enough sleep, a good wash and breakfast – but not what, until her eye lit upon her satchel. She looped it across her body. Markave had already hoisted the pack on his back. She grabbed the lantern and followed him out. As she did so she glimpsed a feline face darting away. She would have liked to say goodbye to the cats. She would have liked a lot of things. But she was out of time.

CHAPTER 10

Dej left the crèche at dawn the next morning.

She and the two others chosen for bonding had been allowed to use as much water and soap as they wanted the previous night. As well as bathing, they'd had their hair shorn. Without the heft of her plait, Dej's head felt light, unbalanced.

She'd been sent back to the dorm after bathing but couldn't sleep, so she'd crept around her various stashes, leaving years' worth of accumulated prizes on floors or shelves or in kitchen cupboards. None of the treasures she'd taken would be any use where she was going.

As was the custom, everyone turned out to see their crèche-mates off, from the olders down to babies carried by the wet-nurses. Dej stood with Min while everyone assembled.

She wanted this moment to go on for ever. She wanted it to have never arrived.

Without looking at her, Min said, "I don't know what'll happen out there, only that it'll be hard. But I believe in you, Dej."

Dej swallowed against the hollowness inside. "What about you? I mean we'll always be friends, won't we? They can't keep us apart, even now."

Min put her arms around her. Dej shut up, collapsing into her friend's embrace. She wouldn't cry; she would be strong, for Min.

Into her ear, Min whispered, "I've taken the easy path. Forgive me."

Then Mam Gerisa was calling her forward. After a last look at the only home she knew, she climbed into the back of the wagon.

The first part of the journey passed in awkward silence. Before they left the crèche one of the skykin pointed out the food, water and chamber pot under the benches along either side of the wagon. Then the door was shut, and the three of them were alone in a dark and airless wooden box.

The highlight of the morning was the rumble of a cart going the other way. The wagon got even dimmer as they entered the umbral forest. Then, suddenly, the world outside caught fire. Dej had expected the heat once they reached the skyland but not the clamminess; the air felt heavy, like a storm was brewing.

Finally, she couldn't stand it any longer. She jumped up onto the bench, trying to see out through the narrow gap just below the wagon's ceiling.

"You shouldn't do that!"

Dej ignored Mev and strained her neck, but she was too short. All she could see was the overhang of the wagon roof.

"Dej, did you hear me?"

She sighed and turned, grabbing a strut to brace herself; there were no proper roads out here, and the wagon dipped and swayed. "No I didn't. Even though all we can hear is the turning of the wheels and Pel's oh-so-attractive mouth breathing, I just went deaf for no reason at all. You were saying?"

Mev looked like she'd had a lemon shoved into her mouth. She was one of Jen's favourites – *had been* one of Jen's favourites – and she wasn't used to Dej answering back. Well, with Min gone, Dej had to fight her own battles. "I said,

'Don't do that'." Mev nodded forward to indicate the pair of skykin driving the wagon. "They wouldn't like it."

"Really? I don't remember them telling us not to look outside."

"It's dangerous to look at the skyland before you're bonded, you know that. Besides, we should use this time to prepare ourselves."

"How, exactly? We don't know what's going to happen."

"There are techniques, if you'd bothered to learn them." Mev meant static meditation, ways of breathing and counting and even sitting which, the tutors claimed, would calm them in body and mind, make them ready to receive their animus. Dej had found meditation lessons as pointless and tedious as ethics.

Pel turned to Mev. "Oh, just ignore her."

Dej decided to ignore them both. Though all she could see on this side was the underside of the wagon roof, by looking across the wagon and narrowing her eyes she could see enough outside to know that the top half of the world was even brighter than the bottom, presumably the division between ground and sky. She couldn't make out anything else.

She looked down to see Mev reach inside her tunic. The other girl brought out a pouch, which she stared at while Dej lowered herself back down to sit opposite. Dej nodded to the pouch, "All right to do a show and tell now, is it?"

Pel, sitting next to Mev, was also pulling out the pouch he'd been wearing around his neck. "Certainly is," he said, then looked up at Dej. "Assuming you've got anything to show."

Now they were openly wearing their parting-gifts, Pel would've noticed she didn't have anything round her neck. She shouldn't have said anything.

Pel turned to Mev. "Perhaps someone stole her parting-gift. That would be a terrible thing, now wouldn't it?"

Mev gave Pel an irritated look. "Let it go, Pel."

Dej suppressed a grin.

Mev upended her pouch to tip a finger of pale pink crystal onto her palm. She stared at it for a moment, then covered it with her other hand, sighed and closed her eyes. She'd probably become a healer or carer; Dej remembered her being good at anatomy and nature classes.

Pel got out his own parting-gift, then bowed his head to stare at the knife on his palm. A knife meant hunter or warrior, according to what they'd been taught, though the tutors said your parting-gift was only a guide, not a sure indication of your final place in skykin society.

Dej had no link to what her mother might have done and been – to what she herself might become. Nothing to focus on while she prepared herself for bonding.

She'd just have to use what she did have. She began to sing under her breath. The tune was a simple one, composed so long ago she'd forgotten when, with no words, just sounds fitted to music: *ta-la-ta-lala, la-ta-la-tata*. Pel looked up from contemplating his knife, and frowned. She didn't falter; she sang louder. Openly. It was time to let the music out. She didn't think it would piss Pel off enough that he'd try to stop her; and if he did, she'd give as good as she got.

Mev opened her eyes too. Dej moved on to the yam-trader's little ditty. She sang it to the end, including the verse about Pel, trying not to feel the lack of Min's voice. Pel was glaring at her now.

When she finished, Mev spoke up. "Where did you learn to do that?"

Dej shrugged. "I just can."

"I never knew." Mev looked down at her crystal. Then she added, "It's rather good."

"Rather useless, more like," growled Pel.

"I like singing. Mev likes it too. You're outnumbered, Pel."

"And you're a loser. I hope your animus rejects you."

Mev drew a sharp, shocked breath.

"What did you say?" Heat rose in Dej's cheeks.

"You heard me."

Dej threw herself across the wagon, fingers outstretched. Mev leaned forward and collided with her, knocking her to one side.

"Ow!" exclaimed Mev, sounding offended, as though she had been Dej's target.

Dej sat back, panting. The urge to scratch Pel's eyes from his face passed as suddenly as it had come, though if that bastard laughed now, if he so much as smiled...

But Pel was sitting back, looking pale. He'd dropped his parting-gift, and his gaze twitched between it and her.

"Just pick it up," said Dej. "You're not worth the effort." She closed her eyes, making like she didn't care.

But she did.

She'd assumed she'd change, somehow, before being bonded. That she'd become ready. Things would start to make sense, or at least she'd learn to accept when they didn't. As her bonding approached she'd be happy to stop stealing, start obeying, and not question. She'd grow up, ready for the future, when she'd be with Min, free, out in the skyland. But that hadn't happened – hadn't had a chance to happen.

This was all too sudden, too soon. She was going to her bonding alone, and unprepared.

CHAPTER 11

They could still beat the cart. It had to use the wide streets that wound around the hill. On foot, Rhia could take a shorter, more direct, route.

The initial cut-through nearly tripped her up. Only Markave's steadying hand stopped her from dropping the lantern and taking a tumble when she stepped on her over-long skirt. She smiled her gratitude then carried on more slowly, her free hand on the wall.

Etyan had come this way, at about this time of the morning, three months back. His path had been unplanned, random. But always downwards.

By the time they reached the middle city the sky was lightening.

In the lower city people were already up and about. Avoiding an open sewer oozing along one side of a narrow alley, Rhia almost tripped over a beggar. Markave shouted at the man to watch himself.

She had followed Etyan on a restday, and the streets had been quiet. He had not headed for the road, and had left home without a cloak or hat; not the actions of someone planning to leave. But leave he had.

They came out onto the north road near the bridge. Rhia looked along the road but saw no carts. She hurried over the bridge. The river, never wholesome, was reduced to a stinking, muddy stream. Just upstream was the low cutting on the bank which channelled water to the dyers' pools. She did not look that way.

Beyond the bridge the road went through open farmland. She made out two carts in the grey pre-dawn, both heading away. One had a lone driver and open sides. The other, farther off, had several people in it.

"Far one?" she said to Markave, panting.

He nodded. "Fenera heard a rumour three men might be sent."

"Then we must run."

Rhia broke into an exhausted lope. They passed the first cart, a farmer on his way to the fields.

Her lantern went out. She flung it away.

As they got closer Rhia saw the second cart had benches down each side, with two passengers and a driver. One of the passengers turned to look at her. His face was distant, and in shadow, but something about the way he tensed alerted Rhia. Although he wore peasant clothes this was no farmer; he was reacting to a possible threat, like a soldier.

"Hold, please!" she called.

Both passengers faced her now. A lantern on a pole lit them from above. The second, younger, man looked to the older one. The driver gave no sign of having heard her, and the cart carried on.

Markave shouted, "Hold in the name of the duke!"

The cart slowed, then stopped.

The men in the back stayed as they were, hands near belts, as Rhia and Markave approached. Rhia pressed a hand to the stitch in her side while she waited for her dignity to catch up with her. Then she stepped up to the cart. Still the men didn't move. From here she could see bundles under the benches, though not as many as she would expect traders – or those posing as traders – to carry.

She reached up and extended a hand over the cart's back flap, as though presenting it to be kissed at court. "Despite appearances," she wheezed, "I am Countess Rhia Harlyn, and I order you to take me with you." She wore her comfortable old mask, the boiled leather faded to almost match her skin tone, but its mere presence should support her claim. Although she doubted any of these men had seen her before, given the interest her life appeared to hold for those at court, they no doubt knew of her disfigurement.

The men did not move. The older one had a thin face and dark hair salted with grey. The younger man was fresh complexioned, with thick fair hair; he looked to his companion who was also, no doubt, his commander. The driver, between the other two in age and the heaviest of the three, was looking over his shoulder at her.

The older man leaned forward and, without touching Rhia, examined the signet ring on her outstretched hand. He gave her a deep and calculating gaze; not the look of a man who believed what he had just been told. Rhia met his eye.

Finally, he leaned back and, still looking at her, said, "This is unexpected." His tone was questioning, as though giving her a chance to change her story.

"I realize that, but I wish to fetch my brother home from Zekt in person."

"The duke did not mention you in connection with our mission."

Rhia enjoyed a moment of smug vindication: she had surprised Francin for once! He hadn't thought she would dare disobey him, or he would have warned his men.

"Nonetheless," she said, "it is my wish to accompany you, and you will respect that." It was disconcerting not to be obeyed without question.

"M'lady?"

Rhia turned her head to see Markave looking back up the

road. "M'lady, I believe your manservant is on the bridge."

Rhia hesitated before turning, aware of the three militiamen's regard. Then she withdrew her hand and looked back towards the city. A lone figure stood at the centre of the bridge, staring out. As they watched he turned away.

Rhia turned to Markave, "Go to him, quickly, I must have what he carries!"

Markave put her pack down then set off back towards the city at a tired run. Rhia turned to the soldiers, composing her face. Though they might not respect her, they would not harm her.

The older one had sat up straight. Something in his manner had changed. It took her a moment to realize that suspicion had given way to deference, presumably because of the way Markave jumped at her command.

"M'lady," said the older man, "our errand is not suitable for a noble, let alone one of the gentler sex."

"Your errand is to fetch my brother, my only family. This matters more than my position or gender." She was aware of the contradiction in her statement: she had asked them to obey her because she was a noble, yet now she asked them to ignore her rank and think instead of a sister's love. She hoped they would not spot the anomaly.

The commander's lips thinned. While he was still considering his response the driver spoke. "Captain, should one of us return to the palace to inform the duke of the countess's request?"

Their commander shook his head. "No time for that."

"I accept full responsibility for any fate that may befall me," said Rhia.

"Begging m'lady's pardon," said the commander, "but His Grace may not see it that way."

"I have prepared a letter stating this, which you may keep on your person in case of... mishap."

For a moment, the commander was silent. Then he said, "M'lady must know we cannot make concessions to her status."

"I accept that. As you see, I am prepared to travel as a commoner."

The man nodded. "Then we will do all we can to ensure m'lady's safety and comfort." He didn't sound happy.

Rhia suppressed a smile of triumph.

The driver looked uneasy, although the other lad smiled.

Sensing movement behind her, Rhia turned to see Markave jogging back. He carried a package in one hand; Rhia tried not to wince at the way he swung it as he ran.

He drew to a halt and huffed, "M'lady, your commission from the woodcarvers."

"Thank you, Markave." She took the paper-wrapped package. "Our militia have agreed to take me with them."

"Very good, m'lady." Markave bent over, then winced and straightened. "Shall I put your luggage in the cart?"

"Yes, please." She had a sudden urge to take her steward's hand. She resisted, but did let him help her onto the cart. She sat next to the smiling young man who let down the flap for her, rather than his grim-faced commander. Much as she itched to see the woodcarvers' handiwork she slid the package into her satchel.

Markave still stood at the back of the cart. "All will be well," she said to him. She meant it as reassurance, but it came out sounding more like an admonishment.

He bowed his head. "Of course, m'lady."

Behind her the commander said, "Let's get going." The cart lurched forward.

Markave watched the cart pull away. Rhia gave him a smile and a small wave. His response was invisible in the dim light. After a while he turned and walked back to the city.

Rhia faced the militiamen. "In case you are concerned, I have my own money. I will not be a burden financially."

"Thank you, m'lady." The commander probably expected her to be a burden in other ways. "I am Captain Sorne," he continued. "And these are my corporals Breen," he indicated the smiling young man who murmured, *m'lady*, "and Lekem." The latter, hunched over the reins, nodded without turning.

Rhia smiled at Breen and Sorne. Silence fell.

She cleared her throat. "I believe you travel as traders?"

"We do, m'lady," said Captain Sorne.

"I cannot see much in the way of trade goods in this cart."

"I'm not sure how much m'lady knows of how business is conducted with Zekt."

Rhia searched her memory for childhood lessons. "The Zekti value our wine, fine cloth and dried fruits."

"So they do, m'lady. And all these items are luxuries, so trade in them is competitive. Perhaps one man with a pack might travel freely, but a cartload would arouse ill-feeling, possibly even open hostility from established traders."

"But why send a cart at all? Why not send just one man?"

"His Grace is a careful planner. And, forgive me if this causes m'lady distress, but we don't know the state and disposition of young Lord Harlyn. He may not be fit to travel."

An unpleasant thought. And there was a worse one: that Etyan might be brought back bound and unwilling. "So, if you are not traders, what story you will give those who show an interest in you?" *In us*, she silently corrected herself.

"Should anyone ask, m'lady, myself and my two nephews are travelling to Zekt to start a new life."

"Our poor mother passed away some years ago," said Corporal Breen, taking up the tale. He had a pleasant voice, matching his easy smile. "Luckily good old Uncle Sorne here took us in." Their commander shook his head at his subordinate's play-acting. "But then our auntie died too, the poor ol' girl. And there were those debts and maybe some other trouble we don't talk about, eh?" he smirked.

"You'd imply you are criminals?" Rhia was shocked.

"My corporal here is trying to impress m'lady, which he can stop doing right now. What he means is that having a dubious reputation can be a good thing when you're amongst strangers. Our actual trade is bakery."

"Bakery?" Rhia wondered if she had misheard. "That's very... ordinary."

"Indeed it is, m'lady. Ordinary and unremarkable. However, as I'm sure m'lady has noticed, Shenese confectioners and bakers are highly skilled."

Rhia had to agree. Those butter biscuits she enjoyed were but one of the delicacies visiting nobles from other nations commented on. "So you will claim to be able to, ah, bake?"

"Both Lekem and Breen can, to some extent. Having heard Zekt lacks decent bakers, we're choosing to resettle there. Unfortunately, we'll find that the local grain is not suitable for our needs, and be forced to return to Shen. If we happened to find a Shenese citizen who wanted to return to his homeland we would encourage him to travel with us."

Rhia liked the words "wanted" and "encourage". It implied they would not coerce Etyan, which in turn implied they were unaware of his possible crime. Then again, what else would they say to her? And Francin had ordered his men to use subterfuge. She knew why. Etyan was a Shenese high noble who had secretly travelled to a shadowland Shen had shaky relations with. To openly demand his return from the Zekti authorities as though he were being held hostage, or even to admit he had fled his homeland, were politically unwise moves in the games of status and power the shadowlands engaged in. "The duke has thought of everything," she conceded aloud.

"Indeed he has, m'lady."

The Sun was rising; Breen lowered the pole and extinguished the lantern.

She wondered what the soldiers' precise orders were. To go to Zekt and find Etyan and bring him back to Shen, yes. But to what fate? And what were these men instructed to do if Etyan tried to run again? Was not letting him get away more important than letting him live?

Whatever the details of their orders – and she could hardly ask – they had not included escorting the sister of their quarry. She stared at Shen city, her home, watching the early light wash over it, until dust kicked up by the cart hazed the view. When the Sun pulled free of the eastern uplands, the day began to heat up.

Rhia reached for her pack.

"May I help, m'lady?" said Breen.

"Ah, yes. Hold this steady for me."

She dug out the wide-brimmed felt hat she wore when visiting the Harlyn estate, one of the few items of clothing she had not borrowed. Breen stowed her pack again.

From under the brim of her hat Rhia observed the land. Crops away from the muddy irrigation ditches were withered and brown. Soon there would be hungry mouths, here and in the city. Hunger, unrest and more riots.

She raised her eyes to the burning sky. How much brighter would it burn in the skyland? The priests claimed the First shaded the shadowlands from the Sun's excesses, but whilst the Church took this on faith, the mechanism was a matter of debate for those natural enquirers who took an interest in the heavens. Presumably some sort of aerial shield followed the Sun across the sky from dawn to dusk. Or rather many such shields, as each shadowland would surely need its own shade.

"M'lady?"

She looked down to see Sorne holding out a waterskin. "Did you want a drink?"

"Thank you." She took the waterskin. The water was warm

and tasted of leather, but she must learn not to be fussy.

"We should consider," she said as she returned the waterskin, "how I might best fit into the necessary fiction you are travelling under."

"M'lady?"

"Could I perhaps be your sister, or failing that, your cousin. I know it is a stretch but I can see no acceptable alternative."

"Indeed not, m'lady." The captain did not mention the unacceptable alternative: that being of a similar age, they might pose as man and wife. "We are not alike in looks so perhaps cousin would be best, m'lady."

"Your widowed and childless cousin, yes. And when we are in company you won't call me m'lady."

"Of course. M'lady."

Was he mocking her? His face was unreadable.

"With m'lady's permission, we are using our real names, as they are unmemorable enough, but yours is from the top of the hill."

"Then perhaps... Rhina." In the space of a morning she had gone from Countess Rhia to Mam Rhina. Quite a transformation.

She returned to surveying the fields. Distant workers shimmered in the morning haze. They passed a field of oilseed, bearing up under the heat, and a sparse olive grove where pigs rooted round under the trees. The soldiers continued to politely ignore her, so she dug in her satchel for the paper she had been reading the day before, a treatise on nightwings, snaredogs and other skyland hunters.

The lunch of hard cheese and cornbread handed out by Captain Sorne took some chewing but stopped her stomach grumbling. During siesta he swapped places with his corporal to take a turn driving the cart. Although Rhia had not expected to sleep, she dozed, lulled by the Sun's warmth and the clop of the horse's hooves. She woke to find beads of sweat oozing out from under her hat and mask. She wished she had thought to ask Fenera for a fan. Her own fans, intricate constructions of stained wood and painted paper, were too conspicuous.

Finally the Sun sank, bringing blessed relief from the heat of the day, though not from the awkward intimacy of the cart.

In the fading light Rhia saw a tight cluster of low buildings past the hunched shoulders of Corporal Lekem. A wayside inn. She had visited such a hostelry over a decade ago, in the company of Uncle Petren and the household guards. It had been an adventure, a chance to experience how the other half lived. She suspected her uncle had done it to bring her out of herself after Father died.

"We'll pass the night there, m'lady," said Captain Sorne, having followed her gaze. She had thought him asleep, but he appeared to be able to go from sleep to wakefulness faster than a cat. "Inns are a good place to gain intelligence, although, if m'lady does not object, it would be wise if you stayed out of sight."

"Right. Yes, of course." This time she could not expect any special treatment.

Chapter 12

By the time darkness fell, Dej and her companions had eaten half the food and drunk most of the water, not to mention using the chamber pot, which did nothing for the atmosphere in the wagon. Pel was asleep, mouth half-open. They hadn't stopped; skykin didn't take siestas.

They carried on in the dark for some time. When the wagon slowed Dej panicked, then calmed. All at once, she knew what she had to do.

Before they came to a halt, she stood up. By the time the skykin unlatched the door, she was on the balls of her feet.

Then she was off, out the back of the wagon, like a hen from a fox.

Just run. Run into the night. She didn't want this, didn't want to live in the skyland, with an animus inside her. She wanted to go home, to Min. She had to get away–

Something whistled through the air behind her. Her feet tangled in each other. She tripped, and slammed into the ground, rolling to a halt.

She drew a breath and howled, once. Then she shut up. What had she been thinking? She couldn't just run back to Shen.

A shadow eclipsed the stars, some of which might just have been in her head. Dej lay still.

The skykin untangled the cord around Dej's legs. In the moonlight Dej made out a flaccid belly and not-quite-flat chest; it was the woman. Up this close she smelled odd, though not unpleasant, like a mixture of old parchment and warm stone.

After winding the cord round the throwing-weights the skykin sat back on her heels and gestured for Dej to stand. When Dej still hesitated, she murmured, "You will have no need of music when the world sings to you."

Dej started but the woman was already standing. She scrambled to her feet.

The others waited by the wagon. Mev looked stricken. Dej didn't look at Pel.

As though nothing had happened the skykin man said, "Relieve yourselves, stretch your limbs, then sleep in the wagon." Like the woman, he had a flat, low voice. He walked off after delivering his instructions.

"Do not stray far," the woman added. "It is not safe for you out here."

Seemed like no one was going to mention her attempt at escape. Dej looked around. The skyland here was barren, which they'd been told to expect; no trees in sight, just the occasional odd-looking patches of what must be plants, some of which glowed a dull greeny blue. Distant hums and whistles drifted in on the wind. The air smelled dry and spicy, like the crèche ovens after they'd had fruitbread baking in them.

Pel sloped off behind the wagon. Mev stretched her arms over her head and walked around in a small circle. Dej turned to the skykin woman. "What did you mean, about the world singing to me?"

"You will see." She nodded, then walked off to help the man attend to the rhinobeast. She had only rested up for a day after the birth but looked fine now. Skykin were as hardy as rumour claimed. As hardy, and as heartless. She would never see the child she'd given birth to again.

Pel came back from behind the wagon. Mev gave an embarrassed grimace and went to relieve herself. When Dej returned from taking her turn at the spot they'd picked as a latrine Mev passed her, holding the pisspot at arm's length. Pel was doing some stretches by the back door. Dej decided she'd had enough exercise for one night. As she went to climb into the wagon Pel said, "So, was your father a shadowkin, or what?"

"How should I know?" But she had considered it. She'd considered lots of possibilities, at various times alone in the hole. Pregnant skykin who came to the crèche to give birth left a parting-gift with their child. Even if her mother gave birth in the skyland she'd have hurried her to the nearest crèche, with a parting-gift. So something must have gone wrong – perhaps her mother had been walking to the crèche alone, as skykin sometimes did, and the baby had come early, killing her – but then whoever brought Dej to the crèche should have checked for a parting-gift. Unless she'd died in the shadowlands and the shadowkin who found her didn't know about the tradition. None of which was relevant to her father; rumour had it skykin didn't worry about who the father was. Assuming skykin and shadowkin could even have children together; they might have been the same people once, but the Separation had been pretty final, if the scriptures were to be believed. "I don't see what difference who my father was would make."

"Maybe none. I just wondered." He put a hand out. "Listen, I'm sorry about what I said this morning."

"Which bit?"

"About hoping your animus rejects you. That was mean."

Dej narrowed her eyes. He looked like he meant the apology. "Yes, it was." But she'd been unreasonable too. "And I'm sorry I went for you. And about what happened with your parting-gift." A lifetime's habit wouldn't let her actually admit she'd stolen his knife. But while he was in the mood to apologize: "I'm not the only one you should've said sorry to, though."

"You mean Min?"

"Yes, I mean Min."

Dej was aware that Mev was back, though she stood off to one side, giving them space.

"I did."

"What?"

"I went to see Min last night. We made our peace." He laughed. "I didn't apologize for screwing her – she wanted that as much as I did – only for the way I treated her afterwards. I was a bit of a prick. But it turned out all right in the end."

"What do you mean? She's probably going to spend the rest of her life on some farm!"

"Easier than facing life in the skyland when you don't know who you really are, or what you want to be."

"Wait, did you…" Dej didn't want to say it in case she was wrong.

"I know she didn't have a parting-gift either. Finding out you didn't today, made me think. I'd wondered how come you two were so close. Now I know. I'm sorry you lost your friend, Dej."

She looked at him hard. "What's got into you? Are you messing with me?"

"No. I wanted to clear the air, to go to my bonding at peace with the world." His voice hardened. "And you should try to do the same."

"It's not that easy!" She hated how Mev and Pel were looking at her now, their patronizing sympathy. "Nothing makes sense!"

"It will when you're joined with your animus," murmured Mev.

"How do I know that for sure? It's not like life's been logical or fair so far."

"I disagree," said Pel. "The crèche staff did their best for us."

"Yes, but, when I think about what they taught us at the crèche … and what they didn't. Like giving us restday off when they told us skykin don't celebrate it. Why do that?"

"Uh, because there'd be no one to teach us?" said Mev.

"We could work in the gardens or something. But that's just one example. There are so many." *Like my music*, she thought, but didn't say. She expected they'd agree with the tutors.

"Well, I never thought that."

"Me neither," said Pel, then added, "The crèches have been bringing up skykin children since the Separation. If they weren't doing a good job the skykin would've had something to say about that, wouldn't they?"

"This isn't helping," said Mev. "We're just getting worked up. Let's do what the driver told us, and get some rest."

Dej nodded. There was no point arguing with these two. As she turned to get into the wagon, Mev came up and gave her a quick, fierce hug. "Don't worry," she said, eyes shining in the skyland night. "Just do what you can to prepare yourself and all will be well."

Dej hoped so. Lying on the bench in the wagon with the other two falling asleep around her, Pel's words rang around her head. He'd meant what he said. He and Mev really didn't see any problem with the crèches. Perhaps they were right. Perhaps she was the only one who did.

Her and Min.

Why hadn't Min told her about Pel's apology? But Dej knew the answer: because it wasn't any of her business, not any more. And the last thing Min said to her was pretty much what Pel had said. Min had chosen the easy way out.

Crèche-mates weren't meant to screw around, but they did. If a girl wanted to do it with a boy she could count the days, or get hold of herbs from one of the traders. That's what Jen did, according to Min. Dej had assumed that was what Min did too. But Min must have known that having a child meant not getting bonded. And recently she'd gone out of her way to change the subject whenever Dej asked what would happen after the baby was born. Like she knew how hurt Dej would be to hear the truth, to find out she'd got pregnant on purpose to escape her skykin heritage.

Dej recalled Min's final words. *Forgive me.*

She'd known all right.

Chapter 13

Rhia's room was cupboard-sized, plain-walled and furnished with a narrow pallet and rickety nightstand. It smelled of dry rot and flatulence, and was lit by a single tallow candle on a rough clay saucer. At least she had her own room, a privilege Captain Sorne had paid extra for. She removed her satchel and was reaching into it when someone knocked on the door.

"Who is it?"

"Sorne. I've brought food." He was taking her at her word, showing no deference when they might be overheard.

The food turned out to be hard bread and lumpy stew, along with a glazed beaker of watered wine. As he left her to it a burst of raucous laughter drifted up the corridor.

She ate as much of the food as she could stomach, dipping the bread into the stew to soften it but leaving the more unidentifiable lumps. The wine was undrinkable.

Returning her attention to her satchel, she extracted the package from the woodcarvers and unwrapped it. The completed sightglass was a sturdy tube of ironwood, or rather two tubes set inside each other, just as she had specified. She examined it, assuring herself they had done as she had asked. Then she picked it up, walked to the door – all of two and a half paces – and turned.

Two faint points of light showed in the patch of night sky visible through the tiny window above the bed. With such a limited view and no idea which direction she faced, she had no idea what stars these might be, but they were enough for a test. She braced her back against the door and raised the sightglass.

Darkness. Was the sightglass flawed? Broken? More likely not pointed in the right direction. She moved it to the right. A bright, blurred light jumped into her vision. She lowered the sightglass and eased the two tubes apart, adjusting the focus. Then she tried again. The light was sharper now, a pinprick not a smear. But still it danced in her vision. She held her breath. The pinprick stabilized. Yes, that was it! A star! And there, right next to it, a second, fainter one.

Rhia smiled. More stars were visible out in the estates, because there was less light than in the city. The sightglass was a device for gathering and focusing light. Therefore, it should show unseen stars. This much she had deduced. And now proved!

She moved her vision farther right, but found no more stars. When the darkness became sheer she opened her left eye, which she had closed instinctively, and confirmed that she was looking at the wall. She moved the sightglass up and to the left, and continued her observations.

In total she saw eight stars where only two had been visible without the sightglass. But the slightest motion – even breathing – made the image jump, and by the time she had covered even this small patch of sky her arm muscles were weak and aching. She would get a far better view outside, and perhaps find something to lean the sightglass on to steady it. Sorne had advised caution, so she would wait until things had quieted down a little.

The hubbub from outside had grown loud enough to hear through the closed door: a babble of voices, more laughter and a harsh female voice singing along to an out-of-tune fiddle. In the common room of the inn she had visited in her youth, what little conversation there had been had fallen away when she and her uncle entered.

Had Etyan stayed here, on his flight from Shen? This inn served the routes to two shadowlands, Zekt and Marn. Marn would have been the easier journey, but he might have had to wait longer for that caravan. Her little brother had lived all his life in the city or on the Harlyn estate. This place was so far outside his experience. Her chest tightened at the thought of silly, soft Etyan, out on the road, among strangers, alone.

She sat on the bed and removed a thick wallet of hardened calfskin from her satchel. As well as selected enquirers' papers, it contained tables of celestial appearances and a folded bankers' draft, though this was a last resort, as to use it she would have to prove her identity. Also, the letter she had promised Captain Sorne.

In searching the bag for her writing materials, her hands brushed her new notebook. She smiled. The sensation of opening a pristine notebook always lifted her spirits. But for tonight she merely wrote the names of the three soldiers on the prepared letter, under the heading, "Be it known that the following act with my authority...". She sealed it with her signet ring, then removed the ring. Someone of the status she now pretended to would not have a signet ring.

She extracted one of her papers – observations on possible social customs of the skykin by Sophist of Jhal – and, leaning close to the guttering candle, read for a while. By the time the sounds from along the corridor began to die down her eyelids were drooping, but she could not resist the lure of the sky.

Sightglass in hand, she opened the door and peered out. The dim corridor was empty. She looked both ways one last time, then made her way outside.

The inn was built around a central courtyard. Rhia stood in the doorway, straining to see if anyone was out there. The only light came from the stars, and from Greymoon, which was still low enough to be hidden behind the inn's buildings. As would much of the sky be. She needed to get somewhere more open.

As far as she could see the courtyard was deserted, so she crept out, trying to recall if there was a well or other obstruction that might trip her up in the dark. She relaxed and sped up once she was far enough across to see out of the gap leading back to the road, where she was heading.

"Evenin'."

She froze, then turned on the spot. A lantern bobbed near the door. To go by the voice, it was held by a man.

He called out again, "Does your man know you're out here?"

"My what?" The indignant response slipped out before she could stop it.

"Your man." The lantern came closer. "Or are you *meeting* a man, hmm?"

"I am not!" Part of her knew how much trouble she was in. But another part was appalled at being spoken to like this by one of the lower orders, and that part had got control of her tongue.

The man was close enough that she could see his features now. About her age, with a wide mouth and heavy brows, though that could just be the way the lamplight illuminated him. He wore something pale over dark clothing. "You should know better, woman of your age with a posh accent like that, you'd be... oh."

For a moment Rhia stared at the suddenly silent man. The foolish part that had made her answer back decided he must have recognized her nobility, and was about to apologize. The sensible part realized he had just seen her mask. If she was, as he appeared to think, a woman of questionable virtue, she was unlikely to cover half her face in an old leather patch.

Trying to keep her voice humble but not cowed, she said,

"I just came out to get some air."

The man laughed. Rhia tensed, wondering if she could outrun him. He lowered the lantern, and she saw a bucket half-full of dark liquid in his other hand. "And I just came out to empty the slops!" That pale cloth he wore was an apron. He worked in the kitchen.

"Then I won't keep you." She hurried past, not looking back.

His voice followed her, still half-laughing, "You city folk, with your airs 'n' graces."

It was all she could do not to run back to her room.

Once inside, she pushed the nightstand up against the door, there being no lock. Not that she expected the man to follow her. But she felt better having put up some sort of barrier.

She sat on the bed and read for a while, letting the words on the paper calm her.

Once she was tired enough to be over her scare she lay down, still fully clothed. The pallet was as uncomfortable as it looked. When her wrist itched she scratched without thinking, then ran her palm over the tender, raised skin of a bite. It appeared she had been incorrect in her assumption that she had the room to herself. The bed, at least, had other residents.

She awoke in darkness, rising from a dream of hair spreading in tangles amongst bubbles and filth; blood welled up from the depths and now she was caught in the hair, it was pulling her down–

The sound came again: a knock on the door. She came fully awake. "Who...?"

"Time to get up. We're off soon." Sorne.

She was stiff and tired, and had bites on her ankles to match the ones on her wrist, but such was only to be expected. When she left the room she found Corporal Lekem outside, not quite standing at attention.

"The others are loading the wagon, so I'm to keep watch over you."

"Thank you," she said. Did he, or more importantly his captain, know she had disobeyed the advice to stay in her room last night? The cook had just been joshing her, but had the encounter been with one of the inn's drunken patrons it might have had a different, more unpleasant, outcome.

As she came out into the courtyard she kept the brim of her hat pulled low against the other travellers' stares. Being cheeked by a stranger – even a harmless one – had brought home to her that these people were as real as she was, not distant peasants to be ignored or commanded. They would not defer to her, nor show any respect; she had no status among them. And she was about to spend a week locked up with them.

She could still turn back. A fraction of the coin she carried would have the innkeeper putting her up in his best room while he sent for an escort from the city.

No. What sort of enquirer let themselves be put off by such a trivial incident? But next time the captain asked her to do something for her own good, she would listen.

Lekem helped her onto the cart, then excused himself to say a prayer at the inn's shrine, a scruffy niche in the wall by the main entrance. Breen saw to their horse and the captain chatted to one of the traders waiting for his ride.

Once horses had been hitched and carts loaded, a tired-looking matron distributed fresh loaves. Rhia was glad it wasn't the male cook.

Captain Sorne climbed aboard the cart and handed her half a loaf. She closed her eyes and breathed in the fresh scent, then ate in delicate nibbles. The bread tasted as good as any at home. *Take joy in small pleasures.* She was halfway through the loaf when the cart set off.

Once she had eaten she gave Sorne the letter of authority, took a drink from the waterskin, then asked, "Did you pick up any useful information last night?"

"Talk of the weather, as ever. The umbral storms are barely reaching beyond the forests now, and they've had no proper rain here for months. Everyone agrees it's the driest rain year they can remember."

"Anything regarding my brother?"

"I'm sorry, m'lady, but many people pass through this inn, and it has been some months. I mentioned a lone boy of noble birth and the landlord said he thought he'd seen such a lad, but could not remember when. He may have been humouring me."

They overtook a pair of traders on foot, carrying heavy packs. Lekem grunted a greeting which was returned. In the back of the cart, silence reigned.

The sky lightened. Ahead, the road divided. They took the leftmost path.

They passed a cart coming the other way, laden with rolls of heavy Zekti paper and, from the smell of it, dried fish. The driver wore a long pale tunic gathered along the shoulders and belted high, but no breeches. Zekti fashion, although plain and travel-worn compared to the pressed and pleated linens of the diplomats who had visited Shen in her youth, back when Francin's uncle had been trying to improve relations between the two shadowlands. She had a stupid urge to call out and ask the man if he had seen a well-dressed Shenese youth, of average height and slender build, with sandy hair. She did not, of course.

CHAPTER 14

Sadakh surveyed the sea of upturned faces. His own face wore a smile as he chanted the familiar words.

He moved his slow and careful gaze over those before him, making brief eye contact with certain members of the crowd, attention always returning to the acolytes at the very front. Several of them sang a little loudly, enthusiasm overcoming ability.

He noted one who did not stand out, whose voice was not too loud and whose recall of the words was perfect; a young man with a face made almost imbecilic by excess joy. He gave the youth the same attention he gave everyone else.

It was firstday, and the sky above the First Light Priory was clear and bright after overnight rain. No doubt the lay members who made up the majority of the congregation had shared their opinions on the weather as they moored their boats at the priory. No doubt some called it a blessing after several wet days. Some, perhaps, even attributed that blessing to him, their spiritual leader and guide. He wished they would not do that. Such talk tipped him from love towards contempt, and he did not want to feel contempt for these people. For his people.

His mind returned to the four individuals lying in the infirmary. His first test had resulted in two speedy and unpleasant deaths, but the dead skykin he had derived that initial extract from had been diseased, tainted. This time the body had been sound, the blood pure. For this new test he had chosen two people of each gender and a selection of ages, though logic said the subject should be young and fit. He had confided his aim in two of his subjects – one of the men and one of the women. They had agreed, of course. The remaining two had no idea their sacramental drink had been tampered with. He could not know what factors made a difference: only by changing the parameters and noting the results could he hope to succeed. He had administered the extract two days ago. As yet, all four subjects lived, albeit in delirium.

The hymn drew to a close. Sadakh waited for the last notes to die away, for the pause, the anticipation. When the moment was right, he began to speak.

"Fellow seekers, we grow. We grow within ourselves and we grow together. Today, we add to our number." He regarded the front row, his expression welcoming, serene. Some of them looked nervous. Not unsure, just daunted. The joyful imbecile blinked, then rekindled his smile.

"Fourteen new seekers have chosen to commit to our path. They have completed the study required, and renounced everything in their old lives that might hamper their search for truth and enlightenment. Let us praise the First and support their choice." This was one of only two direct mentions of the First in the lay initiation ceremony. Like many rites of the Order of the First Light, Sadakh had made subtle changes in the eleven years since he had become the eparch. People needed rituals, but the words must not detract from the intention. Humility and acknowledgment of greater powers were vital, but to constantly invoke a deity whose existence was a matter of faith eroded personal responsibility.

During the next hymn the front row bowed their heads in silent prayer, preparing themselves.

Sadakh felt his ghost stir, but gave her no space to speak. He was making his own mental preparations because, whatever else, he had a sacred duty to those who stood before him. He would fulfil his obligations to his congregation, even though today's ceremony might unfold in a way they did not expect.

The second hymn concluded. Sadakh spoke a short liturgy, then asked the blessing of the First while gesturing over the chalice of oil. Then he stepped down off the dais, trailed by two assistants, one of whom held the chalice.

The first acolyte, a man, was taller than Sadakh. He hunched down, dipping his head to be anointed, smiling awkwardly.

Sadakh used the oil to draw a column-in-a-circle, representing the Pillar of Light, on the man's forehead, then said, "May you find the light within yourself."

"So I will endeavour." The man had an unexpectedly high voice. No doubt the mismatch between size and voice had caused him distress, perhaps even influenced his choice to seek consolation here. Sadakh hoped that one day the new initiate would learn that such external signs were nothing, and would stand tall in his own self-knowledge. Sadly, prior experience suggested otherwise.

The next acolyte was a young and attractive woman. He recognized the look she gave him. The chaplain who instructed her would not have denied the rumours – because Sadakh would not have his clergy lie – and he suspected he would be seeing more of this one.

Two more men, one young, one old.

Another woman next, and then he would be facing the smiling imbecile.

His ghost spoke up as he anointed the second woman.

Have a care now.

Would the ghost have commented if he had not already been in possession of certain facts? Whether she had a true objective reality or merely reflected and voiced his inner thoughts was his defining paradox. As happened when such doubts intruded, he dismissed the uncertainty as counterproductive; improvable. She was unique, and uniquely his.

He sensed, or believed he sensed, her approval at that thought.

Distracted by this lapse, he almost missed the telltale movement. Each acolyte waited with hands clasped under their chin in prayer until the eparch stood before them, at which point they lowered their hands, and their head, ready for his touch. The youth moved a fraction too early.

Another slight movement, this time from behind. His second assistant, to all appearances a mere robed servitor, was a trained bodyguard. The man's nudge was subtle, but Sadakh expected it.

What happened next was fast, and inevitable.

Sadakh stepped back. The acolyte's hand got as far as his belt but, there being no weapons allowed in the compound, he had to reach inside his tunic. The disguised bodyguard stepped forward. The second guard was already behind the attacker: a fierce woman who looked like a stout goodwife in the smock she wore over her leather armour, though Sadakh had seen her bring down men taller than him. She grabbed the acolyte's arm, twisting it behind his back to immobilize him.

A small, shiny object fell from the man's belt: a bronze bodkin.

Sadakh was flattered: no expense spared this time. And he could assume the metal pin was tipped with an equally rare and no doubt lethal toxin.

To the would-be assassin's face Sadakh whispered, "The prince continues to underestimate me."

Those nearby had registered something amiss, but had yet to work out what.

Sadakh nodded over the man's shoulder. The female guard caught his eye, and yelled. "An assassin amongst us!"

The crowd paused, shocked. Then they surged forward. Sadakh's clerical assistant clutched the chalice to his chest, white-faced; unlike Sadakh's guards, he had no advance warning of another possible attempt on the life of the eparch. The male bodyguard shielded Sadakh from the sudden commotion, allowing him to step back onto the dais in safety.

Sadakh turned away from the chaotic scene. The assassin had come here expecting to die. Sadakh had no desire to watch his congregation grant the unfortunate man his wish.

CHAPTER 15

The cart reached the edge of Shen during siesta. Rhia was tired enough to doze despite the heat and the bare wooden seat pressing into her back. She awoke to see a dark barrier curving around the horizon: the umbral forest. Above the great trees towered bastions of fluffy white; huge, bright, impossible. The border between shadowland and skyland was marked by rough winds, permanent clouds and sharp storms. Rhia had seen such clouds on the horizon from the Harlyn estate, but this close they dominated the view. Someone – she forgot which enquirer now – had surmised that the disturbed weather of the umbral related to the great temperature differences between the two zones.

On the ground, the border was not so dramatic. A few stands of ironwoods appeared amongst the fields; then there were more trees than fields; then they were amongst the trees. The treetrunks were smooth and featureless up to a height between two and three times that of a man. Above this, sprays of dark green leaves arranged in overlapping fans jutted out from angular branches. The umbral winds harried the treetops, but beneath the ironwoods the air was as hot and close as a sealed room.

Light showed ahead. Surely they could not be at the skyland yet? No: this section of the forest had just been harvested and replanted with saplings. She wondered which House owned these trees. House Noumen or House Lariend perhaps; their estates were in the north.

When the cart came out from under the full-sized trees, light and heat beat down on them. The Sun had broken through between two pillars of cloud; Rhia squinted against the glare. She now believed the assertion, made by several enquirers, that even in the umbral that edged each shadowland, the Sun was too bright to look at directly.

Ahead, between the ironwood saplings, Rhia saw a pair of identical rectangular buildings. No, not buildings: massive wagons, side-by-side in a clearing just off the road. The caravan.

Although it hurt to look at the world, Rhia noted through watering eyes that even though it was late afternoon in the skyland the light remained pure burning white: silver to shadowland gold.

As they got closer she made out figures, along with horses and carts, congregating under a flapping awning stretched between the wagons.

There were more people than she expected: at least fifty, all men. Some would be the way-traders who served this route. The house-sized wagons had six wheels, each a good three yards high. The massive rhinobeasts who pulled the wagons were corralled on the far side of the clearing.

A dozen or so skykin sat on the ground outside the awning's shade while another half dozen helped traders load their wares onto one of the wagons. In build they were like slender shadowkin but in movement they were fluid and fast. They wore only loincloths and combinations of belts, vests and bandoliers to carry the items they needed.

The casual relaxation of the sitting skykin contrasted with the urgency and energy of the shadowkin. Then again, there was little for the skykin to concern themselves with aside from the loading of luggage. Running caravans between shadowlands was a service they provided in return for having their offspring raised in shadowkin crèches. No money changed hands between the two races.

She had seen a skykin in Shen city once. Travelling with Father to an appointment at one of the guilds they had passed a skykin woman in the backstreets of the middle city. Her gender was obvious by the hat and skirts she wore, and by her cosmetics, enhancing her eyes, her lips and, scandalously, her bare nipples. Rhia's father had hurried past but Rhia had turned to look then asked, with the combined nerve and innocence of a twelve-year-old, whether all skykin dressed like that.

Father had said they did not. This was an outcast skykin who was making her way as best she could, in this case "performing that unsavoury service we discussed". Rhia was still adjusting to the recently acquired knowledge that women, and some men, sold their bodies for a function she herself found perplexing and unappealing. That a skykin might do so had dumbfounded her.

Lekem slowed the cart, shading his eyes to search for space under the awning. Seeing none, he steered the cart into the partial shade cast by one of the wagons. A man in an unbuttoned tunic and straw hat came forward and addressed Sorne. "Good afternoon, Sur. We've not seen you before, have we?"

"That's right."

"So, new traders then?"

"No, we're moving to Zekt."

"Are you now? Well, I imagine you won't be needing this cart much longer."

"We won't, and as soon as we've unloaded you and I will talk."

The man appeared pleased. He nodded and moved off.

A skykin wandered over. Close up their unique features

were obvious. The lack of hair, the small round eyes, the heavy brows and flattened nose; and the skin, pale gold and patterned with scales.

The skykin pointed a too-long finger at one of the wagons. "Do you need assistance?" He – Rhia decided, in the absence of information to the contrary, to think of all skykin as "he" – had a low, even-toned voice.

"No, thanks," said Sorne.

The skykin ambled off, returning to his comrades, more of whom were standing up now.

The soldiers disembarked. "You can stay here while we stash the luggage if you like," suggested Sorne. Rhia nodded and moved to the side of the cart in shade. At least the sharp breeze cooled the air. From her vantage she examined the skykin more closely. They wore no obvious adornment and although there would be males and females here – the skykin were said to share all tasks equally between genders – she could see nothing to indicate such differences. Perhaps this was to be expected given Sophist of Jhal's claim that "the women's dugs wither to stubs during the bonding process", an adaption that sounded most unpleasant.

While the soldiers carried packs from the cart to the back of one of the wagons, Rhia watched a pair of skykin leading a rhinobeast towards the front of the other one. Rhinobeasts came in two sizes; some of the smaller ones, not much larger than a heavy horse, remained in the corral. These ones had hair partially covering their plates of hardened skin. The one being led out was hairless and massive, in proportion to the wagon it would help pull. It moved with head-swinging deliberation, as though it had just decided to wander over to the treetrunk-sized harness pole jutting from the front of the wagon. If it decided to run amok it would crush anything – and anyone – in its path.

"Time to get off, Rhina," said Sorne, returning to the cart.

The way-trader stood at his shoulder.

Clutching her satchel and quashing her nerves, Rhia climbed off the cart. Her gaze fell to the ground underfoot and she started at the sight of damp soil; compacted and bare, but not dried to dust and cracks as she was too used to seeing. She joined Breen and Lekem under the awning while Sorne completed negotiations with the way-trader.

Some of the shadowkin travellers began to climb the short wooden ladder into the wagon. Several of them threw curious glances her way; she tucked herself in between the two soldiers. A pair of skykin led a second rhinobeast up to the wagon. She could see the smaller rhinobeasts more clearly now the large ones had moved. Some of the beasts' hair was plaited or decorated, and jewelled studs and other decorations punched into flaps of loose skin and semi-erect head-frills caught the light. It appeared that skykin decorated their beasts, if not themselves.

Breen elbowed Lekem, grinning. Rhia followed their gaze to find there was another woman with the caravan after all. She wore red and yellow layered skirts and heavy makeup, and was coming round from behind the luggage wagon with a mousy looking man. Seeing Rhia she smiled. When Rhia, realizing what she must be, failed to meet her gaze the other woman looked away and went back to chatting with her companion.

Captain Sorne came over and handed out dried jerky and a wrinkled apple each. Lekem muttered a brief blessing over his food; Breen just tucked in. Rhia chewed the rations and tried not to think about roast beef or honeycake. As she ate, distant thunder rumbled overhead; she found herself hoping it might herald an umbral storm, but the air remained dry, if close.

The last of the way-traders left, taking with them the various carts and mounts people had arrived with. A horse would not last long in the skyland.

The last few skykin stood up. Some moved off towards the smaller rhinobeasts; others went up to the front of the wagons.

Using separate wagons for luggage and people was a precaution against raids by rogue skykin. Should the caravan be attacked the trade goods could be abandoned to the raiders, who would then let the wagon carrying the shadowkin go free. At least, so said Wanderer of Prin. He also claimed such raids were rare. However, he was inconsistent in his claims. Always a risk with enquirers, given they shared a role down the generations, although in his case she suspected the same person made contradictory statements, such as claiming both that the skykin practised marriage and that they did not form permanent bonds. She was not reassured by Wanderer of Prin's claims. She knew so little about what really went on in the skyland.

This was her last chance to turn back.

As though she would. She climbed aboard the passenger wagon.

Inside, the only light came from what Naturalist of Menb referred to as "air vents" – narrow horizontal gaps where the planking of the wagon's wall did not quite meet the ceiling – along with a hanging lamp near a curtained-off section at the back. Everyone else appeared to know the layout, but in the dim light Rhia barked her shins on the bench running down the centre of the wagon before sitting on the bench against a wall, next to Sorne.

When the back door was closed and locked in place she fixed her gaze on the vents.

The wagon lurched forward. Rhia grabbed the seat edge. The wagon stopped. Someone outside said something that sounded like encouragement to an animal. The wagon moved again, this time more smoothly, turning in a tight arc before straightening. The only sound was the heavy crunch of wheels on dirt.

The light level increased. Then, suddenly, it became blinding, brighter than any lamp. Rhia blinked and looked down, her vision filled with violet afterimages of the vents.

When her sight cleared she noticed people staring at her. She ignored them.

With the light came heat. Men unlaced jerkins and removed hats. Rhia sweltered in her oversize dress. She made to take off her hat, then paused. Under cover of its wide brim, she inventoried her fellow travellers. Of the twenty-three besides herself and her companions, eight were Zekti; they sat together and did not engage the Shenese in conversation. Rhia tried not to stare at their bare legs and woven sandals. She could not remember the last time she had seen a grown man's toes.

The Shenese men ranged in age from boys to old men; some travelled alone, some with one, or at most two, companions. Her party of four was the largest group. The soldiers sat around her formed a barrier against casual contact, which she appreciated. She had no idea how to talk to these people.

Captain Sorne had no such issues. He turned to the man beside him and started chatting about skiv-skiv, a brutal ballgame played in the lower city. Lekem, who had ended up on her other side, put his head back against the wall and closed his eyes. Breen sat on the central bench across from her and stared into space, wearing the relaxed half-smile which was his default expression.

Rhia went to fiddle with her signet ring, a habit boredom or nerves sometimes drove her to, before remembering she was no longer wearing it. Instead she removed her hat and fanned herself. She was not looking forward to the next seven days.

CHAPTER 16

All the next day Dej tried to follow the others' lead. She even managed to meditate, or at least to fall into periods of tired numbness. But she kept coming back to how her friend had abandoned her. Min wasn't a coward, but she had taken the easy option. And now Dej had to face the hardest moment of her life without her only friend.

She tried to recall everything she knew about bondings. Very little. The skykin didn't tell outsiders much.

Where lessons ended, dorm rumour took over. She'd heard late-night tales of bondings gone wrong, of madness, agonizing deaths and strange half-formed failures. Which didn't make sense, because how would anyone in the crèche ever know how a bonding had gone? But that didn't stop the thoughts intruding.

Or perhaps that hollowness she'd felt those last few days with Min was a good sign, an opening up of the space she'd need in her heart and mind for her animus. Perhaps all would be well after all, as Mev said.

The wagon halted just after dark. The skykin had told them, before they set off this morning, that the next time they stopped would be at the bonding site.

The woman opened the door, and the man, standing behind her, said, "Follow me."

The skykin set off on foot, the man in front, the woman at the back.

Dej tried to keep her thoughts positive as she fell into step behind the man. Ahead was a rocky outcrop spattered with odd patches of light in shades of mauve and blue. Beyond that, Dej saw a warmer glow, like firelight. The air smelled of dried sage.

No one spoke. The world felt calm, poised. Outside her head, at least.

When they reached the rocks, Dej saw a passage through them. The skykin plunged into the narrow, dark defile. Dej's shoulders tensed as the walls closed in.

After a few dozen steps they emerged into a more open area, though still hemmed in by high rocks. Ahead, a pool lay half under an overhanging rock, like a tongue sticking out of a mouth. Its surface mirrored the stars.

The skykin led them to the pool. "Strip," said the woman, "and bathe."

Apparently a bath before they left the crèche wasn't enough.

Mev and Pel both started by removing the pouches containing their parting-gifts. Dej pulled her tunic over her head.

The skykin gave them tight bundles of sweet-smelling rags. "Use this to cleanse your skin."

The water was cold, but Dej welcomed it. She scrubbed hard, holding her nose and ducking under to immerse herself.

She was the last to get out. She would happily have stayed in the pool longer, perhaps forever. The others had put their parting-gifts back round their necks. There was no sign of anyone's clothes, nor of the male skykin.

The woman passed a small leather flask to Pel. "Drink this." Something else they hadn't been told about at the crèche.

Pel spluttered, and Mev hiccoughed when her turn came. As Dej was last she drained the flask. The burning liquid made her cough.

They set off in silence, led by the skykin woman. The dark shapes of Dej's companions wavered in her streaming vision. Naked and wet, with the ground rough under her bare feet, she had no chance of meditating now. Instead she hummed under her breath; private tunes, her own meditation.

They went through a gap in the rocks opposite the one they'd come through. The stars over there looked odd, golden, and they rushed upwards–

No, that was the fire, and those were embers. She shook her head. It looked really pretty. And she could hear music. Yes, *music*! Up ahead, someone was beating out a complex, insistent rhythm. For the first time since leaving the crèche, Dej didn't want to be somewhere else.

Her body thrummed to the beat. Sparks from the fire eclipsed the stars.

Emerging from the defile, she blinked. The fire was bright as the Sun, and ringed by shadows. People, a dozen or more of them.

"Tonight you become an adult."

After a moment she located the speaker as the woman nearest the fire. Probably a seer. Her life could have been worse: she could have been chosen to be a seer, brought up in a cave, having to take *everything* she was told on trust. She laughed, and someone hissed. She shut up.

People approached her, taking her arms. She didn't resist. Her legs were too long, even as the ground pressed up around her ears. Strong stuff, that drink.

Ahead, the earth was flat and covered in colours: yellow and orange and red and green. The people holding her lowered her to the soft, coloured ground. It was a blanket, of course it was. Her head fell back, and was caught by a pillow. Overhead, specks of burning gold raced into darkness. This wasn't so bad.

"Do you accept the gift of bonding?"

She wasn't sure who'd spoken, or even if anyone had, and for a crazy moment she considered saying *No, I don't – can I go now?* But that wasn't an option so she murmured, "Yes," half nodding, feeling her head move on the pillow.

The bright sky went dark. Her heart stuttered. No, just someone leaning over her. Something cold and hard touched her forehead. She tried to raise a hand but another hand caught it. Her body felt weak, distant. Suddenly afraid, she whimpered.

"There is no shame in fear at this moment," said a soothing voice. "We have all walked this path."

The cold pressure on her head increased. Then the world exploded between her eyes. Surprise as much as pain made her arch her back, bucking against the restraining hands.

Pain rushed in. Huge pain, centred on her forehead, driving out all other sensation. But even so, it was distant, bearable. She didn't have to acknowledge it.

The light returned. Stickiness oozed into the corners of her eyes. Even as she tried to blink her vision clear, a figure leaned over her. They held something in their cupped hands, pale, small as a finger, moving by itself, questing and twisting.

Despite the drugged trance, her fear redoubled. Her bowels knotted and she tried to scream, but all that came out was a gasp.

Cloth dropped over her eyes. An instant later, coldness touched the agony in her forehead. Coldness and slithering, right between her eyes. She wanted to scream, but her body was too far away.

Then the pain was *in her*, no longer distant and escapable. Crashing around inside her skull. In her mind. Experiences unravelled, snatches of the past, scents and tastes and vision and distorted sound; a nauseous, giddying, mind-wrenching rush. The dark, lonely stink of the contemplation room;

sitting in a tree and singing at the sky; reaching out to take Mam Gerisa's pen; praying for Min when she had a fever; crying alone, before Min was her friend; first steps taken across a scrubbed wooden floor; a warm breast, rich milk in the mouth. And always, the pain.

The past visions expanded, deepened. A sky full of stars. Running across the desert. Standing on a high mountain, the world like a map below her. Sitting by a fire, listening to stories of ancient lives. Plunging into an icy stream to come up sputtering and laughing. Shouting a name she no longer knew. The tearing agony of childbirth. Wonder and confusion chased through her head.

The whirling blade of the animus's progress was undoing what she had been. Its presence rose like a flood. She was submerged. She was going to lose herself.

No, this was right; this was how it should be.

But what if I don't come back? She'd never asked for this... She fought the animus, trying to assert herself, to not be overwhelmed. It brushed her aside.

The pain became intensely physical. She could feel her body again but would give anything not to. Her skin grew hot and tight, an unbearable itching racing across it. Bones popped in their sockets. Sinews stretched and muscles contracted.

The bonding was beginning.

Chapter 17

The wagon slowed and stopped soon after full darkness fell. When the door opened Rhia was eager to get out, but had to take her place behind everyone else while they filed down the steps.

Outside, the fat crescent of Greymoon hung bright and low in a clear sky. The wagons had parked side-by-side with a wide gap between them. She inhaled, trying to smell any difference in the skyland air, but found only an absence of smell, compared to the stink of warm, unwashed bodies she'd been immersed in.

Skykin moved around, some with lanterns, unhitching the beasts and fetching items from the luggage wagon. Rhia stuck close to the passenger wagon with the other shadowkin, though instead of facing into the space between the two wagons she looked the other way, out beyond the wagon, into the skyland.

The land glowed. Every enquirer who had travelled through the skyland had written of this and Rhia smiled to see it. The effect was, at first glance, no brighter than a night when both Moons were up: a silvery wash across the nighttime world. But while moonlight was constant and monochrome, the light beyond the wagon concentrated in certain areas – areas, Rhia now saw, where bushes, or amorphous clumps of what must be foliage, grew on the otherwise barren ground – and came in various shades of blue and purple and green; a soft baby-blue from that round clump, a turquoise wash on the patch of whatever-it-was over there. Some of the commonest plants were pale green cages of twisted stems which appeared, as far as scale could be gauged, to be around knee-height.

She turned at the sound of a throat being cleared to see Sorne looking her way. She nodded at him, then faced in like everyone else, ignoring the world at large. But even here there was life. On the bare earth by her feet was a regular patch of deeper shadow. She crouched down, squinting at the interlocking hexagons which covered an area the size of two hands side-by-side. Paving pads, according to Naturalist of Menb. Like many living things in the skyland, this was several creatures combined. Reminded of the apiaries at the family estate with their hexagonal cells, she came up with the analogy of a hive of bees where the hive itself was alive. This same pattern also existed on the largest scale, with the shadowlands themselves distributed in a hexagonal pattern around the widest part of the world. Not for the first time she wondered at the gaps in this pattern: the total of the five rows – three of twenty and two of twenty-one – should give one hundred and two shadowlands. Yet there were only eighty-seven.

Back on the local scale, this particular plant/animal was said to be one of the few skyland organisms it was safe to touch. Rhia pressed down gently. The pads felt like closegrained wood and exuded a faint gingery aroma.

She looked up as light flared. The skykin had lit a fire between the wagons. Loitering shadowkin wandered over to it, carrying folding stools like the one on her observation platform at home. Captain Sorne stood close by, not quite watching her.

She straightened, then looked up farther still. The sky was packed with stars, as many as she would see out in the estates. Not more though: as other enquirers had noted, whatever shaded the Sun by day in the shadowlands had no effect on the night sky. The stars were the same in skyland and shadowland.

She strode over to Sorne and gestured vaguely into the semi-darkness. "I need to, ah..."

He nodded and looked away. Rhia walked round the far side of the wagon. On the northern horizon loomed the dark, distant bulk of the Northern Divide; the mountains they must cross to reach Zekt.

Having checked she was unobserved, she crouched next to a wheel.

When she straightened she realized that she now faced west, with the Moon behind her. She had an excellent view of the sky from here. And, because she never let her satchel out of her sight, she had her sightglass with her.

She turned back to examine the wagon. The main structure was raised up to near head-height by its great wheels; how Father would have marvelled at the skill that went into building such a vehicle.

She ducked underneath, behind the nearest wheel, then got out her sightglass and rested it on one of the spokes. When she smelled something odd she stepped back, wondering if someone else had already used this space to relieve themselves. But this was not human waste, only a scent of ripe rot on the wheel itself, as though the wagon had run over something unpleasant. Careful not to touch the wheel, she stepped close again, and repositioned the sightglass.

Something gave a mournful hoot out in the lambent night. Rhia started, then shook her head. Whatever it was, it was not close. She looked through the sightglass. She had to slouch to bring her eye in line with the lens, but the view was rock-steady.

The bottom quarter of her vision was dark; the sightglass

was shorter than the spoke was deep, so part of her field of view was blocked. Above this the stars in her vision shone bright. She smiled and moved the sightglass along the spoke a fraction, and found more stars. However, she had no idea which stars. In her eagerness she had looked without observing. She raised her eye from the lens and peered out at the sky between the spokes.

The constellation of the Burdened Traveller was dead ahead; the stars she had seen were in the figure's upper chest. That strange, hazy area near the head had always intrigued her. She moved the sightglass up a spoke. In order to line it up with her target she would have to support it with one hand against the steeper angle this spoke lay at. On her return to Shen she must get a proper stand made, some sort of tripod perhaps.

When she looked through the sightglass the fuzziness on the celestial figure's brow sharpened into focus. Rhia was stunned. She expected to catch one or two additional stars through the sightglass, yet here were a dozen distinct points! Some stars were embedded in the haze, while others shone clear through it. She could make out colours too: hints of pink and gold amidst the overall pale blue glow.

Rhia chuckled. The sky was no immutable tableau, as priests and commoners believed. It was a living vision of infinite wonder!

"Hello?"

Rhia jumped, then saw a dark figure standing off to the left of the wagon.

"Captain Sorne."

"Are you all right under there?"

"Yes. Yes, I'm fine."

"You've been gone some time."

"I said I'm fine." But the militiaman was only trying to protect her. There would be other nights. "I'll come back now."

At the fireside the shadowkin had settled near the passenger wagon while the skykin kept to the far side of the fire. Despite the division both races appeared relaxed. Some of the shadowkin were playing dice or knucklebones. As Rhia settled on the dusty ground, one of the boys produced a wooden whistle and began to play. People clapped or beat time on their legs. The skykin looked on, impassive.

When the shadowkin woman got up to dance, Rhia tried not to stare. One never saw stamping feet and swirling skirts like that at court! The woman sat down again when a pair of skykin came forward to ladle stew out of a pot nestling in the fire. The skykin worked efficiently but with no obvious direction. Did they have a leader? One of them was looking across the fire while the others organized the meal. Was looking, in fact, straight at her. Rhia returned the shameless regard.

"Um, did you want this?"

She took the bowl Breen passed her. The stew was pale and starchy, based on white tubers and something beige and mushroom-like, but surprisingly tasty. She had read somewhere that skykin did not eat meat.

As the shadowkin were passing their empty bowls back to the skykin, one of the Shenese traders came over to talk to the woman. After a short discussion overseen by the woman's mousy companion, the pair walked off. They went behind the skykin, who ignored them, and into the luggage wagon. *Well, that confirms my suspicions about how she earns her living.*

Some of the skykin were bedding down for the night, wrapped tight in cloaks. Rhia wished she had thought to fetch her own cloak from the luggage wagon before it was put to its current use. Having no alternative, she hugged her knees for warmth and stared into the fire. She had not sat like this since childhood. It was oddly comforting.

"M'lady?"

She started at Sorne's whisper. Despite the cold night air and hard ground, she had been dozing, lulled by the firelight.

"I have news."

About a third of the traders had retired to the passenger wagon. There were no strangers in earshot.

"Yes, Captain?"

"The way-trader I dealt with back in the umbral confirmed that a young lad matching your brother's description and travelling alone passed through a few months back."

"And how did he seem to them?"

"I'm not sure what you mean."

Had he been hurt on the road? Was he distressed? *Did he have an air of guilt about him?* But Sorne could hardly have interrogated his source; he would have had to pretend to be making a casual enquiry. She settled on, "Just... was he well?"

"The trader didn't mention any injury or malady."

"Thank you, Captain. That's good news." Not really news at all, but she did not want to appear ungrateful.

CHAPTER 18

Rhia woke up with a start. *I'm being strangled!*

No, wait, she was twisted up in a hammock, wound tight like knotted laundry. The wooden ceiling pressed down on her–

Nothing to panic about. She was in a wagon, out in the skyland.

Around her, people were waking up; someone had lit the lantern. It must be morning. Her backside was numb and her shoulders ached from being squeezed by the hammock. But the hammock had looked more comfortable than the bare benches below. She had got *some* sleep.

She eased herself out of her contorted position, wincing at the stab of pins and needles in her legs.

"Need a hand getting down?"

She peered over the hammock's edge to see Breen looking up. "Where's Sorne?"

Breen nodded towards the open door, "Outside, having a necessary. He'll be back soon."

"Right. Yes, some help please..."

Breen was as considerate as a courtier, steadying the hammock and offering an arm for support.

Breakfast was black bread and fruit-water, dispensed from the curtained alcove by the mousy man and the prostitute. The wagon lurched into motion as they were eating. It was still dark outside.

Dawn oozed in. The wagon soon became bright and stuffy.

Rhia would have liked to read her papers, but that would not be appropriate for a poor widow. Instead she mentally reviewed her knowledge of the skyland. In a couple of days' – or rather a couple of nights' – time she might be in a position to confirm the existence of a unique feature mentioned by Wanderer of Prin; whilst he was not the most reliable source, Rhia thought this structure too outlandish, too unexpected to be the product of his imagination.

Lunch was more black bread and smoked meat. Rhia had no idea what meat. The hammocks weren't broken out for siesta; people just slept where they sat. Rhia hunched down, concerned that if she did doze off she would end up with her head on the shoulder of one of the soldiers. She need not have worried. She was too uncomfortable to sleep.

Instead, she returned to the image that had haunted her dreams for months, *pale hair in bloodied water,* and found herself reliving the memory she had hoped the excitement of the journey might drive away.

A rare conjunction, all three Strays in a moonless sky, had kept her up late: watching, sketching, thinking. She had finally headed for bed around the twenty-seventh hour. When the front door opened, she halted on the central staircase, heart thudding. Just Etyan, out all night *again*, coming home.

The noise he made as he lurched into the hall stopped her in her tracks. It sounded like a sob.

She crept down the stairs then called out, "Etyan?" He was heading for the kitchen but looked up at her voice. In the lamplight his expression was furtive, fraught. Rhia smelled kreb-smoke.

"Are you all right?"

He tried to wave her away, the gesture clumsy, uncoordinated. "Fine. Drunk. Need some water."

There was a dark stain on the shoulder of his doublet. "Are you sure you're all right?"

"Yes, sis. I'm sure." His voice was too loud.

She could have let him be, but she had been ignoring his unruly behaviour for too long, unsure what to do now he was too old to listen to nurses or tutors – or her. But she needed to keep him under control, stop him getting in trouble. It was for his own good. "If something's wrong, you know you can talk to me."

"Told you. Nothin's wrong!"

And that was how he repaid her concern these days: disdain and petulant anger. She was getting sick of it. "In that case, Etyan, why don't you try growing up?"

"Why don' I what?"

"Grow up. You're happy enough to tell everyone you're head of House Harlyn now, so why not start acting like it?"

"'S none of your business how I act."

He was still the cheeky, charming boy she'd had Markave slap when he stole food from the kitchen or played pranks on the other servants. That had to change. "Yes it is. I've been managing this household for years, and now, because you were born male, it's yours. But I won't let you fritter away our fortune and family name on feckless companions and dubious women."

"Dubious women…" He'd twitched at that, then shook his head. "Told you, not your business how I spen' my time or money." He looked her blearily in the eye. "You're not my mother."

It hung there between them for a moment. She could have – should have – let his comment go, just turned away. But instead she said, "No. She's dead. Thanks to you."

He tensed, like he was going to leap up the stairs and attack her. Then his face crumpled. He turned and stalked into the kitchen, slamming the door.

She should have gone after him then, should have apologized. But she was tired and infuriated, and he'd be easier to deal with when he was sober.

Except as it turned out, that was the last thing she had said to him.

She sighed, and shifted on the bench to get, if not comfortable, at least a little less uncomfortable. *Oh Etyan, you poor, foolish boy. Where are you? What are you doing now?*

By the end of the day all three soldiers were on friendly terms with their neighbours. Rhia, shielded by their combined presence, had spoken to no one.

When she disembarked that evening, the mountains dominated the northern horizon. The glow of the land appeared dimmer tonight, though that may have been due to Greymoon being brighter. If memory served, the Maiden should be visible in the west.

Lekem and Breen were not paying her any attention. She waited until one of the other travellers distracted Sorne, then ducked under the wagon.

Had anyone asked her – not that anyone had – she would have explained that she had made the sightglass for the Harbinger. However, with the exact time of the erratic star's return unknown, her immediate priority was the Strays. The three most prominent stars in the heavens were named for the wandering courses they described through the field of fixed stars, which foxed the natural enquirers. The Church claimed the Strays' wayward nature was a matter of gender, that these celestial bodies were female, and hence unpredictable. Rhia objected to this on a number of grounds, the two most pressing being that the Strays were *not* unpredictable, merely difficult to chart, and that to assign gender to heavenly bodies made no sense. But the Strays were a mystery she would love to solve.

The Maiden was low, making positioning the sightglass a challenge. Rhia ended up sat cross-legged with it jammed in the angle between spoke and redolent wheel-rim. Different sounds came from out of the fitful dark tonight, mainly rumbles and rustles.

When she finally located the Maiden through the sightglass it shone bright enough to make her gasp. Her gasp became an "oh" of wonder when she saw the star's shape. Not a point of light, but a fat crescent. She blinked and looked again to be sure. It was true. The Maiden was a crescent.

There, in a single glance, was proof of what most enquirers believed against both common knowledge and the implicit teachings of the Church: that the Strays were, like the Moons, like the world itself, *spheres*. Thus, when the Sun was off to one side of them, they showed as crescents.

Although mathematics was not her strong point, now she had this confirmation, she must return to her earlier attempts to model the heavens. A practical approach, perhaps the contraption of balls on sticks she had once discussed with Father. The world in the centre, then balls representing the Moons, the Strays and the Sun arrayed around them in order. The sticks would need to be placed firmly into a medium which allowed them to be moved, to chart the course the heavenly bodies were observed to take. Sand perhaps, in a deep container. No, that would not be stable enough. Ironwood rings, then–

"Hello?"

"Under here, Captain," she said wearily. "And I'm fine. Still."

"In that case, with all due respect, would you mind explaining why you are spending so much time hiding under the wagon?"

Would he care that she had just confirmed a fundamental truth about the physical universe? No, he would not. "I'm not hiding. I'm carrying out observations."

"Observations?"

"Of the sky." From under a wagon: she realized how odd that sounded. "Surely, Captain, you have heard the rumours about crazy Countess Harlyn and her peculiar hobbies?"

"I'm not interested in rumours, only in keeping you safe."

"For which I am grateful. But I am not in any danger."

"We don't know what's out here."

"Actually, I do." She realized how arrogant that sounded – and untrue too, given the sketchy nature of writings on the skyland. "Nevertheless, if it puts your mind at rest, feel free to have one of your men observe me while I observe." If she must have a chaperone she would prefer one of his subordinates.

"That may be for the best."

He showed no sign of going away. "All right, then; for now, I'll return with you."

"Thank you."

She should not try him. And this one observation gave her plenty to think on.

As she entered the firelight the other woman looked up and smiled at her. This time, Rhia smiled back. She had been thinking of her pretence at lower status as a drawback, but it allowed her to talk to people who would otherwise defer and fall silent in her presence. There was more than the life of the skyland to be explored here.

She headed round the fire, towards the prostitute. Sorne trailed her for a few steps, then peeled off.

Unsure of the correct approach, Rhia stood in the woman's eyeline and smiled. The mousy man was playing 'bones with his neighbour; he looked up at Rhia, then back at his game. The woman nodded to her and when Rhia hesitated, said, "Well, sit down if you're going to."

"Thanks." Rhia crouched rather than sat; the prostitute was sitting on a stool and she wanted to look her in the eye. "My name's Rhina." She felt like a five year-old at a party.

"I'm Mella. First time in the skyland?"

"That's right."

"You don't seem scared."

"I've always wanted to see the world."

"Right. More interested in people myself."

Rhia had no answer to that. She supposed she had to be, to do what she did. "So, are you travelling to Zekt to, um, work?" Presumably they had prostitutes in other shadowlands. Perhaps foreigners were considered exotic, like the skykin she had seen with Father, and could charge more for their services.

"Not exactly." Mella waved an expansive hand to take in the camp. "This is where I work."

"Oh." Rhia thought about it for a moment. "Yes, that would be a good arrangement. You don't need to hire rooms and you get new, ah, clients coming along every time the caravan sets out."

Mella nodded. "And a few regulars."

"But the skykin, do they mind?"

"Me plying my trade? Long as I'm not taking the place of a trader with actual goods to move. Not usually a problem on this run. It's not the most popular one."

"Yet you make a good living?"

"Preut and me don't do so bad."

"And Preut is your... brother?"

"Brother and pimp. Don't worry, he doesn't screw me. But he stops anyone getting rough, negotiates deals, and doesn't drink too much of the profit. Also manages things on the wagon, of course. This life beats being stuck in a stinking city whorehouse with a bitch of a madam."

Which, presumably, Mella had once been. If she travelled with every caravan to Zekt, Mella would have met Etyan. But to ask would reveal an interest and all Rhia knew about this woman was her dubious profession.

"You know," Mella was saying, "it's a funny thing for a respectable widow – you're a widow, right? – for a widow like yourself to be asking about, if you don't mind me saying."

"I'm a curious woman. Too curious for my own good, some say."

Mella's smile became cunning. "You don't say."

The prostitute's manner made Rhia uneasy. That and the thought that Etyan might have been one of her clients. She had no idea what else to say to this woman, who lived such a different life from hers. She straightened, feeling her face colour beneath the mask. "It's been very nice talking to you. Good night."

The look Mella gave her as she left was hard to read.

CHAPTER 19

The light burned. Even so, Dej yearned for it. It drew her from the dark place where she'd been hiding. Hiding from...

Smells assaulted her. Lemon and shit, roses and rot, new bread and old blood. When she focused on the smells the humming in her ears grew louder, beat faster. Light was the only constant.

That and life. She was alive. Bare, dusty ground under her, heat on her skin; whatever else, she'd survived.

It was alive too. The thing in her head. Alive, but separate. In her, but not part of her. That wasn't how it was meant to be. *Your bonding will complete you,* the crèche tutors had said. They'd lied. The hollowness inside was still there.

Dej opened her eyes.

The sky was white fire.

She blinked, and something slid across her vision; the world dimmed, became less painful.

She wriggled her toes. They moved. She stretched her fingers, pressing them into the hot, hard earth. Her body obeyed her. Good. Even as she thought this, her stomach contracted. She was ravenous, and so thirsty her tongue had stuck to the top of her mouth.

She raised an arm – it felt light, not quite part of her – and looked at it, a thin dark silhouette against the light. She bent the arm to touch her head. Still there: she had wondered for a moment. Touch distracted her from the impossible smells, the unheard sounds. Touch was under her control. She pressed a hand to her forehead.

Something was stuck there. A leaf? A dressing? Covering the wound. The wound where *it* had gone into her. It was in there for good, now. But not intruding any more. Not causing pain. Just... *there*... on the edge of consciousness. Her animus.

She got her arms under her and sat up. Sounds swirled and smells flashed. Suddenly nauseous, she retched. Nothing came up but at least it unstuck her tongue. She looked around.

The skyland was alive with light and colour. Everything came with its own back-of-the-nose smell, its unique unheard sound, and snippets of knowledge she'd forgotten or never known. *I can't handle this, it's too much!* She wanted to lie down and close her eyes, hide and withdraw.

But she needed water, food. How long had she been out of it? And where was everyone else? She should've woken up amongst her people, her clan, bonded not just to her animus but to them and theirs.

There was a dead point in her vision. The ashes of a fire. And where the earth rose up, those were rocks, the same rocks she'd walked through in the dark. Now, the very stone vibrated when she focused on it, a solid, low hum.

So, she was still at the bonding site. But no one else was.

She looked away from the crazy landscape. Her gaze fell on her hand. It looked wrong. The fingers were too long, the nails thin and clawlike, the skin scaly, covered in a subtle pattern of gold and pale green-brown.

She ran her other palm over the back of her hand, felt the tiny ridges and dimples etched into her skin. But if she hadn't hardened up she'd have fried. She was skykin now, and skykin had scales. All these changes would have hurt like fuck if she'd been conscious when they happened. Her muscles still hurt, like she'd worked too hard in the fields, except it wasn't just her arms and legs, it was *all* her muscles.

Had she taken too long to adjust to her bonding, so the rest of the clan had moved off, taking Pel and Mev with them? But wouldn't they leave someone here for her? That was the skykin way.

Unless something had gone wrong.

Mam Gerisa had sent her off too soon. She hadn't been ready. The bonding hadn't worked as it should.

She realized she was humming to herself, like she did when she was stressed. One thing would make her feel better. She opened her mouth…

… and croaked like a raven.

She tried to sing again. This time she managed a low grunting moan. But even that tore at her throat.

Her animus had taken her voice.

She'd lost her home, her friend, everything she knew. But the loss didn't end there. These changes, the ones she hadn't asked for, hadn't been ready for, they'd reached inside her and *stolen her ability to sing.*

She thumped the ground, then raised her head to scream at the silver sky, "No!" She shouted again, her voice echoing off the rocks, becoming a howl. Her eyes stung but her cheeks stayed dry. Skykin couldn't cry.

The skykin who'd brought her here had said *You will have no need of music when the world itself sings to you*. But the song of the world was chaos. She screamed at the chaos.

She howled until her throat closed, and she had to stop.

There was someone behind her.

She stood up. Her body felt heavy and loose. She curled her fists into her palms, took a deep breath, and turned around.

She was already getting used to the new way of sensing. Bare rock was less distracting than earth, which was crammed with life; growing, writhing, breathing, hunting. The figure stood on the highest point of the rocky outcrop, and she shone like a beacon. Though the woman stood still and silent, when Dej focused on her she felt the pulse of life, vibrating in its own unique rhythm.

This was a skykin, one of her people. And she'd sensed her presence, and the fact it was a she, even with her back to her.

The skykin sprang into motion, leaping down off the rocks. The movement was selfassured, rapid, almost a scamper. *Can I do that now?*

Like the skykin who'd visited the crèche, this one wore only a loincloth, and she was bald. Dej's hand went to her own head. She felt scales, the last of her shorn hair gone. Her final link to what she had been, gone.

"If you really want to die, I'll go away and leave you to it," stated the skykin. Her voice was low and flat, no clues in its tone. But Dej sensed unspoken undercurrents: amusement, an edge of scorn.

"I don't want to die." Her own voice sounded higher than the skykin's. Still off though, still no longer hers. No longer a singer's voice.

The skykin had stopped several paces away. When Dej focused on her she had a sense of unmoving motion, sweeping up all her senses. The two of them circling, appraising, all without physical movement. Finally, the skykin said, "What's so terrible you have to yowl at the sky?"

Dej answered without thinking. "I can't sing anymore."

"Well no. You wouldn't. But that's the least of your problems."

"What do you mean?" This skykin had to be here for her, but this wasn't the welcome she'd expected.

"If you really do want to live, you'll need to come with me now." The skykin turned on her heel and walked off down the defile.

Dej followed.

The rocks provided welcome shade, but even more welcome was the pool at the far end. Dej ran over and threw herself down beside the water. As she looked up from her first few desperate gulps she noticed the other woman watching her. Dej stared back, holding her gaze, before bending down again for another drink. Finally, innards sloshing with chill water, she stood up.

Dej got the impression the skykin was older than her, though not properly *old*. Skykin didn't get old. She could sense how healthy the other skykin was. The skykin was fit and relaxed... and amused. Laughing at her, still.

"What's so fucking funny anyway?" Dej didn't swear. Min swore, and Dej pretended to be shocked; then they'd both laugh. But Min wasn't here.

The skykin strode over. Dej stood her ground. Too fast to see, the skykin raised her hand to strike. Dej tensed but didn't flinch.

The blow didn't come. The skykin dropped her hand. She nodded, like something had been agreed. "You hungry?"

"Yes I am."

"Good." And they were off again, back into the rocks.

The new everything-at-once world was settling down, though it was easy to get distracted by this softly hissing moss-like growth or that mint-scented trace of some large creature's passing.

They came out from the rocks to where a scruffy-looking rhinobeast waited. Its wedge-shaped head swung round to look at Dej and she got the sense of slow chewing, that irritating itch, warm sun on skin. The head swung back, and the rhinobeast's presence receded.

Her companion rummaged in one of the packs strapped across the beast's back.

"Put this on." She flung a bundle of cloth at Dej. She caught it easily – surprisingly easily. It was a rough linen loincloth.

Dej did as she was told while the other woman checked straps on the rhinobeast.

"Breasts hurt?"

"What?" Dej looked up from tying the loincloth. "Uh, yes. They do."

"They're still being reabsorbed. Might take a few days." The woman threw another bundle Dej's way. She caught this too. "That's jerky. Chew it slowly, get all the goodness out of it. Eat too fast and you'll puke. Puke on me and I might decide you're not worth my effort."

Dej mustn't take offence. Without help, she'd die out here. "Thanks," she said. "My name's Dej, by the way."

"I'm Kir."

Just Kir: no title, nothing to show what she was to her clan. Dej recalled whispered rumours, lights-out horror stories to scare crèche-mates.

The other skykin's eyes were fixed on Dej. "Are you..." Dej tried again, "are we clanless?"

Kir nodded. "Yes. You shocked?"

The clanless had been one of the less credible dorm rumours; degenerate, imperfectly bonded half-skykin who sometimes turned on their own. Dej affected a shrug and said carefully, "Beats being dead."

"So it does." Kir put a foot in the rhinobeast's harness and swung herself onto its back, then reached down to help Dej.

Dej took the skykin's hand – the contact sizzled, setting off sensations and emotions gone as soon as Dej focused on them – and let Kir pull her up.

As she settled behind the other woman Kir said, "You have been fed lies."

"All my life." Dej sensed Kir's amused approval. This could work. She was used to being an outcast. Kir was an outcast. Two outcasts together.

Kir kicked the rhinobeast into motion. Dej looked for

something to grab onto, saw only Kir, and concentrated on holding herself upright.

Dej had stuffed the cloth-tied bundle of jerky down her loincloth to climb onto the rhinobeast, and now she eased a strip out. She bit into it, letting her spit soften the dried flesh, then gnawed the jerky down to nothing and licked her fingers.

As she settled back Kir spoke over her shoulder, "You're adjusting well."

"To the bonding, you mean?" She *had* bonded. She only had to look at her hands to know that.

"To the *incomplete* bonding."

"So sometimes… it goes *really* badly?"

"Some die or go insane. I'm glad not to've had a wasted journey."

Rather than agree how inconvenient it would have been for Kir had she died, Dej said, "I'm glad you came for me."

"I came because there's always a chance of a partial rejection."

"At every bonding?"

"Always a chance, like I said. So when we can, we send someone to watch." *We* presumably being the clanless.

Dej ate another piece of jerky. Ahead, past Kir's shoulder, she saw mountains: the Northern Divide. Not that she knew much more than their name: no shadowkin ever saw them by day. Kir's rhinobeast was setting a steady pace and Dej watched the view ahead for a while, in case the mountains got nearer. They didn't. When she couldn't stay silent any longer she asked, "Why didn't they just kill me, if they knew the bonding hadn't worked right? The other skykin, I mean."

She thought Kir wasn't going to answer. Finally, she said, "Kill you and they kill your animus. An animus is sacred, even imperfectly bonded. So, they left you where you fell. You'd have died soon enough, starved or got eaten. But that would have been the world killing you, not the clan."

"They wouldn't have tried to get the animus out of me, to save it?"

"Your animus is like mine. It's flawed. When you die it'll go back to the world."

"Flawed? How?"

"Damaged perhaps. More likely just old."

"Old? I thought an animus lived forever."

"There's another lie. No, they live for a very long time but not forever. Did you have a parting-gift?"

"What? No. No I didn't."

"That'll be the reason you were chosen."

"Chosen?"

"To receive a flawed animus. Most likely your mother was clanless."

She remembered Pel's question. "Or maybe my father was a shadowkin?" Somehow that thought was easier to take than being born to skykin rejects.

"Perhaps. Though no *true* skykin would go with a shadowkin." Kir spat the word *true*.

"You're saying the skykin knew I had no parting-gift, decided that meant I had bad blood, and gave me an old animus?"

"Yes."

So the skykin who'd come to the crèche, who hadn't bothered to get to know her, had set her up to fail.

But they might have known about her. They'd have spoken to Mam Gerisa. The crèche-mother could have told them Dej was no good, so they'd decided she'd get a no-good animus. No, it was worse than that: Mam Gerisa had set her up to fail from the start; she'd known Dej would never be a full skykin from the day she arrived. When skykin came along saying they had a faulty animus, Dej was their girl, even though she was too young. Min would have been the one, if she hadn't been pregnant. Well, in that case, *fuck* them. Even Min. *Fuck them all.*

Kir half turned, and gave her a smile, the meaning of which Dej wasn't sure, but which smelled like approval. "Are we going to meet the other clanless now?" she asked her guide.

"That's right."

"How far is it?"

"Far enough."

"And–"

"There'll be time for questions later."

CHAPTER 20

Soon after dawn the next day, the caravan entered the mountains. The light from the vents dimmed as the ground on the left-hand side rose. Some creature outside gave a daft tittering call, half horse's neigh and half drunken giggle. The sound sparked brief, nervous laughter amongst the travellers.

By midday the wagon was tilting so much Rhia kept sliding down the bench. She followed the lead of the other travellers and grabbed the leather strap attached to the wall just above head height. She had wondered what that was for. People on the central benches had to make do with using the seat edge to keep themselves steady.

No one attempted to sleep during siesta. Conversation died away. The only sound was the huffing of the rhinobeasts and wheels grinding over rock.

She distracted herself by further refining her idea about modelling the sky; yes, a contraption of wooden rings, with pegs and holes to stand the model Sun and Moons and Strays in; that might work. But putting theory into practice would have to wait. In the meantime, what might the sightglass reveal about the other Strays, when they next rose? Logic, and the writings of other enquirers, said they must be spheres too.

They were almost halfway to Zekt. She had travelled farther than any member of her family, save Uncle Petren – and Etyan himself, of course. Father had wanted to see the world, but felt bound to Shen by his duties. Rhia put that thought aside; after all, this was House business.

Petren had been to both Oras and Xuin in his youth, and told her tales of both shadowlands. Her uncle never could settle. When Father's death left him the head of House Harlyn, he had rebelled and run away, though unlike Etyan he had planned his escape. The duke stopped him before he reached the umbral and brought him home to marry a woman he did not love; if the rumours were true he could never love a woman. That was the final straw. Alone at the villa one night, Petren had drunk hemlock, an act of combined bravery and cowardice Rhia could never reconcile.

The caravan did not slow when darkness fell. When Sorne mentioned this to his neighbour the man said, "Not many places flat enough to camp up here, so we keep going till we reach one." Once it became evident that Rhia kept herself to herself, her fellow travellers' curiosity had abated, and they ignored her, which suited her fine.

When they finally halted it was in a steep-sided valley rising to a forbidding escarpment. Even if it had not been too late in the day to see the Maiden, the high walls blocked much of the sky and Greymoon was up, washing out a lot of the stars. Moonlight, and the intrinsic glow of the skyland, revealed a strange landscape of eerie shapes. An orchestra of sounds came from beyond the fire: a murmur like the breeze through trees – except there was no breeze, and no plant out here resembling a tree – low whines, odd hisses and clicks, alongside the familiar sound of running water.

There would be no better night to examine the skyland itself. She walked up to Sorne. "I am going to observe, though not from under the wagon."

"I'll come with you."

"I'll only be over there." She pointed at some relatively flat ground near the back of the passenger wagon. "I won't go out of sight."

"All right, then."

The valley walls were a mixture of bare rock and hanging vegetation. She could tell the difference between the two by the glow the vegetation emitted; dimmer than in the open land, and with a different colour palette, mostly deep red or bruised purple. She turned her attention to the ground.

A soft-looking mat covered a depression a few paces off, glowing a gentle mauve: ground-fur. Naturalist of Menb warned against being lulled by its too-slow-to-see movement: ground-fur exuded a noxious sap that immobilized and poisoned its victim prior to leisurely digestion.

Other plants stuck up from crevices like bunches of pale spikes. She had no idea what they were.

Movement caught her eye. A thin dark line meandered across the pale rock, as though an invisible child was drawing with a thick quill. She crouched down and narrowed her eyes. The front of the line twitched and wavered. Ah yes: follower-worms. Each worm was as long as her hand but no thicker than her little finger. They were said to form chains, travelling nose-to-tail for many miles in search of who-knew-what. She could not remember if they were harmful; probably, as they would need some defence against being eaten. They were heading towards her, so she shuffled to one side. When the creature at the front reached the impacted earth left by the wagon's wheels it stopped. Its dark snout scanned about. Then it made an abrupt turn to the right, leading its followers along the outer edge of the wheel-rut.

Rhia smiled, delighted to observe such peculiar behaviour.

She continued to watch while the rest of the line followed the course set by the leader. She gave up counting how many worms there were when she reached a hundred. Finally, the end of the line emerged from the darkness.

As she stood up she realized how cold she was. She checked on the ground-fur – it had moved a handbreadth, though away rather than towards her – then hurried to the luggage wagon to fetch her cloak, having first checked the wagon was unoccupied. When she emerged, food was being served.

After the meal, Sorne went over to Mella, then off into the wagon with her. Rhia bit her tongue rather than comment in front of his men.

The skykin who had been watching her before still paid her excess attention. Rhia had a theory about him. Before testing it, she wanted to speak to the prostitute again.

Mella and Sorne did not take long, and neither returned looking particularly satisfied. Rhia got up and went over to Mella, who nodded by way of a greeting.

Rhia, trying not to think how odd it must be to make a living doing something so personal and intimate, crouched next to her. "How well do you know the skykin?" she asked, nodding across the gust-pulled fire at their travelling companions.

"Well enough."

"I was wondering whether you might introduce me?"

"Introduce you?" Mella put her head back and guffawed. "What is this, the duke's court?"

"Well, no." Rhia cursed her good manners. "Do I just go up and talk to them, then?"

"Did you want to thank Tan-Ufara for the stew? Particularly tasty tonight, I thought."

Rhia ignored the whore's jibing manner. "That's the cook's name?" It was weird hearing the skykin named. Weirder still, it was only now, halfway through the journey, that she considered they had names.

"Yep."

"Actually, I was more interested in one of the others." Rhia looked past the fire to the skykin. "The one who keeps staring at me. He's doing it now, in fact."

"She."

"That's a she? How can you tell?"

"By paying attention."

Rhia flushed at being called unobservant by a caravan prostitute. "So what differences should I look out for?"

"Well, the women still have breasts, of a sort. That and the voice. A skykin woman's voice is not as low as a man's."

"I see. So why is she so interested in me?"

"Because she's the Yrif and you're going to smell funny to her."

"Yrif is the title for their seer, is that right?"

"That's right."

"Does she have a name, this seer?"

"No, she's their *seer*."

Sophist of Jhal said skykin added a suffix to their birth name on bonding to denote their place in the clan. Except seers. Seers were the wisest amongst the skykin. And this one was female. Rhia looked across at Mella. "What do you mean, I smell funny to her?" Although Rhia most certainly did smell – by now they all did – she suspected this was not what Mella meant.

"How can I put this?" Mella pursed her lips. "I don't know what your story is, but if you're Mam Rhina the poor widow then I'm the duchess of Shen."

Rhia's already hot face flushed further. Several enquirers had noted the skykin talent for sensing – Wanderer of Prin called it *smelling* – deception.

When she said nothing Mella added, "You aren't the first person to pass this way who isn't what they seem, and you won't be the last. Don't worry about it."

Rhia nearly asked Mella outright whether she had seen Etyan. But what would that achieve other than to confirm Mella's suspicions?

She looked up and met the seer's gaze. The skykin did not

look away. Rhia stood and, before she could lose her nerve, strode round the fire. A couple of skykin looked up. The Yrif stood slowly, still watching her.

She stopped in front of the seer. This close she could see how the muscles beneath the skin were normal enough, even though the skin was coarse and scaled. The only changes to the underlying morphology were the flattened nose and heavy brows. And the seer exuded a faint but not unpleasant smell, like a book open under the hot Sun. Rhia realized she was staring, and said, "Can I talk to you?"

For a moment she thought the skykin hadn't heard her. Or maybe was ignoring her. She only had Mella's word that this was how to speak to them. Then the skykin said, "Why do you wear the mask?"

"I... sorry. I'm not sure what you mean."

A shadowkin would explain, or at least repeat themselves, but the skykin just kept staring. Waiting. Rhia wondered how long she would wait. Quite a while, probably.

Rhia took a deep breath. "I wear this mask to cover a scar. When I was younger I burned my face."

"Why?"

"What? No, you don't understand. I mean my face got burnt. In an accident."

"No." The skykin turned, fast as a cat, and walked off.

Rhia stood dumbfounded. Then she walked back round the fire the long way, avoiding Mella. The soldiers watched her approach then looked away as she sat.

Rhia put the warmth of her face down to the fire.

CHAPTER 21

Kir carried on in silence until early evening, by which time they were in the skirts of the mountains.

Dej didn't mind staying quiet; all that howling and screaming had left her throat sore, and talking hurt. Instead she used the ride to get used to the world as it now was. When she focused on this or that *thing* – she wasn't always sure what was a plant and what an animal – from her perch on the rhinobeast's back, knowledge sometimes popped into her head; she knew, by looking, whether it was safe to eat, or dangerous, or its relationship to some other thing. Other times she didn't get any idea of whether she could eat, or be hurt by, whatever she was looking at, or even what it was.

And there was something else. She knew they were heading north, for the mountains, but that wasn't just because she remembered her lessons. She knew because she sensed it, inside. Like knowing up from down, she knew which direction north was.

At one point, as they took a small diversion to avoid a dried-up riverbed, Dej looked back south, but she couldn't see Shen, just the desert. Only now, as evening fell, was the light the colour she was used to in the shadowland, gold rather than silver.

When they stopped for the night Kir dug out more jerky. Dej asked if there was anything else to eat. Kir nodded. "Your belly needs filling. Wait by the beast."

Kir stalked away into the twilight. She stopped a little way off, raising then lowering her head, as though listening, then scenting the air like a dog. She walked a few steps farther, stopped and sensed again. After the third change of direction she whipped out her knife and fell to the ground, stabbing at the earth. Dej wondered if her companion had gone mad, before realizing she was using the ironwood blade to dig a hole.

When Kir straightened she held a pale shape as long as her forearm. Some sort of grub, slow-moving, with a soft beige body and beak-like brown lumps at both ends. Dej's new senses told her it was edible. She wasn't convinced.

"Fetch the bowl from the pack on the top left."

Dej did as Kir asked. The rhinobeast huffed to itself as she rummaged around in its luggage webbing.

"Now hold this end."

Again Dej obeyed, although the grub wriggled disgustingly, exuding a smell like old boots and a not-quite-heard whine that put her teeth on edge. Kir ran her knife along the bug's underside, tipping it up so the liquid that came out – pale brown and thick as honey – drained into the bowl. Kir offered her the bowl and Dej took it, making herself drink without hesitation. It tasted sweet, though with a mushroomy aftertaste. She offered the half-empty bowl to Kir, but she shook her head.

Afterwards her stomach gurgled, but she felt stronger, the aches and pains more distant.

"You need solid food?" asked Kir.

"Yes. Please."

Kir lit a brushwood fire and rolled the bug carcass into it. The dead beast sizzled and popped.

The land around them contained enough life to confuse her still-tender senses, although with night coming on, some of the activity was muted. Dej looked beyond the fire, back down into the darkening desert lowlands.

"No questions?"

She looked over at Kir. "Loads. I'm not sure where to start."

"Hmm." Kir wasn't going to give her any clues.

"All right. How long was I lying out there, before I woke up?"

"Two days."

Min would have left the crèche by now. "And you were waiting there, all that time?"

"Much longer and I'd have left you to it." Something on the bug gave a meaty pop. "That's about ready," said Kir.

Now it was cooked the old boots smell had matured to something more like meat, and the taste wasn't so bad, though the flesh took a lot of chewing.

Afterwards, Kir gave Dej a cloak sewn from strips of cured hide, advising, "Wrap yourself up well; some of the life out here likes bare flesh."

They lay down to sleep, one on either side of the rhinobeast. The creature's solid warmth was comforting, but Dej found herself wriggling in her cloak. The knowledge of which direction was north hadn't left her. If anything, it grew as she drifted towards sleep, and kept her awake. She would be more comfortable if she wasn't lying against the direction of the world. Even so, eventually she slept.

Dej sat bolt upright. Dawn was close, the skyland life around her ramping up to full daylight. But all that mattered was her guts. She threw her cloak off, scuttled away from the rhinobeast, and squatted. When she was done she cleaned herself up as best she could, using plants her animus-given knowledge told her wouldn't sting or fight back.

Kir was up when she finished. Dej braced herself for mockery but the skykin merely held out a flask and said, "Drink."

"What is it?"

"Water. You should try and eat some jerky too."

Dej did as Kir suggested then let Kir help her back onto the rhinobeast. "That jerky… was it beef?" she asked.

"Something like that."

Shadowkin animals died out here so they must have traded for it. "Did you get that for me because it'll take a while to adjust to skyland food?"

"Partly," Kir replied as the rhinobeast ambled into motion. "Though you never will, entirely."

"What do you mean?"

"Being incompletely bonded means some skyland food will take time to get used to. Other things you'll never be able to eat. And you'll need shadowkin food too sometimes."

"Oh." Something else she'd had no idea about. "So what else is different? Between us and, ah, true skykin I mean?"

"'True' skykin. Huh." Kir snorted. "Well, there's the distance to your animus. You'll have felt that."

"Yes. It's like…" she struggled to find a good way of putting it, "… like being able to call on it, but not having it in your face all the time."

"Something like that. And no continuity with past lives. No certainty."

That was one of the animus's greatest gifts, according to the crèche tutors: the comfort of previous lives. "What else?"

"Depends on your animus." Kir kicked the rhinobeast harder, urging it up the slope. "Your animus gives you talents, just like they told you in the crèche, but when you're incompletely bonded you'll lack some, while others can be… out of proportion."

"So, maybe you don't know what all the plants do, but you can see when someone's ill inside."

"Something like that."

"And do you have, uh, a special talent?"

"You should be more worried about yours. Assuming you've got one."

On their second overnight stop Kir went hunting again, this time staying away long enough that Dej started to worry. They were deep in the mountains, in a narrow valley with overhanging cliffs. Kir didn't light a fire before she left so Dej stuck close to the rhinobeast. When her forehead itched she pulled the sticky leaf dressing off and found the wound reduced to a small, sore indentation.

Finally, Kir returned with something slung over her shoulder like a big cousin of the lizards that sunned themselves on the walls of the crèche, though with an extra pair of legs. "What's that?" she asked Kir.

"Rockslither; just a small one."

The rockslither turned out to be three creatures in one, coming apart in segments under Kir's knife, one set of legs per section, with skin smooth and pale as a baby's cheek on the inner face of each piece, and a twisted sinewy cord running down the middle of the whole beast… or beasts. It still looked more like food than the bug had. Tasted more like it too. And it stayed down. When she commented on this the next morning Kir said, "That's good, because you'll be eating a lot of those little bastards."

CHAPTER 22

Rhia gripped the leather strap harder, though her fingers were getting numb. Outside, the rhinobeasts grunted, while their handlers murmured wordless encouragement.

They should reach the plateau soon, with easier going and the possibility of some sightseeing tonight. But first they had to get up this damn mountain.

When the wagon finally levelled out, smiles of relief broke out all round. Rhia released her hold, and shook her hand to get the blood flowing again.

That night hazy cloud obscured much of the sky. The land was flat with sparse, low vegetation, beaten down by the constant winds of the high plateau, giving off a pale glow in shades of purple and azure.

Lekem went over to talk to some of the other travellers while the skykin were setting up camp. Most of those he spoke to shook their heads, but a few followed him. Rhia watched, curious, before realizing what was going on: today was restday.

As Lekem's impromptu congregation formed a circle beside the passenger wagon Sorne muttered, "So much for not drawing attention to ourselves."

The Zekti had gathered near the other wagon – all eight of them – and knelt down, eyes closed, hands clasped under chins. The skykin ignored the various outbreaks of piety. Rhia wondered if Lekem shared the Church-held view that, despite being born looking like shadowkin, skykin were lesser beings, tainted with animal traits.

"Had a lay preacher on one run, we did."

Rhia turned to see one of the other travellers addressing Sorne. It was the trader they sat next to in the wagon, whose name was Olgin. Rhia got the impression he was in the market for a wife. Fortunately, she did not appear to meet his criteria.

"Really?" said Sorne, laconically. "That must have made for entertaining travelling."

"*They* didn't like it much, that's for sure." Olgin nodded at Preut and Mella. "He gave her the evil eye whenever she came back from f– um, being with a man." Olgin leaned forward enough to see Rhia. "Begging your pardon, mam."

"Oh, don't mind me," murmured Rhia, with her best courtly smile.

"So what was this preacher up to?" asked Sorne.

"Reminding those who were straying off the true path, he said. No idea how he got on in Zekt but we never saw him again."

"Mmm. I heard they've got some odd ideas there."

"Certainly do. But their eparch's got the ear of the caliarch. For what that's worth. Our duke might have his foibles but at least he doesn't talk to the dead."

The Shenese worshippers began chanting the First Declaration. "My nephew's quite impressionable," said Sorne. "Should I be worried about him taking against these odd religious practices in Zekt? He'd be going against the caliarch himself, from what you've said."

"Yes, but the caliarch's not the only authority. Delegates most things to those ball-less courtiers. Then there's the prince, though he's a ruthless son of a y'know-what. Anyway, if your boy decides he doesn't like the First Lighters he wouldn't be alone. Do you think he'll do something rash, then?"

"Probably not, when it comes to it. He's just got more devout recently. What with how things are."

"Ack, yes. Damn drought. Shame we can't import water from Zekt. They've got enough of it!"

"It must be quite a sight. I'm looking forward to seeing the floating city."

"It doesn't really float, you know."

"Really?"

And Sorne was off, extracting information from the trader without letting his cover slip. Rhia edged away. Breen shadowed her. She smiled at the soldier. "I want to have a quick look around before supper but promised I wouldn't leave camp alone. Did you want to come along?"

"I'd love to, Mam Rhina."

Greymoon was high and full enough to give decent light, and Whitemoon would rise soon. Rhia led Breen towards the front of the wagons. When she was out of the circle of firelight she extracted her sightglass and raised it to her eye, focusing on the ground ahead. The view was a blurred swirl of pale colour. She adjusted the focus and looked again. Nothing but the flat plateau, broken up by amorphous vegetation.

"M'lady, may I ask what you're doing?"

She lowered the sightglass. "Using a device for magnifying what is far away."

"Ah." Rhia was not sure if he was impressed or confused. She put the sightglass back to her eye. Wanderer of Prin had spoken of the structure she was looking for being "dead centre of the plateau, though some distance from the road". With mountains all around, it was hard to tell how near the centre they were. The road, such as it was, was visible under the moonlight, a bare strip of earth stretching away towards the far peaks. She should use that to make her search more methodical. Sweep out from the road, and back. She moved her view farther up the road. First examine one side, then the other–

Aha! Could that be it? Amongst the chaos and shadows, a regular shape, too big and too geometrical to be natural.

She lowered the sightglass. There was no sign of the cube without it, but now she knew where it was she would get closer, then look again. She pointed up the road and said to Breen. "I am going over there now. You had best come with me."

"Are you sure you–?"

But she had already set off.

"M'lady, is this wise?"

Rhia called over her shoulder, "Surely you're not scared, Corporal?"

Breen caught up with her. "Of the wildlife, no. Of the captain, yes."

"This is a once-in-a-lifetime opportunity. We're going to see the House of the Ancients. Do you know what that is?"

"No, m'lady, I don't. Sounds... old."

"It is said to date to the Separation."

"And it's a house?" He sounded dubious. "How'd it survive?"

As they passed the tethered rhinobeasts the wind brought their smell; musty and warm, though not unpleasant. It reminded her of rising bread. "What do you think the Separation was, exactly?" she asked.

"The day when the disgraced Children of the First completed their fall, and divided into those who sought to keep the form and teachings of the First and those who would make themselves as animals."

Straight out of the scriptures. "With some sort of universal cataclysm, possibly associated with the Pillar of Fire?" The scriptures were vague on the details, though the Church had done much to embellish them down the millennia. "Something capable of destroying houses."

"That's what I was taught. But even if it wasn't such a big disaster at the time, it was so long ago. Surely this house would have just, well, fallen down."

"Perhaps not, given who built it."

"It was actually *built* by the Children of the First?" Breen's tone was a mix of wonder and disbelief.

"By definition, if it predates the Separation." Probably. Wanderer of Prin hadn't said that, as such. But she was annoyed at Breen's thoughtless acceptance of dogma.

"Surely we shouldn't go near it, then!"

Rhia suppressed a sigh. "Have you never wondered why, if the Children of the First were so extraordinary, the Church insists we should avoid or even destroy their works whenever we find them?"

"The Children were great, but through their pride they fell, and all they made was tainted."

Another direct quote. "So the priests tell us." Well, she'd tried. "Right, let's have another look, now we're a bit closer." She stopped and raised her sightglass again. Training it on the location she thought she had seen the cube revealed only moonwashed vegetation. Perhaps the distance had deceived her, this being a flat plain. They would go a little farther and–

"Down, m'lady!"

Breen shoved her forward.

She stumbled. As the ground came up to meet her she dropped the sightglass. Above, the sky exploded in a discordant scream.

She put her hands out just in time to avoid landing flat on her face. She fought to draw breath. *Where was the sightglass?*

The noise came again, somewhere between a choir of young babes in agony and the explosive action of some great infernal pipe organ. With it came a hot downdraft, the reek of rotten flesh.

Rhia gagged, and her guts loosened. *Sightglass. Concentrate on finding the sightglass.*

Overhead, wings beat fast as her heart.

Breen swore.

Something chittered. *I am looking for my sightglass. I am not panicking. I am not looking up.*

But movement to one side caught her eye. Breen, brandishing his dagger, crouching low, slashing upwards.

The awful presence wheeled away. She raised her head and swallowed bile.

Then the hot wind rushed in overhead again, bringing the stink of death.

Last take the damn sightglass, I'm going to die!

She could no longer see Breen. The creature moved through the air like ink in water, blotting out everything else. Its cry tuned down, becoming a soft keening like a choir of dead souls. It was descending, ready to engulf her, destroy her...

A whistling came from one side, cord thrumming through air.

The thing shrieked again, a thousand throats voicing fury and pain. A tendril lashed out from the turbulent, hovering darkness, only to be jerked away as though by an unseen rope.

Light flared.

Someone ran past, silent, half naked. He wielded a pair of swords which gleamed white as bone ... which *were* bone. A skykin warrior.

The skykin thrust upwards with both swords at once. The awful darkness flinched away, exuding a fresh burst of foulness.

A second skykin arrived, holding a flaming torch.

Both skykin struck together, blades and fire.

A screech resonated, then trailed off into a wheezing moan. The living darkness lifted, banked, then slid off into the night.

"Sorry..." breathed Breen beside her. "Thought I'd scared it off but it came back. My knife just went through it. Are you all right?"

"I think so, yes." At least, she would be.

The skykin with the torch looked back at her. She levered herself up onto all fours, while Breen half crouched beside her, ready to help. "Was that a nightwing?" she croaked.

"It was," said the skykin.

Wonder and horror warred in her. "Is it gone?"

"It is."

"Then will someone help me find my sightglass?"

The shock cut in as Rhia walked back to the camp. Her legs went boneless, and she stumbled. When Breen offered his arm, she was happy to put the hand not clutching her recovered sightglass on it.

The skykin took the incident in their stride. The warrior returned his swords to a bandolier on one of the rhinobeasts, then he and his companion walked over to the fire without a backward glance.

The worshippers had finished their devotions, and most of the travellers eyed her up, expressions ranging from shocked to fascinated. Rhia let go of Breen's arm and approached Sorne.

Before he could speak she said, "I'm sorry. I should not have gone off like that."

"You shouldn't, no." He looked her in the face. "Are you all right?"

"Fine. I just need to sit down."

He moved aside. She sat, and stared at the comforting play of flames.

"You should eat."

Rhia started to see Breen holding out a bowl of stew. She took it. "Ah, yes. Thank you. And thank you for what you did."

"I could hardly let you die out there." He grinned across at Sorne, who was tucking into his own meal. "He'd've fed me to the nightwings himself."

Sorne growled over the rim of his bowl. "Damn right I would."

Despite the soldiers' attempts at levity, Rhia felt shaky. Just shock, she told herself.

Perhaps she could try and find the House of the Ancients on the way back. Assuming Sorne let her. Then again, perhaps it was just an oddly shaped rock, talked up into something of significance by Wanderer of Prin – or, given how far away his shadowland was from here, by some other traveller who he had got the tale from third or fourth hand.

But she had seen a nightwing. They were a true wonder. Strange even by skyland standards, they were myriad beings which somehow managed to fly and hunt as one.

And they were quite capable of killing a man. She knew they were found on the high plateau, yet she had not considered the danger. Never mind disappointments and tall tales: she could have died tonight.

What am I doing out here?

The reasons came back at once. *I'm here to see the world and save my brother.* She only hoped she had the strength to survive the first and the wits to achieve the second.

CHAPTER 23

Sadakh had done it again. Or rather, his ghost reminded him as he watched the sleeping girl, he had let it happen again.

Her name was Akbet. Her father was a rice merchant and she had no intention of getting married and raising babies like her older sister. He liked her contrary, questioning nature. He disliked her tendency to fill any silence with speech, no matter how trivial.

The relationship was following the usual path. All new initiates were granted time alone with the eparch to discuss their future spiritual development. During their initial meeting, Akbet had spent more time flirting than listening.

When he first became eparch of the First Light, Sadakh had ignored such behaviour. Power drew adoration but he would not abuse his position by encouraging it. When this did not work, and some of the female (and once, male) initiates sought an intimacy beyond the spiritual, he had taken them aside and suggested they should spend less time in his company, to keep themselves focused.

In most cases, they had been hurt and offended. A couple left the Order as a result.

So, he had reconsidered. Sex was a primal urge. It drove, confounded, even defined. If he wanted to understand people and their relationship to divinity, he had to understand that urge, which often eclipsed other, higher drives. But he made the rules clear to potential partners in advance: entering into a physical relationship would not result in special treatment, and either party could end the relationship without consequence at any time.

This worked, usually. Several of the women who had passed through his bed became trusted members of the Order; one had become a bodyguard. With others the relationship had soured or withered, and the disengagement had been less pleasant. Some stayed in the Order, some left.

This one won't last.

He ignored his ghost: she always said that. Anyone would think she was jealous. Akbet was a skilled and experienced lover, eager to impress. He had let himself enjoy her. Now, as she lay asleep amongst the covers of his bed, he felt the usual shame and sorrow. Shame that he had given in to temptation and justified it, yet again, as the free choice of the other party; sorrow that she had only one currency to trade, a currency most men wanted but few valued.

He eased away from her, and her eyes opened. She smiled and said, playfully, "Holiness." His lovers often toyed with that word, imbuing it with lower meanings. He never gave them permission to use his name.

"Good morning, Akbet."

"Morning already?"

"I'm afraid so."

"I have scripture lessons after prayers, and should bathe first."

"Quite so."

"May I... come back this evening?"

Sadakh had given this inevitable request some thought. Certain experiences could only be explored with a lover, such as how identities blurred at the moment of orgasm and how being so close to another person could nourish and illuminate one's soul. With some of his partners, the shared experience had verged on the mystical. But those had been women who went to bed with a man to find themselves rather than to prove their worth. And even in those cases it never lasted. At some point every woman sensed the part of himself he held back.

Sensed me, his ghost would claim.

He wondered if Akbet would stay long enough – and be sensitive enough – to run up against this inevitable barrier. There was only one way to find out, and for now they both got something they wanted from the relationship.

He smiled. "If you wish."

CHAPTER 24

In some ways the descent was worse. After a morning rolling across relatively flat land the caravan halted. The rhinobeasts were unhitched and moved to the back of the wagon to act as brakes, an activity achieved with a degree of huffing and lowing, and the occasional call from their normally silent handlers.

Several travellers settled on the floor, braced against the benches. Rhia kept her seat but threaded a hand through a strap. They set off again. The first skid had her grabbing for the seat-edge with her other hand. The wagon stopped with a jolt, though it took a moment for her stomach to catch up.

If the traces break...

Think about something else, anything else. Like the morning after the argument with Etyan. *No.* Instead, she went over her mental notes on the journey so far, ready to write them up as soon as she had the chance.

When a jerk or skid set her heart tripping she reminded herself that the caravan went this way every couple of weeks without mishap.

The ground evened out around late afternoon. Zekt was higher than Shen, so at least the descent was shorter than the ascent. While the rhinobeasts were repositioned people climbed back onto benches, sat back, relaxed. As siesta had been impossible, some slept. Mella dozed with her head on

Preut's shoulder; the familial resemblance was obvious. Rhia looked away.

When they stopped for the night the sky was cloudy, although ambient moonlight and the inherent glow of the land showed an abundance of life on this side of the mountains. Away from the road – which was surfaced with gravel here – the ground was covered in fronds and stalks and hairlike tangles, along with regular clusters of solid spheres which looked artificial; these latter had a two-toned glow, brighter, and bluer, at the top. A wall of noise – chirrups and hums and buzzes and clicks – pressed in from the darkness. Odd scents drifted on the light breeze: nutmeg, lilac, something she had no name for.

Last night she had been too wrung out after the nightwing encounter to do more than curl up in her hammock. Tonight there was something she needed to do, before it was too late.

She strode round the fire and up to the seer, who sat staring into the flames.

"I did it," she said.

As the skykin seer looked away from the fire, the membranes protecting her eyes slid back.

"To yourself." The seer's tone gave nothing away.

"That's right. I did this to myself." She half raised a hand to touch her mask.

A shadowkin might show shock, or murmur some apologetic deflection. The skykin did neither. She shuffled round so she no longer faced the fire, and pointed to the ground in front of her.

As she had hoped when she made her bold admission, Rhia was being invited to join the seer. She lowered herself to sit cross-legged.

Still the skykin said nothing. Just stared at her, eyes glistening in the firelight.

Rhia collected her thoughts, then asked, "Is it true that

you can tell when people lie by their smell?" It appeared the "smell" of deception on Rhia had been strong enough to interest this Yrif from afar.

"Yes. Though not as you smell. It is above the nose."

Whatever that meant. "Right." Rhia took a deep breath. Having decided to own up to the lie she had lived with for thirteen years in order to gain the seer's trust, she had better get on with it, and not keep anything back. "I am actually a noblewoman of Shen."

The seer showed no reaction to this revelation.

Rhia carried on. "When I was a girl, I was pledged to a noble in another shadowland." The skykin did not ask which shadowland. Rhia doubted it mattered to her.

"I didn't want the marriage to happen. I wanted to stay in Shen. I had everything I needed there." A tolerant and loving father, her books and papers, even – though she winced to think of it now – the boy she thought was her true love. At the time it had been so simple. Sacrifice appearances to keep the life she wanted. "I had access to substances that burn selectively, so I used one. On myself. Which was stupid. Even being careful I could have damaged my eye. But it worked. The wedding was called off."

She had wanted to confess her terrible act to Father as he lay raving on his deathbed. She had told herself at the time it would only cause him more distress. In the decade since his death, she had buried it deep. And now she had spoken the truth. She had expected to feel unburdened but the seer's lack of reaction gave her conscience no purchase. No matter. She had crossed the fire seeking knowledge, not absolution. She blinked and said, "Now I want to ask you something." It may as well be personal, given the nature of her own admission. "Are you married?"

"No." The seer looked at her. "Are you?"

"No, I'm not, but... will you marry?"

"It is unlikely."

"But not impossible? I mean, do skykin marry, at all?" The accepted wisdom was that most skykin lived in large clans deep in the skyland, with a few choosing, or being chosen, to run the caravans between shadowlands. How the clans worked was a mystery no enquirer had addressed.

"Some make vows. Some do not. Those that do, keep them."

"And is it true they took your name from you when were a child? Because you're an Yrif, that is."

"Just Yrif. That is my name." For a moment Rhia thought that was all she would get. Then the seer continued, "Once able to walk and talk, children who have been chosen as seers are removed from the crèche. Names are taken, though parting-gifts are not." Rhia had not come across parting-gifts in her reading: she made a mental note to ask about those later. "The seer-to-be lives alone in a cave, provided with the necessities of life and visited by clan members of every calling."

"So, healers and trackers and hunters? Everyone who has a... function?"

"All members of the clan have a function. And the wisdom of every function is shared with the growing seer."

Rhia smiled at the thought of so much valued knowledge being passed on so reverently.

"When the seer is mature, ze is bonded."

Rhia resisted the urge to interrupt; Sophist of Jhal had written that although the skykin and shadowkin shared a common language, both had words the other did not, and for skykin some of these related to an individual's identity. Rhia extrapolated that "ze" meant "he or she".

"After bonding, ze is Yrif. That is all that is ever needed."

"And the bonding, I'm interested in that. What is it like, to be bonded?" To have another living creature inside you, changing how you view the world. Controlling you, if Wanderer of Prin was to be believed.

"Ask the sightless what the Sun looks like, or one without hearing to describe the nightwing's cry."

And to think some claimed the skykin lacked imagination! "I understand. You cannot describe it to me because I'm unbonded." But there was so much the seer could tell her. Where to start? Remembering the outbreak of piety on restday she settled on something she would hesitate to discuss with her own people. "Are you aware that shadowkin believe that you, the skykin, are lesser, tainted beings? That you don't have true souls."

To Rhia's amazement and alarm the skykin bared her teeth – they were normallooking, not pointed or discoloured, but the act, suddenly expressive after passive inactivity, was shocking. "Have you seen your soul?" For the first time there was emotion in the seer's tone; amusement? anger? The seer put a finger in the centre of her forehead. "I saw my soul. Every day I feel my soul. I am bonded to my soul."

"The Church has a different idea of souls. A rather less... concrete one."

"It is not my Church."

"No, but it is mine. I lack faith but I am steeped in its beliefs and practices. They define my culture."

This time the pause was appraising. Rhia had an idea that she had, if not impressed the skykin, at least satisfied her. "The comparison of beliefs is rarely productive when cultures differ so greatly."

"You may be right." Rhia smiled, delighted at such quick-minded conversation. "But I would like to know if you believe in heaven?"

"Do you?"

"I'm... not sure I do."

"Then I pity you."

"So skykin do believe in heaven, then?" Was the seer playing with her?

"We do not need heaven. We have our animus: now, always; before, after. Your people need heaven because you are unhappy and discontented with the life you have – so much so that even one born into privilege will maim herself to control her fate. To take such actions yet not believe in continuance of mind after your body dies is contradictory at best, a sad waste at worst."

Rhia had no answer for that. Instead she countered with, "If you do not believe in heaven, does that also mean you do not believe in the First, and that his Children once walked the world?"

"We acknowledge greater powers. As for the Children of the First, I do not know because we were not there."

"So your animus's knowledge doesn't reach back to the Separation?"

"It does not."

It appeared an animus was not immortal.

The rest of the evening passed in a joyous blur of shared information.

Finally, the seer made a brushing motion down her body, and looked past Rhia. Following her gaze Rhia saw the fire had burned to embers, surrounded by sleeping cloakwrapped skykin. "We rest now."

"Of course."

The seer was already standing up.

CHAPTER 25

"What's that noise?"

Rhia looked up at Breen's question. She had spent the morning considering and ordering the information the seer had imparted, just as Father had taught her, prioritizing and cataloguing in her head. Much as she yearned to write some of it down, between Sorne's disapproval and the wagon's motion, this remained impractical.

After Breen's interruption, she listened, and heard a soft insistent drumming from above. "Rain," she murmured.

Breen nodded; he had realized it too. Lekem was praying, no doubt asking the First to send the life-giving rainclouds over the mountains to Shen.

The rain became heavier in the afternoon, sometimes splashing through the vents. Rhia grew downright chilly.

The sky was still cloud-locked when they camped for the night, though the rain had stopped.

The landscape had changed again. The terrain reminded Rhia of Shen's southern pastureland, softly undulating ground covered in what looked like close-bitten grass. Farther off, the diffuse moonlight picked out a dozen broad-headed beasts who appeared to be grazing on the "grass", moving across it line abreast, dark against the glowing land. The creatures ignored the caravan; Rhia assumed that if they were a threat, the skykin would take action.

The sounds this evening bore some resemblance to last night's, though with more squeaks and sighs, and the breeze brought new scents, of parsley and lavender.

Accompanied by Breen, she examined the "grass". It was more like camomile or moss, a tangle of stems and filaments. Some filaments glowed more intensely than others, and when rubbed between two fingers the lavender smell intensified.

As soon as dinner was over she went to see the seer. She took her notebook, and damn anyone who gave her looks for that.

They talked widely, touching on various subjects, from what skykin did for leisure – "Some enjoy competition; others prefer contemplation." – to how the caravan's route was kept free of the febrile, mobile life of the skyland; by dint, Yrif said, of rhinobeast droppings spread along the edge of the road by the wheels of the wagons; even the thinnest smear repelled most creatures and plants. Rhia was glad now she had not touched the wagon's wheels when she used them to rest her sightglass on.

Rhia asked about the House of the Ancients. The seer confirmed its existence although, she said, there is "nothing of interest left now". Rhia would still have welcomed the chance to see for herself.

Some questions the seer would not answer, such as what happened at a bonding ceremony, or details of life in the clans. Rhia did not press her.

Philosophy and theology were also difficult subjects, less because the two of them disagreed than because they saw the world in such different ways. Finding common frames of reference was complicated.

As the hours passed and her wits grew duller, Rhia moved on to simpler matters. When she asked about the skykin diet and used the word "vegetarian" the seer said, "I do not know that term."

Rhia, interested to find a word the skykin did not know even as they performed the act it referred to said, "It means to eat only plants, not animals."

"And is this a common practice in Shen?" The seer was interested in Rhia's home too, though less in the politics and social mores than the plants and animals and the day-to-day lives of the shadowland's people.

"No, but some shadowlands use it as a religious observance, a mixture of abstinence and compassion." They were back at the subject of belief.

"There is much variation in your religious practice, yet you refer to one Church."

"The Church thinks of itself as one edifice, but yes, every shadowland's beliefs are subtly different."

"And I imagine each shadowland's individual Church believes their own practices and rites to be the true ones?"

"I suspect they do."

"Then it is a good job it is so far between shadowlands."

Rhia had to smile at that. She steered the conversation back to the original subject. It transpired that skykin did not have a word for one who ate only plants because they did not hold with the distinction between plants and animals common in the shadowlands; they saw a range of natural life, not a division between two types of life. They did prefer to eat organisms that were, as the seer put it, "nearer to rock than person". She added, when Rhia pressed her, that it was not forbidden to eat creatures with "a discernible mind" in time of need but "to do so may diminish you."

As this was the last night, Rhia was reluctant to go to her rest, but as before, a point came when the seer insisted. Rhia reminded herself that she could continue the conversation on the return journey.

• • •

The caravan set off early the next day. Around noon the light dimmed, and shortly after that the wagon slowed, then turned sharply and stopped. They had reached Zekt's umbral.

When Rhia climbed down the ladder she found they were in a clearing much like the one in Shen. A gaggle of way-traders and others who had business with the caravan waited for them there. Thanks to the overcast sky and fully grown trees, it was dimmer than a sunny day back home, despite the proximity to the skyland.

Sorne directed Lekem and Breen to open negotiations while he wandered over to Mella and Preut. Whatever business they had involved close talk and the exchange of something small, perhaps a purse. Sorne had gone with Mella only the once, and had presumably paid for her services then. This was something else.

Rhia caught the captain's eye when he returned. "Anything I should be concerned with?" she asked.

"I'll tell you later. Right now I need to see what those boys have managed to sort for us."

Not a lot, as it turned out. Because they had not made advance arrangements, they were reduced to hiring a decrepit horse and cart for an exorbitant price. The shifty-looking individual who hired it out no doubt relied on each caravan bringing travellers too disorganized or desperate to have planned ahead.

As she climbed into the cart she saw Mella watching her. Rhia hesitated, then raised a hand to wave. The other woman returned the gesture. Yrif was busy. Rhia was not sure the seer would have bid her farewell anyway.

"So," said Rhia as the cart lurched forward, leaving the bustle of the caravan behind, "what were you speaking to Mella about?"

"Your brother."

Of course Captain Sorne would have realized, as she had,

that Mella must have encountered Etyan. "And did she, ah, meet him?"

"Meet, yes. Have business with, no. He had no interest in her."

"Really?"

"He kept to himself, she said. Looked wretched and hardly spoke a word."

"Oh. Was he unwell? Injured?" She remembered that dark stain on his doublet when she last saw him.

"Not injured or unwell no, but," Sorne, who normally kept his gaze deferentially low, looked her in the eye, "did you know your brother smoked kreb?"

"I did, yes." Rhia felt a sigh building. Out in the skyland she had forgotten some of the complications of life with Etyan.

"The other travellers weren't for letting him smoke in the wagon, which pleased him not at all. First night, he lit his pipe soon as everyone got out. Mella approached him then, looking for business, but he told her to be off. Which put her nose out of joint, and her response to that was to say he should enjoy his weed while he could, as he'd not get any in Zekt."

Rhia hadn't realized that. "What did he say to that?"

"According to Mella, he said 'There's another good reason to go there, then.'"

Given Etyan was, by his own admission, addicted to the vile stimulant, why would he go somewhere he would not be able to get hold of it? She had another thought. Kreb was an upper-class vice, too rare and expensive for the lower city or the villages, and the prostitute had worked out that Rhia came from a class above the one she claimed. "Does Mella know he and I are related?"

"I suspect she'll work it out now."

Which was why Sorne had waited until they were about to part company before making his enquiries. "That was why you gave her money? More money, I mean, for something other than the usual reason. To buy her silence."

"That was their retainer. Those two carry messages for Shen."

"Ah." Perhaps Francin's agents had queried the pair about Etyan when he first went missing. Yet he had never mentioned this to her, never tried to put her mind at rest.

Sorne continued with a wry smile. "But as for buying her silence, I don't rate my chances. There's little enough news out in the skyland and one like her trades in rumour as well as pleasure."

"Well," Rhia said, looking Sorne in the face, "we'll confirm any rumours about Etyan when we return with him."

Sorne's steady gaze gave nothing away, and he replied in a rare moment of piety, "First willing."

When they emerged into Zekt proper, Rhia was shocked by the lush profusion. Flax and beans and beets grew high on both sides of the road, and the irrigation ditches were full. At first this lifted her spirits. Everywhere was life, healthy leaves rustling, flowers open and buzzing with insects, fruits full and ripe. She had forgotten what that was like. Then the contrast began to wear her down, reminding her of how bad things had become in Shen.

Their useless nag made heavy going of the pitted and muddy road, though this did not stop Breen and Sorne taking their siesta. She rummaged in her satchel; although writing was impossible whilst on the move she consulted her tables, confirming the current disposition of the Strays.

As darkness fell they reached an inn, the equivalent of the one in Shen, existing on a mixture of local trade and travellers between shadowlands. Rhia thought it a poor building, with greying lime-washed walls and a moss-grown thatched roof. Most of the other guests were Zekti. There were more women than she expected, mainly servants but also a couple of peasants. Everyone had black or dark brown hair; the grey roots of one elderly trader confirmed Rhia's theory that hair colour was a matter of fashion as much as nature. Alharet's hair was a rich dark brown, un-dyed as far as Rhia knew. Both genders had pierced ears filled with wide earplugs of wood or stone; such an intrusion into the sacred life of the body verged on a forbidden practice at home, but presumably the Church here did not see any problem provided the item being implanted was purely decorative. The Zekti accent sounded laconic to Rhia's ears, with its flat tone and odd downward intonations.

There was no option of a private room. The four of them shared a dormitory, a prospect which would have appalled Rhia a week ago but which she accepted now. The room was cleaner and more comfortable than the one in Shen. The inn even had a bathhouse, though, with no private facilities, a bath could wait.

The sky remained cloudy so she stayed in the room, and started recording her observations while the soldiers caroused in the common room down the corridor.

She would love to meet one of Zekt's natural enquirers. The date on the last correspondence from Meddler of Zekt was over a year ago, implying that role was vacant, but Counsellor of Zekt continued to write eloquently about his shadowland and its unusual capital. She had his name, of course; they needed names to write to each other, though they were discouraged from making direct contact and some enquirers, in authoritarian or overly religious shadowlands, used aliases or got their mail through third parties. Had Counsellor of Zekt worked out that Observer of Shen was a woman? It depended how much he knew of Shenese names. If he knew her gender, she suspected it would make him even less inclined to break enquirers' etiquette in order to meet with her. And to announce her presence so could negate her disguise. No, she would have to forego that pleasure.

She was still hunched over the room's single table when Sorne returned. As he pulled off his boots he called over, "M'lady? I heard something you need to know."

Alerted by the unexpected formality, Rhia put down her quill. "What is it?" The only light in the room was the lamp on her desk, and his face was hard to read.

"I've some news about your brother." There was the hint of a slur in his voice, which was only to be expected after a night's drinking, but also a note of reticence. "This is just rumour, so don't be alarmed, but there was talk of a Shenese noble lad who came through here a few months back and got into trouble."

"What sort of trouble?"

"He snapped at the male staff, tipped the women heavily, and cried into his beer. Said he'd pay well if anyone could get him some kreb. Nothing came of it at the time, but according to the way-traders I was drinking with, someone paid attention. They say he was attacked on the road the next day."

"Attacked! Is he all right?"

"The gents I spoke to said he was robbed and beaten but sent on his way still able to walk. Excuse me for saying so, m'lady, but by their code he deserved no less. A young rake alone, making no secret of having money? They'd say he was asking for it."

"These men you heard this from – could they be the ones who attacked him?"

Sorne grimaced. "Perhaps, but they'd hardly admit it. Nor would whoever did it seriously injure someone of status, for fear of retribution; take his coin and teach him a lesson would be as far as they'd go."

"But do we know he reached Mirror-of-the-Sky safely?"

"We know he was in the city, and have no reason to believe he has left."

"*How* do we know he reached the city, Captain?"

"The duke has informants in all nearby shadowlands, m'lady."

"So I have surmised. What I would like to know are details of your mission." *And your precise orders.*

Sorne looked uncomfortable – an expression not at home on his face – and said, "With all due respect, m'lady, I must ask you to trust me."

"I don't have much choice, do I?" But as she turned away she felt a prick of remorse. She had foisted herself on the militiamen. It was not as though they had wanted her along.

CHAPTER 26

Dej and Kir reached the clanless camp late the next afternoon. At the top of a wide defile cut by a tumbling stream, so steep they had to dismount, the path opened out into a shallow bowl surrounded by mountains. Huts clustered round the stream, built of rough-piled stone with ragged thatched roofs and no windows.

As Dej and Kir dismounted, three figures strode out from the biggest, central hut. Or rather two strode; the third, whom they flanked, moved in a tight, efficient hobble, leaning on a stick. Dej was shocked: an animus kept you healthy, even healing broken bones. But these were the clanless.

"Go meet her," murmured Kir. Leaving Kir with the beast, Dej went forward. As she did so more people emerged, staring at her. She made herself walk tall and slow. The woman flanked by the guards was old. With no hair and skin that didn't wrinkle it was hard to tell, but something about her jarred Dej's new senses. The crèche taught that a bonded skykin lived life to the full, then passed on their animus and died, before the infirmities of old age set in. This woman could not have long to live.

Dej wondered if she was expected to make some gesture of respect, and settled on bowing her head, then waiting for the old woman to speak.

The elder hobbled right up to her. "I'm Mar. What can you

do?" The woman's breath was rancid, and she stank of sweat and age. This person was wrong, broken.

"Do, mam?"

"Yes. Did your animus give you anything of use?"

"I know what's safe to eat."

"Good. You'd die otherwise. Anything else?"

"I know where people are, and when I'm close up I get a feel for their mood."

"Of course you do. Everyone gets that."

"And I can sense direction."

"Hmm. Another one. Well, come with me." Mar turned and hobbled off. Dej followed, flanked by the two guards, neither of whom looked her way.

The old woman led her into the hut, which had to be ten times the size of any of the others. Smoke drifted into shadowed rafters. The only furniture in the central space was a backless seat behind the hearth. Dej jumped when she saw a man standing in the gloom beside the seat, younger but with an air of authority.

"Fetch a belt," commanded Mar, and one of her guards disappeared into a curtained alcove at the back of the hut. Dej tried to relax. The way the man by the seat looked at her didn't help.

The guard came back with a strip of leather. Dej let him tie the belt around her head, covering her eyes. They turned her around, several times one way, several the other.

"Where's north?" asked Mar.

Dej panicked, because she'd become distracted and lost her connection to the world. She took a deep breath and cleared her mind as best she could. Then she raised a hand and pointed to one side.

"Again."

The guard turned her, stopped, turned her the other way. Dej concentrated on not tripping over her own feet. This time she picked up the connection at once. Mar had her find north a third time before the guard removed the belt.

Mar had sat down on the carved wooden seat. "Sometimes an imperfectly bonded animus gives several talents. Have you anything else besides the navigation, and what you need to live? Has your memory sharpened, do you know a lie by its smell, can you sense what an animal wants? Anything like that?"

She'd known how Kir's rhinobeast felt, but not what it wanted. And if Kir had lied to her she hadn't spotted it. "I don't think so, mam."

The elder harrumphed. "It'd be good if the crèches taught useful skills like hunting or fighting. Never mind. You'll learn."

"Yes, mam. I will." So she'd passed the test.

Mar waved a hand in dismissal. "You can stay with Lih and Vay. Cal'll show you."

The man, presumably Cal, led Dej out without a word.

Outside, darkness was falling. They crossed to one of the huts. The two young women loitering in the doorway exchanged glances as she and Cal approached. The shorter of the two said, "With us? Must we?"

"You must," said Cal. "Her name is Dej. Be nice to her."

"Well, we've no spare bedding." The one who'd spoken had a sulky turn to her lip.

"I'll manage," said Dej.

"No one asked you." The girl turned and went back into the hut.

The taller one shrugged and gestured as if to say *come in then*. Dej followed her inside.

Her new hut-mates were preparing a meal on the hut's compact hearth. "Can I help?" she asked.

"Only by staying out of the way," growled the shorter one.

Dej did so, sitting back against an uncluttered section of

hut wall as night closed in outside. The hearth provided the only light. The two girls – or perhaps she should call them women, as they were both older than her – bickered over the stew, then divided it between themselves. After both had eaten the taller one came over with her bowl. "Finish that, then scrape the bowls into the pot and polish them clean."

The bowl only held a couple of spoonfuls, but Dej ate without complaint, then scooted to the hearth to clear up. The other two had retreated to fur-strewn pallets by the wall. "Um, what should I use to polish the bowls?"

The grumpier one pointed to a rag hanging by the door. "That," she said, then looked away.

Dej did the best she could, then curled up in the cloak Kir had given her. Between the hard floor, the cold and the urge to adjust position to match the world's alignment, she found it hard to sleep. Whenever she started wondering how things were at the crèche or what Min was doing now she called up mental maps of where she'd been, or recalled the sights and sounds of the skyland she'd seen getting here.

This is my life now. I need to get used to it.

The next day her hut-mates had her fetch water from the pool behind the settlement, then take a day's worth of rubbish to the communal midden. Dej didn't complain. Being a skivvy beat being ignored, and if she put up and shut up they'd eventually come to accept her.

Somewhat to her surprise Mar herself intercepted her on the way back from the midden. She introduced Dej to a sinewy woman called Jeg. "You need to learn combat skills," said Mar, and left her to it.

Jeg led her to the open area in front of the big hut, where she got Dej to perform the "moving meditation" taught by the crèche to encourage body and mind co-ordination. Step and hold and stand on one leg; pause, twist, and sweep down. All the variations, at different speeds. Over and over again. Dej had no idea what that achieved, aside from providing a spectacle for passing clanless.

In the afternoon Jeg gave her a softwood practice knife, and showed her how to grip it. Then she attacked her. Dej half raised the knife, and backed off. Jeg repeated the procedure with a short staff. Jeg pulled her blows, but Dej still ended up with bruises. Jeg then took Dej through a few basic blocks, moving excruciatingly slowly.

That evening her hut-mates sent her to the pool again. As she unhooked the waterskin Vay, the taller and slightly less unpleasant girl, looked up from the herbs she was sorting and said, "And if you can manage to not bring back any gravel this time that would be *lovely*."

At the pool, Dej kept the lip of the waterskin above the rough pool bottom. It took longer to fill that way, but that was fine, there was something she wanted to try now she was alone. The pool was a few dozen steps upslope of the settlement, and the stream tumbled over rocks above it; between distance and falling water, no one could overhear her here.

Dej hummed. Although she couldn't hear herself over the stream, she felt the sound in her head. The tone, the underlying music, was still there! As she filled the waterskin, her heart lifted and she added a nasal drone, biting back the unheard sound into staccato pops, feeling the noise vibrate through her head and in her throat. She could no longer sing, but music wasn't entirely lost to her.

While she was walking back through the village, Kir stepped out from one of the huts, started, then looked at Dej and said, "You look better than you did when we got here."

Dej smiled, the first real smile she had made with her new face. "Thanks."

Kir smiled back, but while Dej was thinking what to say next, walked off.

On the second day of Dej's combat training, Jeg was joined by a man named Tew. The tutors would show her how to stand or hold the staff or knife, then one would come in to make a slow, easy-to-deal-with attack, while the other stood back and watched, telling Dej what she was doing wrong.

On the third day Tew told her to try the weapon moves she'd learnt so far with her other hand.

Dej stared at him. "You sure? I mean, I can only just do them with my good hand."

Jeg said, "You don't have a good and bad hand anymore. Your animus should've burnt out those reflexes."

Not entirely, as it turned out. She found fight practice harder with her left hand. Harder still when they had her use a weapon in each hand.

Despite the unfamiliar and sometimes painful lessons, the fight tutors' disparaging remarks and the interest Dej's antics provided for the other clanless, she began to enjoy herself. She was so much faster and stronger than she had been – though not as fast and strong as her tutors. And these two were willing to put in the effort to train her. In return, she'd do her best to learn.

When they paused at midday on the third day Jeg went to fetch food while Tew walked over to the stream and bent down to drink. Dej mirrored him, and as they straightened asked, "Where are you from?"

"What?"

"Your accent sounds like mine, so I wondered if you were raised in Shen." Despite their changed voices the clanless had faint accents; some of them sounded flat or used odd clipped vowels. Kir's accent was familiar too, and Dej wondered if they'd been at the same crèche.

"I was." Tew scooped up another mouthful of water. "But you know that doesn't matter any more, don't you?"

"Yes. I do."

Mornings and evenings, she did the chores. Vay cooked, but everything else that needed doing round the hut had become Dej's job.

Lih did as little as possible. She was lazy and vain and loved being right; Dej knew the type from the crèche. Still peeved at having Dej foisted on her, she was also spoiling for a fight. Dej didn't plan to give her the excuse.

At least Vay stuck to gentle sarcasm, and made some concessions.

Dej had come to accept that the hollow left by Min's absence – by her betrayal – would never be filled. She would keep herself curled tight around it, and not let it consume her.

In some ways this place was a bit like the crèche, although there was one difference she must never lose sight of: in the crèche it was Us and Them; the children, future skykin, chafing against the shadowkin staff. Here, it was all Us – or, rather, until she was accepted, all Them.

By the sixth day of training Dej was exhausted and battered, but also getting stronger, faster and more co-ordinated. When Jeg said, "Day off tomorrow," Dej asked if this was because she'd earnt it.

Jeg laughed. "No, just restday. But we'll find out whether you've learnt anything the day after that."

"What happens then?"

"Your first hunt."

CHAPTER 27

In the morning, Rhia revised her judgment of the inn's architecture. Under a sky that promised a soaking, they passed hamlets and, later, a large manor house. Every building used the same materials. Stone and tile must be rare here.

Rain thickened out of the damp air during siesta. Rhia hunched down in her hat and cloak. The hat's brim soon grew waterlogged and began to sag. She took it off rather than have it dissolve around her head, and put it under her seat. When she looked up, Breen, bare-headed and damp, gave her a sympathetic smile.

The cultivation pattern of the flat fields was changing: much of the land was permanently flooded here. Rhia wondered if they suffered from a surfeit of the rain Shen lacked. Then she remembered; these fields were *meant* to be under water. They grew rice, a crop she had once eaten at a diplomatic dinner, finding it dull and a little hard on the teeth.

The rain abated, though the clouds did not disperse. As the overcast day darkened towards evening, she looked past Lekem and saw a humped dark shape rising out of the mist: the Eternal Isle, heart of the Zekti capital.

"So that's Mirror-of-the-Sky, then? More like 'can't see the sky'."

She looked round at Breen's attempt at humour. "The locals just call it 'Mirror' actually." Once, she might have

175

become one of those locals: an odd thought.

Rice gave way to tall reeds that rustled like whispering courtiers and blocked the view to either side. Their horse slowed, its steps dragging.

The Eternal Isle dominated the pale, low buildings of Mirror-of-the-Sky. Mist obscured detail, though she could see the island had been terraced and built on. Although Alharet had grown up there, she never spoke of her childhood; Rhia got the impression there was darkness and pain in those memories.

Closer, and the settlements around the sacred isle came into focus. The islets of Mirror had started as rafts in the shallow lake, places for people to camp or congregate near their ruler's residence. These had become moored, amalgamated together, then, over generations, ballasted to form a network of artificial islands. Such foundations did not allow grand architecture. Most of the city was built of wood and reeds, two storeys high at most.

The causeway extended out into the lake, passing under a freestanding wooden arch painted in green, red and black. Before the arch, it broadened out to a wide platform, with causeways going off to the left and right, around the lake. Along one side of the platform was a cluster of small buildings with several carts hitched up alongside, and horses in a corral.

They headed for the square-cut arch, which was carved with semi-abstract animal and floral designs; feline faces peered from behind curled leaves, and vines twined with snakes. A pair of guards stood at ease under the arch. They wore short tunics and leather skullcaps, and carried obsidian-tipped spears. Lekem stopped the cart. One of the guards approached and asked, "Have you papers?"

Rhia's heart tripped. Bureaucracy was a fact of life in Shen too, but at home she had people for that.

Lekem turned to Sorne, who reached into his jerkin and produced a folded sheet of scruffy vellum. The guard took it, unfolded it and read. "Bakers, yes."

"That's right." Sorne sounded more relaxed than Rhia felt.

The guard glanced at the paper again, then looked at everyone in turn. His gaze lingered on Rhia. "There is no mention of this woman."

"My cousin decided to join us at short notice. She's of little consequence." Sorne smiled at the guard. Rhia bit her tongue and schooled her face to meek submission. "Feel free to up the tariff to reflect her capricious choice." The captain was enjoying this.

The guard nodded and named a price. Sorne paid without complaint.

As they rumbled under the gate, the Sun dropped down far enough to pull free of the clouds. The long, low houses of Mirror shone gold in the evening light, which lit the brightpainted carvings running along their upturned eaves and roof ridges. The houses gave the impression of turning their backs on the lake, and had small, high windows with blue or green shutters.

The causeway ended in another platform. Muscular men in loincloths sat along a bench beside a covered booth, which housed an overweight, bored-looking man in robes. As Lekem pulled up, the man levered himself from his high-backed seat and said, "Welcome to our city. You'll be heading for Arec."

"That's right," said Sorne, climbing off the cart. According to Counsellor of Zekt, Arec was the "strangers' isle". "Can you recommend anywhere good to stay?"

"For Shenese..." the man's mouth twitched, "try Mam Jekrey's." He flicked a finger at the men on the bench, who sat with downcast eyes, ignoring the conversation. "They know where that is. You want how many."

Sorne's face showed a rare moment of confusion. Rhia, used to the odd way Alharet asked questions, realized what the official meant. Those men were slaves. "He means, how many men do we need to carry our luggage," she murmured, hoping the captain would hear her.

Sorne regained his composure. "Just a couple. We can manage most of our stuff ourselves."

"We'll need your names for the register. Follow me."

While Sorne accompanied the man back to his booth the two men at the nearest end of the bench stood up. Once the cart had been unloaded another one came forward to return it to the onshore staging post, ready to be hired by the next travellers unlucky enough not to have made better arrangements.

Three causeways led deeper into the city; the official indicated they should take the shortest, leftmost one, then settled back in his booth.

The slaves picked up a pair of packs each, eyes averted. One went to stand beside Sorne; the other moved to the back of their little group. Slavery was the default punishment here. Some of the more serious crimes were dealt with by the noose, as in Shen, while for others the solution was surgery, including an operation on the brain said to make a person docile as an aged donkey. Despite – or perhaps because of – the alarming uses it was put to, Zekti medicine was held in high regard.

Stepping off the causeway onto the isle of Arec, Rhia found the artificial "ground" firm and dry, though with a disconcerting give. On closer examination she saw it was a combination of compacted reeds, fibrous stems – possibly from rice plants – and soil; Father would have smiled at such ingenious solutions to a hostile environment, although a more sensible solution might have been not to build their city in a lake in the first place. She straightened when Sorne cleared his throat.

With no horses or wheeled vehicles, the thoroughfares were narrow and chaotic. Locals stared at them in a sidelong, politely curious way; Rhia tried not to stare back at the Zekti fashions: lots of pale fabrics, gathers, pleats and bare legs – even the women. Although Zekt was cooler than Shen, out here on the lake the humidity was high, and Rhia saw the logic of loose clothing. They passed more slaves, up on a roof, repairing a brick chimney. There were other outsiders here: Rhia recognized the wide hats of a Xuin couple, the slashed tunic of a Marnese, plus various people whose nationality she could not identify. They saw no other Shenese, and no beggars. Several times she heard music, high pipes and flutes on the wind.

What Rhia had taken to be single large dwellings from a distance turned out to be terraces, much like the lower city back home, where one long building was divided into smaller residences. Some were built round open courtyards.

Mam Jekrey's guesthouse was one such. Their hostess was a corpulent widow with one lazy eye and one wide-open one which gave the impression of missing nothing. She greeted them more warmly than anyone else they had met here. Rhia supposed that was her job.

By default, guests slept two or four to a bedroom, but Sorne negotiated Rhia her own room. As she unpacked, her thoughts returned to their reception. The Zekti were not exactly welcoming, although it was hard to know how much of that was standoffishness towards outsiders and how much was due to ongoing tensions between Zekt and Shen. Etyan had – she assumed – arrived without papers. And, if Sorne's informants at the inn were correct, without money. Her chest tightened at the thought. Her little brother was a bad judge of character, and tended to assume his friendly manner and natural charm would get him through; that and the money and status he was accustomed to having. How had he, a rootless and clueless stranger with no assets, fared with the guards and officials? Was his name recorded in that official's book? And where was he now?

CHAPTER 28

"Hold him down!"

Sadakh stepped back as another hospitaller came forward. After the first test subject had died four days ago – on the very night he first slept with Akbet – he had left instructions that he was to be notified should the condition of any of the remaining three change. The call had come shortly before siesta, while he was in his private study, though little study had been occurring.

It took three people to restrain the man as he thrashed and twitched, convulsions which gave credence to the heretical idea of possession.

Not unlike the travails of a skykin being bonded.

Indeed so, he concurred with his ghost.

The patient's jaw had locked, stifling his screams; tortured groans and hisses escaped from his rigid face. A fortunate situation, if not for the poor wretch himself: screams from the infirmary would cause alarm. The other two patients, at the far end of the room, continued to alternate between feverish sleep and light delirium.

One of the hospitallers glanced back at Sadakh; perhaps he thought the holy presence might bring relief to the suffering patient. Sadakh wished he could.

Or perhaps the man's concern was more prosaic. That four diverse individuals should be struck down with an unexplained fever at the same time caused understandable concern. Sadakh had insisted on isolation and close care, and assured his flock they had nothing to fear, a promise which he could be sure of, given he had caused the condition himself.

The man screamed, a horrific gurgling exclamation of agony.

"His tongue!"

One of the hospitallers grabbed the patient's jaw. Another one leaned forward, armed with the solid leather cylinder placed in the mouths of those undergoing painful operations.

The patient flicked his head away from the hospitallers' attention. For a moment Sadakh was eye-to-eye with his victim, though there was no sense in that flushed and straining face. The man's head jerked back; a feeble spurt of blood sprayed from his mouth. He had indeed bitten his tongue. Unless the blood came from deeper within. One of the hospitallers blocked Sadakh's view and he exhaled.

You did this.

As if he didn't know. He had done this, and that was why he had to be here, to watch, to face up to the consequences of his actions.

The patient began gasping, his limbs quivering.

The head hospitaller looked up and said, "He's dying!"

The duty priest, who had been at the far end of the room watching the other patients, now hurried up between the beds. He snatched up the quartz incense bowl from its stand before the room's shrine, then hesitated, coming face-to-face with his superior.

Sadakh nodded, indicating that the man was to proceed.

The priest stopped at the foot of the bed, perhaps judging it unwise to get closer. Sadakh stepped up to stand next to him.

The patient's struggles were abating and his face was pale under the spattered blood. The noises he made were softer too, though they were not sounds Sadakh had thought a human throat should make.

The priest began intoning the Blessing of Departure, incense bowl held high. Sadakh stood by his side and spoke the words along with him.

Before they had completed the first stanza, the man had fallen silent and stopped moving.

When Sadakh returned to his rooms he found Akbet had waited for him.

"Is all... well?"

"A man died, Akbet. One of the faithful. Just now."

Akbet's hand went to her mouth. "How terrible. Should we pray?"

"Oh, I prayed for him, believe me." Just as he prayed for every other death he caused. Whether it helped, beyond salving his conscience, he would give some of his own diminishing life to know.

"Then," she looked up at him from under long lashes, "perhaps there is another way I may help?"

Sadakh opened his arms.

They went at it there and then, coupling like beasts on the study floor. As they rolled apart, Akbet made some comment about liking it that way. This turned Sadakh's stomach more than his experience in the infirmary, because he had sensed her fear at the violence with which he took her, and she said this only because she thought it was what he wanted to hear. They moved through to the bedroom for gentler lovemaking.

But there was only so long sex could distract for. When they lay quietly together Sadakh said, "Tell me about your other lovers, Akbet."

"Really? Are you sure–"

"I'm sure." No other man would ask her that. Perhaps the request would make her think.

Or not. She gave a brief and embarrassed review of some of the men she had known, none of whom, she claimed, could compare to His Holiness. Then she moved on to talk about her family. For someone who was rebelling against them, Akbet spent a lot of time talking about her family.

Sadakh found himself tuning her out. Then something she said broke through. "I'm sorry," he said, "you said something about enquirers…"

"Yes, Manek's hoping he might." Manek was her older brother; her family had paid for the privilege of having a third child, and being that child had done Akbet no good.

"And he's a scribe?"

"Fully qualified. But he's also apprenticed to an older gentleman and this gentleman is a natural enquirer." Akbet narrowed her eyes. "You know about the natural enquirers, yes?"

Sadakh had heard tantalising rumours of a worldwide network of scholars, not entirely dissimilar to skykin seers. If he could gain access to that level of knowledge he might yet achieve his goal, hopefully without taking another life. But rumours were all he had. Until now. "I know a little."

Akbet looked smug, no doubt pleased to find something she knew more about than he did. "They're very secretive. And to become one you have to be a genius. Manek's always been so clever. The gentleman has others he is tutoring too, but I'm sure when the time comes, Manek will take on the role."

"And do you know this gentleman's name?"

"Manek did tell me." She grimaced. "But I'm not meant to pass it on. Like I say, very secret."

"Of course. But perhaps it is information an eparch might be entitled to know."

"Holiness." She did that dimple thing with her cheeks.

"Everything you tell me is in confidence, child. It would be our little secret."

He had noticed that Akbet loved secrets.

CHAPTER 29

"She doesn't even have a household shrine."

Rhia looked up from her breakfast of sweetened rice at Corporal Lekem's comment. They sat around a low table in the guesthouse's combined dining room and parlour, which Mam Jekrey referred to as "the commons" as though she ran an inn. Other tables were occupied by a pair of merchants from Faro, a Xuin nobleman and a Zekti family from the provinces. People sat or knelt on rush mats on the floor; Rhia had not seen any stools or benches since arriving in the city. Not that she had seen much of the city so far.

"Perhaps it's somewhere you haven't been yet," whispered Breen. "Like her bedroom."

Lekem took no notice of his comrade's innuendo. "If it's not in the hallway, it's not a household shrine."

Rhia pictured the shrine at her townhouse. Around age ten she had taken an interest in Saint Ti. He was said to have brought fire down from heaven after the First cut His Children off from his grace, though to young Rhia, drawing people's attention to a natural phenomenon hardly warranted sainthood. This led her to wonder if there was more to fire than met the eye. This in turn led to a series of experiments, encouraged by Father until they resulted in a burnt thumb and singed hair. Rhia had returned to her initial conclusion: Ti was overrated and fire was dangerous. Remembering this now brought a bittersweet warmth.

"So I guess you're not going to their big restday service?" Breen nodded towards the centre of the city.

"No, I am not." Lekem did not think much of the local Church's practices.

Rhia took a spoonful of rice. In the three days they had been here she had modified her initial impression of the grain: it was soft enough if cooked properly, and it could be interesting if well seasoned. However, it had featured in every meal so far, and she foresaw herself getting bored of it.

She was already bored of the guesthouse, now she had finished writing up her notes from the journey. She had also enjoyed a much-needed bath in water drawn from the lake which, Mam Jekrey assured her, was clean enough to drink, adding rather chillingly, "Anyone caught dumping nightsoil into the lake gets two years indenture." Rhia had not drunk the water but she had tasted it, curious to discover if it was bitter like the world-sea was said to be; it was not.

Now, with her observations from the skyland down on paper, she wanted to see the city. However, when they first arrived at the guesthouse Sorne had "suggested" that she did not go out alone. Remembering the inn in Shen, she had agreed. Given the soldiers left after breakfast and rarely returned before dinner, that meant not going out at all, so far.

Sorne said, "I think I'll go to the service."

Everyone looked at him in surprise. But Rhia saw her chance.

"And I shall come with you," she said.

Sorne was not overjoyed to have Rhia's company. But he could hardly refuse it. Who could object to something as harmless and respectable as attending the restday devotions?

Their hostess had explained that visitors could worship at

the Priory of the Order of the First Light itself "along with the nobility", her tone implying that they should be grateful for this concession. The narrow streets outside the guesthouse were crowded, presumably with people going to local services, and the constant odour of damp reeds was overlaid by incense. Overhead, gaps showed in the clouds. Perhaps the sky might finally clear tonight.

"How are you getting on with Mam Jekrey?" asked Sorne, as they entered an airy square. People were congregating under a red and yellow awning strung across its centre. Odd spots of rain still fell, and some worshippers carried waxed parasols, gaily painted with naturalistic patterns like those adorning the city's eaves and shutters.

"Well enough." Rhia could not resist adding, "Given the limited conversational topics." Sorne had asked Rhia not to mention her brother to their hostess, but then again, they had not spoken much beyond functional pleasantries.

"I'm sorry if you find it stressful to maintain the illusion of being what you are not, m'lady, but we must be careful."

"Careful of what? What are you afraid of?" Rhia bit back her words as a woman carrying a parasol painted with fishes chasing their tails slipped between them on her way to the service in the square.

"I should have said cautious, not careful. There is no specific threat."

"I suppose there cannot be, given how little progress you and your men have made so far."

If Sorne took offence, he gave no sign. "We must maintain our cover, and work from under it."

She had asked both Breen and Lekem privately what they got up to during their days out in the city. Their answers were straightforward, if unhelpful: "looking over premises suitable for baking"; "speaking to a sugar merchant" and – this with a wink, from Breen – "making enquiries".

They left the square, Sorne leading her into another alleyway. Flute music drifted down from above, a mournful air.

"So when will you act?" she asked.

"When we're prepared. If we have to leave suddenly we won't want to wait around between caravans."

That did not sound reassuring. "So you expect a wait of," she did the maths: the caravan would still be on its way back to Shen, where it had to turn round before returning, "over a week, followed by a hasty exit?"

"A *potentially* hasty exit, m'lady."

They entered another square, larger and with no awning, where a man was decrying to the crowd. Rhia assumed he was preaching but he appeared to be complaining about taxes and trade restrictions. "An interesting sermon," she muttered to Sorne as they passed.

"There is someone in this square every day, airing their grievances."

"Really?" Rhia thought of the riot, and the now-dead priest, "Is that wise?"

"It's not for me to judge but if you look to the left of his podium you may notice the guards, and other interested parties."

Rhia looked. Two men in uniform stood there, looking impassive as only guards could, though a well-dressed man not quite standing with them was giving the speaker his full attention. "The guards are here to stop him speaking sedition?"

"More likely to stop the crowd attacking him if they don't like what he's saying. As for the other chap, he'll make sure anything of interest gets reported back."

"To the caliarch?"

"More likely to his eunuchs, given what I've been told about how things work here."

Rhia wondered if Francin would find such a system useful;

it provided a safety valve for the disaffected and a way of monitoring potential subversion. But geography, if nothing else, would defeat such a scheme in Shen, there being no outdoor space large enough to congregate like this in the middle or lower city.

Sorne cut across the square and led her into a gap between houses, where the ground sloped down to a stubby jetty at which two flat-bottomed boats were moored. Sorne haggled with the boatmen, playing them off against each other for the best price.

The boat – a punt, these craft were called – rocked when she stepped into it. Sorne caught her arm and helped her sit, then settled next to her. The boatman stood at the back and propelled the boat with a long pole.

The next islet, Lowck, was no more than twenty yards away. The smell of the lake reasserted itself. Looking down, Rhia saw the silver turn of fish, though the water itself was dark as tea. She wondered how deep it was and then decided she would rather not know. Uncle Petren was the only member of her family who had ever learnt to swim.

They passed four more islets.

The last of the rain cleared, and the clouds thinned.

They came out facing a long, unbroken wall, two storeys high in places; the side of the priory isle. Their boatman poled them round to the front, where a dozen long jetties bustled with recent arrivals. Most appeared of high status, with excessively styled hair, fine linen clothes, green or blue painted eyelids and the flash of metal at throats and ears. She wondered if one of them was Prince Mekteph himself. There was also a sprinkling of outsiders and a few ordinary citizens.

They disembarked and followed the crowd into a huge square compound. They were near the back, and Rhia's main view was of people's heads. However, the acoustics were excellent. After some chanting, accompanied by reed flutes – instruments of the lower classes in Shen, but ubiquitous here – the eparch took to the stage, speaking with a slow, calm authority.

Back home, she attended services only when etiquette demanded it. Father used to say, "Most people who go to Church think they can buy a place in heaven just by standing still and getting preached at." But the eparch's sermon, which took the story of the Separation as its starting point, had a very different flavour. A Shenese priest might stress how the transgressions of those Children who rebelled against the First were a lesson we must never forget, lest we too be punished. The eparch's perspective was different: if even the most blessed can fail and fall if they become arrogant and uncaring, we must always look to our own hearts and moral centre. Despite herself, Rhia was impressed.

Out of the corner of her eye she saw Sorne looking around, subtly checking out the layout of the compound. She had wondered why he wanted to attend the service. Afterwards, as they queued for a boat, she hissed, "He's here, isn't he? In the priory."

Sorne did not have to ask who she meant. After a moment's hesitation, he nodded.

"When were you going to admit you know where my brother is?" Rhia kept her voice low.

"Once I had confirmed it."

"And have you?" It made sense: if Etyan had arrived destitute, the First Light might have taken him in.

"No. But we will."

"And then?"

"Then we'll get him out."

Captain Sorne made it sound so simple. In his world, the soldier's world, it probably was.

That assumed he was telling the full truth; perhaps he just

said what was needed to keep her safe and content. Did the soldiers expect Etyan to resist? What were their orders if he did?

Rhia knew more about the world than Etyan ever would, not to mention having recently discovered the true nature of a heavenly body, yet she did not know the truth about her own brother. Surely Etyan could never have committed the unspeakable deed whose result she had witnessed? But what mattered here was whether the duke thought he had. That poor girl had been a respected merchant's daughter, and her death had roused the middle and lower city. The militia's inability to find the culprit had increased tensions. She had seen where that could lead... seen too, how once the priest blamed for the riot had met his end, those tensions ebbed, for a while at least. Bringing someone to justice for a shameful and unsolved crime would increase the duke's popularity, help him keep order. And she would not put it past Francin to put the stability of his kingdom above family ties.

She had to be there, when they found Etyan. She had to speak to her brother before the soldiers did. She had to uncover the truth.

Chapter 30

Apparently the clanless did observe restday. Not that Dej was sure how it would differ from any other day. Their default activity appeared to be loafing in doorways and griping.

Restday didn't get her off morning chores. But when they were done she went to sit outside the hut, enjoying some rare free time, though dark clouds threatened rain. It had already rained twice since she'd arrived.

She sniffed. Something smelled good. Her stomach gurgled. The size and quality of the nightly stews she shared with her hut-mates had reduced over the last few days.

Clanless began emerging from their huts and drifting towards the big hut. Dej waited until Lih and Vay came out, then tagged along behind. Vay gave Dej the bowl they'd grudgingly allowed as her own.

The fire in the big hut burned a type of sweet earth called peat, and it was always lit. Today it was squashed under a massive smoke-stained clay pot. People sat on the floor, avoiding the curtained-off alcoves round the edges where Mar and her attendants slept. The clanless elder sat in her chair, presiding over her people. Cal stood at her shoulder. Once everyone was settled Mar stood up. Her two attendants came forward. The men ladled out a bowl of stew from the pot, then gave it to Mar. People filed up to the cauldron to get served. Cal was second in line, confirming Dej's suspicion that the clanless had as much of a pecking order as any bunch of squabbling dorm-mates. Cal had watched her practice a couple of times, standing to one side, arms crossed. Unlike some of the clanless, he never commented or laughed. Now, seeing her staring, he smiled. Dej smiled back then looked away, to find she was being watched herself, by Lih. The other girl wore her default half smile, half sneer.

"What?" snapped Dej, before she could catch herself.

Lih narrowed her eyes, and Dej wondered if she was about to get hit. It had to happen sooner or later. But not, apparently, in public. "Oh," crowed Lih, "she's got designs on our seer." She elbowed Vay, who also smiled.

"Ah, so we have a seer; good." Dej put gratitude in her voice, like the girls had done her a favour.

"Well," said Vay, "he's the closest we've got to a seer."

"Not that close," sneered Lih, and laughed.

The stew, when she finally got some, was more tubers than meat, but was hot and tasty. As she was finishing, Mar stood and announced, "The new one there is Dej," Dej spluttered at hearing her name, looking up from her bowl as Mar continued, "though I'm sure you all know that by now. She's another pathfinder."

Dej straightened, but that was all the introduction she got. Looking around the assembled clanless it occurred to her that one of the women here might be her mother. If so it made no difference; skykin didn't bother with such relationships, and the clanless seemed to have all the worst attributes of the skykin, with few of the good ones the crèche had talked about.

Once bowls had been put aside Mar opened her arms and smiled. "Treats, then." The "treats", handed out by her attendants, turned out to be pale starchy cakes and slivers of dried fruit. Dej had been wondering when they'd get shadowkin food. She made sure she savoured her cake and ring of dried apple.

• • •

The hunt left the next morning, led by Cal. Two dozen clanless, about a third of the total settlement, went, including Lih; she was a tracker. Vay, a healer, stayed. Kir travelled at the head of the hunt, on foot, Dej by her side. It was the first chance they'd had to speak all week, and Dej welcomed it, even if Kir didn't appear interested in conversation.

They started down the defile she'd arrived along, then cut up a side valley heading southwest, deeper into the mountains. After an initial scrabble the land opened up enough for Cal to ride the rhinobeast they'd brought to carry the spoils.

After a while Kir halted. Everyone else straggled to a stop behind them. Kir turned to Dej and said, "We turn southwards here. Which way is that?"

Dej concentrated. They were in bogland with no obvious path and the Sun was hidden behind high cloud. After a while she pointed. Kir nodded, and the group adjusted their course.

Later that morning they reached a gentle slope covered in rocks. Trackers and hunters swarmed across it and flushed out the occasional rockslither; these were larger than the one Kir had caught, with four or five segments.

In the afternoon they climbed to high pasture, and the trackers fanned out, circling a herd of grazing creatures like large hairless rabbits with hardened backplates and heavy clawed feet. Those clanless not hunting moved upslope. When Dej opened her mouth to ask Kir why everyone hung so far back, the other skykin said, "Pichons are true herd beasts. Scare one and they all know. They've also a good sense of smell – so stay downwind."

Sure enough, when one pichon raised its head, the others tensed and fled. But the hunters were ready and rushed forward, bringing the animals down with bolas, like the weapon the skykin woman had used on Dej when she ran from her bonding. The pichons died with indignant squeals that set Dej's teeth on edge.

Kir asked Dej to pathfind several more times; mostly she got it right, although on the last occasion, when they were faced with two similar routes over the shoulder of a hill, Kir shook her head at Dej's choice. "The leftmost one," she said shortly, and set off that way.

That night they camped on a hummocky slope, lighting a fire using peat carried by the rhinobeast. Though some of the day's haul had gone into its panniers, there was plenty to roast and it tasted good. People chatted and laughed, even including Dej in some of their banter. When Kir went to relieve herself, Dej followed.

Once they were out of the firelight Dej asked, "So you're a pathfinder too?"

"I navigate, yes."

"Does that make me your apprentice?" Dej liked the idea.

"One of them, yes."

"But still your apprentice."

Kir sighed, then relented and smiled, her teeth pale in the darkness. "Yes. I suppose you are."

On the following day they circled south and skirted a steep valley, found yet more high bogland – this stretch too treacherous for the rhinobeast so they had to go around it – and passed through a wide bowl-shaped valley of reddish rocks, with caves along one side. In the next valley, as evening fell, they came across one of the hunt's targets, though it didn't require much hunting.

Clampers were flat-shelled snails the size of a clenched fist. When smoked, their flesh kept for months, and their empty shells were used as utensils. In the days before the hunt left, Dej had tasted, if not enjoyed, their chewy, smoky meat.

Now she helped prise them off the underside of rocks in a field of fallen stone slabs.

She made no mistakes in her navigation that day, though

she'd found it hard to keep a straight path through the red valley.

That night she sat near Cal; not too close, just enough that he'd spot she was paying him attention. He had a Shenese accent: looked like they had something in common.

The hunt looped northward again, back towards the settlement. This took them onto shallow slopes of jumbled rocks: the best rockslither country, according to campfire talk. The rhinobeast, walking with delicate care, fell behind; the four trackers, including Lih, went ahead.

The morning brought plenty of false alarms, as the trackers circled or froze or crawled between rocks; but no prey. Kir admitted that, being this close to home, the area was heavily hunted.

The trackers finally uncovered a rockslither nest early in the afternoon. One moment they were edging forward, peering into crevices and exchanging handsignals, the next the rocks came alive. Hunters pounced, knives and spears at the ready. Dej hesitated as Kir sprang forward. The action was fast and silent: blows struck, writhing beasts raised on spearpoints, all in frantic moments. Dej, who'd only taken a couple of steps forward, contributed nothing to the hunt.

When, just before evening, the trackers came across another nest, Dej was ready. As the creatures exploded out from their rocky pinnacle she rushed forward, dagger in hand, heart pounding. Something sinuous swept past her foot. She struck out. Missed. Another target, between two rocks. She jabbed at it, and felt the point of her dagger snap. The rockslither escaped.

She looked up to see Lih standing on a rock above her, a dead rockslither baby in one hand. The look the other girl gave her was pure contempt.

CHAPTER 31

That night Rhia's bad dreams returned: pale hair in bloodied water; the lone terror of the break-in; the brutal charge of the city militia. Whatever spell the skyland had cast on her had worn off. The cares of the last few months had returned, and now, confined to a single building in a strange city, she had nothing to distract herself with. She had at least hoped to continue her celestial observations, but the cloud had been constant, and the rain frequent.

However, the next morning was fine, so she went out into the guesthouse's courtyard – which was not, technically, leaving the premises. The maids had hung washing up to take advantage of the dry weather. The Zekti, with their surfeit of water, cleaned both themselves and their clothes often, a habit Rhia approved of, although thanks to the wet climate the guesthouse had a permanent odour of damp washing.

Rhia walked through the miniature maze of flapping linen, looking for the best place to stand. In her room she had tried to deploy her sightglass by day, but the single high window showed only sky or, more often, featureless cloud. Out here she could see the grey bulk of the distant mountains beyond the guesthouse's roof, though when she trained the sightglass on them they simply appeared as less distant grey bulks. She needed a closer target. She moved to

the far corner of the courtyard. Yes, she could see the top of
the Eternal Isle from here. An apt choice, given she could
have ended up living there. She trained her sightglass on it,
steadying her arm by cupping her elbow in the other hand.

She made out individual buildings, low but solid, built
of small blocks of golden stone, many of them roofed with
ochre and black tiles; the overhanging eaves were curved
to funnel the water towards the corners where – ah yes – it
would be channelled away in stone conduits, down to the
lake. Ingenious. Father would have been impressed. Some of
the terraces were green with gardens, tiny manicured patches
cut into the slopes–

"Ahem."

She lowered the sightglass to see Mam Jekrey next to a
linen frame, staring at her.

"Yes?" she snapped, annoyed at the interruption.

She saw her mistake in Mam Jekrey's frown. Rhia thought
of their hostess as "staff", like a housekeeper at another
House's villa. But that was not quite the relationship here.
She smiled and said quickly, "Sorry, I was..." She waved the
sightglass, at a loss to explain her actions.

"What is that thing?"

"It's nothing. A toy."

"Oh. You were pointing it at the Eternal Isle."

"I was trying to see. It's a device to help you see distant
objects. Like I say, just a toy."

"Which you were using to look at the caliarch's halls."

"I was curious and my, ah, cousin doesn't want me going
outside."

"Our streets are safe enough."

"I'm sure they are. He is just being protective." Defending
her confinement stung but she wanted to divert further
questions. "I should go back inside, really." She ducked past,
keeping her eyes down.

Given the interest Mam Jekrey had shown, perhaps she should be more careful in future, and stay indoors.

Her resolve did not even last the night. When the weather improved further and the Sun went down in a cloudless sky Rhia could not resist. She waited until everyone had retired, then crept out.

Mam Jekrey's empty linen frame made a perfect rest for her sightglass. A gibbous Greymoon rode high above the thatched roofs. Through the sightglass the dark patches on the Moon's face she had sketched as a child gained new form and substance. Here were mountains, vast high plains, shadowed ridges. No sign of the celestial skykin settlements she had heard spoken of; then again, the skykin did not build cities, and not everyone agreed they even went to heaven when they died. Had Whitemoon been up she might have seen cities of the blessed shadowkin dead on its surface. But she doubted it.

The Maiden was too low to see from here, and though the Matriarch would rise later she could not stay out all night. She made some brief observations of other stars, then, not wishing to push her luck, went back inside.

Writing up her night's observing occupied the next morning. When she took a break and went to the commons to fetch a drink, she was surprised to hear high laughter coming from beyond the curtained doorway. When she stepped through she was even more surprised at its source.

Captain Sorne sat on the rug-covered floor with two Zekti children; the young sons of fellow guests. The three of them were arranging Mam Jekrey's horn beakers and plates into a rough square, beakers at the corners, plates forming the sides. One of the boys looked up and said proudly, "We're building a manor house."

"So I see." Rhia swallowed. "Actually, I need one of those beakers, please."

"I think we can spare one, can't we, boys?" said Sorne with a smile.

The boy who had spoken nodded; his younger brother picked up a beaker and held it out to her. When Rhia took it, she looked Sorne in the eye. "This is... good of you."

"The boys' parents needed some time alone and I've no appointments until later."

"Yes. So I see." If he was not busy he could have offered to show her around. No: she would not get angry at him, no matter how frustrated she felt. He was not here to serve her.

But the unexpected moment of domesticity left her too restless to return to her room. At home she might seek out the comfortable disdain of her cats, but most Zekti did not appear to keep pets; the practice of caging songbirds which Meddler of Zekt had written of, and which Alharet favoured, must be restricted to the nobility. She ventured back out to the courtyard, where Mam Jekrey's two maids were hanging out more washing. She sat on a bench in the fitful sunlight, pretending to doze in what she hoped was a non-suspicious manner, though she kept her ears open, listening, in the absence of other diversions, to the maids' gossip.

She also considered her unease. She had not, until now, thought about the soldiers' lives, and family situations. Were they missing their wives, their children?

She had never played with Etyan like Sorne played with those children. She had never once sat on the floor and made a mess with him. She wondered if she might, one day, play with children of her own. It was not a strong desire and the idea of Mercal Callorn as a father made her frown. But regret for lost chances added another strand to the tangled ball of emotions lodged in her chest. There had been good reasons for not playing with Etyan, of course: their age difference;

the constant presence of nurses and nannies; the fact that he had been more than capable of making a mess all by himself. But she could not escape the thought that Captain Sorne had been more at ease with these strangers than she had been with her own brother.

That evening she reached a decision. While listening to the maids' chatter, she had overheard something interesting. Over dinner she said to the soldiers, "There is a market tomorrow, two squares across from here. I need more ink so I will be visiting it."

Sorne's lips twitched. "If you insist."

"I do."

"It would not be wise to go alone."

"Our hostess thinks it would. Nonetheless I will accept an escort."

Breen chimed in, "I'm free in the morning."

Sorne nodded heavily. "In that case we may be able to kill two birds with one stone."

"Meaning?" asked Rhia.

Sorne's gaze flicked to their hostess, who was chatting to the Zekti family two tables away. "I'll explain later."

CHAPTER 32

The meeting was not accidental; Sadakh knew that much. Coincidence was rare on the Eternal Isle.

He had arrived via the causeway from the priory, alone save the permitted servitor, actually a bodyguard in clerical robes. By the time they had passed through the eastgate and climbed the first set of steps they had acquired an entourage: four court guards and a pair of administrators, one of whom insisted on briefing Sadakh on the caliarch's current disposition.

The party coming the other way was smaller, just two guards flanking the prince.

They met in an open-sided cloister. The wall to the right was covered in faded murals depicting the deeds of whichever previous caliarch had built or renovated this section of the palace. To the left, staff trimmed low hedges in a terrace garden. Beyond, the clotted mass of islands which made up the rest of the city lay hazy in the low evening Sun.

On entering the cloister, Sadakh noted the number and disposition of the gardeners: three, all carrying diamond-bladed handsaws which could serve as weapons. All, apparently, engrossed in their work.

Prince Mekteph's party descended the steps at the far end of the cloister and stopped. The prince waited for Sadakh's group to approach, then, as a laconic afterthought, sketched an obeisance, hand not quite touching his throat, wrist dipping to miss his heart. Studied disrespect at its best.

"Highness." Sadakh clipped the word.

"Holiness." Prince Mekteph mirrored the eparch's curt intonation.

He wants you to know he watches you whenever you set foot on the Isle.

His ghost was right: Sadakh was in dangerous territory.

"I understand you experienced some disruption at your most recent initiation ceremony." The prince did a passable imitation of concern.

In his head, his ghost laughed, a delicate cadenza of triumph. Sadakh said, "Yes. Unfortunate, though easily dealt with."

The prince's guards tensed. Sadakh felt the change in his own entourage. Out of the corner of his eye he saw one of the gardeners straighten. Could this be the moment civilized deception was swept away, and open conflict broke out? Sadakh, weighing up the pieces in play, the failsafes in place and the current odds, judged it unlikely.

Apparently oblivious of the building tension around him Prince Mekteph enquired, "How go things, generally?"

The prince's concern worried him. His ghost voiced his doubts: *How much does he know?* About the experiment, she meant.

"Things go very well, Highness." Sadakh smiled, "As I am sure they do with you. However, I shan't detain you further. I imagine you have important business to attend to, and I would not want to keep your uncle waiting."

Mekteph gave a courtly nod. "Indeed so. The blessings of the day upon you, Eparch." As the prince swept past, Sadakh's bodyguard kept a position which would allow him to block any attack on his master.

Sadakh wondered if the meeting had actually been

contrived by the damn court administrators, setting the two sides against each other, seeing how the field stood. Sometimes he wondered if they weren't all pawns in the eunuchs' games. The eunuchs themselves appeared to think so.

The caliarch was in the Hall of Eternal Guardians. As Sadakh climbed the steps to the highest point of the Isle one of the sacred gyraptors circling overhead gave a forlorn cry. It was probably hungry. With no nobles of sufficient rank passing away recently, the birds were reduced to a diet of fish and kitchen waste.

Numak the Seventeenth, lord of the Eternal Isle, Glory of the Ancestors, caliarch of Zekt, was sitting cross-legged at a small table; there was no other furniture in the long hall. On the table was a hand-loom.

"Come in, Holiness!" The caliarch's voice echoed off the walls.

Coloured lamps hung from the ceiling and lit walls lined with long niches, each containing the jewelled skeleton of a previous caliarch, bedecked in silks and brocade, accompanied by models and images of people and things important to him during life, and posed to recline in perennial, macabre splendour. Two hundred and thirty-six of them, every caliarch who had reigned long and well enough to warrant the dubious honour of remaining tied to the world to watch over his people. To Sadakh's knowledge no other shadowland employed such a practice, but here it had gone on long enough that the hall had been extended twice.

His bodyguard stayed with the guards at the door. However distasteful Sadakh found this place, it had the advantage that very few were permitted to enter it. The caliarch spent much of his time in the Hall, and Sadakh encouraged him to hold their weekly meetings here where they would not be disturbed or overheard.

The caliarch worked the delicate loom while Sadakh approached. The fabric on the loom was three-quarters finished. It was a design of fish, birds and the noon sky, commissioned from a court artist and woven in priceless gold and silver thread. The caliarch's hand was steady, although the lamplight revealed the wrinkles and spots blemishing the well-cared-for skin. Numak parked the shuttle and sat back; although he did not stand, he gave a rather fuller obeisance than his nephew had. In return, Sadakh bowed low. "The blessings of the First upon you, Majesty."

"Sit down, sit down."

Sadakh obeyed, though he knelt rather than sat, in deference to the presence of a superior. "The piece is almost finished," he observed as he settled back on his heels. "It will be complete in time for Your Majesty's birthday celebrations."

"Quite possibly. Won't be presenting it at the revels, though. Don't want to show favouritism to the weavers." One of Caliarch Numak's many foibles was a desire to know what his subjects actually *did*. To this end he had learned to make bread, to brew, even to gut fish. The people loved it. The eunuchs tolerated it, because Numak was their favoured ruler, and popularity encouraged stability. After the recent misfortunes – natural and manmade – that had divided and reduced the Zekti royal family, the eunuchs were all for stability. Sadakh remained thankful he had backed the right player, however questionable Numak's sanity might be these days.

"Very wise, Majesty."

"So, how goes the Great Search?" The caliarch's emphasis might be comical in other circumstances, but the evasions and euphemisms of court life persisted even up here.

"The news is mixed, Majesty. One of the men died three days ago."

"Oh dear. So that leaves a man and woman, yes? And their

state is unchanged? Any signs of recovery?" Numak searched Sadakh's face for reassurance.

"They receive the best care my people can give, and are watched at all times." And guarded, just in case.

"But," said the caliarch slowly, "is it too soon to know if it works – even if these last two do not die?"

Sadakh heard doubt in the caliarch's voice, and was quick to quash it. "I am confident, Majesty, that if the essence of the animus can be extracted then its longevity will be passed on."

The caliarch's gaze drifted to the niches. "I do it all for them, you know," he said.

In another time and place this might be the cue for Sadakh's ghost to chip in, but she was always silent here – or perhaps her voice was lost amongst the myriad of other dead voices Sadakh was not attuned to.

"I know," replied Sadakh softly. Numak told him often enough. The caliarch's dream of smashing the decorated skulls to release the trapped spirits of his ancestors was a radical, almost heretical aspiration for which he constantly sought approval from the highest spiritual authority in the land.

The caliarch looked back at Sadakh. "You have all you need."

"I do. Your Majesty's generosity is a constant boon." The eunuchs knew Sadakh was up to something. Perhaps they were even aware of his procurement of dead skykin. But no one person had all the facts. And Sadakh must ensure it stayed that way.

CHAPTER 33

Although the weather was fine, Rhia took her hat, jamming it low to hide her mask from casual glances. Breen opened the guesthouse door then fell into step beside her.

It felt good to be outside. "So we are to buy a wig, or failing that, hair dye?" Sorne had admitted he was assembling a disguise good enough to penetrate the priory, but had insisted Rhia did not need the details.

"That's right."

"How about clothes?"

"Oh, we have those."

"Who will be going in?" *And when? And how?*

Breen looked pained. "The captain will tell you everything you need to know."

"Anyone would think he doesn't trust me." Rhia decided to change the subject. "Is he married?"

"Sorry?" Breen's easy stride hitched.

"The captain. I wondered if he was married. I'm guessing not, given his behaviour on the caravan."

"His... oh. Yes. I mean no, not any more."

"But he was?"

"Yes. He lost both his boys to the rain-fever. Before my time, but they say his wife left him because of it."

Had his sons been of an age with the Zekti boys? She thought, briefly, of Father, how, if he had not succumbed during that last outbreak of the periodic plague, everything would be different now. "How about Lekem?"

"Oh, he's married. Got a young kid. Probably glad to get some peace and quiet."

"I'm guessing you're not married?" Breen had gone with Mella more than once.

"Young, free and single, that's me."

They crossed the first square. The Sun painted the reed roofs with a warm golden glow. There were fewer people about than on restday. As they left the square, heading into a narrow alley, Breen whispered, "M'lady, we're being followed."

Rhia's breath caught. "Are you sure?"

"Reasonably." He did not sound overly concerned.

"What should we do?"

"You should keep walking. Take the next left, then carry straight on."

With that, he was gone. Rhia swallowed rising panic and put one foot in front of the other.

She took the left turn, resisting the urge to look over her shoulder.

She passed a turning on the right, but kept straight on. What if he didn't come back? What if Mam Jekrey had been wrong about these strange streets being safe–

"Lost him."

Rhia jumped, hand going to her throat, then turned to see Breen, smiling as ever. "Sorry, didn't mean to startle you. The bas– miscreant saw me and ran off."

"So they know we're onto them?"

"They do now. Hopefully they'll leave us alone. Shall we carry on?" Breen still appeared unconcerned. Rhia tried to be.

The market announced its presence with a low hubbub and the jolly piping of a reed flute. The grid of stalls was larger than Shen's hilly streets could host, though some of the produce was familiar. There were a lot of female stallholders, in keeping with the balance between genders she had seen elsewhere in Zekt. The air smelled of grilled fish and the local variant on tea, which was served with the leaves still in; despite its aromatic scent, it tasted like boiled salad.

They got a few stares, which Rhia ignored; Breen returned the more forward ones with a smile and half wave. Rhia enjoyed his cheeky insouciance.

In the third aisle they found a cosmetics stall with wigs on wooden stands at the back. The stallholder, whose green-painted eyelids and rouged cheeks showed off her wares, looked past Rhia to ask a local woman what she wanted.

Under his breath Breen murmured, "I'll be over here. Might increase your chance of getting served and I can watch your back."

She nodded. He moved off.

Rhia waited while the other customer was served, then stepped into the stallholder's eyeline and pointed to one of the wigs, all of which looked much the same. "How much for that one, please?"

"Fifty marks."

"Fifty marks? I could buy a horse for that!"

"Fifty marks it is."

The lack of written prices gave Rhia no way of challenging the ridiculous price. Some had haggled, so it must be a local custom, but with no experience, nor any clue to the item's truth worth, Rhia was forced to pay up. She fished out an intricately patterned bone disc, only realizing her mistake when the woman's eyes widened. It was a single fifty-mark coin; not something one of her apparent class would have. Too late now. "Where can I buy ink, please?" she asked the stallholder as the woman handed over the paper-wrapped wig.

"Ink?"

"For writing."

"Rheklew sells stuff like that."

"And where would I find this Rheklew?"

The stallholder pointed. "Just to the left of that awning pole."

Rhia laid the wig in the reed basket she had borrowed from Mam Jekrey. "Thank you," she said curtly, before moving off.

Out of the corner of her eye, she saw Breen meandering in the same direction.

Rheklew was a man, writing presumably being men's work. She was his only customer, although when she approached his stall he still favoured her with a brief frown, his eyes going to her mask. When he failed to greet her she said, "I would like to know what inks you have, and their prices please, Sur." Courtesy cost nothing.

The stallholder listed his wares. Rhia asked whether any of the prices were negotiable. He shook his head. Well, she had tried. Damned if she knew why traders didn't just label their wares with the price they expected people to pay. She settled on a pot of lampblack and one of oakgall. As she laid the pots in her basket she heard an odd sound from behind, a rustle and a shuffle. She turned, and found herself toe-to-toe with a stranger.

She opened her mouth to apologize.

The man reached for her.

She raised her free hand to fend him off, found it held an ink pot, and flung the pot into the man's face.

The lid of the pot came off. Oakgall spattered. The man shrieked and clapped his hands to his eyes.

Where was Breen? Over there, wrestling with another man. Passersby paused, stared, drew back. Rhia looked for a way out. Everything was simultaneously too fast and stupidly, frustratingly slow. A voice in her head admonished her, pointing out that the man standing next to her screaming and clawing at his face was her responsibility.

Breen drew back from his opponent and brought his arm back to strike. The man ducked; the punch went wide. The man returned the blow. It looked like it barely landed, but Breen went down.

The man looked her way, eyes narrowing. He strode towards her. He was emptyhanded but young and fit; he could still overpower her. She had to run now. Run or fight. She had fought before, in her study. But that had been her territory, her home. Don't fight! Run! She raised one foot and began to turn, far too slowly.

Movement. Someone else coming up fast beside her. *Not fair, three against two!*

The newcomer stepped forward, blocking the other man as he reached her. The two men connected, twisted, and went down, an oddly fluid motion. The newcomer had grey in his hair and wore a dark tunic. The men rolled. An elbow pistoned back. A flurry of movement. The motion stopped.

Captain Sorne had her attacker pinned to the ground. He knelt on his arm and leant over him, holding his dagger a hair's breadth from the man's throat.

"Who sent you?" Sorne's voice was casual; he wasn't even out of breath.

The man on the ground said nothing, just closed his eyes. Sorne spat, the gob landing on the man's cheek, making him flinch. People were approaching, demanding to know what was going on. Sorne sprang to his feet and kicked the man once in the ribs. The attacker opened his eyes, then, seeing he was not about to die, scrabbled to his feet. Dragging his halfblind companion after him, he staggered off through the gathering crowd, which parted to let them through.

Three other men were coming forward, wearing the skullcaps of city guards. Rhia clutched her basket to her chest and stood her ground.

• • •

The militia did not detain them long. They took statements, then let Rhia and the two soldiers go. They even had their medic look over Breen, who had slipped and fallen while trying to evade his attacker, and hit his head.

Back at the guesthouse Sorne helped his corporal to bed, Rhia following on. As he closed the screen door to the soldiers' room, Rhia said, "I'm not sure what would have happened if you hadn't been there. Thank you."

He inclined his head. "You're welcome."

"Although…"

"Yes?"

"I'm still not clear why you *were* there." When the Zekti militia had asked, Sorne claimed he was accompanying her; Rhia had not said anything to contradict him.

"Can we speak in your room, please?"

"All right."

Her room felt cramped with the captain in it, but she let him shut the door. His paranoia had turned out to be justified. She sat on the bed; he remained standing. "You asked why I was at the market," he said, keeping his voice down against the thin walls. "It's simple enough: if you want to find out who's tailing someone, the best way is to follow them."

"You suspected we were being watched?"

"Yes. And as I don't think every foreign visitor gets such treatment, I've been trying to work out why we might attract particular attention."

"What are you asking, Captain?"

"Simply whether you can think of any reason the Zekti authorities might want to keep tabs on us."

"I …" She sighed. "It may be nothing, but a couple of days ago our hostess caught me using my sightglass to observe the Eternal Isle."

Sorne's lips thinned. "I see. And how did she react?"

"I got the impression she disapproved. But she disapproves

of a lot of things, so I thought nothing of it."

"Right. Thank you for telling me now." His tone implied that "then" would have been preferable.

"And there's something else." On the walk back, she had gone over reasons for the incident in the market, which already felt unreal. Being attacked in public: another thing that never happened to her. She wondered if paying the stallholder with a large coin had alerted chance criminals, but the attack felt coordinated. Given the lack of weapons or threats, she guessed the men were not bent on murder or robbery, but on abduction. Of her, presumably. "It may not be relevant but... at one point I was betrothed to a Zekti noble. He was a minor prince at the time, before all that dynastic unpleasantness a few years back. After my accident," she half raised a hand to indicate her mask, "the betrothal was called off. There was some bad feeling."

Sorne went very still.

She continued, "Diplomacy won out, and the prince's sister married my cousin instead. Which, given how things subsequently went with both our families, was for the best." Her voice sounded brittle in her ears.

"Just to be clear," said Sorne slowly. "You were betrothed to Prince Mekteph?"

"At one point. But we never met."

"And the duchess is only in the position she is because you didn't marry her brother?"

"Yes, though this is not something we dwell on."

Sorne's expression closed down. Finally, Rhia asked, "Why would the prince suddenly be interested in vengeance for deeds over a decade ago?"

"Why indeed, m'lady." Rhia got the impression he was furious, but trying not to show it.

"Even if what happened today was Mekteph's doing," she said, "how would he know I was here?"

Sorne's tone was curt. "Now that, m'lady," he said, "is an excellent question."

"I've told you all I know, Captain." Perhaps she should have shared the information about Mekteph before, but it was nobles' business. As for Mam Jekrey, how was Rhia to know the difference between the general disapproval of a busybody and being spied on? It wasn't as though Sorne kept her informed.

Sorne pulled the door open. "Then I will bid you good night."

Chapter 34

As soon as the hunt returned, the settlement sprang into action, every clanless playing their part in skinning, jointing and preserving the meat.

Dej got clamper duty. It was unpleasant work. The clampers had been stabbed but still exuded a foul and sticky slime. They also came in two parts: an edible fleshy "foot", with a smaller, squishier heart deeper in the shell which provided oil for lamps. Her paring-knife kept slipping, leading to nicked fingertips, and the squishy part of the creature was sometimes still alive, and prone to squirting stinking ichor when pierced.

She finished her work late in the afternoon. After returning the meat, shells and oil to the big hut, she went to the pool to wash, scrubbing her hands and forearms with handfuls of gravel.

Walking back through the village, she met Cal. He stopped and smiled. Dej halted too, hands dripping, and felt a response which might have been a blush – if her skin still did that. "Good afternoon." She kept her voice light.

"And to you." He made to move on, like most clanless did once basic greetings were exchanged, then hesitated and said, "I was wondering where you grew up."

A smile leapt to her lips. "Shen. You too, I'm thinking."

"That's right. Not that it should matter, but you're probably still thinking about your life in the crèche. I know I did, at first. Don't worry, you'll settle in."

No one, in the week and a half she'd been here, had shown any interest in how well she was adjusting to her new life. "I'm doing my best," she ventured, suddenly shy. "I suppose it'll take a while."

"That's the attitude." His smile was constant, even if his gaze wasn't.

She tensed, unsure if that was it, but then he added, "My hut's over there, just behind Mar's. You could come over later, if you like."

Was he asking what she thought? And if he was, should she agree? "Is that 'later' as in… tonight?"

"If you're not too tired."

"I might do that. If you'd like me to." She'd never known how to deal with these conversations at the crèche; boys only spoke to her like this if Min or Jen or someone else more interesting wasn't around.

"I'd like that very much," he said, then nodded to show the conversation was over.

Though Cal's interest pleased her, she knew it for what it was. She'd got looks like that before. Though her post-bonding changes had played out, it appeared her breasts would never be fully absorbed. Cal had noticed that.

But sex was a possible pleasure, and there weren't many pleasures here. She didn't regret never getting beyond the odd fumble with the boys at the crèche, but Cal was older. He'd know what he was doing.

He was also a seer, of sorts. Getting someone like that on her side could make all the difference in this cold and brutal place.

If only he'd managed to look her in the eye, she wouldn't have hesitated.

• • •

When she got back to the hut it was empty. Vay had mentioned extracting fats from the hunt's catch for use in potions and creams. She'd also been teasing Lih about one of the other clanless that Lih was interested in, or perhaps had gone with and might again. Dej didn't much care.

She'd never been in the hut alone, and it made her feel both nervous and powerful. She stoked the fire, and considered fetching the water, but she'd save that task for later as an excuse to get away from her hut-mates. She sat by the hearth and began to hum. She could hear herself properly in the silence of the hut. She closed her eyes, concentrating on the sounds in her head. If she opened her mouth, they became even clearer. She tried to reproduce one of the simplest songs she'd composed at the crèche. It wasn't singing as such, but it was a tuneful noise. Music, of sorts. She tried another tune, humming louder this time.

"What the fuck?"

It was Lih, of course, standing in the doorway.

The other girl strode in. "What d'you think you're doing?"

"Nothing!" Dej sprang to her feet. If Lih was going to make something of this, she'd defend herself.

But Lih just laughed. "That was quite some noise you were making."

"It was nothing." Dej reached past her for the skin on the peg by the door. "I'll fetch the water." She ducked out of the hut, Lih's laughter following her.

When she got back Vay was there, preparing the evening meal. Lih looked up from where she lay on her pallet. "Vay, my dear, you won't believe what she," Lih stabbed a finger at Dej, "was doing when I got back earlier."

"Handstands?"

"No, she was singing. Well, I say singing. Croaking."

Vay didn't look up from the leaves she was shredding. "Hmm, surprised her crèche didn't beat that out of her."

For the rest of the evening Lih kept coming back to Dej's secret, tunelessly parodying the snatch of song Dej had been singing when she came in, then bursting into laughter.

Dej's face burned and she found herself clenching and unclenching her hands. She wanted nothing more than to leap for the bitch's throat, to shut her up. But if she did, Lih would fight back and she'd seen how fast Lih was. She didn't think Vay would join in, but she wasn't sure she'd intervene either. This wasn't the crèche, where fights were quickly broken up by staff. If Lih wanted to beat Dej to a pulp, no one would stop her.

So she ate her meal, wiped the dishes, and stayed silent. When she couldn't stand it any longer she muttered that she was going to the latrines, pulled the curtain aside, and left the hut, Lih's impersonation of a dying crow echoing in her ears.

The night was cloudless, the Moons painting the shabby huts with silver. Hearth fires burned beyond door curtains. From here, they looked warm and welcoming but Dej knew better.

She started walking.

Lih and Vay were just being mean. People had been mean to her before. They would be again. But this had been about the music. Anything else – her fighting skills, her appearance, her failure at the hunt – would have been easier to bear. But not the music. Her secret had become fodder for her hut-mates' mockery.

I'd be crying now, if I could.

Kir had a broken-down and much-repaired hut to herself on the edge of the settlement. Even if she didn't let her stay, even if she didn't want to talk, Dej needed to be somewhere else for a while, until her stupid hut-mates got bored and went to sleep.

"Kir?"

"No, Dej." Kir's voice was quiet but firm.

"Are you... have you got company?" She couldn't sense anyone else in there.

"Dej. I can't... please go away. I just can't see you right now. I'm sorry."

Dej turned away.

She should have grabbed her cloak; the clear mountain night was bitter. She was starting to shiver, great spasms that rocked her to the roots of her teeth.

She'd have to go back to those two vile bitches.

Or she could take up Cal's offer.

Dej cleared her throat outside Cal's hut.

"Dej? Come in."

The seer had a hut to himself too, but about twice the size of Kir's. He smiled up at her from a wooden stool beside the hearth. As he turned in the seat she saw his loincloth twitch. "Why don't you make yourself at home?" He gestured at his pallet. There wasn't anywhere else to sit.

She hesitated, then crossed to the pallet, swaying like Min sometimes used to when boys watched her. Cal stood and caught her arm before she could sit, breathing hard. He turned her towards him.

He reached for her breasts, his smile broadening. Dej resisted the urge to knock his hands aside.

"Ah yes," murmured the seer, and lowered his head to her chest.

As Cal nuzzled and fondled, Dej tried to feel pleasure at his attention, but her breasts were still sore. He looked up, and almost met her eyes. "You know everything will be all right, don't you?"

Dej nodded.

Cal caught her hand and guided it to his crotch. She'd got this far before. One occasion had been awkward and embarrassing, one downright comical. But she needed to do this right. She began to stroke him.

"That's..." he sighed, "...good but, I need to know. Am I your first, Dej?"

Should she lie, pretend to be experienced? Was that what he wanted? She didn't think so. "Yes, you are."

"Ah." His cock jumped in her hand. "Lie down now."

Her knees locked. But what had she expected? She forced herself to move.

She knew the mechanics of the act, and skykin's privates weren't much changed. She let him lay her down, remove her loincloth, then guide himself into her.

When she whimpered at the pain he whispered, "Hush. Hush now."

He settled his weight on her and began to move. Dej looked past his shoulder, up into the smoky rafters, and willed it to be over. He began making a noise between a grunt and a sigh in time to his motion.

All at once he gave a louder, higher grunt and thrust harder. She yelped. He laughed.

After a last spasm he relaxed, becoming an even heavier weight on her. Just as Dej thought she would suffocate he levered himself off and rolled over with a sigh.

Dej lay still for a moment. Despite the fire, the air was cold on her bare skin.

She began to edge away.

Cal grabbed her hand. "Where do you think you're going? The fun's only just begun, my girl."

She pulled free.

He grabbed again. His nails raked her wrist but didn't catch her. She stood and backed off. "That wasn't fun." She scooped up her loincloth, turned, and ran from his hut.

CHAPTER 35

The next day, Breen and Sorne went out while Lekem hung around the guesthouse, not quite on watch. All three men retired to their room after the evening meal. Rhia stayed in the commons until curiosity got the better of her, when she went and rattled the soldiers' door. "Whatever you're up to, I want to know."

Lekem held the door open for her. When she strode past him she was shocked to find a Zekti man sitting on Captain Sorne's bed. Then she looked again. "Ah," she said, "so the wig fits, Captain?"

Sorne nodded. They had even fixed small wooden discs to his ears, imitating the local fashion.

"I take it you're going to the priory?"

"Not exactly. We have a man in the priory. This evening he'll go out to meet his cousin, who's visiting from the country."

"Ah. And will that be permitted?" She recalled the priory's forbidding walls.

"It will." Sorne glanced down. "Can I ask you to return to the commons now? Breen will come with you. If asked, please tell our hostess that Lekem and myself have decided to get an early night."

Rhia's gaze went to the room's small, high window. "All right."

• • •

The evening with Breen in the commons was surprisingly pleasant. They played set-squares, a game of the lower orders Rhia had learnt from the household servants as a child. He laughed good-naturedly when she beat him. But her mind kept wandering, trying to guess where Sorne was, what he was doing. How long would it take to meet his contact in the priory? He would have to be careful, and make sure he wasn't followed. Was Lekem covering his back? What would he do if the man didn't turn up? What would he do if someone else did?

When the commons emptied she returned to her room and dug out her sightglass. The last two nights had been clear, and she had sneaked out to observe the sky from the courtyard. Tonight's high clouds would impede some of the view, but the Matriarch should rise early enough to see.

She spent a while examining a fuzzy area in the constellation of the Stepping Horse, which had just risen above the roof. It was similar to the first misty patch she had viewed on the brow of the Burdened Traveller, if smaller. She dubbed this phenomenon a "star cloud", and added cataloguing all such patches to the growing list of projects to pick up on her return to Shen.

After a while she raised her head from the linen-frame and checked along the roofline. There it was: a bright yellow star. She moved the sightglass and, with some jiggling and shuffling, the Matriarch sprang into focus. It was dimmer than the Maiden – and gibbous. Rhia had assumed its phase would mirror the Maiden's but there was no reason it should: from the Maiden's times of appearance – soon after sunset, or shortly before dawn – it had long ago been deduced that it orbited the world closer and lower in the sky than the Sun did, while the other two Strays, like the fixed stars, had high orbits, out beyond the Sun. Therefore, they could take any phase. This at least made sense; the three Strays' strange retrograde movements in relation to the other stars could not be so easily explained, save by the assumption their orbits traced spirals, rather than following simple, circular paths round the world like the Moons and the Sun. Rhia had no idea why they might do this. But nor did anyone else. She looked again and saw a second star, very faint and surprisingly close by the Matriarch.

"Looking for nightwings?"

"Breen!" Rhia grabbed the sightglass. "You made me jump."

"Sorry." The corporal's face was shadowed.

Rhia straightened. "Is there a problem?"

"No problem. Just getting some air. Lekem snores, you know."

"Not checking up on me, then?"

"Well, yes, that too." She heard the smile in his voice.

"So I'm not as stealthy as I think I am?"

"I'm afraid not."

Rhia sighed. "I was thinking of retiring anyway."

"No need. I can go away again, if you like."

If she reached out now, she could touch him. What if she said, *Why don't you come back to my room?* What was she thinking! She settled on, "You… don't have to go."

"M'lady?" His whisper was breathy, barely audible.

"I…" Did she want this? Did he?

"Was there something you wanted to ask, m'lady?"

Was there? Perhaps there was, now she thought about it… "Hhh-hhgm."

Once again, Rhia jumped. Looking round she saw a Zekti man standing in the courtyard entrance. But she recognized that throat-clearing disapproval. "Captain Sorne. You're back."

"Yes. And you're both outside. Shall we?" He gestured to the door.

"I'll check the coast's clear," said Breen, and slipped into the house.

"How did it go?" she whispered.

"Inside, please."

She followed Breen down corridors lit by horn-fronted lamps to the soldiers' room. When Sorne came in and shut the door, Lekem sat up, blinking.

"Well?" Rhia found her heart racing, from several causes.

"I met our man. He confirms that Etyan Harlyn is in the First Light Priory. Your brother has joined the order as a lay member."

Which was surprising, given Etyan's disdain for religion. "So he's living in the priory? Or somewhere else in the city?" She hoped it was somewhere else. It might even be somewhere close, somewhere they could go tonight.

"He's living in the priory. But he has fallen ill."

"Ill? Ill how? Is he all right?"

"My man has few details. He knows that several lay members developed a fever. Two died but the Shenese youth is on the mend. He is being kept secluded in the priory's infirmary."

"Then we have to get him out." Suddenly everything was simple again.

Sorne nodded. "That's why we're here."

"Can he walk?" *Or run?*

"My contact didn't know that."

"So what is your plan?"

"In essence, go in without being detected and remove him from the priory. If he's unwell, we may have to assist him."

Rhia did not like the word "remove". "When will you act?"

"Twoday."

"But that's five days away!" And it only gave them a day to catch the caravan.

"It's also the caliarch's birthday. A public holiday which brings people out on the streets is the diversion we need."

Which was no doubt the plan all along. "Right." She looked

Sorne in the eye. "And I will, of course, be coming with you into the priory."

The captain opened his mouth but Rhia cut him off. "This is not negotiable."

This must be what prison was like. To be confined, and watched. Sorne rarely left the guesthouse for the next few days. He and Rhia entered a state of polite truce, acknowledging each other's presence but avoiding meaningful conversation. And his paranoia was catching. She was sure Mam Jekrey paid her more attention than any other guest, always watching for odd behaviour to report to whichever official had taken an interest in the foreigners' activities. Rhia found herself grinding her teeth, or pacing her tiny room, in a state of permanent stress.

At the same time, she was bored. Clouds had closed in again, putting a stop to her night-time observations. She had written up all she could, re-read everything she had brought with her and gone over all her notes, twice.

She began talking to their fellow guests. This allowed her to stay in the commons without feeling obliged to speak to Sorne, who appeared to have taken up residence there; more importantly, it gave her something to do, a chance to increase her knowledge of other shadowlands – to get some stimulation, at least. But most conversations never moved beyond the usual social froth. Those that did required an exchange of information, and that meant embroidering lies about her own supposed past in Shen. What few details people were interested in sharing also tended to be mundane and personal. *Never mind how your cousin's canker makes him behave in an unreasonable manner, tell me how they treat such ailments in your shadowland!* She would give all the money in her satchel and several good nights' sleep for one evening in the company of the skykin seer.

Inevitably, she found herself going over the events leading to Etyan's disappearance yet again, and mentally rehearsing her first words to him, along with possible sequences of events that might unfold from there. She couldn't just come out with the accusation, couldn't just say, "Did you kill a stranger?" Assuming the girl had been a stranger to him. No: he hadn't done it; he couldn't have done it. But he had been involved, somehow. She had to give him a chance to tell his side of the story. But first she had to find him.

Etyan was so close, yet until the soldiers made their move, until these long, dull days had passed, he had no idea she was here, and she had no idea what he was thinking, doing. And he was ill. How seriously? Was his life in danger?

One night over dinner Breen reported with mock affront that, "We only find out now that flour made from rice is no good for the kind of baking we know how to do." He affected a sigh and added, in a fair imitation of their landlady, "Such a shame, it just won't rise!" When Rhia smiled at his cheerful double entendre he winked at her.

Sex had stopped mattering to her some years ago. Polain, who she had once loved enough to mutilate herself, was long dead. She had more important things to think about.

But here, the rules were different. Breen was a pleasing-looking young man, and good company. How would it be if they enjoyed a dalliance? Like the time Alharet had introduced her to a handsome young man who would do whatever she wanted and not mention her ravaged face, and who she had not seen before or since.

Though he was younger than her, she was sure Breen would be amenable.

But it would be a diversion, nothing more. She would be using him – much as he had used Mella, albeit without financial exchange.

And Breen was a soldier. If she gave into temptation, no

doubt everyone in the militia back home would hear the
details of the countess's loose morals. Not to mention how
Sorne would react.

The guesthouse took on an air of gaiety at odds with Rhia's
dark mood. The main topic of conversation in the commons
became the best place to watch the caliarch's birthday regatta
from.

On restday, Mam Jekrey produced half a dozen stylized
portraits of previous caliarchs which she hung on pegs
around the commons. Each frame was draped with fresh
green foliage. Lekem refused to look at the display.

Rhia, for her part, urged the time to pass faster.

CHAPTER 36

I'm unravelling.

The thought came to Dej as she walked back from the stream.

Her hut-mates hadn't said anything when she stumbled back in last night, though Lih had pointed to the mess left from dinner. Dej had tidied it up, wrapped herself in her cloak and lain down. What else could she do?

It took a long time to get to sleep, because she was still shaking, whether from cold or shock or despair she didn't know, but she didn't fight it. It was the closest she could get to tears.

In the morning, Lih left to deal with the last of the meat from the hunt. When she was gone Vay said, "Put him from your mind. He's had everyone, has Cal. Probably the rhinobeasts too."

Dej stared, but the healer turned away to rummage in one of the tiny drawers in her wooden chest. She extracted, then held out, a twist of dried green-grey stalk. "You know what this is?"

"Burnheart?"

"That's right. Chew it slowly."

Min had got out of her bonding by falling pregnant. Dej doubted doing the same would help her in any way now.

The sensation of unravelling, coming undone, set in as she

227

swallowed the last of the liquorice-flavoured herb on the way back to the hut. The hollowness Min had left was unpicking her from the inside out.

She'd given away what Min called "the one-off gift the boys all want" because Cal might care, or maybe it might give her some status amongst the clanless, or even just to get some pleasure. She'd been wrong, stupid. She knew how boys – how men – were.

She still thought of Min, whether she wanted to or not. Somewhere in her head the sense of what Min had been to her had tangled with the thought of what Kir could be. Kir wasn't mean and twisted, she was kind, and she cared; compared to most clanless anyway. And Kir was a loner, and outcast even amongst these outcasts, just like Dej. So why not be friends, just like her instincts had said when they first met? But every time Dej got close Kir pushed her away.

Even her music, her first comfort, her secret pleasure, had been reduced to an echo. Reduced, then turned into another stick to beat her with.

She had nothing left.

With most of the hunt's spoils processed, Dej was back to fight practice. The cold fury of her moves surprised, and didn't please, her tutors.

"If you lose yourself your enemy will see that and you'll lose the fight!" chided Jeg.

"What enemy? I didn't think pichons were that smart."

"We don't just hunt rockslithers and pichons," said Tew.

"Then what–"

"Less talk, more practice," barked Jeg.

When, inevitably, Cal joined the gawkers watching her progress, Dej's skin crawled. She kept her back to him, tried to blot him out.

At the same time some small, idiotic part of her wanted

him to be impressed, wanted him to see she was worth more than he thought, wasn't just another naïve and desperate virgin fresh from the crèche, good only to be deflowered and cast aside. And he'd said they could have had fun together. Perhaps they could, even if it was just sex. Maybe if she'd stayed. Maybe if she went back to him now–

No. No man would ever treat her like that again, as a *thing* to be conquered, used.

That evening, having exchanged some of her anger for bruises, and filled some of the emptiness with physical activity, Dej realized there was still one unique and special thing left to her.

She made her move the next day, before she could think better of it.

Mar was a creature of habit. Every morning one of her attendants accompanied her to the latrines. Dej had no idea if it was the same one each time. The two men, Vas and Ryt, appeared identical, and showed an identical lack of wits. Mar called them *my boys* and according to Vay believed they were her actual sons, twins she'd given to a crèche in her youth. Whatever the truth, their hulking presence backed up Mar's authority. She rarely went anywhere without at least one of them.

When Dej went out for water that morning, she loitered and watched Mar and her escort leave the big hut. After a quick look around she scampered up, slinging the empty waterskin over her shoulder. She peered in. The fire was low and the curtains on one of the three sleeping alcoves were closed.

If Vas-or-Ryt woke up and asked why she was there she'd say she'd come to speak to Mar. She'd ask Mar the same question her fight-tutors had refused to answer, about what, aside from small prey, she was being trained to fight. Possibly a stupid question, probably not one Mar would answer, but an excuse for a visit.

That low rasp sounded like snoring. Dej crept over to the wooden cabinet she'd noticed on restday. It had a solid door but no lock. When she raised the latch and opened it a delicious smell wafted out. The fruit was piled high on the top shelf with dozens of the odd cakes, referred to as "rice cakes" on the bottom. She'd palmed a cloth before leaving the hut, and used it to wrap two rice cakes and a handful of dried apple; more than that and someone would notice.

A sound behind her. She jumped, then turned, poised to run or make some excuse, but she was still alone. Just a fart from the sleeping oaf. She grinned to herself and sauntered out.

She went back to the pool and filled the waterskin. As the water trickled in, rather than humming she ate one of the rice cakes and a piece of apple. The treat tasted even better than on restday.

On a previous visit to the pool she'd found a mat of knotted green-grey tendrils which could be lifted like a flap to expose a hand-sized crevice in the rocks. Not a great hiding-place, and she wasn't sure how edible her spoils would be once they'd been in there a day or two, but better than nothing.

On the way back to the hut she tried not to smile.

On the first day after she stole the food, a herb foraging party left, heading east. Kir didn't go with it; instead the clanless's other pathfinder, Gel, acted as their guide. Dej avoided Kir. Kir acted likewise. Dej should have expected that; after all, Min had betrayed her. She'd thought, for a while that Kir might be a friend, but she should have known better.

She ate most of the remaining fruit that day. The second rice cake had gone soggy but that wasn't the point; she ate that too. She left one piece of apple, to prolong the pleasure.

The following day started like any other: fetch water, keep out the way of her hutmates, go to fight practice. Cal turned up to watch her combat moves halfway through the morning. Dej ignored him.

When they broke for lunch Dej willed Cal to go away, walk off, just leave her *the fuck* alone. He didn't. He came over, nodding to the fight tutors. They moved off, leaving him with Dej. Dej stared at the hills behind him.

"So then," said Cal, "did you steal from us?"

Dej looked down and met his eyes, putting as much venom as she could into the tiny word, "No."

But the change in Cal's expression – a softening of the mouth, half-closed eyes, the hint of a nod – told her he knew she was lying. Part of her expected that. Part of her wanted it. But now it'd happened, she wanted to run. Except there was nowhere to run to.

Cal's hand shot out and grabbed her arm. "Come with me."

He dragged her to the big hut. She wanted to hit him, bite him, resist in some way, but it wouldn't do any good. The last part of her was undone.

Inside, Mar sat on her seat while one of her boys tended the fire.

Cal thrust her forward. "Yes, it was her." He sounded more irritated than angry.

Dej looked at Mar, cultivating her best look of innocent confusion. "What was me? What's happened?"

Mar levered herself up to stand and looked Dej in the face. "Do you really think Cal would be our seer if he couldn't smell lies, child? Though it's a talent I've some of too." Her eyes still on Dej's, she pointed to one side, towards the food cabinet. "Did you take food?"

Mam Gerisa had wanted to believe the best of people. These two didn't. And they could sense the truth. Dej met Mar's gaze. "Yes. Yes, I did."

"How incredibly stupid," commented Cal, like this was just one more thing she'd done to disappoint him.

Dej kept looking at Mar. "Took you a while to notice though, didn't it?"

"What?"

"You wanted to know what I'm good at. I'm good at stealing." She hadn't expected to boast about her light fingers but she had nothing left to lose. Perhaps it might even save her skin.

"That's nothing to be proud of," muttered Cal from behind her.

"So where does this food come from, then? I mean, the shadowkin don't just give it to you, do they, so presumably someone who can take things without–"

"Enough!"

Dej shut up at Mar's bark. More quietly, the elder continued, "How we get what we need from the shadowkin is no concern of yours. But even if we were thieves, we'd never steal from each other. I should have my boys take you onto the high plateau, break both your legs and leave you for the nightwings."

Dej's breathing quickened and her throat closed. *I will not show fear, I will not show fear.*

Mar cleared her throat. "But that's not what I'm going to do." She stepped to one side and pointed to her seat. "Kneel behind that."

Dej forced one leg to move, then the other. Without looking at Cal she walked round the seat and knelt. Someone shoved her forward, so her upper body lay across the seat. She looked at the ground and tried to breathe.

A pause, then–

She cried out at the first blow from the leather strap, head jerking up. Cal smiled across the fire at her. She closed her eyes and let her head droop. At the next blow she squealed, then bit off the sound. She closed her eyes tighter, locked her jaw, and dug her nails into her palms. Tears leaked over her cheeks but she didn't look up. And she didn't make another sound.

CHAPTER 37

On the morning of the caliarch's birthday, Lekem climbed out the window of the soldiers' room onto the narrow plank-bound ledge around the islet. Rhia left with Sorne and Breen by the front door. As the three of them passed the commons, Mam Jekrey bustled out. When she frowned to see one of their number missing, Sorne said, "My nephew is unwell, and hopes to join us later." Their hostess nodded, her good eye on him.

The soldiers led her to a jetty on the landward side of the islet. Here they found a single punt, with its steersman waiting, pole in hand. If she hadn't known better Rhia would not have recognized Lekem in the Zekti disguise. Their bundled possessions waited in the bottom of the boat, along with a short wooden ladder.

Rhia had no idea where the boat, or the ladder, had come from, though the punt already had garlands of white flowers and dark green foliage tied across the front and down the sides. The other punts they passed were similarly decorated. Another good reason for choosing this day, as Zekti punts had distinctive painted designs on them, stylized fish and waterweed and pairs of eyes. The garland would hide any markings that might identify the boat to its rightful owner. Assuming its rightful owner was still in a position to make such an identification.

Sorne and Breen sat on the bench at Lekem's feet facing forwards, Rhia opposite them facing back. Just a trio of visitors from Shen off to the regatta. Lekem did not look at his passengers as he planted and raised his pole. After some initial jolts and splashes, he got a feel for the motion, and stopped leaving the pole in too long or pulling it up too soon.

Slow swirls of sediment rose and settled in the brown water. When they passed over a bed of sinuous weed it undulated and spread out like strands of hair. Rhia looked away.

Most boats they saw were heading for the Eternal Isle, where the procession of barges would begin. People in other boats shouted "Joy of the First," to them, a greeting Sorne returned heartily. Aside from that the party was silent.

They passed the next islet. Cheers and faint music drifted across the water. Lekem steered to the left.

"Sir?" Breen broke the silence with a whisper.

Sorne said, "Yes?"

"I think we need to go between those two islets there, just to our right, to get to the priory. That's the most direct route."

"You hear that, boatman?" Sorne sounded almost jolly. Lekem dragged the pole, slowing the punt. His face was flushed and his forehead shone with sweat.

They passed more punts. They were heading against the flow now, earning odd looks. After the third time a group turned to stare at them Sorne said, loudly enough to make Rhia jump, "I told you this wasn't the way!"

"But, Da," said Breen, a mischievous smile on his face, "the girl I was talking to last night said this is a shortcut!"

The locals turned away, embarrassed at the foreigners' antics.

They rounded the back of the priory to find themselves in a narrow, deserted stretch of water.

Lekem brought the punt up alongside the islet about a third of the way along. Though the windows were small and high, the ledge was wide enough for a ladder.

While Lekem pulled himself onto the islet Rhia undid her skirt and pushed it down her legs; the pair of breeches she had packed had finally come in useful.

Sorne passed Lekem the ladder while Breen pulled out weapon bundles from packs. The soldiers worked fast, but Rhia still expected a punt to come round the corner at any moment.

When the ladder was in place Lekem held it steady while Sorne climbed. The captain paused to look in the window, then turned and nodded to show the way was clear.

Before starting up the ladder Breen leaned down to help Rhia out of the boat. She let him grasp her arm and pull her up. Once on the ledge she pressed herself against the wall while Breen climbed, then followed him up. After so long cooped up at the guesthouse, she was enjoying the adventure. She half climbed, half slid through the narrow window and dropped to the floor of a small, warm room. Behind her, she heard the ladder moving and looked at Sorne. "Lekem's staying with the boat," he murmured. That made sense: someone had to ensure it was still there when they got back.

This was a drying room, with clean sheets and tunics draped on wooden frames and a stone hearth in one corner putting out enough heat to keep the damp at bay.

Sorne and Breen unwrapped their weapons. Each had a short stave and ironwood punch-dagger; the glint along the edge of their staves showed they were diamond-dusted. Sorne offered her a flint-edged dagger, sheathed and belted.

"I don't know how to use this."

"And hopefully you won't have to," the captain whispered, "but it may come in useful."

Rhia nodded and strapped the dagger on. It was heavier than she expected.

Sorne went to the door, listened, then opened it a crack.

After a brief look round, he opened it fully. Breen followed. Rhia trailed behind.

Sorne led them left, past several closed doors. The hallway was silent and empty. Rhia listened so hard her ears ached. Though the corridor was not warm, sweat ran down between her shoulder blades. She wished Sorne had not given her a weapon. She had been thinking of herself as a detached observer. Now she was a third of their forces.

They came to steps, going up.

The steps led to another windowless wooden corridor, shadowy in the lamplight. As soon as Sorne turned into it he tensed. Rhia looked past him. Something lay on the floor just up the corridor. The obstruction was the right size and shape for a body. Breen moved to stand beside his captain. Rhia hung back.

Closer, and she could see how the man lay face down, outstretched arm still holding a staff. He wore a leather jerkin like those of the city guard, though he was bare-headed. Sorne and Breen approached, slow and silent. The man did not move. Sorne extended a foot and prodded the body; it gave, rolled a little, settled back.

The door nearest the fallen man was ajar. Sorne thrust it open, dagger in hand. He strode in, then paused and turned to murmur to Breen, "All clear in here. Check him." Breen knelt by the prone figure, allowing Rhia to see into the room, where a second body lay. *Please no, don't let that be…*

But it was another local, though without weaponry or armour. He lay on his side, facing away from the door, a pool of blood spreading out behind him.

Relief that it wasn't Etyan combined with nauseous shame, because this man had had a life and lost it. She looked away to see beds down either wall, and various stands and cupboards. A nightstand had been knocked over and herb-infused water ran into the blood. One bed had the covers dragged half off it. Aside from the man on the floor, there was no one here.

"This one's dead – neck broken," called Breen softly from the corridor. "Wait, got a footprint."

Rhia swallowed bile and turned her back on the carnage. She stepped aside to let Sorne make his exit. Breen was bending over a sandal-shaped damp mark on the scrubbed wooden floor.

"This way," Sorne said, spotting a second print. The two soldiers set off side-by-side, weapons at the ready, at a fast walk. Rhia trailed behind, wondering if she should draw her dagger. Someone else had been here, another intruder – or intruders – and they had taken Etyan. And killed at least two people. She wished she hadn't come.

They reached a set of stairs. Sorne and Breen exchanged nods, then started down, delicate as dancers.

At the bottom they hesitated, leaning out to look both ways along the corridor. A momentary meeting of glances and they set off left, at speed.

Three men were moving away up the corridor, no more than a dozen yards ahead. The one at the back was heavily built and had someone slung over his shoulder, someone slight with fair hair, dressed in a night-robe. Rhia bit down on a cry.

Sorne called out, "Hey, you there."

As the other men turned, Rhia cursed the normally professional captain for giving them away. Then the two unencumbered men stalked back past the one carrying Etyan and Rhia saw Sorne's logic: if the soldiers had attacked from behind they would have had the advantage of surprise, but Etyan might have been hurt.

Without another word, the four men closed.

Rhia enjoyed fencing matches at court, fought by sporting nobles using slender, undusted swords. This was something else.

One of Etyan's abductors had a club and shield, the other a shortsword and dagger. Sorne went for the swordsman. Breen stepped up to the club-wielder.

The corridor erupted into violence.

The soldiers leapt forward together, forcing the two abductors back. Beyond the whirl of limbs Rhia saw the third man bending over. Her heart skipped. She couldn't see Etyan. *Was he all right?*

The other two recovered from their initial surprise. Each side had the measure of the other now. Rhia wondered if she could get past the men to Etyan, but could see no safe way of doing so.

Breen fought laconically, almost playfully. While his opponent swung his club in wide arcs the militiaman dodged and parried, light on his feet, a half smile on his face.

Sorne's moves were faster, dirtier. He pressed forward, then fell back, only to lash out when his opponent came at him again. Both men's punch-daggers had knuckle-guards to parry with. Sorne's stave was longer than his opponent's sword, but the ironwood sword had jagged obsidian teeth set into it. The swordsman's first blow on Sorne was just a touch, yet cloth parted and blood welled above the captain's elbow. Sorne appeared not to notice.

Breen was giving ground. Sorne glanced at his companion, then retreated to stand alongside him.

Sorne stepped back again. Rhia was in his way. She scurried backwards, her mixture of fascination with the silent, intense battle and concern over her brother giving way to stark fear. One step threatened to become desperate flight.

But she could not abandon Etyan. The man who had been carrying him was standing up again. He had a club in his hand and was moving to join the fray.

Rhia almost missed Sorne's next feint. Forward, then back, then forward again. But his opponent wasn't fooled, and they were suddenly toe-to-toe. They whirled round each other, barely avoiding the wall. Another touch, this time on Sorne's flank. Another red line. And the third man was getting in position, behind Sorne. Had the captain noticed?

Rhia opened her mouth to warn Sorne as his first opponent lunged again. Rhia saw Sorne's dire fate in her mind's eye.

Sorne's stave came round from a parry, sweeping down.

His opponent raised his sword, ready to swing.

This was it, the end.

Sorne's stave changed direction, tip bouncing up from the floor too fast to see. Up, inside his opponent's guard. It connected with the man's groin – the man's huffing breath became a squeal – and he jerked forward. Sorne punched up with his dagger hand, pinning the man briefly to the wall. Blood spurted from a chest wound. Even as the swordsman went limp and slid off Sorne's dagger the captain was turning, completing his dirty, crazy move to come round and face his new opponent.

Breen and the club-wielder paused at this decisive stroke. For a moment the only movement in the corridor was the man Sorne had just stabbed, twitching on the floor.

Time, Rhia realized, was at its most mutable in moments like this. When the mind processes *this much*, reality is at its sharpest.

Sorne faced off against his new opponent. She could see Etyan now, lying at the side of the corridor, but it still wasn't safe to go to him. She waited for Breen to lay into his man again.

Instead, Breen looked his opponent in the eye and turned on his heel. Suddenly, he was behind her. Before she could react his stave came round and across her chest; she gasped as Breen pulled her close, diamond-dust rough through the fabric of her shirt. Something pricked her side.

"Still now," he murmured.

This had to be a ploy. The soldiers had not told her

everything, so this must be part of their plan. They hadn't told her in case she couldn't fake the terror she was feeling right now.

More loudly Breen said, "Drop your weapons."

Why would their attackers drop their weapons because Rhia was threatened? A very *devious* ploy. She hoped her knees wouldn't give out before she had played her unwitting part in it.

The fight paused, all three combatants poised. Breen's opponent had already turned to face Sorne. The big man was on Sorne's right-hand side. The captain had his back to the wall, standing next to the fallen swordsman. He had his guard up and his eye on the two men facing him, stave raised to cover one, dagger pointed at the other. He looked surprisingly calm, although there was an odd twist in his expression; not anger but something more complex.

"Captain," said Breen. "Give it up now."

She must have misheard. Breen couldn't be telling his superior officer to surrender.

Without taking his eyes off his two opponents, Sorne said, "Why?"

This isn't a ploy.

"I don't want to hurt her, but–"

"That's not what I'm asking, Corporal, and you know it." Sorne's voice was tight.

"Reasons don't matter. Drop your weapons, Captain."

"You're right, you don't want to hurt her, do you? Those aren't your orders, are they?"

Breen's presence overwhelmed her. His warm breath, stirring her hair, was the only sign he was human.

Human. Fallible. And my enemy.

She had a knife. But no chance of getting to it. Even breathing hurt, against the stave tight across her chest. If she let her legs buckle – as they were threatening to do – would he relax his grip? Maybe she should faint. *And then what?*

Sorne spoke with forced casualness, "So did she sleep with you? Or did she just promise to?"

Did who sleep with Breen?

Breen tensed. The tip of his blade broke the skin of her flank. Despite herself, she whimpered.

"Now, m'lady. Stay calm."

Stay calm? When you have turned traitor and have a knife to me? Anger flashed, but it was a puff of crazy fury, dispersing at once, leaving her boneless with fear. Her legs began to quiver. The prickling in her side intensified. She locked her knees. She had been right not to try fainting.

Breen's head, so close to hers, moved away a fraction. "Why don't we even this out then, hmm? What do you say, my friends?"

The club-wielder spared a glance for Breen. His expression wasn't friendly; more unsure. *How many sides are there in this fight?*

Breen continued, "So I've got the lady. How about one of you fine gents recovers the little brother?"

No. Leave him alone! But all that came from her lips was a pained hiss.

The men hesitated. Perhaps the fallen swordsman was their captain. Without him, faced by one of their opponents switching sides, they were at a loss. Then the larger man nodded and, still covering Sorne, edged back towards Etyan, though not with a raised weapon, thank the First.

Sorne grunted as though someone had just laid down a winning hand of cards. "You've got me. I'll put up my weapons, and accept my fate. But before I do, you owe me an explanation, Corporal."

"What's to explain? I've chosen my side."

"I'd love to know why." Sorne sounded genuinely interested. *How can he be so calm about this?*

"Does it matter?"

"It does to me. And it won't matter to anyone else. After all, you're about to kill me."

"Well I–" Breen jerked. His grip loosened. Rhia stumbled forward, catching herself to land on all fours. She looked up at movement. Sorne lashed out at one opponent. More movement to the other side. She was not sure where Breen had gone, but now he had, she just wanted to get out of here.

But Etyan was undefended. He needed her. She began to crawl towards him. She glimpsed Sorne clubbing his opponent to the ground with his stave, following up with two sharp blows that kept the man down.

The bloody body of the swordsman blocked her path. She needed to stand up. *Come on legs, stand up.*

She looked to one side. The club-wielder was no longer heading for Etyan but had been intercepted by another local. Who? *Lekem!* Where did he come from?

Etyan was not in immediate danger. She sagged against the wall, then turned to sit with her back to it, not looking at the dead man beside her. She'd just stay here a moment.

Sorne moved across; it was two against one now on the man with the club. They had him backed up to the opposite wall. He put up his hands, dropping his club. Sorne, his voice as casual as ever, asked, "Who sent you?"

The man stared at him, white-faced.

"We don't have time for this, do we?" he asked Lekem. Lekem raised his dagger, elbow back, ready to strike the man's throat.

The club-wielder looked terrified, but stayed silent.

"Are you really willing to die for your prince?"

At Sorne's comment the man's eyes widened. Sorne muttered, "Aha." He smashed the man's nose with the heel of his left hand. As blood spurted he grabbed his hair, banging his head on the wall. The man crumpled.

Sorne dropped him and strode back towards Rhia. "Are you all right?"

Compared to nearly everyone else here she was, so she nodded. Fainting looked increasingly attractive but, given the soldiers would have to carry Etyan, that would be unhelpful. She watched Sorne, because what he did decided everything. He went over to Breen, who lay on his side, curled in on himself, one arm caught under his body, the other trying to reach behind for the knife stuck in his back. His eyes glittered and his breath rasped.

Sorne stared at him without a word.

From beside the captain, Lekem called, "You should look away now, m'lady."

Lekem's words made no sense. Then again, very little made sense just now. Rhia stared as Sorne bent over Breen. She could name the captain's expression now: disappointment.

Sorne laid down his stave and put his hand on the side of Breen's head, pressing it to the floor. Breen stopped moving and looked up at him, lips pressed thin. Sorne nodded, and said, "You die as a traitor."

His other hand came round, still holding his punch-dagger. He placed the point in Breen's ear, then pressed down with all his strength.

At which point, Rhia did faint.

CHAPTER 38

For the second year running, the caliarch asked his eparch to join him on the royal barge. For the second year running, Sadakh declined. The offer showed how much Numak valued him, even as it exposed the caliarch's naivety, which grew with age. For the two of them to appear in public side-by-side was an open snub to the prince. Not to mention a temptation: Mekteph had got where he was in part through unattributable "accidents" suffered by other members of the royal family; an incident which removed both the caliarch and the eparch at once would suit his purposes well. The birthday regatta was a security nightmare as it was, with every window, jetty and shoreline along its route occupied and the water packed with boats. How fortunate the caliarch was well loved by his people.

Sadakh took his place at the front of the second barge, by tradition reserved for priests and advisors, in the wooden eparch's chair, which he tried not to think of as a throne despite its high carved back. An oiled mauve and red striped canopy kept the fitful sunlight from him.

In the lead barge, a larger throne under a gold and black canopy allowed Numak to survey his domain and receive the adoration of his subjects. From here Sadakh could see only seatbacks but Mekteph would be sitting just behind his uncle, waving and smiling, throughout their stately progression. The prince's young son and daughter sat either side of their father. Their mother was too unwell to attend; Princess Imkanet, the only surviving child of the late, mad Caliarch Hyrek, was ailing fast and unlikely to be alive this time next year. Once, the canopy would have covered a dozen thrones, each sized and decorated according to the complexities of royal rank, but treachery, madness and disease had taken their toll on the Zekti royal family.

As Numak was childless the transference of the royal line to the prince's family was a given, in Mekteph's mind at least. Yet still the prince plotted. Mekteph was not content to wait for the caliarchy to pass to his son when Numak's earthly rule ended; he wanted to taste power himself, even if only as nominal regent for his child.

Action would have to be taken, once Sadakh's own plans came to fruition. With an eternal ruler there was no need of a successor. Numak might baulk at such expedience but Mekteph was not the only one who had it in his power to arrange accidents. Timing would be key, as once Mekteph saw there was no chance of succeeding to the caliarchy, not even the wiles of the court eunuchs would prevent his machinations exploding into open conflict.

The royal barge pulled away from the wharf at the base of the Eternal Isle with a trilling of flutes and a clash of lyres. A cheer went up. Sadakh forced a smile as his barge followed on. This had not been a good week. Four days ago, another test subject had passed away. Only one remained now.

And then there was Akbet. She had assumed, as she currently had a place in his bed, she would have a place on the ceremonial barge. He had explained that the caliarch's birthday celebrations were a matter of tradition and ritual, as important in their own earthly way as the communions and services of the Church; to use the opportunity to show favour to a lover would be inappropriate. Though she said nothing, from her expression she took his ruling as a personal affront. Why must they always be like this? Despite explaining in advance what the terms of the relationship were, every woman he took to his bed thought she was special, the one who would change him.

She has to go.

Soon, he told his ghost. Her youthful enthusiasm continued to refresh him but she had started asking awkward questions. A few nights ago she had noticed the scar on his forehead. He had said it was old, just as he had told other over-curious lovers before. But she had persisted, and mentioned the other, newer, wound on the inside of his arm, hidden from most eyes by his sleeves. Why did that cut not get better, she wondered? Even had he been minded to tell her, Sadakh doubted she would have understood; doubted, in fact, that she even knew what an animus was. And she had already given him a route into the natural enquirers.

The time to eject the poor foolish creature from his bed was approaching.

The barge was underway now, the shorelines of the islands lined with smiling faces, the air sweet with incense, the water thick with heavensbreath petals. Sadakh's soul was lifted by such massed joy, though as ever he felt the tinge of disdain, which his ghost voiced.

They're cheering because they have a day off work and an excuse to drink rice spirit.

She was oversimplifying, but had a point. How many of these people thought beyond the shallow pleasures of the day? How many of them appreciated how important it was to have a caliarch who valued stability – and who had the eunuchs behind him to ensure he remained in power. Very few of these citizens, he suspected, realized how lucky they were.

CHAPTER 39

"M'lady?"

The skull had cracked. Hearing that sound had done it, had made her slide to the floor for a moment of merciful oblivion. The jaw appeared to have been dislocated as a secondary effect of the blow. Impressive damage for such a short blade.

"M'lady!"

She had only fainted briefly, then woken eye-to-eye with Breen. His eyes were already glassy, all animating force departed. Hard to believe he had been alive so recently.

"Rhia! Are you all right?"

She sat up. There was surprisingly little blood around the dagger in Breen's ear. Presumably that clear liquid running down his cheek was the "essential water" anatomists talked of. Not her area, anatomy.

"M'lady, we have to go."

All very well for him to say, this man of action. He had called her Rhia just now but that was a forgivable lapse, under the circumstances. She tore her attention away from Breen's body.

"Please. We must leave now." Sorne made to touch her arm, then paused. "Can I help you up, m'lady?"

"Oh. Yes. Of course. Thank you." Her own body felt heavy. Despite the thing lying next to her, she wanted to rest here a while, though the captain was having none of it. "Where is...?" She looked up to see someone bending over her brother. She opened her mouth to cry out, before realizing it was Lekem.

"That's right, let's get you up, m'lady."

She let Sorne haul her upright, then called, "How is he, Corporal?"

"Alive, with no sign of injury, m'lady," said Lekem. "He appears to be asleep."

Rhia exhaled. Beside her, Sorne kept hold of her arm. She gave the bodies on the floor one last look. A vile smell was emanating from one or more of them, presumably due to relaxation of the bowels. She had read about that somewhere, with sudden death. She rocked back on her heels, then stabilized herself against Sorne's firm grip.

Seeing the cut on Sorne's arm, she remembered being wounded. Yes, but not much more than a spindle-prick in the side. She could ignore that.

Lekem hoisted Etyan onto his shoulder and they set off, one on either side of her. Somewhat to her surprise, her legs knew what to do.

Sorne released her arm. He examined the wound on his elbow as he strode beside her, then raised his arm to look at the nick in his side.

"Anything serious?" asked Rhia in what passed for polite conversation in the current situation.

"Scratches. You're all right?"

"Oh yes. I'm fine."

They stopped at a door. It was ajar. Rhia tensed, remembering the last such door and what had been within, but worse had happened since, and she was still on her feet.

This door, however, gave onto the drying room. The ladder lay under the high window. Sorne raised it, then climbed up, pausing at the top to check outside.

"Let's get the boy up," he said. Lekem raised Etyan's limp form; Sorne caught his shoulders and they manhandled him out like a sack of grain. Rhia let herself look at her brother for the first time, noting how he had a rash on his face and hands, making the skin look red and raw, how his hair was long but clean, how he looked relaxed, almost content, even if he was limp as a doll. Something began to uncurl in her chest.

She went last. She did not look back.

Outside, Sorne was there to steady her. He helped her into the boat then pulled the ladder down, sliding it off the ledge into the water, where it began to float off.

They laid Etyan in the bottom of the boat, amongst the baggage. It was damp down there, due to drips from Lekem's inexpert poling. He'd get wet.

As Lekem raised the pole and pushed off, Sorne bent down beside her.

"Let's look at your side."

"My side?"

"Yes, you've been wounded."

"Ah, that. Nothing serious."

Sorne lifted her shirt, and she made to slap his hands away before catching herself. She looked down to see a thin smear of blood on the waistband of her breeches.

Sorne grunted. "This'll stop the bleeding." He pressed a leaf to the cut. Numbweed, if she was not mistaken.

While Sorne treated his own cuts, Lekem built up some speed and they cleared the priory isle. The water around them remained deserted. There was noise in the distance. She had no idea what that was. She felt as though she was observing herself, unable to quite connect with reality.

They sat as they had on the way here: she faced Sorne, Lekem faced forward. Except there were two important changes. No Breen – yes, the dagger had gone in through the ear and the skull had cracked; she would never forget that sound – and the addition of Etyan, who did indeed appear asleep.

The first time Rhia had watched her brother sleep she had considered killing him. She had sneaked into the nursery and peered into his crib. She had wanted a brother for so long. Then she had given up wanting one, accepting she was an only child. And finally, after so many confinements ending in whispered sorrow, this tiny pink wrinkled *thing* had come into the world, taking Mother away in the process.

If she killed it now, perhaps Mother would come back.

But at twelve years old, she knew that Mother was gone forever, and that her brother was here to stay. Her fingers had still itched, for a moment. But then he'd stirred and yawned, and opened huge eyes, and she'd wondered what was going on in that tiny head, and what might go on in there in future, and realized that this was her *brother*, the only one she would ever have. And neither of them had a mother.

She loved him in that instant, fully and unconditionally. She would do anything to keep him safe.

"M'lady?" She looked up to see Lekem staring at her. "Are you all right?"

Her eyes prickled. She nodded.

"It's shock," said Sorne. "It will pass, you'll be fine."

She made to shake her head, to say that wasn't it, but lacked the energy to argue.

The noise was clearer now. Cheering, and music. The regatta. She looked up as Lekem brought the punt to a halt. Ahead, the waterway narrowed to a gap between two islets, blocked by a low bridge. A wider passage led off right.

Lekem looked round; Sorne turned in his seat. The noise was getting louder, and seemed to come from all around.

Lekem called down, "I'm not sure it's wide enough to turn safely here."

"Let's go right, then."

Lekem set off. The waterway curved to the right, and narrowed. Lekem slowed, scanning for other options.

The curve sharpened. They came around the corner to find the path ahead blocked. At first Rhia thought this was a dead end, that what they had taken to be a passage was just a long thin inlet. Then she saw what blocked their way. People, dozens of people standing up in punts, facing away from them.

Lekem planted his pole and stopped the punt, then edged it across to one side of the channel.

"Are you going to turn us around?" Rhia had to raise her voice to be heard above the din.

"I can't risk getting stuck halfway, m'lady, so, no."

"Then are we getting off here?" It would not be the most unexpected thing to happen today.

"No," said Sorne. "We're going to wait."

"For what?"

"For the regatta procession to pass and the crowds to leave. Then we'll be able to manoeuvre without attracting attention."

"Ah." Looked at objectively – and she was regaining such abilities – this was the logical course of action.

The music grew louder, and the watchers at the end of the channel began to wave. Many of them had green branches in their hands.

A barge appeared, as big as a skykin wagon, its deck so high that she had no trouble seeing it above the crowd's heads. A small group centred round an elderly man sat under a rich awning. The boat's rails and the awning's poles were adorned with flowers. Everyone on the barge wore pure white robes and gold-coloured headdresses of varying height and complexity. The man waved regally as he passed; those with him smiled.

Although she doubted anyone could have seen them even had they looked their way, Rhia sat low in the boat until the barge passed. Sorne did not even turn in his seat; Lekem's eyes were closed and his lips moved silently.

After the first barge came more, another six in all, carrying courtiers, musicians and various dignitaries. Lekem kept up his prayers.

At last, the final boat passed. As the cheers faded Sorne looked Rhia in the face. "Now we need to remember what we're meant to be."

It took her a moment to register what he meant; reason might have returned but she was damnably tired.

Movement began at the end of the waterway. Most people went forward, out into the larger channel, but one, then a second, punt headed back towards their boat.

The first punt had a family in, the mother and three youngsters chattering excitedly. The father spared a brief, bemused glance for their punt as they passed, leaving a wash of white petals in the water.

The second punt had two young couples in. The man facing their way called out as they approached, "Did you miss it?"

Rhia held her breath.

Sorne answered, "We saw a bit."

"Not from there you wouldn't!"

The punt came alongside and one of those in it, a young woman with flowers in her hair, saw Etyan lying in the bottom of their punt. Her eyes widened, and she turned to her companions.

"We were late," said Rhia with an explosion of pent-up breath. She pointed at the unmoving body in the bottom of their boat. "He got blind drunk."

The couples, who from the smell of spirits were not entirely sober themselves, laughed at this. Then the boy said, "Goes out drinking in his nightclothes, does he?"

"You wouldn't believe what he gets up to," said Rhia, with feeling.

The other punt carried on. From the glance its boatman gave them as he passed, he did not hold a high opinion of foreigners and their odd habits.

Finally, the way ahead was clear. Lekem pushed off.

Rhia's head sank onto her chest.

CHAPTER 40

Rhia came to with a start as the boat bumped land. They were in thick reeds. She looked round. The islets of Mirror were behind them; just ahead, through the reeds, was the causeway that circled the lake. Lekem used his pole to probe the water, then lifted it free and laid it down in the bottom of the punt, on the side away from Etyan.

Sorne raised himself into a crouch. He stepped over the side of the punt, setting it rocking. The lake water came to just above his knees. He addressed Lekem. "You get everything ashore while I fetch the cart." He sounded relaxed, and his face had settled back into its usual impassive but not unfriendly expression. She was comfortable around him. Except, not long ago, he had put a dagger through the head of one of his own men. Breen, who she had almost–

She bent over the side of the boat, gripped the wooden rail, and threw up. When she straightened, Sorne was gone, the only sign of his passing a disturbance in the reeds.

"Can you manage, m'lady?" Lekem looked concerned. "I can carry you, if you need–"

"No. I'll be fine." A string of acrid drool trailed across her lips; she wiped it away with the back of her hand.

"I'll start with the luggage," said Lekem.

"Good. Yes."

Lekem lowered himself over the side and pulled the two

smallest packs after him, balancing one on each shoulder.

Rhia knelt beside Etyan and laid a hand on his forehead, half expecting him to be feverish. Like Father's fever: the slow, awful decline.

Etyan's brow was cool. What she had taken for a rash looked more like burns, the skin raw and peeling.

She felt his skull for bumps and found nothing. Next she checked his hands. On the back of the left one, barely visible in the rough skin, was a line of three parallel scratches. They were recent, the blood barely crusted. She raised his hand to sniff it and caught a sour whiff.

Lekem cleared his throat. When she looked at him he asked, "Can you help me get him over my shoulder, m'lady?"

"Of course." This turned out to be hard work. Etyan would wake with bruises, but for now he slept on, thanks to whatever drug had been applied through those scratches. When Lekem was gone Rhia checked the boat to ensure nothing had fallen from their packs. After he took the last load she dropped into the water in his wake. The lake was chill, and its soft, clinging mud engulfed her feet. She shuffled ashore, grasping the reed stems for support.

Lekem had propped Etyan up against the packs piled at the edge of the causeway, as though he had just decided to sit down and take a nap. As Rhia hauled herself onto the causeway she heard hooves on the planking, and looked up to see a small cart approaching.

She exhaled when she recognized the driver. Sorne had hired a compact carriage such as Rhia herself might have taken to visit the family estate, with a blue-painted canopy and fold-down steps. The benches down the sides were padded and had proper backrests. The horse between the traces was the healthiest animal she had seen since arriving in Zekt.

Sorne and Lekem loaded the cart, carefully looking the

other way while Rhia changed out of her wet breeches. They appeared content to remain damp. She unbelted the knife and returned it to Sorne.

The soldiers laid Etyan along one bench, rolling the canopy down at the sides but leaving the front and back open. Sorne sat behind Lekem who, as usual, drove. It was fortunate Breen was not with them, as it would have been a bit of a squeeze. Then she caught herself, appalled. Had she really accepted Breen's death that easily? The soldiers acted as though nothing had happened. Then again, what else could they do? But when she sat next to Sorne she kept as much distance between them as the seat would allow.

With a flick of the reins and a "geeyup" from Lekem they set off at a brisk trot.

"Water?"

Sorne was holding out a canteen to her. She took it, glad to swill the taste of vomit from her mouth. She spat the water over the back of the cart. As she handed the canteen back to Sorne she said flatly, "You killed them."

At first she thought he hadn't heard her over the clatter of the horse's hooves on the causeway. Then he looked across and said, "I killed Breen, and one of the intruders. The other two should recover if they're found and treated in time."

"Did you know he would..." she shut up as the cart turned; they had reached the crossroads where the lakeside causeway met the main road. As the carriage swung round onto the larger causeway, the guards on the archway came into sight. They were looking their way, though not with any particular interest. Etyan lay below the level of the carriage's backboard, but his crooked knees peeked above it. That must look odd. They might see that and stop them. Rhia found herself wringing her skirt between her hands.

She kept watching until the guards were too far away to make out their faces, and she was sure no one was coming along the causeway. Then she released her skirt and turned to Sorne.

He nodded and said, "I understand your anger and confusion, m'lady. I apologize for keeping things from you."

"You apologize for not mentioning we had a traitor in our midst?" *A traitor I nearly slept with.* "Just how much did you know?"

"I *knew* nothing. I had suspicions. They were confirmed. I acted."

How simple it was to be a solider! "If you had your suspicions about Breen, why in the Last's name was he with us?"

"I had reason to believe he might not be loyal, but reason to believe is not reason to act. Until the attack in the market I hoped I was wrong."

"You think he was in league with the people who were watching us?"

"Breen was a Zekti agent. I believe he tipped off the watchers, identifying himself as an ally and suggesting they make their move."

So rather than the incident in the market being a result of Breen spooking those tailing them, he had caused it. "You could have confronted him then. Why didn't you?"

"I could," conceded Sorne, "but that would have alerted him, and any allies he had. Someone might have done something rash."

"Would they have attacked us in the guesthouse?"

"That would have repercussions. Despite frosty relations, Zekt and Shen benefit from mutual trade. Openly assaulting each other's citizens would be foolish. Besides, there are factions in Zekt. Breen just served one of them."

"The same faction who tried to abduct my brother from the priory?"

"Possibly, though they looked as surprised to see us as we were them. Perhaps there was a communication failure."

"I still don't understand how a possible Zekti agent got on this mission in the first place."

"I believe that is a matter of politics, m'lady. There are foreign influences at court–"

"Are you saying there are Zekti agents in the palace?" An unthinkable possibility presented itself; but a number of unthinkable things had happened today.

Sorne looked uncomfortable – a rare sight. "I'm saying that there is… someone at court whose interests lie with Zekt and not Shen. This person has been known to recruit weak-minded or easily bought individuals. The duke knows this."

"Yet he let Breen come!"

'Forgive me for saying this, m'lady, but the duke is a complicated man, well versed in subterfuge. For His Grace to block Breen's assignment to the mission would show he knew Breen had been turned. Instead, he pretended ignorance."

"So he merely warned you that you might have to thwart a traitor? He must trust you highly."

"I am honoured by the trust His Grace places in me, m'lady."

What had Sorne said when he was taunting Breen at the priory, buying time for Lekem to arrive and save them? *So did she sleep with you?*

"M'lady, are you all right?"

Much as Rhia wished otherwise, there was one obvious "foreign influence" at court. "Is the duchess a traitor, Captain?"

Sorne's mouth twitched, and he kept his gaze forward as he replied, "There is reason to believe so, yes."

Not Alharet. Not her confidant, her best friend, the fellow outsider who made court life bearable. But the duchess was the sister of Zekt's power-hungry prince. And whatever else today had taught her, it was a reminder that sometimes she misjudged people.

CHAPTER 41

Vay fetched the water the day after Dej's beating, sighing and giving Dej a look as if to say, *You can't do it, so I guess I'll have to.*

The following morning, Dej was back on water duty. Up at the pool, she removed the last piece of stolen fruit from its hiding place and flung it away, up into the high rocks.

Restday was unbearable. Everyone in the same space, together but separate, and with nothing to fill the time, no mindless activity to distract her from the emptiness inside.

Fight practice for the next few days was less intense, though whether this was allowing for her wounds or acknowledging she was making progress Dej had no idea. She didn't ask.

Life settled into a numb rhythm. No one mentioned her crime, though the punishment was plain to see on her back. The clanless had done their worst and she was still alive. Out here just surviving was an achievement.

Another expedition set out a few days later. Dej heard Vay and Lih talking about going on "the uplands hunt" but had no idea she was going too until Vay told her the night before. She had become invisible to everyone, including herself, nothing but an empty space, yet still somehow alive.

From the number of clanless gathered in the grey pre-dawn outside the big hunt, it appeared most of them were going though there was no sign of the clan's rhinobeast.

Ryt and Vas distributed weapons. Dej was unsurprised to be issued with the same knife she'd used on the first hunt, its stone tip broken by her clumsy stab at the rockslither. Some of the hunters carried heavy spears, or odd bundles of short, pale sticks. Everyone got a deep wicker basket. When Dej saw people strapping them on their backs she braced herself for pain. But her cuts had almost healed, a reminder rather than a torment when the rough basket rested on them.

Kir strode up to Dej as she was tightening the straps and said, "This isn't a circular trip, it's there and back. I'll lead out, you'll lead on the return journey." Dej nodded, her face blank. This was the most Kir had said to her in a week.

They headed northwest, and were soon scrambling up a ravine the rhinobeast would never have managed. From there it was up and down, bog and slope.

Dej followed a step behind Kir. She stopped when Kir did, listened when Kir talked, spoke only when spoken to. The pattern of the land settled on her as she moved through it. Her sense of direction was broadening into a more complex feel for the terrain, an awareness of the nature of the rock beneath her feet.

That night they slept close and kept a fire burning, with half a dozen clanless awake and on watch. Halfway through the night Dej woke when a screech froze the breath in her chest. She lay paralyzed as it came again, more distant this time. People shifted and woke around her, but the sound died away and the night grew still again. She knew, even without the mutters of those trying to get back to sleep, that it had been a nightwing.

The next day Kir thawed towards Dej, talking more freely, describing how the hunt would progress. Dej concentrated on listening and obeying. But when Kir commented that their prey were dumber than Mar's boys and uglier than Mar herself, Dej felt herself start to smile. Kir returned the smile, and loosened up further. What was going on? One moment Kir was cold and distant, the next she was friendly and open.

They camped early, amongst rocks and shallow caves overlooking the widest valley Dej had ever seen. This was their destination. Now they must wait.

Guards were posted, both against nightwings, and to watch for the annual migration they were taking advantage of. Chakaka were herd beasts the size of large dogs, with a weaker version of the joint mind the pichons shared. They passed this way at this time every rain year, heading towards their birthing grounds in the east. The exact timing varied by a few days, so the clanless had to be camped and ready. Kir said this was the biggest hunt of the year; enough, if successful, to keep them in meat for months.

Late the following day the spotter at the head of the valley gave a short barking cry, and the clanless ran to get into place. Dej grabbed two sticks from the pile kept ready. When she was in position she took out a clump of the stinking moss the healers had provided and rubbed it over her bare skin, concentrating on groin and armpits; it smelled like a mixture of beeswax and old shit. She hunkered down and waited, stock-still, behind a small rock. Chakaka had poor eyesight for anything not moving, but a good sense of smell; if the wind carried the scent of the clanless to them, or if anyone moved, they'd spook.

The clanless had divided into four groups, two on each side of the flat central path through the valley; she was one of four "channellers" in this group. Cal was another, positioned behind and upslope from her. As the distant thunder of the approaching herd grew he called across, "Remember the instructions. And concentrate! Don't screw this up." She ignored him.

She suspected that her position, as the channeller at the front, reflected how little the clanless cared for her fate. But she wouldn't show fear.

The chakaka were in sight now, a mass of pale brown heads and thick legs half obscured by the dust they kicked up. The ground shook.

Though her legs quivered, Dej stayed down, waiting for the lead animals to reach the shoulder-high marker cairn, built by hunters untold generations ago and added to with a new stone on every successive hunt. As the first beasts flowed round the cairn Dej leapt up, arms wide, holding a pair of white-painted sticks. She waved her arms, giving a formless fierce shout to back up the motion. She looked past her waving arms for the right animal; a little smaller, or weaker, or younger; one of those to the side though not one of the fierce bulls on the edge. But all she saw was a waist-high mass of hair and scale and flesh bearing down on her.

That one! A random choice, but better than dithering. She pivoted, ready to channel the animal left, to force it upslope and parallel to the rest of the herd. Once it broke free, Cal and the other channellers would divert it farther up the valley side, driving it into the waiting semicircle of hunters armed with bolas, spears and knives.

The front of the herd saw her, jinking to avoid this strange obstacle. Her chosen beast swerved hard – to the right. It tripped and crashed down, into the path of the beasts farther in. The herd rolled over it.

For the first time in days she felt something beyond numb emptiness. Not fear exactly, more a slight lifting of her spirits, the realization she was still alive. She could sense the herd, the way they moved. Just as she knew how the land was folded and raised around her, just as she could locate every nearby clanless even though they were all behind her, she could feel the herd. Maybe that was why she got the lead

role: not because no one would care if she went under the
chakaka's tough-horned feet, but because her abilities meant
she could read these animals as she read the land. Could Kir
do that? Maybe, but Kir wasn't out here.

Still, she needed to concentrate, just as Cal, damn him, had
said. She focused ahead. Animals rushed past on either side,
the disruption to the flow caused by the fallen beast subsiding
as it was ground into the dust. Cal and the other channellers
had forced one of the herd into the killing circle, but they
needed at least a dozen beasts between the four groups of
hunters to assure the supply of meat and hides. She had to
prove herself. She had to bring in her own kill.

Another possible target, near the edge, small and scrawny,
only hip-high. No, wait! Behind and alongside, covering the
herd's edge, one of the larger bulls, its armoured head lifting
over the other beasts. If she tried for the runt she might
distract the bull, and drive it towards the next channeller.
Towards Cal.

Suddenly her priorities shifted. What Cal had done, the
way he'd treated her...

There would be other hunts. There might only be one
chance for vengeance.

She waved harder, shouted louder, and turned towards the
bull.

Or tried to. Something stopped her motion, and killed
her voice in her throat. For a moment her body was frozen
between heartbeats. Then she asserted her will, and wobbled
wildly, arms tracing a crazy loop, sticks clacking.

The bull broke free, along with two other members of the
herd. Even as Dej shrieked in mingled triumph and terror,
the bull pelted straight up the slope, while the smaller beasts
headed towards the other channellers.

Dej sensed, but did not see, what happened next. Her arms
got their rhythm back, keeping up enough motion to deflect

the herd, but part of her attention moved to the scene behind her, where not one but two animals headed into the hunters' circle; a great bounty if they could secure it, but a risk too, as they were still dealing with the first beast.

Afterwards, she worked out that the bull must've looped round upslope then, sensing herd members in danger, hurtled into the hunters from behind. At the time Dej only felt the shock when it careered into them.

She had to keep waving her arms and shouting, or she'd be trampled. Dust caught in her throat and she coughed, her voice cracking. Then she saw bare ground beyond the mass of brown bodies: the back of the herd. As soon as the last beast passed she lowered her arms and turned around.

There was no sign of the bull; one of the other separated beasts had also dodged back into the receding chakaka. The other was being set upon by hunters, led by Vas – Mar had let one of her boys come on the hunt, it was that important – who as Dej watched drove a spear taller than he was into the fallen beast. Several others, including Cal, were running over to a prone figure at the edge of the circle.

Dej knew, even before her eyes confirmed it, that the fallen clanless was Kir.

For the barley harvest the crèche had brought in local hired help with a strange contraption, wound by a crank, to thresh the crop. Dej had only glimpsed the man whose arm had got caught in this machine, but the sight of mangled flesh had stayed with her. This was worse. Kir must have sensed the danger, and started to turn; the chakaka's armoured head had caught her in the side, where a huge dark bruise covered her flank. But that was nothing compared to her legs. The bull had dragged her along, trampling her as it did so; a white thigh-bone showed through torn flesh. Everything below both knees was bloody pulp.

Dej realized she was calling out: "I'm sorry, I'm so sorry!"

Cal, who had just reached Kir, turned and shouted, "Stop!"

Dej skidded to a halt, in surprise as much as anything, about a dozen paces from Kir's body.

"Back off!" Cal gestured violently, shooing her away. "Now!"

Two more clanless were running up; one of them was Vay, who spared Dej a glance as she passed, and called, "Stay back unless you want to kill her."

Dej stared at Kir and saw, impossibly, that her eyes were open, her chest rising and falling. She was still alive. Dej stood, dumbfounded, while the healers knelt beside the pathfinder. Cal said something to them. Then he stalked over to Dej. She made herself stand her ground and say nothing.

"Do you know what Kir's abilities are?"

The question threw her, but she wasn't going to keep staring like a dumb beast. "She's a pathfinder."

"Yes, and?"

"And what? She never mentioned anything else."

"Well she fucking should have, given how you mooned after her. She's a full empath. Do you know what that is?"

Dej shook her head.

"It means that what you feel, she feels. And right now, the guilt you rightly feel would be enough to finish her off. Now go and help the other hunters!"

Dej obeyed. The fallen chakaka had stopped moving and people were swapping spears for knives and falling on the corpses. The hunt had to come first. A few of the hunters looked up at Dej's approach. She tensed, wondering if they knew what she'd done, but their looks were weary and indifferent.

The other three groups were finishing off their chakaka. The herd had gone, the dust settling. Dej stared at the far group, her mind blank, until one of the nearby clanless shouted at her to start wrapping the meat in the herb-soaked cloths they would use to transport it home. The Sun dipped below the mountains as she worked; she looked up at its last flash and saw Vay and Cal out the corner of her eye. They stood to one side of where Kir lay, arguing.

By the time the kills had been roughly jointed and packed away, it was dark. Dej still couldn't bring herself to look at Kir. She jumped when Vay came over.

"How is she?" She had to ask.

"She's strong, and her animus will try and heal her."

"So she might be all right?' Dej grasped at hope, trying not to think about Mar's badly healed legs; even if Kir lived, she wouldn't be leading anyone anywhere.

Vay shook her head. "I didn't say that."

"But can you help her? Is there something we can do, anything..."

Vay stared past Dej and said quietly, "Something you can do, you mean?"

"Yes. Is there? Because I never meant... yes, anything."

"Wait here." Vay walked off. Fires were being built, burning bones that would otherwise attract scavengers. Exhausted and wrung out, Dej sat down and hugged her knees. Vay returned with a horn beaker which steamed, giving off a bittersweet smell. "This is all we can do," said Vay. "Will you give it to her?"

"Yes. Of course."

Vay looked hard at her, and Dej thought she was going to say something else. Then she handed the beaker over. Once Dej had taken it Vay said, "Remember the good, not the bad, when you go to her, yes? She doesn't need you moping in her face right now."

"I will."

Dej recalled the journey to the clanless camp with Kir, the start of a friendship, all those possibilities. She didn't think about any of her fuckups; certainly not this latest, most terrible one.

When she knelt next to the other girl she thought she was asleep until Kir opened her eyes. She focused on Dej and her lips kinked in what might have been a smile.

"Vay gave me something for you."

"Did she, now?" Kir's voice was a pained whisper. "Give it to me, then."

Dej raised Kir's head and held the beaker to her lips. Kir grimaced at the first taste, and a dribble of pale liquid ran from the corner of her mouth. "Is it too hot?" asked Dej.

Kir made a faint noise in her throat; Dej sensed as much as heard the answer *no*. She held the beaker while Kir drank it dry.

As Dej laid Kir's head back the other girl said, "Do one thing... please. Promise me."

"Anything, yes."

"Forgive yourself." Kir's eyes closed. Dej waited to see if there was more, but Kir had slid into sleep, or unconsciousness.

"I promise," Dej murmured, though she wasn't sure the older girl heard her.

Kir died in the night.

CHAPTER 42

Rhia stared out the back of the cart, starting at every movement on the road, expecting to see horsemen gaining on them from behind. But she saw only peasants and fellow travellers. The reeds gave way to rice fields. She fell into a light doze, fears and unknown possibilities chasing through her head.

When the cart ran over a pothole she twitched awake in time to see Etyan's head loll. He gave a startled grunt.

Rhia almost slid off her seat in her haste to kneel next to her brother.

"Etyan?" she whispered. "Can you hear me?"

Etyan raised a hand, as though fending someone off.

Rhia bent over him. "It's all right. You're safe."

He frowned, eyes still screwed shut. "Wha... where?" His voice was low and feverish.

"Calm now. Shh." He went through a phase, after Father died, of having nightmares; sometimes he would flail and whimper. She used to hold both his hands, and sing to him, just tuneless humming, until he calmed down. She caught herself humming now.

"Ree?" he breathed, his eyes opening to slits.

"That's right."

"How can you be here?"

Captain Sorne was listening at her shoulder. "Don't worry about anything," she said soothingly. "You've been ill. Just rest now."

"But I'm moving, where are–"

"Safe. You're safe." She leaned forward, hugging him. He tensed. He hadn't let her hug him for years. Into his ear she whispered, "Please, you have to trust me. Go back to sleep."

He said nothing, holding himself rigid as a board, but when she withdrew his eyes were closed. She hoped he had enough sense to realize the importance of keeping his own counsel.

Though Etyan remained asleep – or did a good impression of it – Rhia dared not sleep. She could not let Captain Sorne speak to Etyan alone until she had heard his side of the story.

Instead she made herself replay the events in the priory, though considering Breen's death made her gorge rise. There could – there must – be another explanation for his treachery besides Alharet. There were many at court whose motivations were a mystery to her – too many, truth be told.

That assumed Breen had even been a Zekti agent; something else might be going on, something unknown to all of them. Who had those men at the priory been working for? And what had they wanted with Etyan?

Always questions, never answers.

When darkness fell she began to chew the inside of her cheek. If nothing else, it helped keep her awake.

When Lekem pulled over, Rhia looked around; despite herself she had been dozing. There were lights ahead – presumably the inn – beyond the corporal's hunched shoulders. She looked back to Sorne, his face shadowed in the light of the lantern hanging from the carriage ceiling. "Just swapping drivers, m'lady," he murmured.

When Sorne stood up, Etyan blinked and opened his eyes. Rhia wondered how long he had been awake for.

"Good to see you back with us, your lordship."

Etyan gave a groan which might have been an acknowledgment of Sorne's concern or a denial that he really was awake.

"Did you wish for a drink, m'lord?"

"Please." Etyan's voice was hoarse.

Rhia flushed. She should have offered him water when he first awoke. "Let me," she said, and moved across to help Etyan sit up. The way he leaned on her did not feel like fakery. Sorne passed the waterskin and Rhia held it to Etyan's lips.

When he had finished drinking and she returned the waterskin Sorne said, "I'm afraid we won't be stopping at the inn."

Etyan looked up, and she could see the question he wanted to ask – *what inn?* – so she cut him off. "I had assumed not, given the timing."

"However, I have some consolation for his lordship, to make up for the lack of comfort and pleasure."

Rhia was still puzzling over Sorne's words when he reached past her with a smaller flask, of hardened leather. "And what is that?" she barked.

"Something, begging m'lady's pardon, which we did not think to offer you."

Rhia got a whiff of grain spirit from the flask. Etyan's eyes were on it. He had recently discovered the joys of alcohol and had yet to develop the ability to resist it. Rhia helped him drink though she seethed as she did so, angry both at her brother's weakness and at Sorne's assumption that she did not drink. Which she did not, save the occasional fine wine, but she still resented the assumption.

Etyan took a long slug. Rhia eased the flask away when he coughed and liquor dribbled down his chin. She returned the flask to Sorne before Etyan could ask for more, and lowered him back down to rest.

They fell silent as they passed the inn. Rhia wondered whether Sorne would douse the lantern, but a darkened cart would raise more suspicions than one which merely chose not to stop.

As they emerged onto the open road again, Etyan started to snore. Lekem was nodding, and when his head drooped onto his chest Rhia considered trying to rouse Etyan. But Sorne, up front, would still be listening and from the sound of it her brother wasn't feigning sleep. She settled back in her seat and closed her eyes.

She awoke to heat and fuss. The cart had stopped. Lekem was stirring and Etyan's eyes were open, his face drawn. Sorne's voice came from outside, claiming, in his good-natured way, that the offer in question was insulting. They must be at the waystation.

"Etyan, don't worry," hissed Rhia. As he looked her way Sorne stuck his head through the door flap. "Well, we've been ripped off again, but I expected as much. Give us a hand with the luggage, would you, Lekem?"

The other solider stood. Rhia held Sorne's gaze and said, "I'll stay here."

As soon as they were alone she took Etyan's hand.

He stared at her, wide-eyed. "What happened? Where am I?"

"Men came and took you from the priory infirmary–"

"What men?"

"I'm not sure."

"Where's Kefat?"

"Was he looking after you there?"

"He was a healer, yes."

"I'm sorry, but I think the men who took you killed him."

"Oh. That's..." Etyan swallowed. "What's going on, Ree?"

"We followed your abductors and rescued you."

"Why am I in a cart?"

"We're taking you home."

"To Shen? No!"

"Is there a problem here?"

Sorne was all smiles. Rhia clamped her mouth shut.

"Who are you?" asked Etyan.

"I came with your sister to make sure she stayed safe, your lordship. Which she is now, and so are you."

Rhia was not convinced of this, but Sorne continued, "Begging your pardon, but you'll need to change."

"Change?" Etyan looked down at himself. "Oh. Yes."

Rhia said, "I have some of Father's old clothes. Pass that pack please, Sorne." Although there was no one nearby she didn't address Sorne by his rank. She was reluctant to tip Etyan off that these were militiamen, at least until they had had a proper talk. Etyan eyed up the well-worn clothes she extracted from the pack, then his gaze went to Rhia's rough skirt and shirt. Rhia said, "We're travelling incognito."

Etyan nodded slowly, perhaps remembering his experiences on the way to Mirror-of-the-Sky.

He set his mouth, then let his sister help him dress. Sorne and Lekem were in and out ferrying packs, making conversation impossible even if he had been up to it. Outside, the hubbub grew.

When Sorne came back for the final time he held out the flask again. "A drink, m'lord?"

"I had some of this last night, yes?"

"You did, m'lord."

"It's a little early for that, isn't it?" asked Rhia.

"Not as early as you think, m'lady; we had to stop and rest the horse or it'd never have got us here. The caravan will leave soon."

"Then we'd better get on it."

Lekem and Sorne supported Etyan between them, drawing curious glances from the other travellers which Rhia returned with a fierce glare. Mella was nowhere to be seen. Rhia glimpsed Yrif across the camp.

Etyan had accepted Sorne's offer of a drink, and by the time the soldiers settled him in a corner of the passenger wagon he was barely conscious.

"May I have a word outside?" asked Sorne.

"Indeed you may." She had words to say to him. Either her brother was more unwell than he appeared or that flask contained more than spirit.

Sorne grabbed a pack before they left the wagon; Rhia wondered if it contained something else he had kept hidden until now. He led her to the edge of the camp, beyond the awning. The sky was overcast but bright, the light drizzle at odds with the air's silvery glow. "M'lady, there's no way to break this to you gently, so I will just say it. I'm leaving now."

"You're *what*?!"

"You're all but home, and Lekem will look after you and the young lord the rest of the way."

"Where in the Last's name are you going?"

"I have further work I must do for my duke."

"What work?"

"I cannot say. Such are my orders."

"And you knew about this all along? You always planned to abandon us?"

"I knew there would be a parting." He gave a wry smile. "I knew it wouldn't please you."

"It does not!" For a moment she wanted to strike him. But that wouldn't change his mind. "What are your orders?"

"I can't say, the duke–"

"No, not… whatever it is you're about to do." She knew he would never share that; but if he was leaving she had nothing to lose by asking the question which had been eating at her since she accosted the mission to Zekt. "What were your orders regarding my brother?"

"To bring him home."

"And that's all?"

"I'm not sure what you're asking, m'lady."

"If he had refused to come, if he'd resisted when you tried to make him: what then?"

Sorne pursed his lips. "The duke instructed us that, should we be unable to bring him home for any reason, we should ensure he could never be used as a hostage against Shen."

His words sent a chill through her. "Even if that meant killing him?"

"I prayed it would not come to that."

She had known Francin was capable of such expedience, but to hear it spoken of in such a matter-of-fact way... she shivered. "But you would have done it?"

Sorne was silent.

She knew the answer, of course. He was a soldier, and followed orders, as witnessed by Breen's fate. If he had to, he would have killed Etyan. "Did the duke think it likely my brother might not cooperate?"

"He said this was possible, yes." Sorne was not enjoying this.

Neither was she, but she needed the truth. It was her last chance. "But Francin did not say why my brother might not come willingly?"

"No, and it wouldn't be my place to ask."

That was something, at least. But it got her no closer to knowing how much Francin knew about Etyan's possible crime. "And you had drugged spirit to give him."

"The duke advised that the young lord might be distressed or uncooperative."

"Oh, did he? Just that?"

"Just that." Behind them the rhinobeasts were being hitched up. "You should get to the wagon, m'lady."

She would not get more out of him. "And you should go too, if you must." She could not bring herself to wish him luck and turned away, her face hot. Out of the corner of her eye she saw him stride off towards the ironwood trees.

CHAPTER 43

In the cold pre-dawn light, the clanless paid their respects to their dead pathfinder, one at a time. Some spoke to her; some just stood for a moment; a few, including Vay, knelt down and touched Kir's body.

Dej went last. She knew what she had done now and she wanted to throw herself down next to the dead girl and howl, *I killed you*. Instead she locked her knees and made herself look at Kir's slack, dead face.

When they first met, Kir had told her skykin can't kill animuses. That meant they couldn't kill each other. She'd assumed this didn't apply to the clanless, but it did. That was why her body failed her when she tried to drive the bull chakaka towards Cal: her animus had blocked her will.

And that was why Cal and Vay had needed Dej – upset and guilt-ridden, too fucked up to think straight – to give Kir the poison that finished her off. Kir most likely would have died, or at best ended up a cripple; either way she was in no state to be moved, so she'd have had to stay out here, with warriors to guard her, putting them at risk and leaving insufficient clanless to carry home the spoils of the hunt. The needs of the group came first. Had Kir known that? Had she known what was in the cup even if Dej hadn't? Was that why she'd made Dej promise to forgive herself?

The last thing Min had done was ask Dej's forgiveness. Dej

still couldn't forgive Min for her cowardice. Forgiving herself for Kir's death wouldn't be any easier.

As she walked away, not looking back, Cal strode up, a shortsword in his hand. Vay looked up from checking the load in her basket as the seer passed and murmured to Dej, "You won't want to watch this."

Now Kir was dead, they couldn't just leave the animus to rot inside her. Dej asked, "Will he eat it?"

"That's a privilege for the elder, once it dies."

"It's not dead?"

"No. When we die they live on for days, weeks sometimes."

"So we take it back and give it to Mar? Is that why she's so old, because she gets to eat the animuses of dead clan members?" Dej wanted to be appalled, but something – shock, her animus, Kir's last words – made her accept this crazy practice.

"Yes, though it won't keep her going forever."

"And who'll be in charge then? Cal?" Dej was aware of what Cal was doing now, in the corner of her eye, or possibly in her imagination.

"Unlikely. He's got a seer's animus, not an elder's. I imagine there'll be quite a contest when Mar does go. You might want to back Lih."

"Lih?"

"She's slept with both Mar's boys, and whatever else, she's no fool."

The thought of Lih being in charge of the clanless did nothing to improve Dej's mood.

Cal returned with a cloth-wrapped bundle; red dripped from it. "This is your responsibility," he said, and handed the bundle to Dej.

Dej made herself take Kir's severed head, and nod. Because it *was* her responsibility, in so many ways.

• • •

As the clanless were preparing to leave, a fuss went through them. People looked north, to where a lone figure picked its way down the valley. Dej didn't remember anyone leaving the group, and from the attention this person was getting, their arrival wasn't expected. As the figure got closer Dej saw he was all skin and bone, with a withered arm hanging useless by his side. After their initial interest, the clanless looked away, deliberately turning their backs on the new arrival.

Dej went over to Vay. Since their unspoken complicity in Kir's death the healer hadn't said a harsh word to her, and had even deflected Lih's casual malice when the other girl had muttered about Dej's basket being lighter, but stinking worse, than everyone else's.

"Who's that?" Dej asked.

"He has no name now." Vay sounded tired.

Cal was walking out to meet the new arrival.

"But you knew him once?"

"Once. Now we don't. Only Cal can speak with him. He's dead to the rest of us."

"He was clanless?"

Cal stood facing the scrawny skykin; everyone else save Dej was ignoring him.

Vay looked at Dej. "Yes, and now he's nameless too. Look if you have to but remember this: you're looking at failure, at what will happen to you if you're not careful. Do you understand?"

"You cast him out."

"He was disruptive even before the hunt – this hunt, five years back – when he screwed up and got trampled."

"How does he live now?"

"I don't know and I don't care."

Cal must care: he was deep in conversation with the outcast. It looked more like negotiation than argument.

Dej could see ulcers, or possibly grazes, on the outcast's face and arms.

"If he's an outcast, why is Cal talking to him?"

"You need to stop asking questions, Dej. Stop questioning, obey those wiser than you, and learn by your mistakes. You make enough of them."

Dej shut up. The clanless might not be able to kill her, but she had evidence of what they could do right there, in the form of this pathetic outcast.

Cal and the scrawny man spoke for some time. Afterwards, the outcast wandered off to look out over the valley, eyes fixed away from the clanless. Cal came over to the rest of the group, calling out selected individuals including, Dej was unhappy to note, Lih. He took them to one side and spoke to them. Dej strained to hear, but caught only the odd word – "diversion" and "priorities" and "yes, all".

Lih returned with an odd expression on her face. Dej got out of her way and then, when the preparations to leave resumed, shouldered her backpack; she had a disconcerting compulsion to handle the basket as though it were fragile, to shield the animus in its grisly case.

She turned to face upslope once she'd fastened the straps over her shoulders. Lih called out, "Not that way." Dej turned, confused and angry because whatever else, she knew where she was going.

"We're not going back yet." Lih addressed the immediate group. "We're leaving now, and we've got a hard march in front of us."

"Where to?"

Dej was glad Vay asked the question, so she didn't have to.

"Wherever Cal and that one lead us. We need to hurry."

CHAPTER 44

Etyan remained subdued all day, though alert enough once the drugged spirit wore off.

Mella and Preut were in the wagon, and Rhia recognized a handful of others from the journey out; presumably regular traders. There was a higher proportion of Zekti going this way.

When people disembarked to sit round the fire in the evening, she and Lekem helped her brother to the edge of the group. She settled him on the ground, wrapped in her cloak, then turned to Lekem. "We'd like some time alone now please."

Lekem hesitated, looking between the two of them. No doubt Sorne had ordered him to keep a close eye on Lord Harlyn.

Rhia gestured to the noisy darkness beyond the fire. "It's not as though anyone will be going anywhere, will they?"

"As you wish."

Etyan looked up. "See if you can find us some food, will you? I'm famished and that stew looks like it'll be ages yet."

His peremptory tone jarred, but Lekem's nod, before he left, was halfway to a small bow.

When they were alone Rhia sat down and said, "So, why did you leave?" She had decided, during her ruminations in the guesthouse, to try the direct approach. She had waited too long for answers.

Etyan shrugged, one of his favourite gestures.

"Etyan! I need to know."

"Personal stuff."

"Like what? You ran away from your home, from me–"

"I can't face that now. I'm tired."

"You owe me an explanation."

"Why, because you came all this way to get me? You always wanted to see the world."

She ignored this cutting, if accurate, observation. "This isn't about me. I need to know why you ran away to Zekt."

"That's easy: the first caravan I found was going that way. Who are those men, Ree?"

"What men?"

"The two in the cart. The lummox over there and the other one – where is the other one, anyway?"

"If you want me to answer your questions, then you'll need to start answering mine." The conversation was following an all-too-familiar pattern: ignore her, stall her or change the subject; sometimes all three. But they weren't talking about gambling debts or family heirlooms broken by drunken "friends". He had to see how important this was. "Why did you leave Shen? Was it because of the girl?"

Etyan's head whipped round. "What girl?"

"The night – no, the morning – you left, a girl was found dead in the dyers' pools."

Etyan's throat bobbed. Staring into the fire, he said stiffly, "That's a shame. Who was this girl?"

"Her father is a guildmaster in the tanners. She was engaged to a journeyman tailor; they were to be married the next month. Her name was Derry." Though Rhia found it easier to think of her as "the girl", that was unfair, cowardly. And perhaps making her brother consider a young life taken too soon would jolt him into opening up.

"That's very sad." She knew that tone of fake unconcern;

he was upset but refusing to show it. "Ree, people die all the time in the lower city."

"This girl was a guildmaster's daughter. And she didn't just die, Etyan. She was murdered. She was stabbed, then her throat was cut; she may have been... assaulted... too."

Etyan kept his gaze forward but from his expression, she had shocked him. Finally, he said, "I need to rest. Please, I want to lie down before I eat."

Rhia huffed out a breath, conceding defeat. For now. "All right."

Etyan pulled the cloak tight and lay down on his side, shoulders pulled up to his ears. When Rhia looked up she saw they had become the centre of attention. She wanted to drop the humble pretence and tell the other travellers to mind their own business. After all, they were on the way home. She was among, if not friends, then at least people who meant her no harm. But she had thought that in Mirror-of-the-Sky.

Lekem had found a handful of dried fruit; Rhia told him to give it to her for now.

Etyan roused when the stew was served. He sat in silence, miserable and withdrawn, but ate everything put in front of him. When Rhia gave him the fruit afterwards he nodded vague thanks then looked away.

As soon as he had eaten he asked to go back to the wagon. Lekem helped him, and Rhia followed. She hung back in the wagon's doorway, using the time alone to check the wound in her side. It was healing cleanly, just a little sore. The discomfort in her chest was not going away though; she no longer felt that tight, immediate fear for her brother, but a complex and heavy knot of emotions, accumulated from a lifetime of dealing with him, had settled back inside her.

When Lekem returned from helping Etyan into his hammock she took him aside and asked, "Did Sorne tell you he was going to leave us?"

"Yes, m'lady, shortly before we reached the waystation."

"Did he say why?"

"He did not, no."

Well, she had to ask.

In some ways Sorne's betrayal hurt more than Breen's. Breen had acted according to his own code, however misguided that was. But Sorne had known Breen was a traitor, and still let Rhia go into danger, albeit danger he had then saved her from. And he'd planned to abandon her all along. She'd assumed the soldiers' mission was to get her brother back but there must be more to it than that. She thought of all the times the soldiers had been out and about in Mirror, leaving her alone at the guesthouse. They said they were working to maintain their cover. But what else were they doing?

Mella and Preut were laughing by the fire. On impulse, Rhia went over and crouched next to Mella. The pair greeted her, and then Mella observed, "Less coming back than going out, I see."

"I'm sorry?"

"You've lost two of your party. But it looks like you have your young relative back."

"I do, yes." So the prostitute had worked it out. Rhia wished she hadn't.

"He don't look too well," observed Preut from Mella's far side.

"He'll be fine." This wasn't what she wanted to talk about. "How was the last run to Shen?"

"Quiet enough," said Preut, and Mella nodded.

"I don't suppose the drought's broken back home?" *First help me, I'm talking about the weather!*

"Heard they had thunderstorms east of the city," said Preut, then added, "Mind you, that wasn't from a reliable source."

"Ah well." Rhia looked around. Yrif was on the far side of

the fire, helping scour the dinner bowls clean. Suddenly the seer looked up, straight at Rhia. "Think I'll just..."

"You do that, then," said Mella. She sounded amused.

The seer stepped away from her companions as Rhia approached, and sat down, following Rhia's progress with her gaze. Rhia went over and sat next to her.

The seer said, "He is your kin."

"What?" No pleasantries, of course. "Oh, yes, the boy. He's my brother." Had the seer seen the resemblance? Or somehow smelled their connection? Or was there a more mundane explanation, involving Mella's loose tongue.

"He is why you came?"

It took Rhia a moment to realize she was being asked a question. "Yes. I came to bring him home. He's my only living relative."

"He is damaged."

"Damaged? He's been ill."

"No. This is something more. A change is upon him."

"A change? What do you mean?"

Yrif spread her hands; a small gesture, but Rhia thought it signified high emotion. "It is beyond us."

"What do you mean?" She noted the use of *us* – was the seer drawing on the knowledge of ages, held by her animus?

"We have no experience, no comparison, for this. I would look closer, examine him."

Rhia could imagine Etyan's response to that. "Perhaps later. Right now he isn't at his best."

The skykin gave a curt nod. "Yes. Later." For a moment Rhia thought she was being dismissed, but Yrif's face settled back into its usual implacable expression and she said, "Let us converse, Rhia of Shen."

Rhia got out her notebook. She had devoted some time in Mirror-of-the-Sky to preparing a list of questions for the seer.

• • •

The next day brought them to the foothills leading up into the Northern Divide. Etyan remained taciturn, though when they disembarked for the night he said he could walk unaided. Rhia took that as a good sign. "You're feeling better, then?"

"Yes."

"What ailed you? A fever?"

"A fever. Yes."

She thought that was all she would get, but then Etyan said, "How are the cats?"

"They're fine. Jili had six kittens." This was frivolous talk, but it beat sullen silence.

"Did you keep any?"

"One, like last time." She needed to keep him talking. "The new housemaid is settling in, though she can still be a bit of a scatterbrain."

"And everyone at court?"

"Much the same." He took more of an interest in court than she did; she searched for something else to say. "The Orasians came. Alharet has worked her magic, so Yorisa's due to be betrothed to Lord Magran as soon as she's old enough." *And Alharet might be a traitor to Shen.*

She took a deep breath, because such banality burned when there was so much of import to be said. "And Mercal Callorn has asked for my hand in marriage."

He looked away, the ghost of a grimace on his face.

The "marriage conversation", as she thought of it, had been one of several she had put off, or that Etyan had evaded, back home. But they had ground to make up before they could even get back to where they had been. And, after the direct approach had made him shut down, she needed to make concessions. One was obvious. "Etyan, I'm sorry for what I said to you."

"You are?" He looked surprised; was an apology from her really so rare? "What you said when?"

"That last night, before you left. When we argued. You were drunk, so I'm not sure you remember..."

"I remember. You made it about Mother."

"I did. And I shouldn't have."

"No, but... you were angry."

"Yes. I'm sorry."

He nodded. "I wish I'd known her."

"I wish you had too."

"So tell me about her."

He had never asked this before. When Father was alive, bearing his loss every day, it had been too painful. After Father died, Rhia had come to think of herself as the substitute parent, fulfilling both roles for her younger brother. They rarely spoke of their real parents.

"Well, she was beautiful." Rhia wasn't sure of that, having little to judge against, but in this case a little lie was permissible. "But frail too. My first memory of her is one of my earliest memories. We were sitting in the villa gardens. It was a dry year, so I must have been about four years old. She made lace, did you know that? I wanted to see, and she tipped the cushion towards me, and smiled..." Rhia had never spoken about this to anyone. Homely memories welled up from some deep bright place where they had sat, unexamined, for years. She recalled what she could of the mother Etyan had never met, and told him about her. He listened without interruption.

When Lekem cleared his throat apologetically and held out two bowls of stew, she stopped and focused on Etyan's face. She found his expression hard to read. But she thought she saw grief for what was lost, much as she felt herself at that moment.

After the meal, Rhia searched for some way to restart the conversation. They had gone straight from mundane fripperies to an emotionally difficult subject they had been avoiding for years, but still had not tackled the current issue.

Before she could speak, Etyan said, "I need time to think things through, Ree. Get some perspective."

"Of course." What else could she say? And she had other business, matters of the mind to distract her from the raw pain of her suddenly exposed heart. "Do you want to be alone?"

"I... yes, I think I do."

"I'll leave you be, then." She stood up.

"Where are you going?"

"To speak to the skykin seer."

"Really?" Etyan looked confused, and a little disdainful – what Rhia thought of as his *unable to grasp my eccentric sister's odd obsessions* face. They had slipped back onto old ground already. "Why?"

"Because she knows some amazing things." That came out wrong. Disdain for his disdain would not help. "If you need me, just wave, or come over. I'd rather talk to you." Another small but necessary lie.

CHAPTER 45

The following night they camped up on the plateau, which put them in the vicinity of the House of the Ancients. Rhia considered asking Yrif if she could spare an escort to look for it, though the thought of meeting another nightwing made her shudder. But she needed to be available for Etyan, in case he felt ready to talk.

Tonight's skies were the clearest she had seen in weeks, and before she went to talk to the seer she decided to spend a while observing the heavens.

The Matriarch had already risen. When she knelt down to balance her sightglass on the wagon's central wheel she found the star was still gibbous. And there was another small star close to it again, in the same position as before; no, a little farther out. Quite a coincidence, considering the Stray was in a different part of the sky this time.

She looked down as something pricked her leg, then yelped. A glowing blue sphere the size and texture of a cat's hairball was stuck to her bare shin. She brushed it off, making her hand tingle, then looked up to see another half dozen, rolling in on the wind.

"Everyone inside."

She recognized Yrif's voice, and backed out from under the wagon. Skykin were guiding the shadowkin into the passenger wagon; the experienced travellers took it in their stride, muttering about how dinner would be late tonight. Some skykin set about crushing the glowing balls with bone blades or bare feet. They must be blowballs. Not a serious danger but they could sting bare flesh; shadowkin flesh anyway. When a small one came to rest just in front of her Rhia paused and stamped on it; it gave off a whiff like rotten wood. She scraped her boot off on the wagon steps to dislodge the garish filaments and went inside.

After a short while Preut, watching from the doorway, announced that the swarm had passed. The shadowkin emerged from the wagon. The ground was spattered with blowball remnants. Etyan swung the cloak off his shoulders to cover the mess, sitting on one edge, leaving enough room for her.

As Rhia settled next to him she said, "You're looking better." Other than his skin, which remained raw and flaky, he appeared healthy enough now. Perhaps whatever oddness Yrif had scented on him was also fading, as the seer had made no further comment.

"I feel pretty good." He looked past her to where Lekem crouched on the bare ground. "We'd like to speak alone now, please."

Lekem nodded and stood. Rhia stayed silent, letting her brother lead the conversation, relieved he finally was.

Etyan sighed and said, "I don't want to go back."

Rhia resisted the urge to point out that, given they travelled with the caravan, he didn't have much choice. She certainly was not going to mention the possibility that the duke would send men to meet them at the waystation. Instead she asked, "Why not?"

"The life I had... it's not what I want."

Again Rhia bit her tongue. Talk of duty and obligation would drive him away. "So do you want to return to Zekt?"

"I... The eparch's amazing. It's like he sees into you, sees what you really are. And he doesn't judge. He wants everyone to find their own path. He helped me give up the kreb, and start to look at my life, think about where I was heading."

That Etyan had kicked a bad habit was good news. That he might start taking personal responsibility was even better. If only she could get him to come home willingly too. "I heard him preach while I was in Zekt. I was impressed."

"You were at the priory? When?"

"We visited on a restday to, ah, see what the setup was."

"You and your 'guards'? How did you know where I was?"

"The duke has his spies." There was no point denying it.

Etyan pressed his lips together.

"Is that what you want?" she asked, when it became obvious he wasn't going to say any more. "A religious life, in Zekt?" She kept her voice gentle, taking care not to express her considerable scepticism at the idea of her feckless little brother taking holy vows.

He stared ahead and whispered. "I don't know."

After the meal Rhia asked him if he wanted to come and meet the seer, both in case it helped him, and because she wanted to know what the seer made of the "change" she had referred to. But he shook his head, and fixed his gaze on the flames.

Light rain set in overnight. The next day Rhia took advantage of the flat terrain to get out her papers. Her fellow travellers stared at this unexpected behaviour. Lekem did a passable impression of his absent captain when he cleared his throat disapprovingly; Etyan looked on in amusement. She ignored them all. She wanted to get down her notes from the previous few nights' conversations with the seer while their talk was still fresh in her mind.

Some of the seer's information supported what Rhia already knew. For example, Yrif confirmed that skykin children were sent to crèches because they were born into a place too hot and bright for them, needing milk the mother could no longer produce. Abandoning them was an act of kindness, not cruelty; as Yrif put it, "To keep them is to kill them."

They also spoke of subjects not covered by the enquirers' writings, such as personal decoration. The skykin did not enhance or ornament their bodies; such clothes as they wore were purely functional, covering their delicate parts, protecting themselves from their environment, carrying items of use. When Rhia asked why this was, Yrif asked her, in return, whether she wore her mask for others or for herself. Rhia thought for a while, then said, "Both, I think."

"Yet you never see yourself."

This was not entirely true; one of Alharet's most treasured possessions was a mirror of beaten bronze, which she had let Rhia use. But she knew what the seer meant. "No, but people can recognize me by it. So though I wear it in part to save their feelings when they see my scars, my mask is also part of my identity." She thought for a moment. "Ah, I see. You do not need such external trappings to know each other, nor such individualistic habits to know yourself, because of your animuses."

"Quite so."

Rhia knew better than to ask *how* the skykin knew each other without physical signifiers; another case of describing colour to a blind man. "Yet you decorate your rhinobeasts with studs and plaits and suchlike. Is it because they have no animus, so are not so easy to identify?"

"In part. But it is also self-expression, done for our own amusement."

"Ah!" Rhia had read discussions of whether the skykin had art; the consensus was that they did not. "So you... indulge your artistic drive in this way?"

"Those who wish to, yes. Some interests and urges can be retained from the human part of the symbiote–"

"The what? Symbiote?"

Yrif brushed a long-fingered hand across her bare chest. "This. What was once shadowkin. Any who retain such desires after bonding may express them by personalizing things in their lives that matter to them, such as animal companions, or parting-gifts."

"Yes, you mentioned those..."

And Yrif went on to explain this intimate skykin custom, which no enquirer had ever written about.

Rhia also asked whether it was true skykin did not take a daily siesta. Yrif confirmed this, and Rhia asked whether needing less sleep was another benefit conferred by the animus. Given she often spent much of the night up on her observation platform, she usually took a siesta at home. Father, on the other hand, had disliked breaking up his day with a nap when he was deep in a project; however, if he did not rest, he found he was less productive the next day.

"Perhaps," Yrif had said. "Certainly we feel no need to sleep during daylight hours. We sleep when we do, and wake when we do, because that is what the world tells us."

Rhia had been brought up to believe the shadowkin were the true descendants of the Children of the First, and the skykin were degenerates. Surely those with the most right to the world would be those most in tune with its natural rhythms? It was a disturbing thought, challenging a fundamental tenet of shadowkin existence.

Other conversations openly contradicted accepted knowledge. One of these was about the Harbinger. Rhia had assumed that the lack of reference to the hopefully-soon-to-return "bearded star" in her older papers was down to chance, that there did not happen to be any such writings in the collection she had inherited – after all, even the best parchment degenerated over time. She had assumed that, like every other heavenly body, the Harbinger had always been present, albeit intermittently. But assumption was a symptom of a lazy mind. The seer – or rather her animus – recalled a time before the "nightflower", as the skykin poetically described it, had graced the sky for a few months every three or four shadowkin generations.

Rhia was used to uncritically devouring the wisdom of the natural enquirers but perhaps she put too much faith in words written by men she would never meet.

The caravan reached the head of the pass in late afternoon, by which time the rain beat solidly on the wagon roof. When the caravan stopped for the beasts to be unhitched she put her papers back into her satchel. As they started off again her thoughts returned to the star which appeared so close to the Matriarch. She must observe again tonight, if the rain abated and if that part of the sky was not hidden by the ravine walls.

A shout came from outside. Rhia frowned at the interruption to her thoughts.

The next shout was closer, and clear enough to make out the words.

"Hold, or pay the price!"

Chapter 46

Dej hurtled down the slope, mud and rocks sliding away from her as she half ran, half fell towards the caravan.

"I said, hold, or pay the price!"

The wagons lurched to a halt at Cal's third cry. Dej stopped ankle deep in muck, breathing hard, and drew her knife.

Around her the other clanless were emerging from their positions. The ambush site had been picked with care: on the flat the caravan could outrun the clanless but on the slope, the wagons were vulnerable.

She had a good view of the three skykin sitting up front of the lead wagon. These "true" skykin weren't so different to the clanless when viewed through what she now thought of as her "old" vision. But her other senses picked up an additional aspect to their being, a vibrant sense of connection the clanless lacked.

The skykin in the middle of the three stood up, then looked down at Cal and the halfdozen warriors flanking him. With the rhinobeasts hitched at the back of the wagon to act as brakes, there was nothing except height between them. The woman had an air of easy authority.

For a while no one spoke. Dej shifted, trying to keep a stable footing in the mud.

Finally, the skykin leader said, "The luggage is in this wagon." Beside her, the other two skykin stood too, ready to jump down.

Cal shook his head. "We don't want shadowkin gear."

Dej started; when Lih had told her they were attacking a shadowkin caravan she'd assumed it was to get the shadowkin food they needed.

"Are you here for one of our beasts, then?"

"No," said Cal, "we're not here to steal from you."

"Then why have you disrupted our journey?"

"We want one of your passengers."

The skykin considered for a moment. "The clans accept that sometimes your people will rob us. But assaulting those we convey breaks our covenant with the shadowkin nations. This is a grave crime."

"We don't want to assault him, just return him to Zekt, where he belongs."

That made sense, given the direction their outcast guide had come from.

When the skykin leader didn't respond, Cal continued, "We outnumber you three to one. If we cut the traces on your beasts the wagons will crash and none of the shadowkin will survive. Let us have this boy and the rest of your passengers can continue on their way."

The silence stretched. Dej blinked water out of her eyes. The rain was getting harder.

Finally, the skykin pointed at Cal. "This will be remembered," she said.

Cal threw up a hand as though to say he didn't much care, then pointed to Jeg and Vas. "Come with me you two." Leaving four warriors armed with bolas and throwing clubs to cover the skykin at the front he walked round the wagon. As he passed Dej's position he nodded at her. "You too." She tagged along behind. Her position with the clanless, such as it was, hung by a thread. Or as Lih had put it: *Given the choice I'd throw you out but Cal wants to give you another chance to prove yourself – or fuck up again.*

Cal walked upslope to the passenger wagon. A dozen clanless surrounded the two rhinobeasts attached to the back of it, though at a safe distance; the animals shifted in the traces, and their musk was strong. Dej tensed as she, Cal, and the two warriors ducked between the animals. The door in the back of the wagon was closed. Vas looked to Cal, who nodded. He wrenched it open.

Cries of surprise and consternation came from inside. Vas and Jeg brandished batons and swords in the doorway as Cal shouted, "Stay calm and you'll all be fine."

The shouts died down. The two warriors went first, then Cal. When she followed him, she was briefly overwhelmed by the dark stink of stale sweat and sudden fear. As her senses adjusted, vague figures in the dim interior resolved into shadowkin; half wore light, loose clothing and had dark hair; the rest looked like the staff at the crèche, with paler hair and brighter, tighter-fitting clothing.

The shadowkin pressed themselves back, staring in wide-eyed terror at the intruders.

"I am looking," said Cal, "for a young man named Etyan. Is he here?"

The shadowkin's eyes darted, looking to each other in fear and confusion. None of them spoke.

Cal strode up to the nearest young man, one of those with dark hair, and asked softly, "Are you Etyan?"

The youth and his older companion both shook their heads, not quite in time, the older man murmuring, "No, no. We don't know any Etyan." His companion's glance darted away, across the wagon. Cal spotted this, and turned. There were three people over that side who Dej would describe as young men: one who sat rigid next to an old man and a pair who sat together, next to a woman who had something wrong with her face. The first was of the dark-haired shadowkin, the other two were fair-haired, one lightly built, one well muscled enough to put up a fight.

Cal strode across the wagon to the dark-haired young man. "So, are you Etyan?" he asked. He kept his question low and calm.

"No, I'm not." The young man's voice came out as a high squeak.

Cal nodded and turned to the pair of young men. Before he could speak the larger one stood, hand going to his waist. He was fast, and managed to draw his dagger, but the clanless were faster. Vas swept in with a heavy slash, knocking the dagger away. Jeg's staff connected with his wrist and the man staggered back. She followed up with a brutal jab to his chest which floored him.

Pandemonium erupted. Shadowkin leapt to their feet, or cowered back, crying and begging.

"Quiet!" roared Cal. "Calm down!"

His shout filled the wagon. People sat, hands out in surrender. Vas and Jeg stood back to back, covering the assembled shadowkin with raised weapons. Dej brandished her knife and tried to look threatening.

Cal leant down to the man on the floor and said, "I really hope that the answer to the question I'm about to ask you is "No". Are you Etyan?"

"Last take you," gasped the man.

Cal gestured to Dej. "If he tries anything, stab him." Dej came over, though her training hadn't covered situations like this. Cal put a foot on the man's shoulder then bent over him. "I'll ask again: are you Etyan?"

The man closed his eyes. "Yes. I am."

"Did you know we can smell lies?" asked Cal conversationally. He stepped over the wounded man to face the other young man. This one had a rash on his face and a smell at once unnerving and intriguing. "Are you Etyan?"

The woman next to the boy said, "Leave us alone. You

have no right to disrupt our journey." She wore a tanned leather mask over the left-hand side of her face.

"Yet here we are. If the boy won't speak I'll ask you. Is he Etyan?"

"He is, damn you," said the woman. "And if you want him you'll have to come through me."

"That's an option."

The fallen man coughed; blood sprayed from his mouth. Jeg's blow must have damaged something inside. Cal frowned at him then said, "I don't think you'll make it home, my friend. You've got a long slow death ahead of you, I fear. Let us help." He looked up and murmured, "Dej, finish him."

Dej stared, shocked and unsure. The masked woman gasped. The boy huddled close to her; Dej had never seen anyone look so scared.

Beside her Jeg growled, "You deaf, girl?"

Jeg said she was too reluctant to commit in a fight, that she was squeamish. Now she had to prove otherwise.

Dej knelt. The man on the floor was muttering under his breath, blowing bubbles of blood. Coward: he was begging for mercy. She couldn't afford to show mercy. No, this was mercy, as Cal had said. And to survive, she must do what Cal said. For now.

She knew where the heart was. She brought her knife round to his chest. Then she pushed it in, hard.

The knife, lacking a point, caught. She hammered the pommel, driving it in. The blade broke skin, sawed past bone, buried itself in softness. Blood welled. The man's muttering become loud enough for Dej to make out the words "...in the hands of the First...." before his breath hitched and stuttered, making a hard *huh-huh-huh* sound, then wheezing away. He'd been praying, not begging. His body went slack, and a last surge of red rose around the knife. She smelled blood and shit and a nameless absence.

Cal and the woman were still talking, but she couldn't look away from the man she'd just killed. It had been easy. He hadn't fought back. He'd been defenceless.

Overhead Cal said, "As you wish. You'll be the guarantee." Then to Vas, "Bring them both."

Beside her Jeg muttered, "Come on, girl," and kicked her, just hard enough to break the spell. Dej began to struggle to her feet. "Your knife!"

Cal and his captives moved past her – the woman was coming as well, it appeared. None of them looked at her. Dej tugged the knife. It came free with a gush of dark blood. There being nothing else to clean it on she wiped the knife on the dead man's clothing.

She stood on legs suddenly too long for her. The two shadowkin had been bundled up in cloaks and were being pushed out the wagon door. Dej followed, the last to leave. As she emerged from between the rhinobeasts, she tried to sheathe her knife. But her hands trembled, and the handle was sticky with blood. She leant over, bracing her free hand on her thigh, and threw up.

CHAPTER 47

I'm dreaming. This is a nightmare. Any moment now I'll wake up.
But Rhia knew better.

Even through the cloak – made of supple leather, unlike the caravan skykin's woven ones – the air burned. She squinted out from under the hood as they emerged onto the road. The world was unbelievably bright, fine details seared to vague white – and that was with an overcast sky.

The rogue skykin filed up the road, taking her and Etyan with them; the caravan skykin hung back, letting them go.

Any moment now Yrif would order her people to attack, and mount a rescue.

Again, Rhia knew better. The rogues outnumbered Yrif's people, and the seer had to put the safety of the caravan first. If saving it meant sacrificing some of the travellers, she would. The duke's logic: the few suffer so the majority may thrive.

As they left the caravan behind, Etyan dodged out of the line and began to run back down the road.

"Etyan! No!" *What was he thinking?*

A hand clamped round Rhia's arm. Something whistled off to one side and Etyan went down with a shriek. He had managed less than a dozen steps.

Someone grasped Rhia's other arm. She turned to say they could stop that, as she had no intention of trying anything, and found herself facing the bandit who had killed Lekem.

Female, by the look of her chest, and with something about her eyes that made Rhia think she was young.

The rogues retrieved Etyan. They'd brought him down with a string between weighted gourds – bolas; she had read of such weapons.

The rogue's leader, a male, came over and addressed Etyan, "I didn't realize you were an idiot." He drew his dagger. "Perhaps we need to be clearer, spell things out." He stepped up to Rhia and brought his knifepoint up to her neck. Rhia stiffened but didn't flinch. "If you misbehave, she suffers." This man was a bully. She hated bullies.

He stepped back, sheathing his knife. To the rest of the group he said, "Just in case these two are as dumb as they seem, let's keep a tighter rein on them."

A skykin came forward with a coil of dark fibrous rope, and tied Rhia's hands together in front of her with one end, then did the same to Etyan, who stood like all hope, all fight, had gone out of him. The skykin girl took the middle of the rope, leaving Etyan and her to be dragged along like the helpless baggage they had become.

As they set off again Rhia heard the caravan moving away behind them. She refused to despair.

When they came up to the head of the pass they left the road, skirting the plateau's edge. They were heading east, or perhaps northeast. Rhia watched her footing, aware of how the life out here could hurt her. Etyan reeled and stumbled. He fell twice, once with a yelp, once in silence, and had to be helped up by their captors.

Why was this happening? These rogues, these *bandits* were a poor-looking lot; one of them, who was walking up front with the leader, appeared half dead. Someone must be offering them a reward for Etyan's capture. Had whoever hired the men in the priory also hired these skykin? It had to be someone with influence. And she still had no idea why.

What made her brother so valuable?

They carried on when darkness fell, leaving the plateau to head along a rocky gorge. Although the rain had thinned to a light drizzle, the ground was soaked, the rocks slippery. Rhia feared for her ability to get through such terrain in the dark with her hands tied, and was relieved when the bandits stopped and made camp. Bizarrely, the first stage of this involved rummaging around amongst tumbled rocks for half-buried baskets, one for each bandit. How far had they come, to need to leave so many supplies? Could they not live off the land, as the caravan skykin did? The ripe, meaty smell from the baskets added further mystery.

The skykin girl handed the rope to another bandit and went to retrieve her basket. This second bandit told Rhia and Etyan to sit. Rhia was glad to, and even gladder when the younger skykin returned with a waterskin, which she offered round.

The girl pointed to her satchel. "What's in there?" She sounded as young as Rhia had thought, though also like she was trying to be fierce.

"Just papers."

"Papers?" From her tone this girl had even less respect for learning than Etyan did.

"Yes. And when you ransom me I'll be a lot more valuable if I still have them."

The skykin sounded dubious. "Let me see."

Rhia was in no position to object. The young rogue knelt next to her and rummaged around in her satchel; even if this skykin could read, in this darkness she would not be able to see what the papers said. When the girl pulled out the sightglass, Rhia bit her lip.

"What's this, then?"

"Just a toy. A trinket."

The skykin shook the sightglass, held it up to look at – though not through – and finally said, "Looks pointless."

Rhia was not going to argue. The skykin glanced across to where their leader was directing the building of a fire, a task made harder by the persistent damp. Then she strode over to where her basket was propped against a rock and put the sightglass in it, placing it with unexpected care. "It's safe with me," she assured Rhia. Rhia doubted that, but bit her tongue.

Once the fire was lit, cloth-wrapped meat was taken from backpacks and rolled into the flames. The smell of cooking made Rhia's stomach grumble. Their guard stayed close. When she was called over to fetch food Rhia hissed to Etyan, "We'll get out of this, I promise."

"I can't see how." His tone was desolate.

"Do you have any idea who hired these bandits?"

"No. Wish I did."

Their young guard returned with a roll of meat which she was already tearing into. As she finished her meal she looked over and shrugged, which was not a gesture Rhia had seen any other skykin make. "We don't have any shadowkin food."

This struck Rhia as bad planning, though she said nothing.

Another of the rogues called the girl called over. The two of them came back shortly afterwards and re-tied her and Etyan's hands behind their backs. Then they bound them together back-to-back, wrapped in a single cloak.

Etyan held himself tense during the process but when their captors moved off she felt his shoulders, pressed into hers, begin to shake. She reached for his hands, and managed to catch hold of his bound fingers; he grasped at her hand so hard she winced.

"It's a nightmare, Ree." His voice was a tearful whisper.

Having thought the same earlier, she decided not to point out that nightmares ended in thankful waking. Instead, she searched for hope. "The duke will hear of this, and act."

"Hear of it how?"

"Mella and Preut – the, ah, lady of the night and her brother

– they're his agents. They'll report to the duke as soon as the caravan reaches Shen. We're in Shenese jurisdiction on this side of the mountains."

"Even this far from home?"

"Yes." Rhia answered with more certainty than she felt; the extension of a shadowland's influence into the skyland nearby was a nebulous arrangement the skykin barely acknowledged, and Rhia did not recall it ever being tested. But they needed all the comfort they could get.

"And how will anyone find us out here?"

Rhia had been thinking the same. And she was not going to share Sorne's admission that the duke would rather his relatives were dead than used against him as political hostages. "I don't know," she admitted, "but he will come for us. Until he does we have to stay alert, act smart and not lose hope."

"I'll try."

Unless she wanted to give him unrealistic reassurances there was nothing more to say. She kept hold of his hand until his breathing evened out and he released her fingers.

Rhia thought she would be too uncomfortable to sleep, but finally she fell into an uneasy dream-haunted doze.

CHAPTER 48

Whenever she closed her eyes, Dej saw blood, welling up round her knife. Cal would've noticed how she hesitated today. At the time she'd only cared about proving herself, but now she wondered if he'd set her up. The order to kill had been quiet; she doubted the shadowkin had heard it. But they'd seen who stabbed the defenceless man. That they were probably doing him a mercy wasn't what the shadowkin would remember. They'd remember what she did, not why. And if the shadowkin came looking for the clanless who'd struck the lethal blow, she had no doubt Cal and Mar would give her up.

Assuming she didn't fuck up again before then. Looking after the prisoners was humiliating work, but it was work she had to do right. She probably shouldn't have taken the shadowkin woman's wooden tube, but it was some small thing for herself, and no one would challenge her taking it.

The next day the rain was back, harder than ever. According to campfire chatter last night, it didn't usually rain here, at least not like this.

After the rope was nearly jerked out of her hand when the boy prisoner stumbled yesterday, and knowing the sort of country ahead, Dej decided to re-tie the pair along the rope rather than at the ends, leaving them a free hand to reduce the chance of falling over. Lih had made it clear that Dej had to get approval for any decision, no matter how trivial, so she discussed it with her hut-mate first, gritting her teeth at Lih's insistence that she double-check the knots.

The shadowkin had to be helped to their feet, and the woman had a rash on her chin where she'd got stung or bitten overnight. She watched Dej re-tie the rope in silence. The boy barely noticed what was going on. He looked so miserable. Pretty though, better looking than any of the boys in the crèche, though with that oddness about him. Seen side-by-side, the two shadowkin looked similar; crèche tattle said that was the case with relatives, so maybe they were related. Mother and son? No, the woman wasn't that old. Brother and sister, then? Whoever the woman was, she cared about the boy enough to risk her life for him.

Dej quashed that line of thought. She couldn't afford to think of these shadowkin as people. They were booty, and a test she had to pass.

Rhia lowered her hand from scratching her itchy chin, then rubbed at her other wrist where the rope chafed. The backs of her hands were sore and hot to the touch.

"Leave the rope alone!" Their guard turned. She must have felt the rope jerk. Rhia held her free hand up to show she wasn't trying to escape. Where would they go, out here? She glanced behind, where Etyan staggered along, eyes on the ground.

At least the Sun was still behind clouds, though the rain was so persistent that the leather cloak had soaked through, leaving her sweltering in warm dampness. At one point, straightening from hauling herself up between two boulders, she almost threw her hood back, just to get some air. Fortunately, common sense cut in.

The land here was barren but not lifeless. Knobbly hand-sized patches of something like lichen spattered the grey rocks with mauve and dark green. Touching one in passing she noted how it gave then sprang back; she was reminded of the bath sponge she had bought from a merchant who claimed to have got it from the skyland. Perhaps he had. And as she heaved herself across a tilted slab, she saw movement in a crack in the rock, something as long as her arm, turning sinuously.

Whatever else, she was seeing the skyland by day. Few shadowkin did that and lived.

The gorge widened, allowing for the growing stream running down its centre. The skykin veered up the slope, until they were walking along the valley's side, halfway between stream and skyline.

The land opened out further, and then the valley floor dropped away. The stream tumbled over a rocky lip to disappear into a dark ravine. The distant thunder of water came from below, along with puffs of fine mist.

The valley side was covered in low vegetation, a saffron-coloured grasslike plant with patches of dark orange. It smelled a bit like wild thyme and was thin and springy enough to step on, though slippery in the damp. The slope was made more treacherous by rocky outcrops varying in size from a person's head to a small house.

The bandits leaned left, into the slope, as they traversed it. Rhia followed suit, careful to step where their jailer did. Even so, several times her feet slipped, and she had to catch herself on the slope, grabbing at the sort-of grass for purchase.

The rope jerked again. Dej looked back to see the shadowkin woman making heavy weather of the slope. Dej looped the rope tighter around her wrist. If the stupid cow fell there'd be trouble. She should have used two separate ropes, one for the boy and one for the woman, and made the boy go ahead rather than dragging along at the back. That way if the woman fell, she could let her go without risking the main prize. Too late now.

Not that they'd be her problem much longer. Once they were through this valley Cal, together with half a dozen hunters and the outcast guide, would cut northwest to drop the captives off at the eastern edge of Zekt, from where they'd return loaded down with food. Mar hadn't been lying when she said they didn't steal food from the shadowkin; they got paid in it by shadowkin who needed agents out in the skyland. To hear the clanless talk, this job was the most important for years.

Dej would head northeast with the bulk of the clanless. Gel had been one of the dozen or so clanless who'd stayed at the settlement, so Dej hoped she'd get to pathfind the way back, though if the clanless had raided the caravan before they probably knew the route. She realized she'd already adjusted to Kir's death. Forgiving herself was another matter.

The mountains enfolded her, and while her feet found their way she took comfort in the land's stable, uncritical endurance. Soil over rock; plants binding soil. Stable, fixed, safe.

And then it wasn't.

Far upslope, a tiny movement at first, sodden roots and earth easing free of the bedrock below. Easing became slipping became ripping, the movement slow as a falling leaf, inevitable as a dropped stone.

She stopped dead.

Between one breath and the next, the weight of sodden soil and plants pulled a huge slab of ground away from the mountain.

Landslide! Dej threw herself down flat.

The roar of tearing earth drowned out the thunder of water from below. Someone shouted. Everything slid away. Dej began to slide with it, fingers digging into the treacherous ground even as it shifted under her. Soil and small stones pelted her. But she had a grip on the land. She could ride this out.

Or so she thought.

Something pulled at her wrist, tugging her free of the slope. She fell faster, no longer moving with the land but half falling, half tumbling, grasping at the stupid scrap of rope tied round her wrist just for something to grab onto.

She was heading for the ravine. She was going to die. *No! I got this far, I can't die like this!*

She hit something. Bounced off. A moment later her wrist jerked upwards. She cried out and got a mouthful of mud.

Debris rained over her. But she was no longer falling.

I'm falling, I'm going to die!

Rhia flailed for purchase. There was none. She was turning even as she hurtled down the slope.

Falling!

This is it, I'm–

Not falling.

Breath exploded out of her. She'd landed on something soft and damp over something hard and unyielding. Something safe. She inhaled and pressed herself into mud while the mountain washed past her.

Eventually, the fall of soil and gravel became a trickle. She raised her head, blinking loose earth out of her eyes.

Everything was at the wrong angle.

She closed her eyes again, gathered her strength, then tried looking round again, more carefully.

Her fall had been broken by a massive object poking up from the valley side. A big rock? Probably, and hitting it might have killed her if not for the mass of mud and sodden vegetation already caught on it, cushioning her fall. She'd landed sideways, with the mountain on her left, draped along the flat surface like a ragdoll.

Her right arm hurt. Broken? No, just trapped under her at an awkward angle. She eased her left arm back and levered herself up enough to look around. The top of the rock was flat, or made so by the muck and debris caught on it, forming a ledge wide enough to sit up on. Brilliance beat down from above; she kept her gaze low.

Something was pulling on the arm she was lying on. Of course: the rope! And Etyan was on the other end of it. She lowered herself again, using the weight of her body to pin her arm, rather than have to support Etyan's weight. Her body felt weak and fragile.

"Etyan!" Her feeble call was barely audible over the tumult of water below. She drew breath and shouted louder, "Etyan, are you all right!"

"I'm here!"

Thank the First! She raised herself again, hoping for a sight of him. The strain on her wrist increased – and it was from two directions. The bandit girl must still be attached to the other end of the rope. Etyan and the skykin were strung either side of the rock that had broken Rhia's fall, like a pair of market scales.

"Etyan, are you injured?"

"I'm... I'm not hurt. Dangling like a party treat though."

"Stay calm, we can get out of this."

Hauling him up was not an option. Even if she could free her arm, she doubted she was strong enough. And there was the pull coming from the other side. "Hey, you down there, skykin girl!" Rhia called.

A pause, then, "Yes?"

"Are you hurt?"

Silence, then, "No."

Good. So, this just came down to an engineering problem. "Are you facing in or out?"

"What?"

"Can you see the sky?"

"All I can see is dirt."

"Right. There should be a rock to your left. Reach out for it!"

"Why?"

"Because the alternative is that I use this sharp rock up here to cut through the rope you're holding onto, and you fall. Makes no difference to me." Rhia hoped this wasn't one of the skykin who sensed lies.

"Uh, I can see the rock."

"Good. You need to get onto it, and cling on. Etyan?"

"Yes."

"The rock's on your right, so it's the same for you. Except," she laughed a little hysterically, "there's no risk of me cutting you free."

"Glad to hear it." He sounded pretty hysterical himself.

This would be easier without her pack. But even now, Dej couldn't bring herself to ditch Kir's possibly still-living animus.

She kicked out to the left, and on the second attempt stubbed her toes on rock; she winced. On the third attempt she got her foot into a gap in the rock. She clung with her toes, then used her left hand to get a hold farther up. Her right arm, which she hung by, was going numb.

She turned her head round to face the rock. It was dark grey, shot through with seams of pale crystal. She felt the shock of small lives disrupted by the landslide.

She gripped the rock tighter, working her fingers into crevices, gripping with her toes until they cramped. Then she hauled herself closer.

From above, the shadowkin woman called, "That's it, both of you. Now you need to climb up."

She brought her right foot round, twisting herself into a

knot, found an indentation, and jammed her foot into it. She pressed herself to the rock, clinging close with three limbs, cheek against the rough stone.

She could hear the woman shouting encouragement to the boy, though her words were hard to make out over the rushing water from below. Then she called down, "I don't know your name."

The woman was talking to her. "I'm Dej."

"Right, Dej. I need you to climb now. Use the rope for support."

Who did this shadowkin think she was? Dej answered her own question: someone who knew what she was doing. And someone she was still attached to. "All right," she called up. Having to hold the rope was a hindrance, leaving only three limbs to climb with. But if she screwed up, it might save her. She bent her left elbow and hauled herself up across the rock, toes feeling for a hold.

As she pulled herself higher the pressure on her right arm lessened. Her right shoulder popped. Suddenly she had full control of that arm again. It ached, but worked.

From above the woman called, "Etyan, keep going, you're nearly there."

Dej raised her raw wrist high enough to put some slack in the rope and shook her hand to get the blood flowing. She brought her right arm round, ignoring the pins and needles, and gripped the stone with it. This rock was bigger than her hut. Secure now, she risked looking over her shoulder.

The ravine was no more than two dozen steps away. Those two dozen steps were a slanted ruin of mud-churned earth and debris. A pale shape stuck up from the devastated land over to one side, just short of the precipice. It looked like an arm.

It was just possible, if the stream was deep enough, and not as full of rocks as it sounded, that someone might survive the fall into the ravine. But even if they did, they had no way to get back up. She extended her senses, trying to find some glimmer of other, familiar lives, but there was nothing. The clanless were gone. She was on her own.

Except, of course, for the pair of shadowkin she was tied to.

She turned back, and looked up.

The two shadowkin were only a body's length away, on the highest point of the rock. The boy was sitting down; next to him the woman was unclasping her cloak. The boy, who'd lost his own cloak, looked at Dej. His desperate dare-to-hope expression made her look away.

The woman eased her cloak around both of them. They sat pressed together under it. She turned her narrow gaze on Dej and called. "Can you find us shelter?"

"Shelter?" She'd overheard Cal talking to Tew on the journey here, something about allowing for the cloudy skies not holding on the way back. At the time, she'd been confused as to why the state of the sky mattered. Tew had mentioned the red valley; she'd only visited it once, but reckoned she could find it from here. "Yes," she said, "Yes, I can."

"How far is it?" The woman was pale and Dej smelled the fear on her, though she kept her voice even.

"Less than a day's walk."

The woman nodded. "Good."

She appeared to assume that the fact Dej *could* lead them to safely meant that she *would*.

CHAPTER 49

"Which way, then?"

At first Rhia thought the skykin girl hadn't heard her. She sat at the edge of the rock, facing downslope. She turned slowly, her expression hard to read. "Over there," she said, pointing up in the direction the bandits had been heading. "We'll have to crawl."

"That's fine. We'll manage." Both she and Etyan had cuts and bruises, and her right arm was still numb from being trapped under her, but these were minor inconveniences.

"We should get this rope off first. If one falls, we all will."

The girl – Dej – was right. What had saved them before could kill them now. "Good idea. And, um, your backpack...?" From her perch just above the girl Rhia could see the pack was only half full; it contained a red-stained bundle, presumably more of the meat the skykin had eaten the night before. And, somewhere, her sightglass.

The girl said nothing. Then she undid the straps on the basket and eased it round in front of her. She stared into its depths.

"I don't suppose," said Rhia, "you've got a spare cloak in there."

"No. We only had one spare. You're wearing mine."

"Ah. And can I have my sightglass back, please?"

"Your what?"

"The wooden tube you took from me last night."

"Why?"

"I'm sorry: why what?"

"Why should I give it back to you? You threatened to cut me loose just now, Mam Shadowkin."

"My name's Rhia, and this is my brother Etyan. Yes, I threatened to cut you loose. And you were planning to sell us to the highest bidder. But that was then. I'm sorry, Dej, but your people are gone. It's just the three of us now."

"I know that."

When Dej cut the ropes off their wrists Rhia tried not to flinch. If she turned her knife on them, they were dead. If she chose to leave them, they were dead. They had to trust her.

The skykin re-sheathed her knife and reached into the basket, drew out the sightglass and passed it up to Rhia, who tucked it in her satchel. Then she jammed the basket into a crevice in the rock, leaving it upright and open to the sky. "I'll lead."

"Yes, please." She turned to Etyan. "We can't both have the cloak, so you take it."

"Are you sure?"

"Yes." Here was one thing she could do to protect her brother, even if it left her exposed to the sky. She would be all right for a while, as long as the Sun stayed behind those clouds. She massaged her arm to get it working properly.

"Follow me down," called Dej.

The same coating of loose earth and vegetation that had stopped the rock killing her made getting off it tricky. She took it slowly. Below her, Dej slid off the rock to spreadeagle herself facedown on the slope.

"You'll have to go on your bellies, like snakes." Dej demonstrated, working her way up and along the loose earth by pressing into the slope with her lead foot, at the same time reaching up with both hands, grasping for handholds. When she found a rocky outcrop or bit of vegetation still attached to the mountain, she held onto it while pushing off and up with her back foot.

Once off the rock Rhia followed Dej's lead and pressed herself into the mud. Her arm ached. She ignored it. The land had settled, though the ground beneath her felt treacherously loose, and every tiny trickle of earth dislodged by her weight made her breath catch.

Dej called, "Don't get too close." Not much risk of that: the skykin was already some way ahead.

Dej led them diagonally up the slope. This half crawl, half paddle was an undignified, stressful, filthy way to travel but it was the only way if they didn't want to end up in the ravine below. Rhia turned her head to check Etyan was following.

Her body began to ache in strange new places: buttocks, ankles, upper arms. Fear gave way to frustration. She reached higher, eager for this to be over.

Her arm skidded through earth. Suddenly she was sliding. She pressed herself into the slope, ignoring the soil in eyes and mouth, her hands outstretched, fingers clawing for purchase.

She slowed. Stopped. Raised her head.

Dej and Etyan were looking down the slope at her. She wanted to call out that she was all right but her mouth was full of muck and she lacked the energy to state the obvious.

She spat out the mud and began to crawl back up the slope.

Dej hauled herself off the loose earth onto undamaged land. The two shadowkin had fallen behind. If she wanted, she could get up and walk away now. Just leave them. They were nothing to her.

She still wasn't sure whether she should've left Kir's animus. She hadn't been sure it was dead, but when she'd got to safety and thought about discarding the head, her own animus hadn't objected. Kir was dead and gone. And so was everyone else.

Leaving her with these two. At least they – well, he – had value. And not all the clanless were lost. Mar was back at the camp, waiting for news only Dej could bring. Dej could bring more than that. She could lead these two not to shelter in the red valley as they expected, but back to the clanless camp.

Except they'd never make it that far. The rain was easing off; she had to get them to shelter before the Sun broke through, if she wanted them to be worth anything to anyone.

When Rhia finally felt firm ground beneath her she stopped and closed her eyes, getting her breath back. She rolled over to sit up and saw Dej standing against the skyline, staring down into the ravine. Etyan was sitting nearby, his chest heaving.

"We're just coming," she called to the girl.

Dej looked at Rhia, then away. Rhia crawled over to Etyan. They leant on each other for support, and stood up. Once she saw they were upright, Dej turned and started up the hillside, moving in a low crouch which Rhia did her best to copy, eyes on the ground, hands poised to catch herself if she slipped.

When they reached the top Rhia was relieved to see flat moorland.

The rain had loosened to drizzle. Rhia shaded her eyes and looked around. The moorland – she thought of it as such, even if the vegetation consisted of purple sort-of moss dotted with upright orange-brown coils – stretched to distant hills. The girl turned to them and said, "Walk in my footsteps. If you see movement, freeze." Without waiting for an answer, she set off.

Dej stepped delicately on the moss and avoided the snake-like coils, which expanded and contracted in a disturbingly breath-like rhythm. Rhia took care to follow close. Her boots

were soon wet; the mats of mossy tendrils were waterlogged.
A lot of skyland plants favoured tendrils and stems over leaves.
Rhia had no idea why. She should check if any enquirer had a
theory about that when she got home. If she got home.

Her head grew warm and itchy, as though she was too close
to a fire. She could feel the Sun's heat through the clouds.

During a brief stop while Dej found a safe path, Rhia noticed
that they were heading for a cleft between two hills. As they
started off again one of the coils sprang open, lofting a vivid
orange stalk in an eye-blink. Rhia froze. The stalk rebounded,
waved – once, twice – and then the clubbed end, the size of
a baby's fist, exploded into a cloud of tiny dark spots. Seeds.
Rhia held her breath. There was little wind but the specks
took to the air and rose. Rhia wondered if she should call out
to their guide, but decided to take the girl's advice. She did
nothing, said nothing. Behind her Etyan called out "Ree?"

"Stay where you are, Etyan," she murmured.

The seeds lofted onto a high breeze – or perhaps they
had some way of propelling themselves? – and began to
disperse. Up ahead, Dej turned to watch. Rhia waited until
the air around her was clear then nodded to Dej, who, after a
moment's hesitation, nodded back. They carried on.

Rhia's throat began to hurt: the moisture soaking into her
boots mocked her growing thirst. The clouds were thinning,
she could feel it. Burning hurt: what sort of agony would
slow immolation be? Or perhaps it would not be that bad.
Like dying in snow, perhaps. According to Pathfinder of Keft
that was an easy death, like falling asleep. She would like to
see snow; it sounded fascinating. Of course, the enquirer who
claimed snow gave an easy death could not know for sure,
given he had lived to write about it.

She paused, realizing she was about to walk into Dej. The
skykin had stopped and turned. Ahead of them, the land ran
out. "We're nearly there."

Rhia nodded numbly. Etyan looked exhausted and afraid, but said nothing.

They descended into a great, shallow bowl scooped into the mountainside. The mountains on the far side were lower. The foliage was sparse but varied. Rhia was sure they were still on the Shenese side of the mountains. If she saw the Sun she could be sure. But if she saw the Sun she would die.

Dej picked her way between large red rocks, working her way down the slope.

Rhia almost missed the cleft in the land. Her eyes ached from squinting against the light and her head was tight, hot and painful. When Dej's legs disappeared she stopped, confused, then shaded her eyes and saw that the girl was descending a steep slope.

"Is there shelter down there?" Rhia wasn't sure how much longer she could go on.

"No, but there's water."

Rhia licked her lips. The stream was in a ravine whose sides were mercifully shallow enough to scramble, rather than climb, down. Even so, Rhia nearly fell in her haste to get to it. The base of the ravine was in shadow. Rhia threw herself down beside the tumbling stream and drank deep. The water tasted odd, and made her tongue tingle. She looked up and saw, where the Sun still shone further up the ravine, how the rocks beside the stream were crusted with red. Had she just poisoned herself? Too late now, and Etyan was gulping the water down too. She looked up at Dej. "Is it safe?" she asked.

"For us, yes." Dej lifted her cupped hand to her mouth.

Not a reassuring answer, but it was too late now. When they had drunk their fill the three of them scrambled up the far slope. At the top Rhia saw dark holes in the hillside a few hundred yards ahead. Only exhaustion stopped her breaking into a run. When she reached the first cave she ducked inside and was confronted by darkness. She blinked, bright afterimages dancing in her vision. Through them she made out the back of the cave; it was barely deep enough to lie flat in, with a deeply pitted floor.

The next cave was a good five yards deep and nearly as wide, with a relatively flat if rock-strewn floor. Rhia wondered if there was some inimical beast or plant, or some other reason they could not stop here. But Dej went right in, then turned and sat on the ground in the mouth of the cave. Rhia followed, and lowered herself to sit against the back wall. Her eyes started to close, but she snapped her head forward and looked to Etyan, who was sitting on a rock. "How are you doing?" she asked gently.

Etyan tried for a smile. "Nothing wrong with me a big plate of roast pork and a flagon of chilled wine wouldn't fix."

Rhia nodded. Dej sat with one leg tucked under her, staring out at the landscape. Rhia let her head fall back.

Her last thought, before exhaustion claimed her, was that they should be careful, because whilst the girl had led them here, she had made no promises.

CHAPTER 50

So here they were: two shadowkin. Her problem. Apparently.

Dej looked over her shoulder to see the woman leaning back against the cave wall, eyes closed. The boy was still alert, and looking her way. Rather than endure his gaze, she murmured, "You're safe here."

He nodded, then lay down next to the woman and closed his eyes. They trusted her. Or perhaps they were just too exhausted to care.

She'd done what they asked. She'd saved their lives.

What the fuck was she supposed to do with them now?

She should take the boy to Mar. That was what she was here for, what the other clanless had died for. But she couldn't manage both of them.

Behind her, the pair breathed slow and even. They were asleep. She stood quietly. The woman was stroppy, and of no value; they'd only brought her along to ensure the boy's good behaviour. And she was sure to object to Dej handing her brother over to the clanless. She should deal with her now, while they were both off guard, unable to defend themselves.

Her hand went to her knife. A blow to the heart? She had killed a man like that already. But he had been wounded. Slit her throat then? The knife's tip might be damaged, but it still had a keen edge.

Those were messy options, and tricky when the target wasn't lying down. A stone to the head? Again, messy and uncertain. Choking was better: quieter, cleaner. Jeg had said you could choke anything with a neck and a nose by applying pressure where the neck bulged. She was strong enough. Just pin the woman's neck against the wall until the life went out of her.

She turned around, ready to act.

The two shadowkin still lay sprawled by the wall, exhausted. Helpless.

What am I thinking?

They weren't some *prize*, some *problem*. They were *people*. Shadowkin, yes, but until recently she'd lived with shadowkin. She'd live *as* a shadowkin. Min still did.

For a moment she stared at the sleeping pair. Then she turned and walked out into the evening light.

Why was this so hard? In the last few days she'd killed a brave stranger and her almost-friend.

Would Kir have spotted the landslide in time, maybe told them to go around the valley? Perhaps Dej was indirectly responsible for *all* the clanless deaths.

Stop finding reasons to hate yourself.

If she killed the shadowkin woman now that would be one more reason.

Maybe she could have if she hadn't known her name. And this woman – Rhia – who she was thinking of murdering in cold blood, had said she was sorry Dej'd lost her people. She'd sounded like she meant it, even though they were the same people who'd kidnapped her.

So, she couldn't bring herself to deal with the woman. She could still take the boy back to the clanless. Or what was left of them.

But the settlement was nearly two days away. He was soft and unsuited to the wilds. She doubted he'd survive in the open for that long. She'd have to leave him here and go back to the settlement.

And the shadowkin woman? When she fetched them back here the clanless would do what she'd been too weak to do, and kill her. They only wanted the boy.

And if she left these two here alone she wouldn't put it past the woman to convince the boy they should take their chances out in the skyland rather than wait for the people who'd abducted them to come back.

It all came back to the woman. She had to get rid of her.

But she couldn't. Not in cold blood.

She stalked around the valley, paying just enough attention to her surroundings to stay safe. She found herself thinking about the boy. He was needy and weak and soft. But there was something else about him, something intriguing she had no name for. If she killed the woman, killed *Rhia*, how would he, how would *Etyan*, react? She was his sister. She'd put herself at risk for him. Dej suspected Etyan would do the same for her.

The Sun broke free of the clouds just before it set, painting the land in silver. Dej sat down, listening to the chirrups and croaks of unseen creatures, until darkness fell and the chill crept into her bones.

When she returned to the cave the two of them were still asleep. She stared at their shadowy forms, willing herself to go back to thinking of them just as problems to be dealt with. But she was past that.

She sat down cross-legged in the cave entrance, looking out into the skyland night.

After a while she began tapping her thigh with the flat of her hand. She couldn't face humming, not after last time, but the rhythm was a welcome distraction.

"Is that a skykin tune?"

Dej started, then looked over her shoulder. Etyan was

awake. He hadn't moved but he was looking up at her, his face a pale oval in the gloom. She scooted round and said, "Skykin don't have tunes." She realized she should have said "we" not "skykin". She kept her voice low to avoid waking his sister. She didn't want to deal with her right now.

"Oh. Right."

"It's not our way." That was meant to impress him but came out sounding pompous.

"I didn't know that."

"Why would you? You're a shadowkin."

He grunted, maybe taking offence at her tone. "All right, so if you don't have music, how come you're good at drumming?"

"Drumming?"

"Yes, like you were doing on your leg just now."

Dej hadn't known it was called that. "It's just something I do. It doesn't mean anything."

She thought that was it, but then he said, "I used to sing."

Despite herself, she was intrigued. "Were you any good?"

"I was. Really good. People would have paid money to hear me, though obviously they didn't."

Obviously. Why obviously? "So what happened?"

"What do you mean?"

"You don't sing any more, why is that?"

"My balls dropped."

"Your what?"

"I became a man and my voice broke. Doesn't that happen to the boys in the crèches before they get, uh, bonded?" He sounded confused.

She'd noticed voices getting deeper, but not related that to singing. Or to boys' balls for that matter. "We aren't encouraged to go around examining each other's privates."

He giggled; a nervy, sharp sound. "So what do you do?"

"Do?"

"In the crèches."

"Learn how to be skykin."

"Right. Which doesn't include music."

"No. It doesn't."

"But... it does include how to fight other skykin."

"What?"

"When you attacked the caravan. I didn't think skykin robbed each other."

She'd walked into that. "You'll live longer if you don't say things like that, Etyan."

"I'm sorry, I shouldn't have. Sorry." Dej realized how scared he was. All this talk was just bravado.

"Damn right you shouldn't. Now go back to sleep!"

He shut up and closed his eyes. Just like that.

No one *ever* obeyed her straight off, doing what she said without talking back. Even younger children in the crèche gave her lip. He was scared of her: she had power over him. Power over both of them. It felt good.

But she was tired, and though skykin needed less sleep than shadowkin she wanted to be awake when they both woke up.

She felt for north, then lay down in line with it, though the world's pull seemed oddly weak. She put a hand on the knife at her waist as she closed her eyes, but felt it slip off before sleep claimed her.

CHAPTER 51

"I think you have been misled. You appear to believe I am one of these natural enquirers, heh."

Sadakh suppressed a sigh. "So I have heard, Sur."

"From whom, may I ask?" Tamen Ikharon steepled his fingers and looked at Sadakh over them. He was probably wondering why this stranger was presuming upon his time.

Sadakh had travelled to Ikharon's house incognito, accompanied by a single bodyguard dressed as a servant, with two more disguised guards trailing them in a second punt. When he had written to request this meeting he had only signed the note E.S. – his initials, or rather the initial of his title and name, given he had just the one name. The response had come back two days ago, but his duties, and other matters, had kept him from this meeting.

"I would prefer not to say how I came by this knowledge." Although his relationship with Akbet was doomed, Sadakh would not cause trouble for her. "I know how much your organization values discretion, so I hope you will forgive me for practicing it myself, and not naming names."

"Organization, heh. That's a formal word for something so informal. Assuming it exists."

He had hoped this meeting would distract him from concerns over what might be happening in the skyland right now but it looked like being hard work. "I have it on good authority that the natural enquirers do exist." Technically a lie; he had only hearsay and rumour to confirm the existence of the network.

At least this was not a trap. Although Akbet was no agent of the prince – if she was, he would be dead – she could have been fooled or blackmailed into providing incorrect information to draw him out from the priory. But no armed men had assaulted him, and his host's annoyance at having his work interrupted spoke of a genuine scholar. Then there were the books and scrolls Sadakh had glimpsed through the open door of his study before being shown to this austere parlour. The man before him was a kindred spirit. Albeit a stubborn one.

"If the enquirers did exist, and I was one, then your interest would be what, heh."

"I would like to join."

"You would, would you?"

How long is it since someone spoke to you like that?

His ghost was amused. So was Sadakh, a little. If this had been purely an intellectual exercise he might have given up. But despite his care in operating on the animus, and despite sustaining it with his own blood, it was ailing. And his final test subject was missing. He needed access to the deep well of wisdom and learning this man guarded. "Yes, Sur, I would. I am a seeker of knowledge, as I said in my note."

"That is all you said. Not why, or who." Ikharon scratched his chin. "Before we go any further I must know who I'm dealing with."

Sadakh had considered using a false name but if the ruse was exposed it would destroy any chance of acceptance. "I am," he said, putting on a self-effacing smile, "Eparch Sadakh of the First Light." His smile said he knew how hard that was to believe.

Tamen Ikharon sat back in his chair, his face falling into

a comical expression of shock, then glanced at the door, perhaps fearing he was alone with a crazy fantasist.

You can't blame him.

Ignoring his ghost and keeping his hands spread Sadakh said, "Naturally you are sceptical and you would be within your rights to call a servant to throw me out." His own "servant" waited in the hall, in case of trouble.

"I am considering it."

They sat in silence. Sadakh made himself wait without comment or movement.

Finally, Ikharon said, "My own area of interest is people. How we interact, what we believe, why we do what we do. A case study of extreme self-delusion would be a new area of investigation, but quite fruitful, heh."

Sadakh let his smile widen, showing no distress or offence. "I came hoping to join the enquirers. If, instead, I am to provide an increase in their collective wisdom, who am I to disagree."

"You don't protest at being taken for a madman, heh."

He's enjoying this.

Sadakh agreed. And he did not mind, much. "Protesting would do no good. However, realizing that you would need convincing, I have brought proof."

"Have you now."

Sadakh reached for his leather shoulderbag, swinging it onto his lap to pull out a flat object wrapped in padded cloth. "This is a little heavy: may I use your table?"

Ikharon gestured to show he could, and Sadakh leant over and unwrapped the earthly symbol of his office, a palm-sized pectoral of pure iron, in the shape of the bisected circle of the Pillar of Light, rendered with enough ornate flourishes that the original motif was hard to distinguish.

The scholar leaned over the table to examine the item. "May I touch it?"

"Please do."

Ikharon ran his hands over the pectoral, and under it. He felt its weight. Then he sat back, pulled at his lip, and stared at Sadakh. "I can see three possible explanations," he said slowly. "The first is that you are delusional but rich enough to get your hands on a considerable quantity of metal which you have then had crafted into a facsimile of the eparch's pectoral. This is unlikely, not least because I'm on nodding acquaintance with all those in the city with means to create such a treasure.

"The second possibility is that you stole the pectoral. This would be a near-impossible heist to pull off, and having done so, I can think of no reason under heaven you would bring it to me.

"This leaves the possibility that you are telling the truth, heh." Ikharon inclined his head. "If that is so, then I hope Your Holiness will forgive this humble scholar's scepticism."

"I expected nothing else, Sur."

"I am not yet convinced. I simply chose the most logical explanation, heh. So, assuming I am correct, what might His Holiness the Eparch have to bring to the network of natural enquirers? We have scholars of the scriptures amongst us but – please do not take offence – not all enquirers are devout."

"I take no offence at others' beliefs."

"So I have heard, heh."

"I was not planning to share my thoughts on the scriptures; that I can do with my flock."

"Then what subject would you specialize in?"

Sadakh had considered this at length. Although he had one unique area of expertise, he preferred not to mention it. "Anatomy," he said instead.

Ikharon raised a bushy eyebrow. "Now that's not an answer I expected, heh."

"But is it an acceptable one? Our nation prides itself on medical knowledge. I would be honoured to share my investigations into the workings of the body."

"I see. Are you aware of the enquirers' titles?"

"I fear not."

"We use inherited titles for both discretion and continuity. Discretion is necessary in shadowlands that do not approve of our investigations, though that is not a problem here. To my fellow scholars I am Counsellor of Zekt. Before I go to my celestial reward I will hand this title to one who has a mind for such things, heh. The First did not see fit to bless me with children but I have apprentices, all of whom strive to be worthy of such an honour."

"I understand." Sadakh hid his disappointment at finding there was no opening for him in the organization.

"Most shadowlands have two active enquirers. Zekt's other enquirer rejoiced in the title of Meddler of Zekt. This was not the title he inherited, but one he took on as he became increasingly... mischievous. He was not always a credit to the network, heh. This individual died suddenly, a few months back."

"How, may I ask?" Sadakh tried not to sound too pleased at finding there might be a position for him after all.

"He choked on a fishbone."

Not the prince's doing, then. That was a relief.

Ikharon continued, "Meddler of Zekt had not yet taken on apprentices and both of his offspring were daughters and hence of no use."

Pah! Sadakh shared, but did not show, his ghost's irritation with that statement: notwithstanding creatures like Akbet, conditioned to believe their own inadequacy, many women had sharp minds. To dismiss half the population due to their gender struck Sadakh as wasteful.

Ikharon concluded, "For some months now, I have been

Zekt's only natural enquirer. I had considered appointing one of my apprentices to take my late colleague's place, but none of them are yet ready for such responsibility, heh."

"Which means there might be space for me in the network."

"It is possible, subject to proof that, and forgive me for this, Your Holiness's mind is of a sufficient calibre. Our standards are high."

"I would expect nothing less. If I am found wanting, I will accept the judgment of my intellectual betters."

"Forgive me for this also, but would Your Holiness's duties not impinge on your enquiries?"

"I can always make time for knowledge."

Ikharon smiled. "Heh. Now that is what I like to hear."

CHAPTER 52

For a brief moment before full consciousness returned, Rhia thought she was still in the wagon. But she was curled up against rough rock and all her muscles ached. With an indrawn breath, she remembered where she was.

She opened her eyes to darkness. The view outside showed a star-spattered night sky over a dark land relieved by the occasional soft glowing patch. The only sound was the peculiar night chorus of the skyland – currently a low trilling overlaid by soft chirrups and a repeated three-tone croak – and Etyan's light snores. The low shape lying in the cave's mouth must be Dej.

Rhia stretched. She needed to pee, was thirsty again and had a headache. Her stomach felt like it was flapping against her backbone. Her shoulder was stiff and sore and the top of her head and backs of her hands felt hot and itchy.

She pulled herself up on the wall, pausing to wait for her head to stop spinning. Then she crept past the sleeping skykin girl, who was lying diagonally across the entrance.

She took a few cautious steps out of the cave, wary of disturbing any wildlife, then squatted by the light of a glowing bush. Much as she needed a drink, trying to find the stream at night, alone, would be unwise.

Once she was done, she got the sightglass out of her satchel and sat on a rock, elbows on knees. Both Moons had set, so it must be, what, the twenty-eighth hour? She wondered how far away the nearest clock was.

She held her breath when she lifted the sightglass to her eye.

The stars blazed in her sight, pure and clear. Rhia exhaled. The device was undamaged. She wanted to observe the land itself in daylight as there was something about the rocks here... but for now she focused on the stars. Whatever else, the heavens were here for her. None of the Strays were visible, but the act of observing calmed and comforted her.

On returning to the cave she heard movement in the darkness and Etyan whispered, "Can we trust her?" He meant the still-sleeping skykin.

Rhia sat down next to him. "I don't think we have any choice."

"She killed your guard. Lekem, that was his name, wasn't it?"

Rhia's face flushed. She hadn't thought of the dead militiaman since being snatched from the caravan. Breen had said he had a family. That innocent conversation felt like a lifetime ago. Lekem's wife would even now be assuming he was on his way home. And Etyan called him a guard; she hadn't admitted the truth about her travelling companions, just as he had not yet shared his reasons for leaving Shen.

"Ree?"

"Sorry. Yes, Dej killed Lekem. But I don't think it was her idea." Rhia recalled the bandit leader saying something to Dej, and Dej hesitating, though she might be misremembering; she'd had other priorities at the time.

"Assuming we don't die horrible deaths out here," Etyan spoke with false jollity, "Would you let me go back to Zekt, if that's what I wanted?"

Rhia considered the duke's orders to Sorne, House Callorn's marriage proposal and, not least, the girl – Derry – dead in the dyers' pools. She wanted to say no, for all those reasons. But saying no to Etyan often had the opposite effect. And much had happened over these last few weeks. "I won't stop you. It's your choice, and your responsibility."

Rhia heard movement and looked over to see Dej sitting up. She wondered how much the girl had heard. "Any chance we can get a drink?" she asked.

Dej looked out the cave mouth where the sky was lightening. "We'll have to hurry."

"Then let's go."

Dej did not hang around; Rhia struggled to keep up without tripping in the dark. From the occasional curse behind her Etyan was having similar problems. At the stream Rhia drank as much as she could as fast as she could, although the liquid sloshed around inside her. When they climbed out of the shallow ravine the sky ahead was pale grey.

Back in the safety of the cave Rhia said, "Dej, is there stuff here we can eat?"

"Maybe."

"Will you look?"

She stared at them for a while, then said, "All right," and left.

Rhia considered how they might store water. The skykin's cloak was leather, but it was made of strips, roughly stitched. It would not be watertight.

The Sun rose, washing the land in brilliance. By its light Rhia examined her satchel in case that would work, but though the leather had been waxed the seams were not sealed. "Hmm, that'll dribble."

"It's good that you're thinking about this, Ree." She looked up to see Etyan's worried face, "But shouldn't we be worrying about how we're going to get out of here?"

He was right. She put the satchel down. "There's only one way we can do that."

• • •

So now she was going to forage for them? These two were her prisoners, at her mercy. They had to do what she wanted!

But wonderful though it had felt when Etyan obeyed her last night, things weren't that simple. Whether she liked it or not, she had a connection to him and his sister, and the longer she stayed around them, the stronger it'd grow.

If she wanted to break free, she should walk away now. Leave everything behind. But without the clanless she was on her own. Could she live as a total outcast, like that pathetic creature who'd spoken to Cal, so far gone no one else would even look at him?

And if she abandoned them now, the two shadowkin would die anyway. They'd starve or get bitten or stung, probably suffering long, agonizing deaths worse than anything she or the clanless could inflict.

Kir's fate was on her. Maybe the clanless's too. She wasn't ready to add two more deaths to her conscience.

She couldn't kill them, and she couldn't leave them to die. She may as well feed them.

Meat wasn't an option. Even if she managed to catch something, they had no fire to cook with. She picked some tasty stem tips but they'd wilt quickly so she ate them as she went. Then she spotted a yellow creeper draped down a slanted rockface. A scrabble up the slope showed this to be palefruit. The fist-sized fruits were shaped like two shallow bowls pushed together and the flesh inside was moist, if stringy. Vay had mentioned that palefruit was "about as harmless as you got" so it should be fine for shadowkin. Dej cut a vine with half a dozen fruits on and looped it around her neck. Two of the fruits fell off during the trip back to the cave, but she picked them up, leaving them two each, enough to keep hunger at bay.

The shadowkin were deep in conversation when she returned, though they were keeping their voices down. They shut up when her shadow fell across them.

While Dej split the fruits and used her knife to ease the flesh free of the rind, Rhia said, "Are these plentiful here?"

"Plentiful enough." The vine'd had another half dozen fruits ready to eat, with a dozen more ripening.

"Would you be able to fetch more, enough for us to live on for a few days?"

"I could."

"Good, because we're hoping you might go and get help."

"What do you mean?"

"You can travel safely through the skyland. We can't. And even with food and water, we can't stay here forever."

Dej grunted, then handed the split fruit across. This woman wasn't going to sit still and await her fate. Just as Dej suspected, Rhia would take things into her own hands.

Etyan dug his fingers into the pink-white fruit and scooped out a handful of flesh, cramming it into his mouth. From his expression he didn't think much of the taste. Rhia followed suit, grimacing as she swallowed. Dej ate her own fruit in silence.

The meal left their hands sticky. Rhia wiped her fingers down her already filthy skirt and said casually, "So, will you help us?"

Dej shrugged. "Perhaps."

"I imagine you were being paid to take my brother to Zekt?"

"What if we were?"

"We have the means to pay you well if you get us to safety."

"Do you? Because right now, that's hard to believe."

"I have considerable resources back home."

Was she lying? Possibly not, given they'd had someone willing to die to defend them on the caravan. Money could probably buy that. "Then maybe we could come to an arrangement." This power she now held, literally that of life or death, made her lightheaded. "Where is home?"

"Shen."

She'd thought their accents sounded familiar, though not quite right. Finding out they came from the place she'd lived most of her life tightened the bond between them, made it even harder to leave them to die. "I'll think about it," she conceded.

She took the empty seedcases outside to dump them away from the cave, and relieved herself behind a rock.

With enough money she could make her own way in the world, maybe even in shadowkin society. But she'd be alone, if she accepted this woman's offer instead of taking the boy to the clanless. Rich or not, she wouldn't belong anywhere.

"Ree!"

Dej hurried back at Etyan's cry. She found Rhia hunched over, retching, Etyan bent over her, one hand on her back. He looked up as Dej blocked the light.

"What did you give us?" He looked like he might throw up himself.

"Palefruit. It's good, nothing wrong with it."

"Then why is she like this? I feel like shit too."

"I thought shadowkin could eat it!"

"Well, we can't." He grimaced and gulped.

His sister leaned forward, then half collapsed. Etyan caught her, narrowly saving her from banging her head on the wall. She retched again, but only bile came up.

Dej had saved them, only to accidentally kill them.

Etyan looked around in panic. "We have to help her!"

Do we? If Rhia died now, then assuming Etyan survived Dej would be better off. *And it wouldn't be me killing her, but the world.* Like the skykin did with faulty animuses.

"Please! Do something!"

The boy was desperate, as animated as she'd seen him. He'd do anything for his sister. Would Min have cared so much, if this had been Dej throwing her guts up? "I'm not sure what I can do."

"Aren't skykin good healers? I heard that somewhere."

He had no idea. But if she just let Rhia die, he'd hate her.

There'd been a bad batch of meat at the crèche once, and several youngers got sick. She'd helped the staff tend them. "We need to make sure she doesn't choke on her puke. Help me lay her on her side."

Rhia groaned when they moved her, but didn't open her eyes. They got her onto her side, as far away from the pool of rancid vomit as possible.

"Now what?" asked Etyan.

"She needs water."

"Yes. Right. How?"

"Her satchel—"

"No good, she already thought of that."

Dej looked around. They had nothing. Then she remembered one of her least favourite chores from the crèche. "Take your shirt off."

"What?"

"Just do it! Then give it to me."

Etyan shrugged free of his shirt and handed it to Dej.

"I'll soak this in the stream and bring it back. Rhia can drink the water I wring out of it."

"You might want to wash it first." Etyan looked embarrassed. "I haven't exactly been able to perform my daily toilette."

"I'll manage." Etyan's shirt did smell but not unpleasantly so. His body was soft and his skin looked odd, like he had the shadow of a rash on it. When he noticed her staring she jumped to her feet.

At the stream she cleaned the shirt, wringing it out and beating it on a rock, just like washday. Then she let it soak in the deepest pool, after which she draped it around her neck; chill water dripped down her back all the way to the cave.

The stench of Rhia's puke made Dej's nostrils close when she returned, a feeling she still found weird. Etyan lifted his sister to sit back against him, her head flopping on his shoulder. He looked better, at least.

Dej lifted the sopping shirt from her shoulders and squeezed it into the shadowkin's mouth. Water dribbled over her lips. She licked and then gulped. Etyan licked his own lips, no doubt thirsty himself.

When the shirt was wrung dry Etyan lowered Rhia to the floor. "Sleep now," he murmured. "It'll be all right."

"Help me clear this up," said Dej, nodding at the mess Rhia'd made.

"Uh, sure."

Dej fetched two empty palefruit rinds, and got Etyan to hold them while she scraped up the soiled earth. When she returned from dumping them outside she asked Etyan, who sat watching Rhia, whether he wanted water. He looked up then said, "I'll be all right."

"That wasn't what I asked."

"Yes, I would. If you don't mind."

"Wouldn't have offered if I did."

When she returned Rhia was asleep and Etyan was dozing. She shook him awake and handed him the shirt.

"Given how hot it is I'm going to leave this off," he said, when he'd wrung all the water out of it. "Unless you're offended by the sight of naked shadowkin flesh."

"I'm not offended by much."

Etyan smiled.

"Why were you in Zekt?"

"What do you mean?" His smile died.

"I overheard heard you talking to Rhia about going back there."

Etyan said nothing.

"Well?"

"It's complicated."

"I'll listen carefully while you explain it then."

"I'd rather not."

Could she make him tell her? Maybe, but she didn't want it to come to that. "All right. Can you tell me why you left Zekt, then?" Someone in Zekt wanted him back.

He nodded to his sister. "She came to get me."

"All the way across the skyland?"

"All the way across the skyland. Once Ree gets an idea into her head... I'll tell you one reason I left Shen: because of her."

"Really? What did she do?"

"Nothing. Everything. She stifled me. She paid for the best tutors so if I didn't do well in lessons it was my fault. She didn't like me going out with my friends, but we never had visitors, not any of my own age, anyway. And she goes on about me being immature and irresponsible all the time."

"Are you?"

"Am I what?"

"Immature and irresponsible?"

"No! I don't know. Maybe I was a bit wild. Some stuff I did wasn't... oh, can we talk about something else?"

"You can tell me about your life in Shen."

"I said I didn't want to talk about that."

"Very mature." She liked how he got all fired up, even if it made him seem younger than his years. And she was curious about his life, so different from hers. "Some of it must be all right, especially if you've got money. Tell me about those bits. What was it like, where you lived?"

"You mean the city?"

"Yes, the city. Did you ever meet the duke?"

"Only about once a week!"

He was showing off: typical boy. But she was impressed, even if that was just a lowly crèche-kid's response. "Really? What's he like?"

"Well…"

They talked while Rhia slept, and the day grew hotter. When Etyan grew hoarse Dej fetched more water, and when he wanted to take a siesta Dej let him. She stayed where she was, staring out over the skyland.

CHAPTER 53

Father is alive. Father is alive and he's calling her name. He wants to show her a marvellous contraption that he's built. But she can't go see because Etyan has fallen in the lake, and the weed and the hair are dragging him down. Uncle Petren says she should come away with him and see the world instead, but she has to get her stupid brother out of trouble yet again, because without her he'll be hung like a common criminal–

Rhia woke in sweltering darkness, nightmarish dream giving way to nightmarish reality. Her guts were an empty sucking hole and she was dizzy and weak. Her throat felt like she had been breathing diamond dust.

She lay still, then rolled onto her back, massaging her numb arm where she had slept on it.

Etyan slept beside her. From what she could recall, he had not been as sick as her, thank the First.

So she, and possibly he, could not eat skyland food. How long did it take to starve to death? A week? Two? Thirst killed you faster, if she recalled. It certainly felt like it would.

Etyan looked oddly pale in the skyland night. She realized he was bare-chested. Rhia worked back through blurred memories. So that was where the lifesaving water had come from! She licked her lips and whispered, "Etyan!"

Etyan stirred and raised his head. "Ree? How are you?"

"All right but really thirsty. Can... can you help me get to the stream?"

"If you're up to it."

"I'm going to try."

He had to pull her to her feet and provide a shoulder to support her. She held her breath as he helped her past the sleeping skykin, but Dej didn't wake.

Outside, thin cloud masked the high stars, though both Whitemoon and the Matriarch were low in the west; the Maiden was in the sky too. Shame she wasn't up to making any observations. She shivered in the chill night air.

"Ree, are you sure you can make it to the stream?"

"Possibly not," she admitted. "But we need to talk, alone." Dej had interrupted an important discussion when she had returned with that damned fruit.

"Then let's sit down."

As he helped her onto a rock she asked, "Did you keep your meal down?"

"I did, though I'd still prefer that roast pork dinner."

"And has Dej said anything about our proposition?"

"Our–? Oh, going for help, you mean. No, we didn't talk about that, not directly."

"We have to assume she will." *Given the alternative.* "And we have to decide where to send her."

"I know that." He thought she was nagging him; didn't he see how important this was?

"It must be Shen," said Rhia.

"Why?"

"Firstly, because it's closer. Secondly, because Zekt isn't safe."

"Not safe how?"

"Well, someone tried to abduct you from your sickbed. And I was attacked. Twice."

"Attacked? Who by?"

"Different people, but in both cases they may have been working for the same person. Someone wants me as a hostage, which isn't a fate I fancy. So Zekt isn't the logical choice. Shen is. And it's your home. Unless," she wanted to give him a chance to confess; if there was anything to confess, "there is something waiting for you there you can't face?"

Etyan was silent.

"What happened the night you left, Etyan? You have to tell me." Her voice was growing hoarse.

"I don't know!"

"How can you just *not know*?"

"Surprisingly easily."

"You–" A coughing fit took her.

Etyan stood. "I'll get the shirt and fetch some water."

"Wh–" Now her voice had died, damnit.

He was already striding off.

"Etyan?"

Rhia looked up at the skykin girl's voice. She stood in the mouth of the cave.

Etyan told her, "Ree wanted to get some air, and a drink."

"You shouldn't go out alone."

"She wasn't up to going to the stream anyway. We'll come back in."

He offered her his arm. She let him help her back to the cave. Neither of them said anything.

"It'll be dawn soon," said the skykin, "but there's still time to get to the stream."

"Yes, let's," said Etyan as he lowered Rhia to the floor. "I'll fetch you some water, Ree." Rhia didn't argue.

"I heard shouting."

Dej waited until they were out of earshot of the cave before she spoke. "Were you and your sister arguing about where to go back to?"

Out of the corner of her eye she saw his head whip round. "Yes. We were."

"Because you want to go to Zekt?"

"I don't know. I found something in Zekt, something amazing. Well, a person."

"A girl?" Dej was surprised at how that made her feel.

"No, nothing like that. A religious leader. Sounds odd, I'm not a religious person. But he was amazing." They reached the ravine, "Uh, can you show me the best way down here?"

"Of course."

As Etyan was soaking his shirt at the pool Dej said, "So, this religious leader in Zekt?"

"The eparch. I was going to get initiated. Then I fell ill."

Dej remembered the sickness she'd sensed on him. It was still there, if she concentrated, though he wasn't acting unwell. "Ill, how?"

"That's the thing. One night after the evening service I felt feverish, and collapsed. And so did three others, according to the priest who was looking after me. They all died. I nearly did. It was horrible. Everything hurt. And I remember, after the others died, how the eparch came to visit. He sent the priest away, and he prayed over me, but before he left he said something, I'm not even sure I heard it right but... I thought he said, 'You have to live. I can't fail.'"

"What did he mean?"

"I don't know but... it was weird, four people who barely know each other all getting ill at once like that. Almost like it wasn't an illness at all. I'd put it from my mind, until Ree got ill, but you know what?"

"What?"

"I think I was poisoned."

"Why?"

"I wish I knew. Can I ask you something?"

"You can."

"Do you know who hired you, Dej?"

"I can't tell you that."

"Can't or won't?"

She wouldn't take offence or refuse to answer. "Actually I wondered if you might have some idea. Could it be this eparch?" What if she bypassed the clanless and took Etyan to whoever had hired them in the first place? But she had no idea who that was. And she'd be selling him out.

"Perhaps, though I'm not sure why. More likely something to do with politics... I told you a bit about life at the duke's court, but Zekti nobles are something else. They marry their sisters and assassinate their rivals. The only reason they haven't killed each other off entirely is because the eunuchs stop the craziness from getting out of hand."

"Eunuchs?"

"They're men who've... let's just say they often have fine singing voices."

Dej wasn't sure what he was getting at, but he seemed to be attempting a joke. "So you don't really want to go back to Zekt?"

"No. It has to be Shen. There's stuff there I don't want to face, but the eparch was always talking about taking personal responsibility and to be honest I've been pretty shit at that for most of my life."

"You're assuming I'll do what your sister wants."

"If you don't, then me and Ree are going to die out here. You do know that, don't you?"

She certainly did.

Rhia looked up as the pair returned. Behind them, the sky was pale. Dej handed over the sopping shirt. As Rhia wrung it out over her mouth her arms quivered with effort. The water tasted faintly of sweat but she didn't care.

As she lowered the shirt Dej said, "I'll do it."

"You'll go for help?"

Dej nodded. From the way Etyan looked at her she had not shared her decision with him.

"Thank you."

"And I'm going to Shen, not Zekt?"

"That's right." Rhia looked up at her brother, but he turned on his heel and went to stand at the mouth of the cave.

"Will your people believe me?"

"Yes: they'll know we're missing. And I'll give you a letter."

"Can I take the cloak?"

"The cloak? Well, I guess it's not much use to us. Yes, that's a good idea, it'll make you less conspicuous once you reach Shen."

Dej looked unsure. "Will there be trouble?"

Rhia shook her head. Even if Alharet was the traitor Sorne had intimated, Rhia could see no link to their current predicament. "No, no, I'm sure there won't be."

CHAPTER 54

"Slow down! I'm not used to having to remember so much stuff." Dej tried not to sound as pissed off as she felt. The shadowkin was making her feel stupid, expecting her to repeat complicated instructions after only hearing them once.

"I'd write it down but..."

"...but what?"

Rhia narrowed her eyes. "Can you read?"

"Of course I can read!"

"Ah, I'm an idiot. You were educated in a crèche. Yes, yes, I'll write it all down. I can draw you a map too."

"No need. I just find my way back to the caravan route then follow it south, don't I?"

"Yes. Will you be able to work out which way's south?"

"I always know which way I'm going."

"You do? How?"

Dej tried not to grin at the shadowkin's expression. "My animus tells me." *Whether I want it to or not.*

"Really? I had no idea they did that. Fascinating. That'll certainly help. But you'll need a map of the city."

Rhia tore blank pages from a book, and used them to draw the map, and write what she called "a letter of introduction". She wrote a list of names on the back of the letter. "Only hand this letter to one of the people listed here, do you understand?"

Dej nodded. That there were people the shadowkin didn't trust enough to rescue her wasn't reassuring.

Finally, Rhia gave her a pouch of coins and a chunky ring with a complex design of feathers and flowers cut into it. From the weight Dej guessed the ring was made of solid metal.

"I'm not sure how I'll carry all this," said Dej.

After a moment's pause Rhia emptied her satchel, putting the papers and the strange tube in a neat pile behind a rock. "It's not as though we'll be going anywhere for a while." The shadowkin's voice was brittle.

Dej left around mid-morning. Rhia took her hand when she said farewell, a very shadowkin gesture. So did Etyan. "Stay safe," he said. Dej nodded, unsure how to respond.

She paused to drink at the stream. When she reached the far side of the ravine she had a choice. If she really was going to Shen she should head southwest. If she struck north she would be heading back towards the clanless settlement.

Last chance to decide.

She could just take news of the shadowkin's location to the surviving clanless. The shadowkin had let her go. They'd even given her money. But what would Etyan's fate be then? It depended on who in Zekt wanted him, and why. And Rhia would most likely end up dead.

Then again, not wanting Rhia dead didn't mean she had to obey her without question. The shadowkin noble's manner pissed her off, with her assumption that Dej would obey her, would remember everything, would do everything she wanted. Would behave, in fact, like a servant. She was no one's servant. And if she did walk away from the clanless now, they'd never have her back.

A simple choice. Southwest to save the shadowkin and shed her old life. North to damn them and reclaim it.

● ● ●

Rhia watched Dej leave, following her progress until she lost sight of the skykin in the bright landscape. She caught herself scratching the back of her hand; where it had been hot and sore, now it was itchy, the skin peeling. Seeker of Thir had written of the unshaded Sun burning not just the skin but the very blood, and causing cankers and other maladies even after the burns had faded. Not a pleasant thought, but she had more pressing concerns.

From the shade at the back of the cave Etyan said, "You're not thinking of going outside?" With the skies cloud-free, the light was blinding.

"No, I can see from here." Something still nagged at her about this strange valley. Her sightglass would make observation easier but it would be dangerous to use in these light levels. Instead she shaded her eyes with her hand and stared out, down the slope and across the bowl of the valley, hoping her vision would adjust. But the intense sunlight washed out colour and made her blink. She would have to wait to confirm her suspicions.

Even at the back of the cave it was hotter than midday in the shadowlands, as well as being close and airless; she pulled her skirt up as high as was decent, rolled up her shirt and removed her mask. She would kill for a fan. Although she had got Dej to fetch more water before she left, the thirst was back. And she was exhausted. Perhaps she could sleep. "I'm going to rest now," she told Etyan, who nodded. His own eyes were half closed.

She lay down, making herself ignore the hard floor, the dust encrusting her sweaty skin, her hollow and aching guts.

She closed her eyes. But her mind refused to rest. They had over a week before they could expect rescue. Four days for Dej to get to Shen city, four days back. Possibly a day to get the expedition together, although she hoped Francin might prepare a search party as soon as he heard they had been taken from the caravan. She decided to give him the benefit of the doubt. Eight days was not so long. They would survive. They just had to conserve their energy during the day, and make sure they got plenty of water once the Sun went down.

At some point, Etyan would open up. She knew her brother; if nothing else, boredom would drive him to make conversation.

She must have slept, as she started awake at Etyan's gasp.

"What's that?" Etyan was pointing at a hand-sized creature crawling diagonally up the cave wall. It had two parallel bodies, long and hard-shelled, connected by a lacy integument; its many legs and red-brown colour reminded Rhia of a centipede.

"I have no idea," she admitted.

"Is it dangerous?"

"I have no idea of that either. I'd advise watching, but not bothering it."

They observed the creature's silent traverse: up, across, over. Etyan edged away as it came down the far wall. Rhia got up and looked more closely. It appeared to be two creatures, possibly mating. One end of each had a cluster of what looked like eyes. At opposite ends, interestingly. The bug-thing/ things found a crack between floor and wall and crawled into it. She turned to Etyan and smiled. He looked embarrassed for a moment then smiled back.

Outside, the shadows had shifted towards evening, and though the Sun still burned bright she decided to risk examining their surroundings.

When she picked up the sightglass from her pile of papers Etyan asked, "What is that?"

"It's for looking at distant objects. I can show you how to use it, if you like."

He shrugged. "Maybe later."

He felt rejected in favour of her other interests. Well, he

only had to speak to her and he would have her undivided interest. She made her observations methodically, starting with the leftmost part of the field of view and working across, concentrating on rocky outcroppings and bare patches where the soil was free of vegetation. Even the soil was red. But the red markings were not uniform. It was as though something had been washed from the rocks and earth, staining the land.

Analyst of Durn had written of such landscapes. Durn was the richest shadowland, its wealth legendary.

"Etyan?"

"Yes?"

"You might want to look at this."

Etyan got to his feet.

Rhia handed the sightglass to him when he joined her at the cave mouth. "So I just look through it?"

"That's right."

Etyan raised the tube. "View's a bit blurry."

She showed him how to adjust the focus. "Ah," he said. "That's clearer." He smiled without lowering the sightglass. "This is a clever little device. Did you make it?"

"I designed it. I got the glassblowers to grind the lenses. Do you see how red the rocks are, over there where you're looking now?"

"Um, yes."

"There's a reason for that."

Etyan must have heard the excitement in her voice, as he lowered the sightglass and looked at her.

"Those rocks," she said, "the red ones. They're the raw material which, when heated, yields iron."

"Iron? But they're everywhere."

"Yes. Yes, they are."

In this bleak, strange valley was a treasure beyond imagining.

CHAPTER 55

There was no easy answer, so Dej did what she'd always done: she followed her heart. She'd been pleasantly surprised to find she still had one.

The two shadowkin, despite their noble arrogance, had treated her better than the clanless had. It'd felt good to have power over them, for a while. Good to know she still had choices tooo, no matter how hard. And talking with Etyan had made her happy in a way she couldn't remember since saying goodbye to Min.

She couldn't sell him out, then go back to living with Mar and the dregs of the clanless, surrounded by empty huts to remind her of a disaster that might have been her fault. And she couldn't abandon him to die.

She would save his life – being owed a favour by shadowland nobility wouldn't do her any harm – and then she would make her own way in the world.

After cutting south to avoid the landslide, she headed for the shadowkin road. When she reached it, she ate a handful of fruit from a bush-like plant which smelled safe and bedded down beneath an overhanging crag.

She awoke in the deep dark, tired, chilly and uncertain. She wanted to pull the cloak tighter and go back to sleep. But time wasn't on her side. She could rest properly when she reached Shen. She listened to the night sounds of the skyland for a while, then got up and carried on walking.

They went back to the stream as soon as the Sun set. Rhia wondered if the iron in the water would harm them if they drank too much, then discarded the thought. Not drinking at all would kill them.

The night remained clear, and the Matriarch rose. Rhia settled herself at the mouth of the cave. Her sightglass revealed a star close to the Stray, yet again. Three times was more than coincidence. What did this odd conjunction signify?

An amazing possibility occurred to her as she was observing Greymoon a while later. What if it was a moon? If the Strays were indeed spheres they might they have other, smaller, spheres going around them, as the Moons went round the world. Accepted wisdom said the world was orbited by the Moons, then the Strays and the Sun and finally the fixed stars. But if the Strays had moons of their own, what would it mean for that view of the physical universe?

She stayed up late observing, though exhaustion claimed her before the Maiden, now heralding morning rather than evening, rose.

She woke when the heat grew too intense. Clouds had closed in, and the cave was stifling. She did not feel hungry this morning. Did not, in fact, feel like she had a stomach at all. When she said as much to Etyan he grunted.

They were falling into a daze. She had recovered from her sickness and now the revelation about the Matriarch's moon sat deep inside her, a small and shining joy. But without food they would fade, becoming lethargic in mind and body, while they waited for rescue. Before they embraced this torpor, she must address their unfinished business.

She raised her head; a bead of sweat dripped from her chin. "Etyan?"

He looked up.

"We need to talk about what will happen when we get back to Shen."

"Now?"

"Yes, now."

"I have no idea what will happen when we get back to Shen." He sounded exhausted.

"No. Which is why I need to ask you some questions which I hope you're willing to answer."

"Are you willing to answer mine?"

"That would only be fair."

"All right. Those guards of yours, who were they?"

"They were militiamen, Etyan."

"Ah. Well that would be the logical choice for guards."

She knew that infuriating, evasive tone too well. "What are you afraid of? I have to know. Is it because of the girl in the lower city? What do you know about Derry's death?"

He hunched in on himself. "Why do you assume I know anything?"

"Because I followed you, that morning."

"You did what?"

"I followed you, down the hill." She hadn't been able to concentrate after their row, and had gone to her room, intending to nap before daylight. But she had been too agitated. Not as agitated as Etyan; she had heard him pacing and muttering. Then the front door opened. "Why did you go out again?"

"I was still messed up, Ree. I didn't know what I was doing."

She could believe that, given how he'd lurched and staggered down the hill. But previous binges had ended up in unconsciousness, not wanderlust. "You knew where you were going. You headed straight to the lower city."

"I like it down there."

"What where you looking for? What were you doing?"

"You really did watch me, didn't you? Just watched." Bitterness crept into his voice.

He was right. She should have called out, intervened, asked him what he was up to. Would things have gone differently then? "Yes. And I saw her."

"Saw who?"

"I lost you near the river, in the backstreets, but then I heard you somewhere up ahead. I couldn't find you – First knows how anyone manages to find their way around down there – and I came out at the dyers' pools. That's where I saw her. She... she was face down, in the water, with her hair loose. There was blood in the water." Rhia's already tight throat constricted at the memory. "I thought at the time she must have died in a brawl." An assumption she was later ashamed of, when she learned the truth. "What do you know about the death of Derry, the master tanner's daughter, Etyan?"

"I didn't kill her!"

"What was that stain on your shoulder? It was dark as blood."

"It was puke! I was drunk and I threw up."

"But the girl–"

"Stop going on about her!" He might have stormed out, had there been anywhere to storm to. As it was he hunched down and looked past her. "Just leave it, Ree. Please. It's bad enough that we're stuck out here in this awful place, not knowing if we'll ever get home. And I can't think straight in this heat. Just leave me alone. Please."

What choice did she have? She stared out over the lethal, beautiful landscape.

When she came down from the mountains Dej found herself in familiar terrain, with sparse vegetation and rocky outcrops. A speckling of purple and red blooms and drying patches of mud showed the rain had reached this far. She remembered the last time she had been in a place like this, with Kir. But that was the past.

The farther south she got, the drier the land became, although she heard distant rumbles of thunder behind her.

Ahead, a smudge grew on the horizon, like a static cloud: the shadowland of Shen.

She was hungry, as she only picked fruits and stems she was sure wouldn't harm her. Thirsty too, after setting a fast pace since drinking from a stream first thing. But that was fine; she could go for longer than a shadowkin without food or water. And the pair she'd left in the cave would be worse off than her. She considered them, or rather, considered Etyan. Her thoughts kept coming back to their conversations, and to him, the way he looked, the way he moved. He was an orphan of sorts too, pushed onto a path he had no choice about.

She pressed on and reached Shen's umbral not long after dark. She was tempted to continue, but wanted to be fresh when she entered the shadowland.

She rested under the tall trees of the umbral, lulled to sleep by the night winds sighing through their tops.

Chapter 56

When the day cooled enough to move, Rhia wrote up her theory about the Matriarch's moons. At sunset the clouds finally released their rain, a few drops, then a pounding torrent, as violent as any rain-year storm at home. When full darkness fell Etyan got up and walked out. Rhia tensed, but he stopped just outside the cave and turned his face to the sky, then opened his mouth. After a moment's hesitation Rhia joined him. Very little water actually went down her throat and though the rain was warm she soon began to shiver. "Let's get back inside," she suggested. He shrugged but complied.

They were soaked through and Rhia insisted they wrung their clothes out. As she got the worst of the water out of her skirt she said, "I suggest we don't try and go to the stream in this weather."

"Fine by me."

The rain eased off and the Moons rose behind the clouds.

When the rain finally stopped they dressed in their wet clothes, for protection against the local wildlife.

With the Moons and stars hidden behind cloud, the night pressed in. Far from helping her see, the patchy skyland glow confused Rhia's night sight, and damp vegetation dragged at her sodden skirt. Etyan reached the stream before her.

He also finished drinking before her. She raised her head from the water to see him already scrambling back up the side of the ravine. He was probably enjoying being able to evade her, if only for a while, but they needed to stick together out here. She called softly, "Wait for me, I'm just coming."

Hearing her voice, he turned.

Darkness fell on him.

The screech was deafening, more so for coming from nowhere. But Rhia recognized the carrion stench. She jumped up.

Etyan's scream joined the nightwing's cry. He batted at the dark mass whirling round his head, then tottered and half fell, stumbling down the slope, limbs flailing.

The dark cloud flowed after him.

Rhia ran towards the nightwing. It was smaller than the one she had met on the plateau, not much bigger than Etyan himself. But it could still kill him. She met it halfway but misjudged its location, dark on dark, and only brushed the edge of its oily darkness. Membranes slapped her palms, stinging like wasps. Then it was past her.

She turned and staggered downslope, after the creature. At the same moment, she heard a scream and a splash.

The stream butted close to the edge of the ravine here, with a small rocky ledge fringing a deep pool. Etyan, out of control, had tumbled over the ledge and into the water.

Rhia ran faster, tripping in her haste to outpace the nightwing. She threw herself into the pool after her brother.

Cold water stole her breath. Her legs found rock, straightened, pushed her up to stand. The water came up to her chest. All she could see of Etyan was thrashing limbs and wild spray.

The nightwing hovered overhead, sending tendrils of darkness down towards the water. But not into it.

Rhia remembered the skykin seeing off the nightwing on the plateau, the bone sword and firebrand. No sword or fire here–

She gulped a breath and threw herself over Etyan, clapping a hand across his mouth and nose. Something sharp whipped the back of her neck as both of them went under. He struggled but she held him tight and close. She willed him to understand what she was trying to do, to cooperate; to save himself. The water overhead frothed. Her knees and one elbow bumped the bottom. Would they float? Whatever her instincts, they had to stay under.

Etyan's struggles grew feebler. Was she drowning him? Her own chest began to ache. His lips pressed against her palm: he was still trying to scream.

Overhead, the commotion in the water was easing off.

Her lungs began to burn. Etyan went limp in her grasp.

Enough. That had to be enough. She pushed off the rocky bottom, pulling Etyan with her. His head broke the surface a moment after hers. She tensed, expecting stinging darkness, but there was only cold night air.

She drew a huge, sobbing breath and released her hold on Etyan's face. He gasped, coughed, then moaned.

"There, it's gone now, it's gone."

"What… what…" his voice was a strained whimper.

"Nightwing. Small one. Doesn't like water. Stay quiet, in case it's still around." She risked a glance up, and saw a deeper darkness far overhead, receding against the clouds.

"Can't, can't feel…" he sobbed, words breaking down.

"We need to get out of the water." For all she knew something equally unpleasant lived there. "Can you stand?"

"No…" it was a low, pathetic groan.

"Then I'll support you." Even in the bad light she could see the dark spots on his skin – on hers too, where her hands had brushed the nightwing. Given the stinging numbness emanating from these patches, and given how many more Etyan had, no wonder he was moaning. "Lean on me."

He pressed his lips together and nodded dumbly, the whites

of his eyes clear in the night.

He got one leg under himself with her support, then squealed. "My knee!"

"All right. I'm going to pull you out. Hold onto the rock here."

Once he had a grip on the rocky ledge she waded past him and pulled herself out, somewhat surprised at how easy it was. Some enquirer had written about that, how mothers saved their babies with impossible feats in the face of sudden danger. Apparently it worked with little brothers too.

Lying flat on the rock, she leant down and grasped his upper arms, ignoring how the nightwing stings burned. "You have to help me, Etyan. Push off with your good leg."

He nodded. Then, half climbing up her, half being pulled by her, he hauled himself out of the pool. For a few moments they lay side by side on the rocky ledge, dripping and panting. Then Rhia sat up.

Etyan's panting was becoming more pained. "Can't breathe..." he gasped.

Nightwings had paralyzing poison. They had no mouth, no teeth; they were many small parts yet all one creature. Sting; paralyze and numb; dissolve and digest. That was how they hunted.

"No one's going to digest you if I can help it."

She did not realize she had spoken aloud until Etyan frowned up at her. "You have to sit up. Sit up and keep breathing!" She pulled him upright; the manic strength still infected her. Compared to this, seeing off intruders in her study was nothing.

His breath became more laboured. It couldn't end like this! His eyes closed. She held him, not tight enough to constrict his breathing, and muttered, "First of the Universe, I don't generally have much time for you, and I'm sorry about that, but please don't let my brother die. Please save him. Just save him. *Please.*"

Her arms had gone numb, though how much was from the nightwing's poison and how much from supporting Etyan she could not say.

His breathing weakened, and she feared to breathe herself. But it didn't catch, didn't stop. "That's right," she murmured, "hold on." For what, though. Dawn? But dawn would kill him. She looked down his body. His left knee was swollen. Even without the nightwing poison, she wasn't sure he could get back to the cave.

"Ree?" She barely heard his whisper over the rush of the stream.

"Yes, Etyan!"

His eyes were closed but his mouth worked again. She bent down to put her ear close.

Etyan murmured, "You want to know what happened?"

"What happened when? Oh." He meant Derry. "You don't have to tell me now if you don't want to. You can just lie here." And not die. Don't die, don't die, *don't die*.

"I'm scared, Ree."

"I'm here."

She thought he had changed his mind about speaking, or perhaps lost the ability to, when he said, "I can't... I have to tell you. Before... before I go."

"All right. If... whatever you want, Etyan. Whatever you need to do."

"Wanted to say before but... wasn't sure you'd understand."

"I'll try, now."

"That morning. Found her like that."

"I believe you!" Why hadn't he just said that in the first place?

"But I knew her. Who she was. The reason I went back was... to pay her family off. Because of what we did."

Rhia's heart slowed. "When you say 'we'?"

"Me, Phillum and Aspel. I was so out of it... 's no excuse.

She was out late, dressed up, we thought she was a... y'know. She was scared. But they said she was playing and... that made it more exciting. I shouldn't have... they wanted me to prove myself."

I don't want to hear this. But she had to.

"Let us be clear, Etyan. Are you saying you... attacked that poor girl?" She couldn't use the word she was thinking of. Her little brother would never do that.

"Yes. While they watched. I hate myself."

How could you? She pulled away. She didn't want to touch him.

He groaned.

He was dying. She had to stay.

She said, "Don't hate yourself." She wanted to say *I hate that you could do that* but if this was it, if he *was* dying, she couldn't let him die hating himself. She searched for some consolation, something to focus on other than what he had done. Like what he had *not* done. "You didn't kill her. Remember that."

"No, but..." Etyan drew a long rasping breath. "They said... if I blabbed they'd say... all my idea, treating her like that... Felt so shitty. When I went back in the morning... to say sorry, make amends..." His voice was dying away, "... saw her just lying there, in the dyers' pool. All that blood. I ran. Kept running."

"Oh Etyan."

His eyelids fluttered and he whispered, "Maybe I deserve this."

"You don't!" Some twisted, dark part of her thought maybe he did, but she knew what he needed to hear right now. "I understand. And I forgive you, Etyan."

"Thank you, Ree."

He was thanking her for the last comfortable lie she would ever tell him.

She felt his lips move against her cheek. "You have to go. Save yourself."

"No. I'm not leaving you." She wanted to hold him tight forever, to save him, despite what he'd done.

"Sun'll kill you."

For once, his logic beat hers. He couldn't move: she could. One of them could survive. Tears pricked her eyes. "I love you, little brother." She couldn't remember the last time she had told him that.

His murmured, "Love you too, sis," was barely audible.

His breathing slowed. She held him, waiting, dreading the final breath. His chest was barely moving when the sky began to lighten, and she prayed again, because if he woke up now, if the poison wore off, she might still get him to safety before the Sun rose. But he didn't wake up.

Finally, with dawn creeping up the sky, she kissed his forehead, stood, and lurched back up the slope.

CHAPTER 57

Halfway back, Rhia fell. She lay in the mud and looked up at the fading stars. She had no desire to move.

But something inside would not let her give in. She rolled over and got up, then staggered the rest of the way to the cave. She threw herself down beside the back wall as the first rays of the Sun touched the land outside.

She lay there, numb in body and mind, until the heat made her itch, and thirst made her gasp. Then she got angry. She cursed the First and Last, cursed herself, the Sun. And Etyan. Etyan, and the awful thing he had done. Etyan, dying alone outside.

Curses turned to tears, and once they started she thought she would never stop crying. When the tears ran out, she lay in a stupor. The double-bodied bug emerged from its hidey-hole. She watched it crawl around, her mind empty.

Evening came.

She levered herself up onto her arms, and from there to her feet. She staggered outside. She had to know.

The ravine gave some shade. And she had been outside without protection for a while on the way here, and got away nothing worse than burnt skin. Perhaps if the Sun had been hidden behind clouds... but it hadn't. She remembered, even through her daze, how bright the day had burned.

It took an age to get to the stream. She could manage no

more than a few steps before she had to rest, and she kept tripping over her skirt, which hung low on her hips. No need for a corset next time she visited Alharet. Not that she expected to do that again, for a number of reasons.

After nearly falling, she crouched and shuffled down the slope, hands to either side to catch her when she wobbled.

At the bottom, she took a deep breath before focusing on the pool.

The rock ledge was empty.

Had he fallen in the water? Or climbed in deliberately, to protect himself from the Sun?

Perhaps she should search the pool, in case.

But last night's manic strength was gone. If she went into the water now, she wouldn't come out again. She brushed her hand across the rock ledge, not sure what she expected to find. Blood? Some residual warmth? Some more arcane sign that her brother had been here? But there was nothing.

Most likely his body had been carried off by something. That was how it was out here.

Thirst got the better of grief and she lay down on the rock to drink. She was tempted to stay there, stretched out on the rocky ledge, ending her own life where Etyan had ended his.

Unless he'd crawled into cover nearby. She pulled herself upright and tried calling his name, but the sound that came out was a pathetic rasp. She tried again, and managed a loud croak. No one answered. She waited a while anyway.

Then she crawled back to the cave.

She must have been at the stream longer than she'd thought; the Maiden was up. It would be light soon. She wondered if she would have the strength to reach the ravine the next time darkness came. Or the strength to do anything. Death had come to Etyan. It would come to her, soon. But while she waited she would take one last opportunity to see heaven, before she found out for herself what went on up there.

It took a while to find the sightglass amongst her piled papers. It took longer still to position it, her arm shook so. She ended up lying on her front just outside the cave entrance, chin on a low rock, elbows on the ground, both hands holding the sightglass. She was delighted when the limited view included the Maiden, then bemused at what she saw.

The Maiden was gibbous. At first she thought she was hallucinating. She focused again, made sure elbows and hands and head were as firmly planted as they could be. No, it was gibbous, three-quarters full. Which it couldn't be, because the Sun was on the far side of it. The Maiden orbited nearer the world than the Sun did. It could only *ever* show a crescent, because the Sun was beyond it, so the sphere's side was the only part the Sun could illuminate.

Damn you, universe. She grimaced, which made her sore lips crack; tears stung her eyes. She didn't want to cry; she couldn't afford to waste the water.

She rolled away from her makeshift observatory. Time to get back to the cave. Time to rest. She must leave this latest mystery unsolved: annoying, ironic, but it was something she had to accept. Just like she accepted that Etyan was gone, and she was dying. She was all done with the stupidity and illogicality of the universe.

She sat slumped in the cave entrance and watched dawn steal over the valley, the landscape going from grey to gold to the painful blue-white of full daylight. Movement caught her eye. A flock of flying things wheeled and dipped in perfect synchrony over the silver-painted land: they moved like starlings, but were shaped like tiny darts, trailing ribbons of azure and emerald. It was beautiful here, in its way. Beautiful, and deadly.

When the flying creatures were gone she crawled to the back of the cave and lay down, sightglass clasped to her chest.

• • •

Dej came out of the umbral into parched fields. Everything was so dim! A few weeks ago, this would've been normal but now she felt the shadow between her and the Sun as a physical presence. She doubted she could go back to living in a shadowland.

She didn't see any shadowkin, but she still pulled the cloak tight and raised the hood.

When she reached the inn Rhia had told her about she walked in and threw her hood back. The way the room fell silent made her want to grin, but she kept her face stern.

The first coin she produced got a look of disdain from the man behind the bar. She took a larger, darker coin from the bag Rhia had given her. The way he snatched it implied she'd overpaid. Never mind.

She ate her bread and cheese in a corner while watched by everyone and approached by no one. Rhia said harming a skykin was a crime, thanks to the ages-old pact following the Separation, but that didn't mean she'd be welcomed.

On Rhia's advice she asked for a private room; she moved the chair to block the door, and slept with her knife under her pillow.

The Sun is Life. The Sun is Death. The Sun is the centre of all things.

Rhia's whispered "Hah!" blew a puff of dust across the ground under her cheek.

The universe doesn't work like I thought it did.

The Sun is the centre of all things.

It was obvious. Simple. Moons went round the world – round the *worlds*, given the Matriarch had a moon too. And the worlds, *all of them*, went round the Sun.

Of course the Strays traced spiral paths, when viewed from the world's surface. In moving around the Sun they appeared to come closer, and go farther away, because they took their own courses, unrelated to the world's. Their apparent changes of direction were optical illusions.

The world is just one world among many. The Sun is the centre of all things.

This revelation must not die with her.

She opened her eyes, released her hold on the sightglass, and pushed herself upright. The movement sent cramps through her body. She held herself erect and still until they passed.

I have the measure of you, Sun. I solved you.

When she had gathered her strength, she rummaged through her possessions for her notebook and pen. Her hand shook as she unscrewed the inkpot.

Has my whole life led up to this revelation? Or have I gone mad? And would anyone ever read her words? Perhaps some foraging skykin unaware of its significance might one day use this book for kindling.

But she had to record her findings. It was what she did.

"The Sun is the centre of all things…"

Her pen caught and slid, leaving the words barely legible. But she drew on the last of her strength, and wrote until the ink ran out. Then she lay down and watched the world turn.

Soon it would be dark, and safe to get water, to quench the thirst that had expanded to fill her head, her body, her soul. But the journey was beyond her. Right now, a trip to the stream was about as feasible as walking to Shen.

She risked another prayer, asking that her writings be found one day.

Then she closed her eyes.

CHAPTER 58

Dej stared at the impossible sight. A hill covered in houses. She knew a lot of people lived in the city, but knowing and *seeing* were different things. Hundreds of buildings crammed together, so close and tight it was impossible to see where one ended and the next began. How could anyone live like that?

And so many people on the road, heading towards the city as evening drew closer. Most of them stared at her. Another small group passed now, where she stood gawking at the view; they gawked back at her. She gave them what she hoped was a *don't-mess-with-me* look, then raised her hood and carried on.

Once she crossed the bridge she kept one hand on Rhia's satchel, and one on her knife. She was amazed at the variety and number of people bustling through the gaps between buildings; the streets, Rhia had called them.

She worked her way up the hill into the richer area, using Rhia's map. Everyone stared at her now. Sometimes people looked like they might speak to her when she stopped to check her map, but no one did.

Nearer the top of the hill the roads had a surface of small stones, and everything was cleaner and bigger. Half a dozen young boys in bright, tight breeches followed her for a while, whispering and pointing, until she turned and glared at them. They ran off down a narrow stairway.

Rhia's map included notes Dej couldn't make head nor tail of: what did *the silver stair (steep)* or *the courtesans' guild (avoid)* mean? After wandering through streets of tallastrees houses she gave up and asked for directions. She chose a less well-dressed older man, and asked the way to the Harlyn house in what she hoped was a firm and commanding tone. The man gave her directions then hurried off.

The house, when she found it, was one she'd already passed, just one more blankfaced mansion. The first time she saw it she'd discounted it as being the Harlyn house due to its shuttered windows, but if she hadn't been so befuddled by the city she'd have realized that if the owners of a house went away, their house would be shuttered. She hoped someone was in.

She rapped on the door. After a long pause, it was opened by a young girl dressed in clothes which wouldn't have been out of place in the crèche. "I must see Steward Markave," said Dej with as much confidence as she could muster.

The girl stared at her, then pulled the door closed. Dej resisted the urge to kick it.

The door opened again, and an older woman scowled at her. "Steward Markave is not here. What business do you have with him?"

Rhia had said Markave was her first choice to give the letter to, but that any member of the household could be trusted. "Who are you?"

The woman harrumphed at the impertinent question, then said, "I'm his wife. So, what do you want with my husband?"

"I have a letter for him."

"Then you may give it to me– Where did you get that?" The woman had spotted the ring Dej wore.

"The countess gave it to me."

"I doubt that." The woman shook her head. "Give me one reason why I shouldn't call the militia."

"Because I have this letter!" It made a change to be accused of stealing something she *hadn't* stolen.

"Let me see."

Dej handed over Rhia's letter.

The woman studied the letter, her lips moving as she read. Then she said, "You'd better come in."

Inside, the hall was high and clean and dim. The woman said, "Wait here, I'll fetch someone."

"Who?"

"Someone in authority."

Dej looked around for somewhere to wait.

"No, stay right here. Don't go anywhere."

The woman smelled agitated. Having no other choice, Dej stayed where she was while the steward's wife hurried out the door, slamming it behind her.

Alone again, Dej stared up into the shadowed heights of the hall. A staircase wide enough for three people to walk side-by-side ran up the walls to the top of the house; Dej saw rafters up there. The hall was lit fitfully by lanterns hung from the underside of the staircase. A tabby cat peered through the wooden banister halfway up to the next storey.

At ground level the hall contained a shrine in a niche like those at the crèche and a spindly, useless-looking table. There were three doors. The first, when she opened it, gave into a grand room with shuttered windows; Dej made out a large table in the centre. The second room, also shuttered, contained high-backed chairs and smelled of dried flowers. The final, plainer door was locked – or rather, there was some resistance when she tried it, as though someone had jammed it shut.

Rather than disobey and explore further, Dej looked out of the tiny window beside the door. Though the window on the other side of the door was boarded over, this one had actual glass in it, like guests drank from at the crèche. Bubbles and impurities gave a weird and warped view of the outside world.

Not so warped Dej couldn't spot the steward's wife on her way back. She marched alongside a man in heavy dark clothing who carried a drawn sword. Behind them were half a dozen similarly dressed men, moving with precise and menacing confidence.

This didn't look good. Or perhaps it was normal; perhaps she should wait meekly like she'd been told to. But the steward's wife had kept the letter. Dej still had the ring but without the letter, who'd think she had been given it, when the more likely – and often correct – assumption was that she was a thief?

Dej ran up the stairs. The cat turned and fled into a half-open door on the first landing.

Dej threw open the door, to be faced with a dark bedroom with shuttered windows. She ducked out. The next room along was the same, dark and shuttered.

The front door opened. The men marched in. Dej pressed herself into the wall, away from a casual glance, and crept up to the next landing.

"Nerilyn!"

The woman's shout echoed through the stairwell but she wasn't looking up. Dej continued her ascent.

"Nerilyn, it didn't escape out the back, did it?"

It. Charming. She reached the top landing and tried the first door. It was unlocked, and she tumbled through, pushing it shut behind her.

This room was shuttered too. She was screwed anyway; in her panic she'd climbed too high to jump out of a window even if she could open the shutters. Despite the dim light she could see this room was full of clutter.

On the far side a ladder was propped up against the wall; above it a trapdoor was cut into the wooden ceiling. Dej dodged junk to run across the room. She climbed the ladder, and hit the trapdoor with the heel of her hand. Perhaps she could hide up there.

The trapdoor banged open. Dej winced. What passed for daylight flooded in. She stuck her head through and found herself looking across a small platform set into a pitched roof.

She hauled herself up onto the platform and closed the trapdoor. As it snicked shut she heard the door open below.

Ahead was a flimsy wooden railing; beyond that a long drop to the street. The house down the hill from here was too far away; she'd never jump that gap. Behind her was a wall of weathered wood with a folded stool resting against it; to either side, two wooden walls slanted down where the platform was cut into the roof.

Dej crept to the wall on the far side of the platform and climbed, with slow care and a pounding heart, up onto the roof. The angle was no steeper than the slope she'd climbed after the landslide, and covered in rugged tiles. Easy. She leaned into the roof and half crawled, half scuttled upwards. When she reached the roof ridge she looked both ways. To the left was a chimney of heavy brick. The nearest house, to the right, was closer than the one at the front. That leap was doable.

She stood up on the peak of the roof. It was less than two handsbreadths wide. She suspected the view from up here would be impressive but had no intention of checking.

Below, the trapdoor clattered open.

She began to run along the roof.

Just before she jumped she saw a shocked face at an open window set into the roof ahead.

A moment in the air, then the far roof lurched up to meet her. She flailed for purchase, scraping knees and hands. Her left leg caught, and she reached out, hand brushing a tile, then catching hold of its edge. She jerked to a painful stop.

Dej caught her breath. She was straddling the small peak above the window she'd glimpsed.

"Hey," she called softly, "You still in there?"

The face had been a girl about her own age, shaking something – a rug? bedding? – out the window. She heard a gasp, and movement.

"Wait!" Left hand splayed across the tiles to support her, Dej reached into the satchel and fumbled a coin out. "Look, look what I've got!"

Her throw – backhanded and blind – was never going to be accurate, but she thought the coin flew past the window.

"I've got money. Lots of it. It's yours if you get me out of here."

"I should tell my mistress..." the girl's voice was uncertain.

"Then she'd get the money. And you'd probably get in trouble."

A pause. Then, "Where are you? I can't see you."

"I'm above you. When I climb down I'll need your help to get inside."

"All right."

Dej hoped the girl meant it. She got a firm grip with her hands, then unhooked her left leg, easing it round. She lowered herself along the tiles beside the window whose little peaked roof had broken her fall. Looking in she saw a pale-faced girl, wielding a stick – Dej recognized it as a rug beater. For a moment she thought the girl was going to attack her, especially as she couldn't have been expecting the stranger on the roof to be a skykin. But then the girl held the rug beater out. Dej grasped it and used it to brace herself. Then she climbed, with exquisite care, in through the window.

She found herself in a child's nursery. The girl stepped back and smiled nervously. Dej fished Rhia's purse out from the satchel. "When I leave here safely, the money's yours," said Dej.

The girl nodded and turned on her heel.

Dej followed the servant through the house. When the girl ducked into a room without warning, Dej followed. They stared at each other as heavy footsteps passed the door. When they reached the ground floor the girl opened the back door, which led into a small yard. Dej tossed a handful of coins at her and ran through the back gate.

Downhill, to the right, she heard voices, men giving orders. Could she lose them and get out of the city? Probably, with care and a little luck.

And go where?

Uphill, at the very top of the city, was the palace. Rhia had admitted that not everyone in the palace could be trusted, and Dej no longer had her letter with its list of those who could. And her reception so far hadn't been good.

Perhaps this was far enough.

CHAPTER 59

A shadow made her flinch. Rhia blinked her eyes open, annoyed at being disturbed now she had made her peace with the universe.

It took several attempts to focus. When she did she saw someone standing in the mouth of the cave.

Her heart leapt. *Etyan!* He wasn't dead; he had come back! She levered herself up onto one arm and focused.

It wasn't Etyan.

This person was tall, wiry and half naked: a skykin. Had the girl returned already? But this skykin was a stranger. A hallucination? She would have expected to hallucinate someone recognizable, and useful. Sorne or Markave or Father.

The skykin grunted and peered into the cave.

Rhia held her breath.

The skykin spoke. "How about this, then?" The voice was lower than Dej's. Something about it tickled Rhia's memory.

"Go 'way," croaked Rhia, her lips cracking.

"Don't think I will."

Though the skykin had the light behind him, Rhia knew him now. The leader of the bandits. She shrank back against the wall.

"You remember me, then?" Rhia got the impression the rogue skykin was smiling. He strode into the cave. The evening light caught his face, showing a half-healed gash running from chin to forehead; the eye socket on that side was empty, red and puckered. "I've had a really shit week," he said conversationally, "how about you?"

The universe had surprised her again. She had thought things could not get any worse. It appeared they could.

"I'll take that as a yes. Thought I was dead when I washed up downstream. Must've been out of it for days. Woke up to find a rockslither eating my eye. It's a long walk home and I was thinking I'd use the caves to rest up. And here you are, sister of the boy who caused all this trouble. Where is he?"

"Lea' me alone."

He lunged forward and grasped her throat, not so tight she couldn't breathe, but tight enough she couldn't move. "I said, where is your brother?"

"Dead!" she croaked.

The skykin paused, then said, "Didn't you hear me say, when we first met, that we can smell lies?"

Rhia said nothing. She noted with cold detachment this foible of skykin ability, or of her own mind: because she did not want to believe Etyan was dead, her assertion smacked of untruth.

The skykin released his hold and leant back. "So, he may or may not be around, but I do have you. Perhaps you'll be worth something. If nothing else, to draw him out." He looked at her. "Considering how much you had to say before, you're very quiet now. How about coming back with me, and we'll see if the boy follows?"

"He's dead." Rhia drew a breath, "And you... you can just *fuck off*."

He slapped her face. Her head flopped to one side.

She couldn't remember the last time someone had hit her. She couldn't remember ever saying that word, used once by a bully, out loud. It was turning into quite a day.

She didn't realize she was giggling until the skykin shouted, "Stop that!" He grabbed her arm, dragging her away from the wall. She flopped onto the earth, too weak to resist.

He let go of her, then leaned over to place a hand on either side of her head. "We can't leave this cave until it gets dark or you'll fry, so we've some time to pass together. And I must say, you've got far too much cheek for my liking. I think you need to be taught some respect." He grabbed her skirt, and pulled it up. Rhia thought, incongruously, of the poor dead girl, of what she had endured before she lost her life. The skykin lifted a leg, bringing his knee down between hers, forcing them apart.

With the last of her strength Rhia jerked her knee up, hard, into his groin.

He yelped and fell back.

Before Rhia could draw breath, he sprang forward again and punched her on the jaw. Rhia's teeth snapped together and she tasted blood. The next blow battered her ribs. Then the side of her head. A blow to her stomach made her entire body spasm.

His blows hurt so much she didn't care that he was going to kill her. She just wanted him to stop. When darkness crept in from the edge of her vision, she welcomed it.

The guard stared at Dej. "You want to *what*?"

"See the duke. Now, please."

The guards wore the same colours as the men who'd come to Rhia's house, with short staves on their belts. They didn't look like they were going to draw them, which was good, but she'd had to show them Rhia's ring before they'd stop shouting at her to be off. She hoped they had the wit to work out that if she *had* stolen a noble's ring she'd hardly be turning herself in at the palace.

"What makes you think he wants to see you, scaly?"

Ohh, an insult. She wasn't surprised, but was disappointed at how unimaginative it was. "Because," she said, meeting his gaze while keeping half an eye on the other one, "I know where Lord and Lady Harlyn are."

The two men exchanged glances. Dej stepped back, ready to draw her knife, or run. One of them said, "Wait right here." Then he turned and marched into the dark corridor beyond.

The next blow didn't land. Something fell across Rhia's legs, and there was a shout from nearby. Weight rolled off her. She wished she had died, because everything hurt *so very much*, and the pain wasn't going to stop until she was dead.

"Ree!"

She prised her eyes open – one stung like she'd got chemical fumes in it – to see the impossible vision of a new face over hers. Etyan's. Except, not Etyan. "Ree, stay with me!"

Someone groaned, off to one side. Her dead brother's face moved away. There was a scuffle, then Etyan's voice, "Oh no you don't, you piece of shit."

Reality broke through the pain. Rhia forced herself to focus.

Etyan – it really was Etyan – was crouching over the rogue skykin, who was curled up on the floor. Her brother held a large stone in one hand, poised to strike. At that moment, Rhia wanted him to smash the bastard's head to a pulp. But then Etyan stood, and kicked the skykin hard enough to propel him to his feet. Another kick and the skykin staggered away, swaying. There was a fresh, gaping wound between his shoulderblades, white bone visible through the blood streaming down his back.

"Get out!" shouted Etyan. "Get out and don't come back."

Etyan kept shouting, kept brandishing the stone, as the bandit staggered out of the cave. Etyan limped after him.

Rhia watched them disappear into the Sun's glare. A few moments later Etyan returned and hobbled across to her. "How badly did he hurt you?"

"You're alive." Her voice was a rasping whisper. "You're alive, Etyan. *You're alive!*"

"Yes, I am."

"How?" She reached up.

He caught her hand in his. "I don't know. Whatever happened to me in Zekt, it changed me. I hadn't realized how much." His skin looked coarsely but regularly patterned, almost like scales.

"You survived... the Sun."

"When I could move again I got into the water to avoid getting burned. But I was so weak the current washed me downstream. Washed me up somewhere with even less cover. It hurt like f–, like you wouldn't believe. Burning, just burning, for days. Felt like days anyway. But I could feel my body changing. The Sun woke something inside me. Finally, the burning stopped, and instead of the Sun being painful it was... sustaining."

"Your leg..."

"Knee's still dodgy, though it's healing fast. Other than that, I feel amazing." He looked hard at her. "But you look awful, sis."

"Thanks."

She wanted to lie down and close her eyes but he said she had to sit up, and stay awake. He helped her get upright. The pain in her ribs put all the other small pains in the shade. Every breath hurt. Leaving the stone he had used on the bandit with her "just in case" Etyan went to fetch water.

Rhia put a hand on the stone – it was unpleasantly slippery, and she'd never lift it – then, despite Etyan's warning, closed her eyes.

• • •

What a room! All these padded seats – and the furnishings! Mam Gerisa would've wet herself. Some of the fittings were, Dej noted, removable, like the dainty carved candleholders shaped like sitting dogs or the ribbon-tied herb bundles hanging in the drapery.

She had no doubt the man sitting across from her was the duke of Shen. Leaving aside the fact he claimed he was, his amazing if impractical clothes and the number of attendants fussing around him, there was how he smelled. Not just the smells a shadowkin could pick up, the soaps and spices and perfumed hair, but the more arcane scent of power.

She told him about the abduction and the landslide and the cave. He listened, fingers steepled under this chin, then asked Dej, "So, were you in the group that attacked the caravan, then?"

Rhia had warned her to be honest with the duke. "Yes, but everyone else who was is dead."

"And how do you feel," asked the duke, "about saving the very prize that got your people killed?"

She didn't flinch. "Etyan and Rhia had nothing to do with what happened to the clanless. It was an accident. I have no people now."

"And can you lead my men back to these red caves?"

"I could, yes."

The duke raised an eyebrow. "You could? Meaning you might not?"

If someone had said to her, back at the crèche, that one day she'd be haggling with the duke of Shen, she'd have told them they'd lost their mind. From the intakes of breath around her, some of the courtiers would agree. "I didn't say that. I'd just like you to do something for me in return. Please."

"What sort of thing?"

They probably expected her to ask for a massive sum

of money or a house of her own. "A really small thing. Nothing really."

She explained.

The duke listened, nodded and then said, "Consider it done, Mam Dej."

Dej grinned. No one had ever called her "Mam" before.

Chapter 60

Why no news? The caravan must have reached Shen days ago, yet still Sadakh had heard nothing.

Nothing regarding the prince's reasons for sending men into the priory either. All he had got from the surviving intruders was the name of the now-untraceable third party who had hired them, and their orders to steal the Shenese boy from the infirmary. Did Mekteph know of Sadakh's plan to assure an eternal caliarchy for Numak, and the young man's unwitting part in it? A chilling thought.

And then there were the other intruders. Whoever would have thought one foreign lad, noble though he might be, was worth so much trouble? More importantly: where was he now? The agent given the job of recovering the boy was a feckless type, but even so–

"Akbet! You startled me."

He rounded a corner to find her just standing there. She carried a stack of washing, so perhaps it was a matter of chance, but ever since he had told her not to visit his rooms he kept running into her.

"Holiness." She dimpled, and dipped her head, and he knew he was meant to melt. Or harden.

This had gone on long enough. "Is your burden urgent?"

She blinked, as though just noticing the folded linen in her arms. "Oh no, I just, I was…"

"Then let us talk, privately."

"Holiness."

He led her to an empty prayer-room, from her expression not where she was hoping for. He took the linen from her, and sat her down on one of the benches. "Do you remember when we first became close?"

"It was the greatest moment of my life, Holiness."

Oh dear.

Sadakh ignored his ghost. "And do you remember what I said at the time…?"

He had been putting this conversation off, knowing how it would go.

"That sex is merely part of life, and that either of us was free to end the relationship at any time." Her eyes widened. "But this is different, Holiness."

Save us from foolish children.

"I fear it is not."

"No!" Tears began to roll down her cheeks. "I'll do whatever you ask, anything at all!"

For a moment, he considered asking her to do something that would test her avowed love to its limits.

The animus, in its bath of warm blood, would not survive much longer. Unless he found it a new host. The difference between skykin and shadowkin was not as great as people believed, so a shadowkin might suffice. But even if it worked, he would have difficulty extracting the animus's essence, as to access it he would have to operate on the host. Whilst working on bodies away from the priory, guarded by discreet servants, was concealable, it would be a different matter to operate, repeatedly, on one of his own people. Even one who claimed she was willing to do anything for him.

He held up his hands. "You have my prayers and my sympathy. You have given me devotion, and been hurt in return. But our relationship is over. I need you to accept that."

She looked at her clasped hands while tears fell on them.

"Can you accept it, Akbet? Are you strong enough?"

"Never!" She leapt to her feet and ran from the room.

Sadakh sighed. In some ways he envied Akbet, even as he pitied her. Perhaps one day he would feel that strongly about another person, and understand this deepest of human mysteries. Perhaps that was the last piece in the puzzle. Perhaps once he had felt mature and lasting "love" he would finally understand.

Or perhaps love was one of the many things that had been taken from him, and he would always be alone.

The response from his ghost was predictable and inevitable. *Not while you have me.*

He went to find the guards, to order them to eject Akbet from the priory isle.

The next day one of his bodyguards handed him a note. He broke the seal eagerly, hoping for news of the Shenese boy, but it was from Tamen Ikharon, asking him to visit "at the earliest convenient time". He had sent his treatise to the enquirer four days ago: a distillation of his notes on how the blood circulated in the head and body, culminating in an argument that the brain was the seat of bodily control.

After assuring Ikharon he would make time for his studies, to delay his visit could count against him. Besides, it would take his mind off his other concerns. He sent an immediate reply. Then he took all the usual precautions, and left the priory isle.

When he arrived, this time accompanied by a pair of disguised guards, Sur Ikharon insisted on serving him chocatl, assembling the drink himself as they spoke. "I was most impressed with your treatise, heh," he said, as he poured the warm milk onto the cake of beans. "Not my area of expertise, but on initial reading, yes, very impressed."

Creep. Would he say that if you were not the eparch?

Sadakh hoped he would, if the work justified it. Such was the nature of the enquirers. That was why he wanted to join them.

"However," continued Ikharon, dribbling honey into the drink, "I am a little perplexed."

"Perplexed? About what?"

"Well, to be frank, about where you got your knowledge from. One gets the impression some of it was acquired, heh, practically." Ikharon stirred the drink with a wooden paddle and handed it over.

Sadakh put the bowl to his lips but did not drink; despite his love of chocatl and high hopes that Ikharon was what he seemed, he would never be so foolish as to accept an untested drink from a stranger. He put it back on the low table between them. "It was. I confess an interest in the workings of the body. I think of it as counterbalancing my interest in the immortal and imperishable soul. The body is the house of the soul, and hence of lesser concern, but still a fascinating subject in its own right."

Ikharon sat back with his own drink. "I understand. I am assuming this is not a hobby you advertise, heh."

"I am discreet." Could this be a prelude to blackmail? Sadakh would be disappointed if it was. And Sur Ikharon would live to regret it, albeit not for long.

"Of course. I am merely curious. Such study stems from a comprehensive education, heh. And here, I fear, I came across an anomaly."

"What sort of anomaly?" Sadakh kept his tone light.

"When new members of our network are not the sons or apprentices of existing enquirers, it is beholden on us to do our research. I would have been remiss had I not checked what the public records have to say of your history before you assumed your current position, heh."

Oh, here we go.

"Please, Holiness, I hope I have not caused offence."

"Not at all. You discovered, no doubt, that I was not born in Mirror."

"I did. You came to the city in your late adolescence, from one of the villages."

"That's right." To his knowledge the last person to check up on him was Prince Mekteph. One of his objections to Sadakh's current position was that he had been born a peasant.

"Nine years after arriving you took up the position of eparch of the newly rejuvenated Order of the First Light. An impressive progression, heh."

"The First called me. I did my best to answer." Sadakh smiled. "But yes, it was quite a journey. One which still amazes me." He had not initially sought power. But when he realized how easily people could be swayed by his words, it had been hard to resist – even as, at the same time, he tried to use his growing status to spread a genuine message of selfdiscovery. The support of the man who later became caliarch also helped.

"I would never argue with the will of the First. But given your priorities must be with matters spiritual, I find myself wondering when and where you developed your intellect and gained the more... physical knowledge, heh, as shown in your treatise."

Tell him he just accepts you as you are or you leave now!

For once, Sadakh broke his own rule, and answered his ghost. *No. I am going to give him the truth.*

Her alarm manifested as a pain between his eyes.

"Holiness? Are you unwell?"

"Just a little tired." Sadakh took a long, slow breath. "I did not get my training in Zekt. I was brought up, and educated, in the skyland."

"I am not sure I understand."

"I was trained to be a skykin seer."

Ikharon's eyebrows went up again, as they had when Sadakh first confessed who he was. "I cannot see how that can be. How you got from there, to what you are now, heh."

"Do you know what a nightwing is, Sur Ikharon?"

"I have heard of them."

"Pray you never meet one. I was trained as a skykin seer but my bonding was disrupted by a nightwing attack. I was the only survivor and my animus was lost before the process was complete."

"Lost, as in… died?"

Sadakh nodded. The pain between his eyes intensified. He ignored it, pushed the ghost to the back of his consciousness. He was the master here.

"Yet you survived." Ikharon looked thoughtful. "It must have been traumatic–"

"It was. I would rather not talk about it. But that is where I got my initial education. From the skykin."

"Which means you would be a great authority on them, heh."

"And perhaps I may share that knowledge one day. But not yet. I look to the future, Sur Ikharon, not the past."

"I understand."

Sadakh doubted he did, but concerns about what skykin secrets he might choose to share could come later. "So, will you put me forward to join the enquirers?"

"I will give it serious consideration, in the light of what you have told me. If I decide to sponsor you, the final stage is to send a copy of your treatise to the enquirers in the nearest six shadowlands."

"And if you do that, would you be obliged to tell them my real name?"

"It is necessary for us to know each other's real names in order to correspond."

He had feared as much. "Could I not receive my writings through yourself?"

"You could, but were anything to happen to me then your conduit to the enquirers would be lost. At which point, that would be the end of the natural enquirers in Zekt, which is not an acceptable situation, heh." Sur Ikharon looked thoughtful. "Perhaps, under the circumstances, I could confide your secret in one of my staff, so should the worst happen they could forward your enquirers' correspondence."

"No, thank you." The fewer people who knew this particular secret the better. It was not as though any enquirers from other shadowlands would ever visit Zekt. "I wish to keep my work for the enquirers and my spiritual vocation entirely separate."

You're used to that.

Sadakh ignored his ghost's observation. At least she had stopped torturing him.

Ikharon said, "There is one thing, rather delicate – and I promise I won't return to this subject again, but now we have touched upon the durability of the network, I have to ask. It is said that the skykin do not live as long as we shadowkin, heh."

"That is true. The animus burns bright, but fast."

"I realize your animus, that you… this may not be relevant, but I need to know whether you, well, how long you might have, heh. I mean, you are only a decade younger than I, so if you live only a skykin's span… You understand why I need to know this."

"I do."

"And can you tell whether your animus changed you in that way? Have you any idea at all how long you have left?"

Sadakh spoke from the heart when he said, "I wish I knew."

CHAPTER 61

The duke wasted no time; his rescue party set out that evening. He provided a pair of solidsided wooden wagons pulled by horses; the leader of the rescue party, Captain Remeth, rode alongside. One wagon was given over to the drivers not on duty – and Dej – to let them rest, while the other was full of equipment and supplies.

Captain Remeth and his four companions were militia. Dej had seen militiamen before, when two soldiers visited the crèche in search of a fugitive. That pair had been impressive enough to the children, with their cudgels and leather armour, but these were a different breed. They moved with quiet efficiency and carried diamond-toothed swords.

The men who'd come to the Harlyn house had been militia too. The steward's wife had hurried to the palace claiming a rogue skykin was running amok in the household. The militia, not knowing any better, had turned out to deal with the threat. Rhia had been wrong to think everyone in her household could be trusted.

The soldiers treated Dej with a courtesy and respect that disconcerted her, until she saw how it worked with these people: they followed orders, and if that meant they were on your side you could be sure of their support; if not, you were in trouble. She was also valuable. She'd brought news of the lost nobles, and only she could find them.

They retraced Dej's journey through the shadowland, reaching the umbral as dawn was approaching and waiting out the heat of the day in the shelter of the forest.

They set off into the skyland at dusk. The wagons rattled along at a fierce pace throughout the night, sticking to the caravan route.

The militiamen stopped as the sky went from black to grey, and pulled a huge construction of heavy canvas – a tent – from the supply wagon, erecting it speedily. The horses went into the tent, the men went into the wagon. And that was how they waited out the day's heat. Dej stayed outside, sitting against the wagon and dozing.

The next day, they left the road and cut up into the foothills. Dej went ahead, checking landmarks from memory and direction from instinct. Weirdly, whilst her sense of direction had been dulled by the red valley, she had a strong sense of where it was now, as though she was somehow drawn to it. *Or someone in it*, she thought, before mocking herself for being so soft.

When the ground got too rough and steep for the wagons, the militia unhitched the horses. Two men stayed with the wagons, while the remaining three took all five horses up into the hills.

With no wagon or tent to shelter in, the party had to reach the caves before sunrise. Captain Remeth insisted Dej rode whenever the ground was flat enough, to avoid her getting left behind. She sat behind him awkwardly. On the steeper sections, Dej dismounted to scout ahead while the men led the horses.

They were on a relatively even path when one of the horses stumbled. Dej heard a familiar hiss and tensed. The party stopped and calmed the horse. It had disturbed a rockslither, and the beast had bitten the horse's leg.

The party's medical expert, Gerthen, examined the horse.

If it was too badly injured to carry on they would have to leave it behind, though they'd cut its throat rather than let it fry under the open sky. But Gerthen produced bandages and bound the horse's leg, and they carried on, hurrying to make up lost time.

They had to approach the red valley from the south, that being the only route suitable for horses, though not a way Dej knew and twice she led them up false trails by mistake. By the time she saw the familiar line of holes in the hillside the horizon showed a line of silver.

"Which one are they in?" shouted Captain Remeth, kicking his horse into a gallop.

"Second from the left."

"Will the horses fit in that cave too?"

"No, but there should be room for them in the fourth cave along."

The captain barked orders as they halted outside the caves. While he and the medic followed Dej to the cave where she'd left Rhia and Etyan, the third man, Hithim, hurried the horses into the shelter of the fourth cave.

Dej entered the cave to see two bodies lying at the back, stretched out side-by-side. She gasped and hurried forward.

The nearest one stirred and sat up. It was Etyan. She grinned at him. "You're alive!"

"Very much so." Etyan looked to the militiaman. "Captain…?

"Remeth, m'lord."

Dej started at the deference in his voice.

"Captain Remeth, my sister needs urgent help."

"I'll see to her, m'lord." The medic bent over Rhia.

Dej looked at Etyan over the medic's head. He glowed with health. And his skin had changed. He didn't have scales, but there was a bronzed patterning which could make you think so at a glance.

"Have you managed to get her to drink, m'lord?" asked the medic.

Etyan looked down, his face twisted with worry. "I've tried, but she fell into a doze two days ago and I can't rouse her. I've wet her lips since."

"That was wise, m'lord."

"She has also been beaten."

"Beaten?" Dej looked at Etyan in confusion.

"One of… those we encountered came back. The leader, I think. I saw him off."

So Cal had survived the landslide. Dej kept her expression neutral.

"Is he likely to return?" asked Captain Remeth.

"I doubt it. Certainly not now you're here."

"We'll set a watch anyway. Mam Dej, please go and tell Corporal Hithim to stay sharp during the morning, and shout out if he sees any skykin; we'll cover the afternoon."

She did as the captain asked. The Sun was up fully now.

When she got back the medic was smearing something on Rhia's lips. Etyan was chewing on jerky, eyes closed. Captain Remeth looked like he had fallen asleep sitting up against the side wall.

Dej sat against the opposite wall, out of the way. The medic turned his attention to Rhia's other injuries, getting Etyan to lift her gently, then binding her ribs. When he was done he told Etyan she was stable but must be watched. Then he went to sit next to the captain, and closed his eyes. The militiamen could sleep, and wake, near instantly, but Dej still waited until she was sure the medic was asleep before crawling over to Etyan and whispering, "What happened to you?"

"I'm not sure. But I can go out in the sun, and eat skyland food. And I feel great!"

"That's amazing!" And it was. She hadn't been sure of her feelings for him before but now she found him fascinating.

Irresistible, even.

Rhia stirred, and Etyan got up to drip water onto her lips. When he returned he sat close, his leg pressing against Dej's. Dej smiled. "She'll be fine," said Dej, though she had no idea whether the shadowkin woman would recover.

He asked her about her journey to the city. He was shocked at the reception she'd got at his house. When Dej grew tired she let her head loll onto Etyan's shoulder. He didn't move away.

She awoke in the afternoon to find Etyan snoring gently, his head resting on hers. The captain was on watch. She doubted Cal would come back now the soldiers were here, but she enjoyed thinking about what might happen if he did.

They left as soon as darkness fell. Rhia, still out of it, was lifted like a fragile package, strapped onto a horse behind the medic. Etyan asked Dej if she wanted to sit behind him on his horse. She was happy to accept.

CHAPTER 62

Rhia opened her eyes. Above her a wooden ceiling was lit by a gently swinging lamp. Everything ached, but she was alive.

"Ree?"

She turned her head to see Etyan's face. Her brother was alive too. She was alive, he was alive and the universe did not work the way everyone thought it did. She smiled, then remembered the other recent revelation. Etyan had raped an innocent girl.

"Ree, this is Gerthen." She focused on the man standing near her feet. "He says we need to get some food and water into you."

"Wh–?" They were in a wagon, a smaller version of those the skykin used.

"Don't try to talk."

Etyan and the other man, whose name she had already forgotten, lifted her up. Beyond them the skykin girl, Dej, looked on.

Rhia's body felt light and delicate, except for her chest, which ached like one big bruise. Etyan squeezed water into her mouth and fed her a sweet yet salty paste which tasted wrong, and then wonderful. "Captain Remeth hopes to reach the umbral before daybreak," he said as she gulped the stuff down.

She grunted to show she understood.

"You should rest."

"Been asleep too long." Rhia focused on the skykin girl. "Thank you."

Dej looked startled, then grinned and nodded.

"Dej had some trouble." Etyan's voice was halting. Rhia looked at him. He shrugged. "Maybe when you're stronger."

"No, tell... me now."

"Our housekeeper tried to set the militia on her. The militia captain says the duke took Fenera into custody. She was still being questioned when he and his men left, but has confessed to spying on our household, passing information to a lover. A foreigner. I'm sorry, this isn't news you need right now."

"Markave?"

"I don't think there's any question of his loyalty."

She never thought there was. But his first wife had died, and now his second wife had betrayed him. "He's all right?"

"Oh, yes, as far as I know everyone else is fine. Ree, you need to rest."

Everything, even speech, took so much effort. "Yes." Etyan and the medic helped her lie down.

"I should probably give you this back," said Etyan as she settled. He held up her signet ring. "I'll put it on your finger." The ring was too big for her now; she slid it onto her thumb, wrapped her fingers round it to stop it slipping off, and closed her eyes.

Will he ever look at me the way he looks at her?

But that was different: they were brother and sister; Dej had no idea what that felt like. She did know what love felt like. It burned like the Sun.

The last two days had been sweet torture. So close to Etyan, but never alone. The soldiers treated her better than the clanless had, but Etyan they treated like his every wish was a command. She wasn't sure what he'd done to earn such respect.

They'd sat together, and talked when the soldiers were asleep. But it had been vague, harmless chatter, about life in Shen or her life with the clanless; not that she said much about that. She was happy to forget it.

They reached Shen's umbral just before sunrise. Captain Remeth stopped at a clearing in the forest which, Etyan told her, was where the caravans departed.

For the first time, it was safe for everyone to spend the day outside, though the soldiers appeared happy to rest up in the wagons with the doors open for air. When Etyan said he was going out, Gerthen said he'd keep an eye on his sister.

Dej followed Etyan. He stopped outside the wagon, and looked up at the solid ceiling of cloud pressing down overhead. The air was heavy and moist. "Shall we walk in the umbral?" she asked.

"Why not?"

Side-by-side, they headed into the shade of the trees. Dej felt stupidly self-conscious. The hollow inside her had been filled, by this boy, but she had no idea what to do next.

They both started speaking at once.

"Sorry," said Etyan, "you first."

"No, you."

"All right. I don't know exactly what happened to make me... what I am now. It must have been the eparch, I guess, whatever he gave me. However it happened, I've noticed changes in the way I see the world. I wanted to ask you about them."

"Sure." What had she been hoping for, a declaration of undying love?

"I think I'm sort-of part skykin now."

"One way to find out. Follow me." Dej strode off towards the brilliance to the north.

She led him to the edge of the umbral forest. The border wasn't sharp: the ironwoods thinned, and then it was just the odd stunted tree shading damp ground dotted with skyland plants, and then there were no more trees, just open skyland. He hesitated for a moment in the last of the shade, then stepped out into the light.

"Does that answer your question?" she asked with a grin.

"I knew the Sun wouldn't kill me. I had to walk back to the cave in daylight."

Well, if he'd said that… "All right, let's try something else."

She led him farther out; the landscape here was lush compared to the dry farmlands on the far side of the umbral. When she spotted a low-lying mat lying in a depression she asked, "What do you see when you look at that?"

"I see… a squishy-looking mat thing. But I get the feeling it would be dangerous to touch it."

"It would. When I look at it I also know that it'll leave me alone if I leave it alone, but that it can move so I shouldn't take a nap anywhere near it."

"So I sense extra stuff I couldn't before, but you sense *and* know stuff?"

"Looks like it."

"So I was right: I'm part skykin."

It wasn't as though she was a full skykin, a *true* skykin, herself. "Sounds like you got the most useful stuff. Trust me, some of it's a pain."

"Like what?"

"Having to sleep with my head to the north."

"Oh, so that's why you didn't sleep against the wall in the cave. But not every skykin has to do that. They didn't on the caravan."

"Not every one, no. We've got… different skills." She wanted to exaggerate, to try and impress him. But then, she'd got to Shen alone, evaded the militia, and led the party that saved his life. That was impressive enough.

"I see."

She wanted him. Leaving aside what he did to her heart and head, when she looked at Etyan she got an ache in her groin, just like Min said she got over some of the boys back at the crèche. Even the image of Cal, looming above her, wasn't enough to kill the desire. Should she take the initiative, just grab him?

"Shall we go back, then?"

Dej looked up. "What?"

"I don't want to leave Ree alone for too long."

"All right. I suppose we'd better."

Damn, but this was hard, painful work. Grabbing him would have been too much, so maybe if she just came out with how she felt... But what if he laughed in her face?

Etyan turned back to the umbralumbra. She took a last look at the skyland, then sighed and followed.

Rhia woke doubting her insight. What if the Sun was not the centre of the physical universe? What if her revelation had been a fever dream? But it made sense of other anomalies, like the Strays.

How did the shadowlands fit in? Could they be, as dogma claimed, the result of heavenly shades that followed the Sun? How would that work if the Sun was the point around which everything else orbited? And then there was the matter of rotation, as postulated by Skywatcher of Liyr. Would this model work if heavenly bodies rotated? Yes, in fact the world had to, for day and night to occur. And if the world, a sphere, rotated as it went around the Sun, these celestial sun-shades must be structures of massive complexity, moving in ways it hurt her head to consider. They were a niggling complication in this elegant new system.

Two things were certain. Firstly, she had a lot of work to do to prove her theory. Secondly, if she did prove it, the Church would not be happy.

Beyond her closed eyelids the soldiers were talking but she couldn't hear Etyan. He had told her his awful secret. Would he run away again? Would the militia stop him?

She opened her eyes. The medic was at her side a moment later. "Where is my brother?" Speech came easier today.

"I'm not sure, m'lady."

"Could you find him, please? I need to speak to him, alone."

"You should have some more food and water first."

"I'll go and find the young lord," said one of the other soldiers.

She managed to sit up unaided to eat and drink. The only remaining pain was from her ribs which the medic – Gerthen, that was his name – assured her had been badly bruised but not broken.

She needed to see beyond Etyan's confession. He had done something terrible, but not as terrible as she feared. And he had not acted alone. Had, in fact, been led on by his noble cronies, as he so often was. By Phillum and Aspel, he had said. Phillum Escar and Aspel Callorn, that would be. A suspicion began to form in Rhia's mind.

She saw Etyan approaching, in the company of Dej and the militiaman, both of whom peeled off before he climbed into the wagon. Gerthen left after Etyan entered.

"How are you?" Etyan asked, sitting on the end of her makeshift bed.

"Better. Etyan, we have to talk about what you told me at the pool."

"When I thought I was going to die."

"Yes, when you thought you were going to die. But you didn't." No: he had survived to become something new, something unique. "But now I know what happened the night you left, I can't unknow it."

"But you can choose what you do with that knowledge." His voice was quiet.

"Yes. I can, and I will. But it will depend on what happens when we get to Shen."

"What do you expect to happen?"

"I don't know. Francin investigated the girl's death, *Derry's* death, but chose not to share his findings with me."

"Right." He looked uncomfortable. As well he might. "And those militiamen with you? Were they sent to arrest me?"

"Their orders were to bring you home. They were not given reasons."

"So," he exhaled. "The question is, given you love knowledge so much, are you going to share everything you now know?"

He was asking her to cover up his crime. "If questioned I won't lie. But if there is any way of bringing Derry's real killer to justice, I will."

"You do know there's a logical contradiction in what you've just said. You might not be able to protect me and still get full justice. Whatever else," he looked away, "I was one of the last people to see her alive."

"I know that. But you didn't kill her."

"And what if the duke knows more than he's said? He often does, doesn't he?"

"We'll deal with that if we have to. For now, I need you to know that I'll stand by you." *Despite what you did.* "And I need you to assure me that you won't run off again."

Etyan stared out the back of the wagon, towards the light. Then he said, "The skyland is fascinating. I never knew."

"Etyan! This is no time for your games."

"I know." He looked back at her. "I'll come back to Shen with you. I can't promise more than that."

And she could ask no more of him than that.

CHAPTER 63

The next morning, Rhia watched the umbral clouds spill over into Shen's skies through the open back door of the wagon. She was strong enough to sit up by herself today.

They had set off during the night, stopping at the inn around dawn to water the horses. Rhia took the opportunity to change into the clothes the militia had brought; plain garb, but clean. She left her filthy skirt and shirt in the inn's outhouse. She had lost her mask; presumably it was still in the cave somewhere. The militia had brought the only possessions that mattered: her notes and her sightglass.

Fat drops of rain began to fall around mid-morning. The militia sent the horses into a full trot; if the drought broke now, the dusty road would become a quagmire.

Nothing came of the initial shower. In the afternoon, with the city on the horizon, lightning began to flash through the clouds behind them. Rhia, watching from the back of the wagon, saw the storm roll up, distant grumbles becoming sharp bangs. Then, with only a few spatters to herald it, a torrent came beating out of the sky.

The road turned to mud in moments, and the wagons slowed. The militiamen whipped the horses on. Just when it seemed they would have to concede defeat and pull over to wait out the storm, they reached the paved section of road. With stone under their wheels they sped up. When they crossed the bridge into the city Rhia looked down to see brown water foaming; the air smelled of cold earth and dislodged sewage.

The rain had transformed the city. The soaking streets were full of half-crazy people, some singing praises to the First, some dancing in the downpour, some holding impromptu parties, some just staring up in wonder at the heavens. The wagons had to halt to allow processions to pass, or slow to weave through joyful crowds.

The carnival atmosphere persisted into the upper city, with gangs of youths singing and drinking, and more sedate household outings under awnings previously used to keeping the sun off. Children splashed through puddles and raced paper boats down overflowing gutters.

When they pulled up outside her house Rhia thanked the militiamen, remembering the three soldiers she had left the city with: two now dead, one First knew where. Then she, Etyan and Dej made an undignified dash for the front door. The first-floor shutters were closed and without her key Rhia was reduced to knocking on her own door.

Nerilyn answered, her initial confusion dissolving into amazed relief when she recognized her mistress. "I'll fetch Markave!"

Markave bustled in and stopped short at the sight of the damp and poorly dressed trio hurrying into the hallway out of the rain. He gasped as he realized who they were. "Welcome home, m'lady, m'lord. I shall instruct Nerilyn to draw baths, and will make some supper."

"Thank you. Where is Brynan?"

"This is his day off. We had no idea you would make such good time. The bedrooms are aired but..." his gaze settled on the skykin girl.

"Yes please, Markave, the spare one too." She turned to Dej. "You're free to leave whenever you want, and I will ensure you are well rewarded when you do, but I would advise waiting until morning, and better weather, before going anywhere."

"Thank you, I will." From the look she gave Etyan, Rhia had an idea the second bedroom might not be needed. She was not sure how she felt about that.

"I'll be in my room." Etyan started towards the foot of the stairs, then looked back and smiled at Dej. "Coming?"

She nodded and followed him.

As the pair disappeared, Rhia turned to Markave. "I'm so sorry about Fenera."

Her steward's gaze dropped to the tiled floor. "So am I. For this to happen in your household–"

"No, I mean, she was your wife, and now..." Now, at best, Fenera would be dismissed, whipped and branded; at worst, executed.

"Things had not been right between us for a while. She still wanted children of her own." Markave's two sons from his first marriage had been brought up by his sister after he was widowed. Markave continued, "I suspected there might be... another man." Markave's twisted expression said he was not comfortable discussing this, but then he added in a voice hard as ironwood, "I hear he fled the city before he could be apprehended."

So they might never know who was behind Fenera's treachery. "Please let me know if I can help in any way."

"M'lady, do not make allowances for this unfortunate situation. It will not affect the service I give you."

"Thank you, Markave. I know that. I just... I wanted you to know you have my gratitude and support. Now, while the water heats for our baths I think we will eat."

"The, um, skyland visitor, will she require any special foodstuffs?"

"I don't believe so, but you can ask her. She doesn't bite.

I'll change out of these clothes, then I need to visit my study."

"M'lady, about your study, there was–"

A sharp knock interrupted him.

Markave looked to Rhia, who nodded. He opened the front door. Beyond him, Rhia saw uniformed men. For a moment she wondered if Captain Remeth had come back for some reason. Then the militiaman wearing a captain's insignia, a stranger, said, "We have a warrant for the arrest of Etyan Harlyn."

Rhia strode over. "You have a *what*?"

"A warrant. For Lord Harlyn's arrest." There were three of them, and they looked surprised, going on shocked. Then again, she must be quite a sight, with her travel clothes, emaciated body and scarred face. Perhaps he did not realize who she was.

"Let me see." Rhia held out a hand.

The men exchanged glances.

"I'm Countess Harlyn. Who else would I be, in this house? But if you doubt it..." she thrust her thumb, with the signet ring on, in their faces. "Now, give me this warrant." The captain produced a roll of vellum from an inside pocket. It was somewhat crushed, but dry, unlike the men themselves.

Rhia unrolled the vellum and read it. She had never seen an arrest warrant, but it looked official, and had the duke's seal. This made no sense. Captain Remeth had no orders to detain Etyan. Unless something had changed in the last few days.

"This is unexpected and irregular. We have just returned from an arduous journey."

"We have our orders, m'lady."

They were not going to go away. "Come in, and wait in the parlour."

"We were told to fetch the young lord–"

"You will wait in the parlour." She nodded to indicate

the parlour door. "No one is going anywhere yet, do you understand?"

"But, m'lady–"

"This way, please." Markave shepherded the soldiers out of the hall. "Shall I fetch cloths for the furniture?"

"What? Oh yes. Let them sit." Rhia climbed the first few stairs, calling Etyan's name. After a few moments he stuck his head out of his room. "Uh, yes?"

"There appears to be a misunderstanding. Some militiamen have arrived with a warrant for your arrest."

"What? No!"

"Stay calm! We have to cooperate." Should she insist on accompanying him to the palace? But once within those walls they were out of safe territory. "You stay here, and I'll sort everything out." *I hope.*

"All right." He made to close the door, looking pale.

"You had best wait with them."

"I really don't–"

"They're just following orders. Please."

"I suppose I don't have much choice." He came out of his room, then looked back over his shoulder. "Uh, Dej, it's probably best if you stay here."

Rhia didn't hear the skykin's reply, though Etyan had left the door ajar. In the parlour, the trio of soldiers were standing not remotely at ease. "This is Lord Harlyn. You, and he, can wait here, because no one is arresting anyone right now."

"But–"

"Do not press me, Captain. My patience is all used up. So you can keep sight of him, Etyan will stay in this room with you. You can all sit down and wait in a civilized manner until I get back."

"I'm sure there is nothing to worry about," she said to Etyan as she left. He nodded but said nothing.

Markave passed her at the door, carrying cloths and towels.

She thought of asking him to fetch a cloak, but decided not to; despite her weakened state a manic energy infected her. Let the rain come. Then she remembered what her steward had said earlier, "Markave, I'm going out, was there something else, regarding my study?"

"Yes. Someone came for your ironwood chest two days after you left."

"What? Who?"

"Someone from the palace, I believe."

"Were you in when they arrived?"

"No, m'lady, I was out settling accounts at–"

"Was Fenera?"

"I'm not sure, I think she may have been here."

"No one is to leave this house until I get back!"

CHAPTER 64

"Where are my papers?"

"Cousin! You're back!" Francin stood up from the table where he was conferring with one of his small councils. "And wet. Yes, I was told the rains had finally come, thank the First."

"My papers. Where are they?"

"Leave us, please." He gestured to the half dozen gentlemen around the table, who wore expressions ranging from shock to disgust to outrage. They stood, a couple staring at Rhia's unmasked face as they passed. "My apologies, we shall reconvene tomorrow," murmured the duke. "And kindly tell the guards that the countess and I are not to be disturbed."

He gestured to one of the empty chairs. Rhia ignored it and began to pace. Francin resumed his seat and said, "Papers? Oh, you mean the ones in that great big chest with the awfully nice lock on it?"

"Yes!"

"They're safe."

"Safe where?"

"Safe here, in the palace. Now you're back I'll return them. It is lovely to see you, by the way; you've looked better, smelled better too, if you don't mind me saying, but even so—"

"Francin! Why did you take my papers?"

"To protect them, which is what you would have wanted,

I'm sure. After that break-in and with you running off to Zekt like that – I'm embarrassed to say I underestimated your persistence – I just thought they would be safer here."

"You *just thought*. And you didn't think to tell my staff what you were doing?"

"Well, no. Which turned out to be a good idea, didn't it? Shame about your housekeeper. Are you sure you won't sit down? All that pacing is making me dizzy."

Now her initial fear and fury was spent, exhaustion crept back in. She pulled out the chair across the table from Francin. After weeks of wooden benches and bare earth the padded seat felt ridiculously decadent. As she settled into it the duke asked, "Where are my men?"

"Your men? Oh. The two corporals are, I'm afraid to say, dead. As for Captain Sorne: you tell me. He abandoned us on the Zekti border, on your orders. I don't suppose you'd care to tell me what he's up to?"

"Nothing to concern you, cousin. How did his men die?"

"Lekem died defending us from the rogue skykin." Rhia had no intention of incriminating Dej.

"Oh dear. I'll make sure his family is well compensated. And the other one, Breen, wasn't it?"

"He betrayed us. Captain Sorne executed him."

"How awful." Francin did a convincing job of looking shocked. Rhia was not convinced.

"You knew he was a traitor, yet you sent him with us! Why?"

"I didn't *know* he was a traitor. I rarely know anything for certain. I do not see the world as you do, full of certainty and order. Every decision I make is a judgment, based on the facts I have at the time, and the likely outcome."

"But you suspected Breen had his own agenda!"

"Yes, I did. And I am sorry to be proved correct. What form did his betrayal take?"

"He tried to take me hostage. Who was he working for, Francin? And what did they want with me?" She would get to Etyan, but right now she wanted to take advantage of Francin's unusual candour. Which was due, she realized, to her having information he did not, for once.

Francin put his elbows on the table, and rested his chin on his hands. "I don't know for sure why you were targeted. But I will say that you underestimate your own value."

"What? As a political hostage? But Zekt and Shen hardly speak as it is! What leverage would the Zekti royals expect to gain by holding a Shenese noble?"

"Hhhmm. You've become rather more worldly wise since we last spoke politics."

Rhia wasn't sure she had ever spoken politics with Francin; his aunt had brokered her marriage to Mekteph, and his uncle had told her how it damaged Shen's interests when the wedding was called off. Then again, her cousin's definition of politics was somewhat wider than hers. "I'll take that as the compliment you intended. But my question remains: what would the Zekti want with me?"

Francin gestured, taking in the room and everything beyond it. "The world is changing, Rhia."

Don't I know it.

"The droughts are more frequent. Unrest is building. Historically the Harbinger has always brought change, and often chaos. When it arrives, I want to be in the best position to serve – maybe save – my people."

"Meaning what?"

"Meaning many things. For a start, we must not underestimate the value of knowledge. That chest I had removed for safekeeping is irreplaceable. In the wrong hands it could be used to damage Shen. It is a valuable resource. You yourself, with your quick mind, wide knowledge and ability to think laterally, are also a valuable resource. Even more so given your position."

"My position? As a noble?"

"Don't be coy, Rhia. We're past that."

"The natural enquirers."

"Yes, the natural enquirers. As an enquirer you have access to a web of wisdom and expertise greater than any one shadowland holds. So, when you willingly if unexpectedly went to Zekt, it was an opportunity to be exploited. The Zekti could put you to great use."

"When you say 'the Zekti' you mean Prince Mekteph, don't you?"

Francin inclined his head.

"I doubt he would be particularly well disposed towards me, given… past events. So why would I assist him now?" Even as the words left her mouth Rhia answered her own question. "Ah. He tried to take Etyan hostage too." Which meant, she realized, that Mekteph could not have been behind their abduction from the caravan: far from coming after her, the rogue skykin had wanted Etyan, only taking her as well to ensure his good behaviour.

"Did he now? A logical move, I'm sure you will agree. People who refuse to cooperate with their captors, even when threatened with harm, often change their mind when the threat is to a loved one."

"But Breen wasn't working for Mekteph. He never met him." Though he must have made contact with the prince's agents in Zekt. Mekteph had found out Etyan was in the priory from Breen, and sent men to snatch him, to use against her. How well coordinated this was with their own infiltration she could not say; it was likely the two groups met by chance, both taking advantage of the regatta, prompting Breen to make his move. Which brought her back to the conclusion she had been hiding from ever since she left Zekt. She looked Francin in the eye. "Breen was working for Alharet."

To his credit, Francin did not flinch. "An interesting assertion."

"Who else could it be? She's so fond of deflecting any discussion of her old homeland, so good at implying she wasn't happy there. I chose to believe that, given it was my fault she had to leave it. But she was telling me what I wanted to hear. She was lying to me." Rhia felt emotion break through, and fought to quash it. "I was fooled by her. But you aren't so easy to fool."

Francin looked at his hands, then back at Rhia. "I am also the ruler of this land."

It took Rhia a moment to catch the implications of that statement. "You mean, you would allow a traitor the freedom to condemn themselves? Even when that traitor shares your bed?"

"I cannot act without evidence."

"And now you have it. The duchess has acted against you, against us; against Shen." Now she had acknowledged the truth – that her best friend had been using her, felt nothing for her, possibly even hated her – the pain was near physical. While she needed to bring the subject round to Etyan soon, she could not let this go yet.

The duke said nothing, but his silence was confirmation enough.

"You must arrest her, Francin!" Alharet's betrayal hurt more than Polain's had, when the boy she had mutilated herself for had said he didn't really love her.

"No, Rhia. Not yet. I play the long game. A tipping point will come. Then I will act."

"I can't accept that!"

"I feel for you. But this isn't about feelings. It's about politics, about weighing costs against benefits."

"And you would gain no benefit from acting now, so you won't." At that moment, she hated her cousin; or rather she understood him, and hated what he was, what he had to be. She had nothing to persuade him with except her pain, and pain was a weakness in his world.

Or maybe she did.

"Francin, what if I were to offer you access to more iron than you've ever dreamed of?"

She had never seen him look surprised. It was a comical expression on a face which rarely revealed his true thoughts. "What are you talking about?"

"Iron ore. There is a place, out in the skyland, where iron lies around for the taking. It is located in territory Shen has a claim to. I can lead you there." She was reasonably sure of this; the route from the road had been hard, but not complex; Dej could certainly find the red valley again. Possibly the men who had rescued her and Etyan could, though it was unlikely, as they had travelled by night, led by Dej.

Francin sat back, eyes wide and mouth slightly open. "Are you trying to *bargain* with me, cousin?"

"It appears I am, yes. I don't like this game, Francin, but if you insist on playing it, I will participate."

"So you *could* tell me where to find this source of iron, but you *won't* unless I arrest my wife?"

"That's right. It's that simple." She swallowed. "Unless you would have me tortured, or hurt Etyan to ensure my cooperation." Given her other reason for being here, could Francin have predicted this whole conversation, and arrested Etyan as part of a deeper game? But his shock appeared genuine.

Francin's gaze narrowed. Then his mouth twitched and he said, "I am an expedient, some would say hard, man. But I have boundaries. I do not hurt my own."

Rhia hoped never to test that assertion. "So, will you arrest her?"

"Would the promise that Alharet will pay for what she has

done when the time is right be enough for you?"

"You know we are beyond that. Act now, before she does. Once she is in custody, I will tell you where to find the iron."

Francin was silent. Then he got up and walked to the door. He pulled it open, and Rhia drew a sharp breath. To the men outside he said, "Both of you, go now to the duchess's chambers. Confine her there, and search her rooms for weapons or poisons. Let no one enter unless they are in my company."

Now she must clear up the other matter. While Francin was still walking back she said, "My brother didn't kill the girl in the lower city."

For a moment Rhia thought she had flummoxed him again. Then he smiled and said, "I know that. Well, when I say know, I am as certain as I can be, given–"

"Then why in the Last's name do you want to arrest him?"

"Arrest him? What are you talking about?"

Ice gripped Rhia's heart. "Guards turned up at my house shortly after we arrived, saying they had come for my brother."

Francin turned and strode back towards the door. "Not on my orders, they didn't."

CHAPTER 65

Dej looked at the cat. The cat looked at Dej. The cat was black and white and was called Yithi. The crèche kept cats to control vermin but they didn't have names, and letting them come indoors was forbidden. This cat, Yithi, looked entirely at home on Etyan's bed.

Etyan's first priority, on getting her alone in his room, had been clothes. Not the removing of them, which she'd have been happy to do, but finding some clean ones. "You should probably cover up too," he said with a grimace, before adding, "Not for my sake, it's just the servants. You know..."

She didn't, but when he threw a clean shirt to her she put it on.

The cat had slinked in shortly afterwards, leaping onto the bed like it owned it. Etyan had rushed over to fuss the animal then, when Dej sat beside it, smiled over at Dej and pointed at the cat. "Dej, this is Yithi, she likes having her stomach rubbed but watch her claws."

He looked at the cat, and pointed at Dej. "Yithi, this is Dej. She's like no one else I've ever met."

At which point Dej leaned across the sprawled cat, grabbed Etyan's face, and kissed him with all her might.

He'd been surprised, and had taken a moment to respond. When he did the warmth flowed out of her chest to fill her entire being. She was on fire. This wasn't like those fumblings at the crèche. He really knew what he was doing.

And then his sister had called him.

Now, alone in Etyan's room, Dej scratched the cat's stomach. It looked at her with disdain, then closed its eyes. Dej stroked the soft fur, enjoying the simple pleasure of fussing an animal, but snatched her hand away when she saw claws being unsheathed. The cat licked a curled paw as though that was what it'd intended all along.

Dej stood up, and looked around the room. Light from the unshuttered windows fell on chests and boxes and shelves. Etyan had so much stuff. Some of it looked like toys: carved and painted militiamen in ranks on a shelf, a stuffed dog with button eyes on the nightstand.

She moved over to the window. Rain spattered the sill and splashed in, soaking the thickly woven rug. She should probably close the shutters. But being in the city, crowded by strangers, was bad enough. To seal herself in darkness was too much.

As she turned away from the window, the cat started. A moment later someone downstairs shouted, "The countess was quite clear!"

Dej rushed over to the door and flung it open. She looked over the banister to see the steward, Markave, backed up against the outside door, blocking the path of a militiaman who had his sword out and raised. Etyan stood behind the solider, his back to her – and to another militiaman, who was advancing on him from behind, shortsword poised. The man was about to stab him in the back.

Dej vaulted over the banister.

She landed on flesh. Something cracked beneath her. She rolled free, winded but unhurt, coming up into a crouch on the far side of the hallway.

Etyan turned, his face a picture of shock. "Get back!" she yelled, going for her knife. Etyan obscured her view of the other soldier. He gawped, but moved.

Her hand found fabric instead of her leather sheath. Damn shirt!

Movement by the door. The steward raised his hands, crying out.

Her fingers grasped her knife, and she drew it, just as Markave gave a burbling grunt and slid to the floor.

The second soldier pulled his blade from the steward's guts, and turned towards her.

Knife against sword: not ideal. And what if there were more of them?

Perhaps this wasn't such a good idea...

But she had to save Etyan.

The militiaman charged her. Dej dodged, twisting away from the attack. The sword sliced the air by her ear.

She stepped back, putting her against the wall. The swordsman came at her with a chest-high cut. She ducked and stabbed upwards. They both missed.

She was fast and fit. She could win this. She just needed to get her hands on the fallen man's sword.

Etyan had pressed himself into a corner, the useless little table held out in front of him like an ineffectual shield.

Her opponent pressed home another attack. She slashed up inside his guard. Her blade snagged... But didn't cut, damn its broken tip.

His next attack came in low. Something nicked her thigh.

The groaning militiaman she'd landed on began to crawl away, dragging one leg. He'd left his shortsword behind. Good.

Movement to the left: an opening door. Less good.

Her opponent stepped back, taking stock. He saw his companion coming through the door, and also saw Etyan, cornered and defenceless. He grinned.

Go for the sword or save Etyan?

She feinted, ducked, and turned, moving faster than a shadowkin ever could, putting herself between the militiaman and Etyan.

After a momentary look of surprise her opponent attacked again. He was sure of himself now, with his ally about to arrive. Jeg had warned Dej about over-confidence. It made you sloppy. She could use that.

She ducked back. Diamond grazed her cheek.

Stay focused and look for an opening. Dej could hear Tew's words in her ears.

An exuberant downswing, barely avoided. He was getting cocky now.

She brought her knife up and across, a backhanded cut. She half expected to come in too low, maybe catch on his leather armour, but the knife skittered up the man's chest, then met flesh. Its flint edge opened his throat from shoulder to ear; Dej felt the knife catch the edge of his jawbone.

She pulled it free. He span away from her in a spray of blood.

"Dej!"

She looked up at Etyan's shout to find the other militiaman at her shoulder. She raised her right arm to parry. His short-stave came down on it. She both felt and heard the bone snap.

He shuffled back, poised to come in again and finish her off. Her arm didn't hurt but it was numb, and she had no idea where her knife was.

But she could see a shortsword.

She ducked down and forward, under her new opponent's swing, and snatched up the discarded sword from the floor in her left hand. Even as her opponent adjusted to this unexpected move, bringing his stave round for another blow, she brought the sword up under his ribcage.

He made a surprisingly mellow grunt of surprise, and

folded. Dej stepped back and let go of the sword. It remained impaled in the man's soft innards.

Someone shrieked.

Dej looked up, dazed, to see the maidservant standing in the other doorway, hand covering her open mouth.

"Nerilyn!" bellowed Etyan, "It's all right! Be quiet!"

Conditioning over-rode the girl's shock; she shut up.

Etyan dropped the table and emerged from his corner.

"Dej! You're covered in blood."

She looked down. He wasn't wrong. "Mostly not mine."

Etyan stared around the hallway wide-eyed. "You killed them."

"I had to. They were going to kill you."

"I... I think I'm going to be sick." He staggered to his feet and threw up on a bit of floor not covered by other fluids. He straightened and wiped his hand across his mouth. Then he saw the fallen servant by the door. "Markave!" He turned to the girl. "Nerilyn, fetch clean cloths and, uh, water..." Etyan didn't sound sure; to Dej he admitted, "I don't know what to do."

Dej remembered something Tew had said about dealing with injuries. "We need to keep gentle pressure on the wound."

Etyan did so, initially with his bare hands, then with the cloth the maid brought, which was soon red through. The man's breaths came out as groans, but didn't stop. The bleeding slowed. "Now we need to bind fresh cloths in place."

"How?" asked Etyan.

"Unlace his jerkin, put the dressings under it, and lace it up again. Then we can go get proper help."

Etyan nodded.

While he re-laced the jerkin, Dej looked across at the two men she'd stabbed. They weren't moving and there was a lot of blood. Nausea stirred. The third man, the one she'd landed on, lay at the foot of the stairs, half conscious.

She risked a look at her broken arm but it was mercifully hidden by the shirt; that sleeve had no blood on it, unlike her left leg and, from the feel of it, her face. The arm was still numb so she decided to ignore it for now.

The front door rattled.

Etyan staggered to his feet and peered through the glass-paned window. He turned to Dej, "It's Ree! Help me move him."

They dragged the unconscious man by his arms as gently as they could. He left a bloody smear on the tiles.

Rhia came in, leading four more militia. Dej tensed. Both other times she'd encountered soldiers in the city, they'd been hostile. The militiamen's hands went to their belts at the sight of a blood-soaked skykin amongst fallen bodies.

Rhia barked, "Stop that, all of you!" She knelt beside her steward. "Markave!" She looked up from the floor. "Have you a medic, Captain?"

The lead militiaman called one of his people forward. The others looked round the hall, taking in the carnage, checking for further threats.

"They attacked us," said Etyan. "Dej saved me. Dealt with all three of them."

Rhia threw a grateful glance Dej's way. "You're hurt too."

"My arm's broken but most of this blood isn't mine."

"Etyan? Are you—"

"Shaken, nothing more."

The militia captain said, "M'lady, we'll see to your steward and then look after the skykin gentleman."

"She's a girl." Etyan, despite the quiver in his voice, sounded amused.

"Perhaps if the young lord and the skykin, ah, girl, could wait somewhere else?"

"The parlour," said Rhia.

The wounded man at the bottom of the stairs groaned.

The captain gestured to two of his men. "Why don't you have a word with our imposter there?"

"So they aren't real militia?" Dej had thought as much.

"I don't recognize them, and I have it on the highest authority that no warrant for the young lord's arrest has been issued. So yes: imposters."

They moved into the parlour, the room with the high-backed chairs Dej had peered into before, now light, and with damp patches on the furniture and floor. Etyan chose a seat big enough for two. When Dej sat next to him he took her good hand. She grasped his in return.

Shock settled on them. Etyan shivered. Dej gritted her teeth against the blossoming pain of her injured arm. They leaned into each other.

Rhia came into the parlour, sitting pale-faced on the edge of a seat.

"Who were they?" Etyan's voice was small.

"I'm not sure," Rhia sounded equally stunned.

A cry of pain from outside sent tension through the room.

A few minutes later the militia captain entered. Rhia leapt to her feet.

"We've bound your man's wound. The thrust missed his vitals, thank the First. He's lost a lot of blood, but with care he should live." Rhia's face collapsed into relief.

The medic came in and moved up to Dej, but she was focused on the captain, who was speaking to Rhia. "We also managed to confirm our suspicions regarding these imposters. They're mercenary types, the sort of men certain Houses have been known to hire to do unsavoury work."

"Which House, Captain?"

"The imposter didn't know as they're hired through intermediaries. However, this job was hastily organized. Their usual contact told them to go to a certain place in order to get the stolen uniforms and forged warrant they would need. The uniforms were brought by a maidservant from the palace. One of the mercenaries recognized her."

"Who was she?"

"He didn't tell the individual we've been questioning her name. All he said was that she works for the duchess."

Rhia's expression hardened. "Oh, does she now."

Chapter 66

At noon the following day, a long-overdue enquiry was held into the murder of Derry, the master tanner's daughter. Rhia appreciated the speed of its convening and even more, its discretion. It was held in a lesser chamber, off the main Council hall.

The presiding magistrate was an elderly viscount from House Abenar, chosen for his relatively low rank – hence lack of agenda – and for his House's reputation for solid neutrality. The Church sent an observer, as was their right; even more unusually, the duke himself was present.

Derry's father was invited but chose not to attend. Representatives from House Harlyn, House Escar and House Callorn were required to attend. In the former case, this meant Rhia, given Etyan's link to the incident. The other two Houses both sent their heads. Rhia wondered how much they knew. All three of them swore, on copies of the Book of Separation, to tell the full and accurate truth. Although the wrath of the First was not a major consideration, Rhia had no intention of lying – whatever the cost.

No one else was permitted in the chamber. This did not stop dozens of courtiers and nobles from packing the hall itself, awaiting news.

Outside, the rain abated after falling through the night, washing filth from the streets and leaving humidity and fecundity in its wake.

After the oaths and a brief preamble, Viscount Abenar described the finding of the girl's body by one of the dyers, the militia's response, and what little the original investigation had revealed about Derry's death. Then he asked, "Do any of those present have anything they wish to add to these known facts?"

Rhia looked at the two counts; they did not look at her. No one spoke. Tell the truth about Derry's death, yes; offer her brother up to the wolves, no. Rhia said nothing.

Francin stood. "I have some additional information, Viscount."

"A whore, perhaps?"

Dej stood, shaking off Etyan's hand. The huge room was packed with overdressed people, sitting in huddles and groups on the wooden benches, whispering and staring at other huddles and groups. Their own small group consisted of the two of them and the two able servants from Rhia's household. Dej hadn't been sure about coming, but Etyan was expected to, and she had no intention of letting him out of her sight.

Now she strode over to the woman who'd spoken, a pinch-faced matron with a ridiculous bunch of feathers stuck to the side of her head, and said loudly enough to be heard over the surrounding murmurs, "I'm sorry, Mam, but my race, being inferior, doesn't have such good hearing as you shadow-dwellers. Could you repeat what you just said about me, for everyone's benefit?"

Perhaps the woman would. Perhaps everyone would laugh when she did. If that happened Dej would laugh too, harder than anyone. She and Etyan had, after all, spent much of the previous night fucking. Despite her memories of Cal, it was what she wanted. What he wanted too. She now knew what all the fuss was about.

The woman drew a sharp breath, but said nothing. She went white, and raised her fan to cover her face.

Dej grinned, turned on her heel, and walked back to her lover. Etyan looked as shocked as everyone else, until she caught his eye. Then he smiled.

As she sat down the small door to the side chamber opened. The whispers became louder, surprise going round the room. Etyan had said these things took time but Rhia and the nobles hadn't been in there for very long at all.

Francin cleared his throat, an unnecessary gesture considering he already had the full attention of everyone in the Council hall. "Dear friends and fellow nobles, we have, I am glad to say, finally got to the bottom of an unfortunate incident in the lower city."

Not exactly, thought Rhia, keeping her expression fixed as she stood, with the two counts, behind Francin.

"I am gratified to see such interest being taken in the untimely death of one of our common citizens." Rhia suspected that, had she been able to see his face, the duke would be wearing his best apparently vacuous smile, the one that had fooled many a foreign diplomat and insulted many a courtier, "A death, sad to say, which was the result of murder."

A predictable susurrus went round the hall. Rumour would abound amongst the Houses, though the girl's life and death were of far less interest than the potential involvement of their fellow nobles.

"The act was carried out by low criminal types. These men have now been brought to justice."

Thanks to Dej. The surviving, wounded mercenary had been taken to the palace, where he had enjoyed the ministrations of the duke's inquisitors throughout the night, finally confessing that he and his companions had put the knife to poor Derry. He would be dead by now.

"However, it appears the thugs were hired on the orders of two young scions of noble houses, House Callorn and House Escar. Their intention was to blame the murder on the head of a third house, House Harlyn. Sadly, Lord Harlyn, being an impressionable young man, did not come to me at once with his concerns, but chose instead to run away. Had his sister not bravely insisted on fetching him home, his guilt might have been presumed in his absence."

An interesting twist on the truth, but from Francin she expected nothing less.

"Our esteemed judge-viscount, on hearing these facts, did not insist on custodial or corporal punishment for the nobles involved, a lenient judgment we should all be thankful for." Because, the duke did not say, being noble will only save your neck up to a point. "However, both guilty Houses are to pay fines: five hundred marks each to the girl's family, and two thousand marks apiece to House Harlyn."

Rhia was tempted to request the entire fine be paid to the girl's family. A month ago she might have. But leaving aside the consequences of suddenly making an ordinary craftsman rich beyond reason, the other Houses would be insulted by this gesture. She would instead ask Markave, when he recovered, about non-Church-affiliated charities in the lower city to which anonymous donations might be made.

Francin concluded, "I leave it up to the heads of House Escar and House Callorn what punishment, if any, they choose to visit upon their errant sons."

None, Rhia suspected, given the two boys had acted with the sanction of their elders, possibly even at their suggestion. The unseemly haste with which House Callorn put their marriage proposal to her confirmed that; no doubt they would have preferred Etyan tried, disgraced and punished, but they had been desperate enough to settle for self-exile. And then there was Alharet's involvement.

Oh yes, Alharet.

"The matter is now closed." With that, the duke swept down the stairs to cross the hall, scattering courtiers.

And that would be that, publicly. Francin had told her the hearing would "resolve what can be resolved whilst minimizing disruption". The guilty parties would get off lightly. All of them, including Etyan. Even in private Francin had not mentioned the full extent of the girl's ordeal.

Etyan and Dej were holding hands now, oblivious of the looks that got them. Did this skykin girl, who obviously loved her brother, need to know what he had done that night, what he was capable of? *Should I tell her?* How would she react? *No: I can't face it. Not right now.*

No mention was made of the impersonation of militiamen by the hired criminals. Their orders had been to make sure Lord Harlyn's side of the story remained unheard after his unexpected return from Zekt; once Rhia went to see the duke they had tried to take Etyan from the house. Had they succeeded that would have been the last anyone saw of him; perhaps they would have made his death look like suicide or perhaps he would just have disappeared without trace. When Rhia had asked the duke who had given them their orders, he had told her, in a typically patronizing tone, that as such matters were handled by intermediaries there was no way to know for sure. Rhia resisted the temptation to ask how, if this was the case, he could be sure the young Lords of Houses Callorn and Escar were ultimately to blame, but she knew better.

The exit from the hall was a disorganized scrum. Rhia stuck close to Etyan and Dej. When their path brought them close to members of House Callorn, Rhia spotted a half-bowed head amongst the Callorn nobles. "Lord Mercal?" she called.

The viscount turned, surprised. Rhia probably should not be doing this in public, but he too had been badly used. "I am sorry, but I do not think I can accept your kind offer of marriage, under the circumstances."

He nodded his over-heavy head. "I u-understand, Countess."

He looked so miserable that she did not add the obvious addendum; that it would never have worked anyway.

Chapter 67

I could stay here forever.

But Etyan had got up, leaving Dej alone in his bed. When he was gone she became aware of the wrongness in the light and the seething mass of strangers at the edge of thought. She should get up too and leave this comforting nest, even though it was the first place she'd ever been truly happy. The world was still out there, with all its shit and trouble.

The door opened and Etyan came in. Dej loved the way her heart flipped when she saw his face. "A letter's been delivered," he said, holding out a folded parchment, still sealed. She wasn't sure why he was telling her this until he added, his tone puzzled, "It's for you."

Dej knew what this must be. Etyan came over, but hesitated before handing the paper over. "Um, is there something I don't know?"

"No. Yes. Sorry. I asked the duke to write to my old crèche for news of someone I once cared for there."

"A boy?"

Was that jealousy? "No, a girl in my dorm."

He passed her the letter, and sat on the edge of the bed. The address was "Dej, of the skykin, under the protection of Francin, Duke of Shen." The writing was neat and even; Dej wondered if Mam Gerisa had used her newly recovered bronze-nibbed pen.

She broke the seal and read the letter:

Dej,
   I was touched and delighted to receive a direct missive from our noble duke.

Dej smiled. More like stunned, then smug as a cat with stolen cream.

   Min went to the farmstead of East Grain, a quarter-day south from the crèche. The mistress of the house was sympathetic to her unfortunate condition and had taken on another girl in a similar state some years back. She is a midwife and after the birth Min was to stay on, with her baby, as a servant on the farm.

Dej's smile became a smirk at the phrase "unfortunate condition", then settled back to contentment. Some part of her had doubted the she-goat would keep her word, that Min would be sent off to be a whore, or a slave, or some other vile fate as punishment for her disobedience. But the crèche-mother *had* kept her word. Then she read the final sentence.

   Sadly, the baby came too early, and died. Despite the midwife's efforts Min also went to the First.
   Yours,
      Mam Gerisa

Dej let the letter fall. Min had seen something in Dej others missed, and taught her that it was all right to be different, and that you had to stand up for yourself. She'd been her rock. She'd also been a fallible, ordinary, scared girl. And she'd made her choice. It was no one's fault that, in the end, that choice killed her. Under her breath Dej murmured, "Oh Min. I forgive you."

"Dej? Are you all right?"

The hollowness Min had left in Dej's soul was gone now, filled by this boy right here, looking at her with concern and love. "It wasn't good news, but I can deal with it. I'll be fine."

"Come here." Etyan hugged her, careful of her damaged arm. Dej clung to him until her eyes stopped stinging, then murmured, "Come back to bed."

"I'd love to, but I've got House stuff to do."

"Like what?" He'd spent some of the day since the hearing talking with his sister in the parlour, but when Dej showed an interest he'd said it was nothing worth boring her with.

"Just stuff Ree can't do."

"Is there anything your sister can't do?"

"She'd like to think not. But some of the guilds and counting houses disagree. Now the man of the House is back they need me to look over the papers she's been dealing with on my behalf."

"So she can't do certain things without a man approving them, even though she knows what she's doing?" This struck Dej as a stupid arrangement.

"That's right."

"Does that mean you're going back to your old life?" Dej had been too busy enjoying the present to give the future much thought.

"No. I can't. I'm not that person anymore."

And Dej wasn't the same person who'd left the crèche. She was free, though that freedom frightened her. Min was gone, Kir was gone. But Etyan was here. And "here" was his home. But not hers. "So will you stay in this house, in the city?"

"I don't know, Dej. I just don't." She realized he was upset too, for different reasons. She hugged him again.

When they sat back he got up to go. "Wait." She put a hand

on his arm. "We need to think about the future."

He sighed. "I don't want to."

"Me neither. But we have to."

They found Rhia in the room that Dej had fled through when she first came to the townhouse. Rhia's study, Etyan called it, adding that she spent a lot of time in there.

Etyan knocked on the door. From inside Rhia called, "What is it?"

"It's me, Ree. Us."

"I'm a little busy. Can it wait?"

"Not really." Part of Dej still wished it could, wished she could retreat into the warm cocoon of Etyan's love and forget everything else. But then, she didn't want him to fall back into the routine of his life here, a life she hadn't been part of.

"Come in, then."

The room was even untidier than the first time she'd seen it, with almost every surface covered in paper. The only clear surface was a massive ironwood chest, near the door. "Sit there if you like," said Rhia, turning in her seat. They sat on the chest.

She shuffled her chair around further. "What's so urgent?"

Etyan said, "I need to think about my future. I never have, before now. It's always been about the moment, or trying to escape the past. But the past makes the future."

Dej had come up with that phrase, in their discussions.

"A perceptive assessment," said Rhia. "But I know you. You're working up to asking me something. Please, whatever it is, just say it."

"It's not asking, so much as telling. I, we, are leaving."

"No!" Rhia's face fell. "You can't. I only just got you back!"

"I know. What you did, coming to get me… it's amazing. But I can't stay here. I've changed. I mean, everyone can see that…" he held out the hand Dej wasn't holding, with its patterning of scales, "... but it's not just physical. I can't go back to the way things were."

Rhia's shoulders dropped. "What about your obligations? You're running away from them. Again."

"I'll finish all the paperwork. And I'll write letters, saying you're authorized to carry out House business in my name. Hopefully at least some of the people we deal with will accept that."

"And what about you? What will you do, if you're not being the head of House Harlyn?"

"Whatever happened left me able to survive in the skyland. So I want to explore it, with Dej." He squeezed her hand.

"It's not safe. Even for skykin, proper skykin like Dej, it's dangerous out there."

"I know," said Dej. "Which is why we're going to visit but not live there." She'd kept a straight face when Rhia said "proper" skykin. Etyan's sister didn't need to know that Dej wasn't one. She'd have to tell Etyan, at some point. But not yet.

"Then where will you live?" Rhia stared at Etyan.

"Not in the city. Dej hates it here. And I'm not sure it's somewhere I want to be right now. In fact, we'll leave as soon as I'm done with the House business, assuming the rain lets us. By the end of the week, hopefully."

"So soon! Where will you go?"

"To the villa, out on our estate. At least at first. Then to the umbral. From there I can get out, and see the world."

"But you'll come back, sometimes, to visit."

"Sometimes, yes."

Rhia turned to Dej. "And you'll be with him?"

Dej had an inkling that Rhia wanted to ask if this was her idea – which it was, originally. "Etyan has made his own choice."

"Which just happens to be the same as yours." She looked back at her brother. "Then I won't stop you, Etyan. Just...

please take care. And don't go too far, not without letting me know." She frowned. "You're not considering going back to Zekt, are you?"

"Never."

"That's something, at least."

Dej'd had enough of this conversation. She wouldn't put it past Rhia to come up with some great new reason why Etyan had to stay. "We'll let you get back to your papers, then."

"Yes. Thank you. Etyan, please tell Nerilyn I'll come down for supper today. It looks like we won't have many more meals together."

On the landing Etyan turned to her. Dej put her good arm around him, and he returned her embrace. They kissed, and nothing else mattered.

They'd make this work.

CHAPTER 68

It could almost be a social visit on a twoday. Except this was not twoday, and Rhia had needed the duke's permission to see the woman who had once been her best friend.

Even so, Alharet greeted her at the door to her chambers with a smile. She did not look at the pair of guards posted outside the door and instead exclaimed, "How delightful to see you!"

"May I come in?" Did the duchess not know Rhia was responsible for her imprisonment?

"Of course. I can even send a guard for tisane and biscuits. I am not being starved or beaten." Her smiled widened as though she had made a joke.

"No, not on my account." As Rhia followed the duchess through to her parlour she questioned her decision to visit. But the longer she left it, the harder this conversation would be.

They sat in their usual chairs. Rhia did not look at the duchess's caged bird. She decided to start with the obvious question. "How much do you know? About your situation, I mean?"

"Guards came five days ago and told me I was to be confined to these rooms for my own safety. They also searched my chambers, presumably also for my safety. My husband visited me two days ago and said he believed I had been plotting against his nation and that I would therefore be kept under house arrest for the foreseeable future."

"And have you?"

"Have I 'been plotting against his nation'? What do you think, Rhia?"

"I don't know what to think."

"So it was pure coincidence that my arrest came immediately after your return to Shen?" Though the duchess's smile did not waver her words were hard as ironwood. Francin had offered Rhia an escort for this visit; she half wished she had accepted one now.

"Perhaps not." Rhia fought to hold onto the calm fury Alharet's treachery evoked in her. It was hard, now she was face-to-face with the woman. "Or perhaps it was just time for what you did to come into the light."

"And what precisely have I done?" Alharet appeared interested in Rhia's opinion.

Rhia refused to let herself be pressured. "For a start I believe you tried to steal my papers."

Alharet's pale brow furrowed. "Your papers? Oh, you mean that break-in at your house, a month or two back? I thought you said it was lower city types."

"Who you might well have hired."

"What an accusation!" Alharet looked genuinely hurt. Then she smiled, "And completely unprovable."

Rhia hoped her shock did not show on her face. Keeping her voice even she said, "Just as my housekeeper's foreign lover will never be found, and just as I may never know who tried to abduct me in Zekt, or why."

Alharet laid one hand on top of the other in her lap. Her fan had, apparently, been one of the items confiscated. "Just so," she said, then looked at Rhia with a friendly smile, "You should realize your own value, my dear. Perhaps now you do. If you were not so enquiring you would be more innocuous, less of a threat – or prize. If you were happily married off, to a decent, quiet man your life would be safe and happy, and that would make me happy."

Rhia ignored the last part of that sentence, focusing instead on Alharet's near-admission. "There was a plot to discredit my brother. I believe you had a hand in it."

And Alharet ignored the last part of her reply, saying instead, "A plot, you say? Is Etyan all right?"

"He's fine, and the hearing–" Rhia bit off her words, realizing Alharet might not know there had been a hearing; perhaps she did not even know Etyan had survived the attempt on his life.

Alharet inclined her head, as though acknowledging a minor victory in a board game.

Rhia would need to admit one more thing to confirm the last part of the puzzle. "Men came to my house on my return. They wore militia uniforms. Your maid gave these uniforms to them."

Alharet looked thoughtful at this latest accusation. "You know where my servants are now."

Rhia realized it was a question. "No. I don't." Most likely they were being questioned by the duke's men.

"Nor I, except the girl I had to dismiss."

"Dismiss? When?"

"Five days back, shortly before," Alharet spread her hands, "all this. Stealing palace property indeed. So hard to get good staff."

Rhia stared. Had Alharet known the rope was shortening? If so, how? She was suddenly sick of the games the duke and duchess played with each other, and with everyone else around them. "Why do you do it, Alharet?"

She did not expect an answer, but Alharet said, "Because our early life makes us what we are." She looked Rhia in the face. "Your father has been dead over a decade, but you still think of him a lot, yes."

"Yes." Rhia was unsure where this was going.

"And your brother; he is far younger than you, and causes you much stress, yet you love him."

"I do." An unpleasant possibility was suggesting itself.

"My father was a cold and distant figure; I am not sure I ever loved him. But my brother and I were born within moments of each other. Mekteph and I are two halves of the same being. Despite having married others since, we were, and in our hearts remain, as close as two people can ever be."

Rhia felt sick. She had always assumed that the books on Zekt exaggerated when they spoke of the ancient tradition of the Zekti royals taking their sisters as wives. She stood up on stiff legs.

"I wanted to hate you," said Alharet, her voice showing emotion for the first time, "because your selfishness ripped me from everything, and everyone, that I loved. From Mekteph, though time and distance cannot kill love like ours. But you are honest and smart – too smart for your own good – and I found I liked you. I still do, believe it or not."

Rhia looked away, determined to show neither anger nor revulsion. To the wall she said, "The feeling is no longer mutual."

Then she walked out.

As she hurried down the corridor the duke was coming the other way. Irked at this latest contrivance, she was tempted to bustle past him, but he opened his arms and said, "How are you, dear cousin?"

"I am well. A little busy, though."

"Then I won't keep you long." He nodded at the pair of couriers trailing him. "Catch up with us in a moment, please." He offered his arm. Rhia took it. She would not get away without some sort of exchange. At least he had ensured they would not be overheard.

"That must have been hard for you." His sympathy sounded genuine. And it probably was; she was being unfair to Francin. She was one of the few people he let down his guard with – a little at least.

"It was. It was as though she didn't know what she'd done."

"She might not, fully. I heard a doctor of the mind refer to such a condition once. He called it – now let me make sure I pronounce this correctly – compartmentalization."

"So one part of the mind does not know what is going on in another part?" Perhaps Alharet's final claim to be her friend might even be true, as the duchess saw it. Which made things worse, in some ways.

"Quite so."

"What will happen to her, Francin?"

"For now, she will remain in her rooms, with all the comforts she is accustomed to."

"Will there be a trial?" Part of Rhia was appalled at the idea of her damaged friend being put through such an ordeal. Part of her wanted Alharet to pay for her duplicity, for the pain she had been willing to cause those close to her. Compartmentalization in action.

"I think we have had enough of such proceedings for now. Perhaps if more evidence comes to light... but there was something else I wanted to talk to you about. The expedition to the red valley is setting off today."

"That didn't take long to organize."

"Well, this is a historic discovery. I believe there is even an apposite aphorism for such prompt action, something about striking while the iron is hot. Regarding that, I wondered what your enquirer friends have to say regarding iron? I've consulted our coppersmith but iron appears to be an altogether trickier metal to work with."

"Analyst of Durn has written on the extraction and processing of many metals, although I only have a few of his papers."

"Might he be able to provide more, if you ask? I am assuming this enquirer is a man, for which I hope you will forgive me."

"He is. And yes, I am happy to write to him for more details."

"As a purely intellectual enquiry, of course."

Rhia smiled to herself. Durn was halfway round the world, yet Francin did not want anyone there to know about the iron. Everything he did came down to politics.

She thought that was it, and opened her mouth to say farewell, but Francin held up a hand.

"Just one more thing, if I may. I'm hoping the map you provided will allow my men to find the valley, but if not, do you think we might prevail upon your skykin friend as a guide?"

"You'd have to ask her."

"I believe she left for your estate yesterday?"

"She did." Not that Rhia remembered telling Francin this.

"And I believe she and your brother are planning to set up home in the umbral?"

"So they say." Crises often brought people together, for a while, and she would not begrudge Etyan – or Dej, for that matter – the happiness they had. For now. She did however hope this would not be a lasting attachment. And now was the perfect time to mention her concerns in that area. "Francin, you do know that if I marry, I may no longer be able to pursue my enquiries freely."

"That depends on who you marry."

"Please don't tell me you have someone in mind!"

"Not at the moment. But do not worry about the future of your House, or your studies. I will take whatever action is necessary to protect both these things."

He knew her value. And so, now, did she.

When she got back, the townhouse was under the same silence she had become accustomed to. Markave was resting in his room; he was able to walk unaided now, though Rhia had no intention of letting him return to his duties until he was fully healed. She waved off Nerilyn's offer of food, but took a pitcher of water up to her study.

She rummaged through the ironwood chest, and extracted the treatise she had mentioned to Francin. She would re-read it in bed tonight, and write to Analyst of Durn tomorrow.

First she would continue her observations, as she had done every night since her return from the skyland. She had confirmed her fever-dream revelation in the cave: the Maiden was growing increasingly gibbous, filling out like a Maiden who had lost her maidenhood.

But before she could put her startling theory about the nature of the universe to the enquirers, she must make and record many more observations, and start to pin down the mechanics of this new model of the heavens. She had no love of numbers, but acknowledged their place in backing up observation. Her back to the new sandclock, she took the tables she would need tonight from her ironwood chest, and unwrapped her sightglass.

She had work to do.

CHAPTER 69

"You shouldn't have come."

The injured skykin spread his hands. "I was out of other options."

He looks like a man out of options. Sadakh's ghost was cutting and accurate in her appraisal, as ever. However the skykin had lost his eye, it was a recent injury. "How did you get to the city?"

"I went to the location in the umbral where we pick up the food you pay us with. The shadowkin waiting there brought me here, but says he expects additional payment."

"I've no doubt he does." Though most loyalty was for sale, that of his now-dead agent had been absolute. His ability to pathfind and his web of contacts amongst both races had combined to make that unimpressive-looking individual Sadakh's greatest asset outside the priory. "And you're sure my messenger didn't survive?"

"He died in the landslide, along with most of my people."

"I'm sorry to hear that." And he was, both because the deaths of strangers gave him no pleasure, and because the clanless as a group had been a useful resource. He and the injured clanless sat in a back room in the launderers' house. Sadakh had been due to visit yesterday but put it off; instinct, and his ghost, told him he would find bad news here. The day had brought one piece of good news: Ikharon confirmed that he had dispatched copies of Sadakh's treatise to all nearby enquirers, with a strong recommendation that he be awarded the post of Meddler of Zekt.

Today brought no such joy. "And you say the boy was heading for Shen?"

"Yes. I went to get help from our settlement, to go after him. We arrived back at the valley just as the soldiers were taking him and his sister south."

"I assume these soldiers outnumbered your party."

The skykin refugee shifted on the wooden stool. "They had horses, and weapons."

"And Shenese livery?"

"They were not Zekti. And there's something else you need to know. The boy, he was changed."

Sadakh went cold. "Changed, how?"

"It was almost as though he'd become part skykin."

Sadakh said nothing. The skykin looked uneasy. His ghost spoke up: *This one is a broken seer, like you.*

Whilst the skykin's account of the botched kidnap had not been detailed, Sadakh knew enough. And he did not want to spend any more time in this person's company. He stood. "I will see that you leave with all the food you can carry."

Even before he opened the door to the warm and fetid room, Sadakh knew his fears were justified. The room was kept sealed, but a fly had got in; he could hear it buzzing around. And he could smell the corruption.

When he lifted the lid on the heavy stone vessel, the smell got worse. The dead skykin's head had started to rot a couple of weeks ago, but the bath of his blood which he kept it in had been enough to sustain the animus. Not any longer. He did not have to reach into the soft matter inside the skull to know the creature was dead.

At times like this his ghost's voice would have been

welcome, but she was silent. He should have expected that.

He could eat the dead animus. But at best it would prolong his life by a few months. And it was possible it would just kill him.

But all was not lost. On the contrary: his experiment had worked. He had living proof of that, and he now knew where the individual who held the key to his success might be found.

Out loud he assured himself, his ghost, and the world, "I will not give up."

ACKNOWLEDGMENTS

This story took a while getting where it needed to be and had a lot of help along the way.

Thanks firstly to the Tripod writers group – currently Mike Lewis, Jim Anderson, Marion Pitman, Andrew Bland and Mark Bilsborough – who saw way too much of this novel. Thanks also to the One Step Beyond writers who gave feedback on various aspects of the book and to beta-readers Sue Oke, Alys Sterling and Jacey Bedford, who went through the whole first draft and gently pointed out just how much needed changing. For technical advice, some of which I actually listened to, my thanks to Dr Dave Clements and most especially to Dr Mark Thompson.

Thanks too to my lovely patrons, whose ongoing support helps me keep writing even in the lean times, most particularly to James Anderson, Chris Banks, Shirley Bell, John Dallman, Gemma Holliday, Cathy Holroyd, Dave Mansfield, Sara Mulryan, Pete Randall, Martin Reed and Teddy. If you'd like to join them, please check out patreon.com/jainefenn.

I'm grateful to Marc Gascoigne and the Robots for taking a punt on this book once I'd licked it into shape. Last but not least, thanks to my husband, Dave, who never lost faith and remains the centre of my personal universe.